ZERO LIGHT

ALEX KNOWLES

Zero Light
Copyright © 2022 by Alex Knowles

Published by Alex Knowles

Cover Design by Rashedjrs

All rights reserved.

No part of this publication may be reproduced or transmitted in any form or by any means, electronic or mechanical, including photocopy, recording, or any information storage and retrieval system without the prior written consent from the author, except in the instance of quotes for reviews. No part of this book may be scanned, uploaded, or distributed via the internet without the permission of the author and is a violation of the International copyright law, which subjects the violator to severe fines and imprisonment.

This is a work of fiction. The names, characters, incidents, and place are products of the author's imagination and are not to be construed as real except where noted, and authorized. Any resemblance to persons, living or dead, or actual events are entirely coincidental. Any trademarks, service marks, product names, or names featured are assumed to be the property of their respective owners and are used only for reference. There is no implied endorsement if any of these terms are used.

The author and editor have taken great effort in presenting a manuscript free of errors. However, editing errors are ultimately the responsibility of the author. This book is written in American English and includes relative diction.

1

Saturday, December 12th *Early Morning*
Year - 27514

Brotok City Race Track

My breath misted before me as I bounced from one foot to the other. Balsy stood next to me, blowing on his hands even though he had thick gloves on. It was biting cold weather.

"Why do they insist on racing in these conditions?" I asked him.

Our garage was alive, as was the city race track.

"The conditions vary as much as the tracks," Balsy said. "If they didn't test them, they'd never learn how to cope up there."

When he pointed upward, my stomach flipped. I looked up, sucked in an icy breath. Then, circulating my Azris, I regulated my temperature better.

Alek was nowhere to be seen. Ezra kept eyeing the door, and Tatsuno paced from one side of Ren to the other.

I waited, hoping he'd make his own appearance. It didn't look like he was going to.

"Nerves," Balsy said. "First race, pure adrenaline takes you through. This one . . . this is business. There's nothing like it. The pressure, the stress." He cast me a "Shit," his face flushing, adding fast, "Sorry."

"Not your fault. We were forfeiting these so I could learn more either way. The fact Ivori's still in bits is just frustrating. I've lost all the prep time I hoped for."

Balsy clapped his hands together again. "Yeah, this sucks. So you can understand the pressure on him even more then. He can't lose. Not one race."

Tatsuno glanced once more at Hara, who threw his head to the bathroom. When he went to move, I intercepted him. "I've got this."

At the back of the garage were two sets of showers. Alek had locked himself in the first.

I knocked loud, then leaned back on the wall. "You coming out?"

No answer.

"Then just listen," I said. I put my hand to the door; my hand vibrated with Azris as I let it flow out into the structure and toward my best friend. "You think you're going to let everyone down. You think you haven't trained enough, hard enough. You think you aren't good enough. You think everyone out there's watching you."

I heard a noise, the slight scrunch of leather. The door thunked. "Everyone is watching you." I paused, heard him sigh. "They're watching you, because you not only won Mote Lerate for us, you nailed the other racers to the wall."

"I'm scared." His voice was so low I could barely hear it.

"Honestly," I replied. "I'm scared for you. I have no idea how you do those speeds out there on two wheels. But we all believe in you."

"You don't know how I do it . . ." His chuckle was real. "You don't recall the Canillion run?"

Shit, he had me there. I stepped back from the door as the lock clicked and he opened it. Dressed in full form-fitting leathers, he stood with his shoulders low. "You know I disassociate from that. Sometimes I don't think I was actually there, right?"

"I wouldn't be here now if you weren't." His eyes met mine, and those nerves danced in his irises, rich dark shadows.

"We've come a long way from the start. Don't go all mushy on me now," I said, and forced a smile. His fear, so real, it hit me on a level I'd never expected. "Together. We need each other, remember?" I held out my hand for him.

Alek glanced at the garage, then took my hand in his, his grip light at first, then stronger. He pulled me to him, slapped my back. "Thanks, man." Then he went for it, bouncing on his feet out into the garage, taking his helmet from Tatsuno with a grin, a lingering kiss and a wink back at me.

I chuckled to myself and moved back to my spot with Balsy. "We should go watch this from the spectators' boxes," he said. "Garage needs to be as free as possible."

Hara also noted this. "Everyone out. Race ready!"

While everyone that wasn't essential left, I hung back. Tatsuno waved me to his side, though Hara shot him a glare. "Don't speak, don't react. Let us do our jobs, and you can stay."

I just nodded.

Red lights flashed around the garage. "Thirty minute call," a voice announced.

Engines fired up around the track. Unlike us, with only six drivers, there were twelve here. I could pick out the sound of Ren's engine from all the others. He had a tiny underlying hum. Maybe I was just a little more used to him, or attuned to him; it made sense to me at least.

I glanced at Alek, only seeing his back, the contrast of bright orange against dark blues, and his number "1" etched into his leather, with beautiful swirling waves of the ocean.

Ren had many a tune up, just as Ivori had, or, well, was having.

I swallowed as his clamps were detached. Hara's voice, cool, calm, started running through pre-checks with Alek through comms.

Alek's voice was calm now, and though Tatsuno never asked me, or said anything, he gently leaned into me, just touching the once. I caught his eyes with mine, blinked slowly.

We both believed in Alek, but his love, his worry, exceeded mine.

His professionalism as he turned focused and then with deft speed and attention to detail, continued with Hara through the system checks.

Alek, Tatsuno, Ezra, and I had since Mote Lerate played every video of the races here, night after night. We'd run through the corners, the speeds, the timing. What the other riders were doing, over the years, things had improved tons. Tech, speeds—we'd tracked them all.

Ren had raced this track a few times, he knew it. The old ways.

Now we watched Alek for the first time as he paced through it. Every gear switch, every drop, or climb. He warmed the tires; he tested all the tech, the balance.

"All green," Hara said.

All we could do was wait then.

Waiting was a killer.

My stomach churned, my mind in turmoil. Tatsuno turned to me. "They're not going to mess around here," he said. "First race is a test on all of them. They never bring it."

"Trust them," I said and focused on the screens. I'd gotten enough practice in with the team in seeing things from all angles. "They can do this. No other Icarian here knows the track. Not like Ren."

"The old track," Hara added, coming in on my other side.

"Yeah," I could only hope it was enough.

When the lights finally turned to let us know this was it. We were all on edge.

A sense of warmth washed over me.

Ivori? I asked on the inside.

I'm here, linking us to Alek and Ren.

Wait? That might not be a good idea.

Trust them and me—they need us.

I swallowed, thinking, knowing we'd have an inside view.

When my view really did change and I could see the track through Ren's eyes, I almost fell over.

Shit. Could have warned me.

Sorry, maybe it's best you find a seat?

No, Tatsuno will know something is off.

Good to have you both aboard, Ren said.

4

Isn't this cheating? I asked Ivori.

We're not giving them any advantage over the track or anything extra, so no. Not in my mind, at least.

I let out a laugh, but it was just nerves. Tatsuno glared at me, and I lowered my head.

Even I know that got you the death stare, Alek said.

The lights turned green on top.

Eight red lights showed.

Fifteen seconds.

Then we were going backward across the board, five seconds.

Two.
Four.
Six.

Ren's engine revved.

Eight lights
Ten lights.
All green! Go!

They were off. Twenty-two laps to go. 4.45 kilometers for each one. Every single one of was going to pass slow as all hell, even if they were less than a couple of minutes in comparison. All Icarian settled in really well, the first turns, the first few laps, nice, steady. Alek wouldn't worry about lead place right now. But he was there, front and center. All he had to do was keep it, right?

The number 1 suited him, and Ren and I couldn't help but hope that no one would even try to take it from him.

My hope didn't last long.

The two closest riders to him were already cutting it rather fine.

Watching how close left my heart beating almost as fast as Alek's on the track.

Hearing his gear changes, feeling Ren's actual revs, it was too much. I really needed to sit down. No matter what Tatsuno thought of me.

When I made for the chair, my legs wobbled, and he caught me, hand under my arm. He leaned in. "Whatever you're doing, steady. Even I saw Alek's heartbeat miss them."

I met his eyes with mine, nodded, and sat. Closing my eyes, I knew Hara might see me sitting there, not looking at the screens. I didn't care. My focus was on my friend, on his reactions, his feelings.

My breathing steadied and at least I was safe like this, even if Alek's speed had me worried.

What's the average on the track? I asked Ivori.

286 kilometers per hour average, she replied. *Fastest point 319.5. Fastest lap recorded was 1.29.999 last year.*

That was faster than anything we'd been already. I cringed as Alek approached the straight flying out of that last turn at almost two hundred kilometers per hour already.

I swallowed. *They're pushing it something wicked,* I said. Ren's speedometer hit 327 before he reacted and throttled down, hitting the brakes hard.

They don't have a choice, she replied. *The others are hitting just the same speeds if not more trying to keep up.*

Lap fifteen and number 7, who had stayed really steady behind Alek, made a move for it, opening up on the straight and cutting in before the bend.

Fuck. I felt Alek's pain at the position loss.

You can take it back, I said through to them. *Don't panic.*

I didn't know who it was for sure, but I felt someone come up behind me, put a hand on my shoulder. "I need to see what you're seeing," Hara said.

I opened my eyes to look up at him. He didn't seem upset. But he knew.

"I'm not sure I can share it?"

I can share it, Ivori said, *but it will use a lot of Azris.*

Do it, I said to her.

The screen before us flickered and then projected—there with my

Azris was Alek's view. I saw the look Tatsuno and Hara shared. But Hara got down to my level. "We can use this. I'll relay instructions to you, if you can pass them to Alek."

I nodded the once.

They didn't speak for another two minutes.

Lap seventeen.

Alek pushed number seven, but he wasn't letting up. He had that lead and he wasn't giving an inch.

Hara stood, moved to Tatsuno. Sweat dripped down my back, off my nose. I heard them whispering, then arguing. They couldn't argue. Fuck. I needed them both. Alek needed them.

"Guys!" I shouted. "Whatever you're wanting to try, share it. Let Alek make the decision."

Tatsuno was shaking his head, but he lowered it to me. Hara came back to my side, cocked his head at me, then put his hand to my arm. A calm wash of Azris flowed over me. "I don't have much, but I can ease it a little." I breathed in deep. "Now relay this through too Alek."

I listened to his precise instructions. "Sean's low on Azris. He can't take much more pushing. Increase the pressure and speed up on the next laps ten kilometers per hour each."

The world Alek experienced was already flying past me at speeds I couldn't comprehend, not used to the feel of sharing point of view. "Sean's too unsteady on the bends. He's coasting too much, lazy on the controls. He might have got the lead. But he won't keep it. You need to take him on turn ten. It's the slowest on the track; the speed will have him braking harder than he has. He doesn't like it. He can't do that and watch you. Tap your Azris on the out, and you'll get past him."

Alek didn't respond, but I saw him etch the throttle up more.

Eyes glued to the screen, we watched his speeds increase. Instead of that 327, they hit 334, then the next lap 338. Average speed increased to 294.

I wish I could see what the other guy does, I said to Ivori.

I'm good—she laughed—*I'm not that good.*

I wanted to hold my breath for the next pass, but I'd have suffocated.

Instead, like the others, I just watched. Alek continued the pressure.

Into lap twenty-one's straight and into the final lap twenty-two, he hit a top speed of 345.

Going for it, bend ten, he said to me.

I looked at Tatsuno, whose fists were clenched. I understood. Turning back inside, I said, *We're all here for you. You've got this.*

Turn ten approached fast, and number 7—though even at these high speeds—was just, well, all over the place. His lines were off; his bike wobbled. Even I could see it.

Alek did exactly as Hara had asked, pushed him in even further so he had to hammer his brakes. Ren's brakes glowed red hot, and I glanced to Tatsuno whose brows furrowed. He'd seen that too. *Hold it together, Ren,* I said inside. *Please to all the gods out there, hold it together.* I gripped the arm of my chair, my knuckles turning white.

Alek flicked his wrist. Ren banked sharply right into the bend, so fucking close to Sean. If they looked at each other, they were less than an inch apart. Sean couldn't take it as he pulled back. Alek straightened up out of the bend, hit his Azris just slightly. He didn't need it. He was already clear.

With moments to spare, building speed right back up again, he slipped into the next sweeping bend with absolute precision. Then, as they came rocketing out of the last one, he let Ren tap his Azris in full, and I couldn't even see the speedometer as he shot over that finish line, fast to throttle off and hit the brakes.

I couldn't help myself. I shot up, screaming into the air. He'd won, he'd done it.

Number 1 was number 1 again.

Hara hugged me. And then Tatsuno too, jumping up and down with pure adrenaline.

Then my legs gave way.

The others couldn't react fast enough. I hit the floor, and Ivori lost the connection to Alek.

Tatsuno offered me a hand, and within the next moment I was back in my chair panting. Hara passed me a drink, which I gulped down.

"I don't know how you did that, but I'm glad you could."

"Thanks," I said to him.

He winked at me. "You know Alek; I know how to watch the track a little more. We did good." He held his hand out for me to shake, and I did.

"Teamwork," he said.

"Teamwork."

2

Tuesday, December 22nd *Lunch*
Year - 27514

The screen before me played, again and again. Brotok City track, December the twelfth. How Alek and Ren had pushed Sean, number 7.

Tatsuno and Alek were talking it through again. I listened, and my heart sank.

I'd missed two races now.

Mote Lerate - the City Capitol . . .

I mean, I knew it was on the cards to get Ivori up and to get me ready for anything. But missing Brotok as well, that hurt a lot, and hurt our chances of winning even more.

These were the real racing tracks, not like the tryouts, and part of our cities for Amalia and Camran. They were so very different; both excited me and made my stomach churn. The stats flashed up before me, our races different than Alek's but still so severe. I read over them again. While the team heads pulled everything to pieces again and again.

This sucked.

Mote Lerate - Track 1 - 5.8 km

Laps 73 - Fastest time – 1 min 42 seconds

Brotok City - Track 3 - 5.4 km

Laps 61 - Fastest time – 1 min 36 seconds

Our next chance, our only chance of being anywhere where we needed to be. I had to do this. There was no choice.

Okburg City - Track 1 - 5.2 km

Laps 60 - Fastest time – 1 min 29 seconds

Even if I had forfeited, I couldn't hold Alek back. We might not have been fit to race, but he sure as hell was. I truly hadn't known the both of us were needed to score high enough to be classed as a win.

It had then taken some studying to learn how and why both of us were, and that Alek needed to place really well for us to even have a chance to move on.

We'd all been there and watched the first live full-on motorcycle races he had ever taken part of, and then the cars in Mote Lerate. But to miss Brotok as well . . . I sighed.

Alek had done fantastic. He'd taken the top spot on both tracks, setting us up already for a good lead. We needed it.

Bike racing had my heart in my throat and my stomach in knots the whole time they were flat out, though. It was really hard to watch.

And I mean flat out. The way they flipped those tiny two-wheeled machines around fascinated and terrified me.

My entire team's frustration was coming through now though.

Nothing was working to get Ivori back up and running. Nothing. Her nites were gone, her metal structure all changed. Nothing was the same, and anything we tried to give her was rejected. Every single time.

We needed nites inside her. But I'd just not got enough to spare. That took time, and time was something we were struggling with.

Now the more my friends watched and talked, the more of a failure I thought we were.

Even if we weren't.

Bodil's fresh pastry smells drifted through the break room while I had my nose deep in the new engine parts for Ivori.

"Food's in," Alek shouted.

I pulled my head out. "Smells amazing," I said.

"Always does," Lena said, spinning on the chair at my side. "Far too good. Geo needs to get us some salads in instead. I swear I'm putting so much weight on here."

"You mean despite all the training you all force on me . . . I'm eating like a horse."

Lena rolled her eyes at me. "Force? I seem to recall you were the one who wanted to keep up the 4 a.m. regime even though we don't really need to."

I couldn't help but laugh at her and when I moved to wash my hands, I threw a towel her way. "You train too hard for any of that," I said.

She threw the towel back at me. "I don't get a choice. I have to make sure your sorry ass is out there putting the effort in."

I rolled my eyes and sneaked past her to the break room. The smell really was good, and I helped myself to some pie and fresh veggies. It wasn't long before the rest of the teams were coming in, grabbing food and sitting to talk.

Balsy and Itoh argued over something on the way in. Itoh ran a hand over his shaved head, itching it. "We don't have a choice."

Balsy threw his hands in the air. "There's always a choice," he retaliated.

They saw me and closed off.

"Everything okay?" I asked.

"Ivori's shell still isn't cooperating. We're missing something. I just can't see the way. Nothing's taking. There's no strength to it anymore. We can't seem to get it right."

I knew they'd not let anyone else over to their side of the track to help. "Can I see?" I asked, poking the pie on my plate.

"Yeah, we're not going to be able to put her back together like this. We need to figure out what's causing the issue within the metals."

Ivori piped up through the comms. "I'm sorry," she said. "Oto needed the time. We can try again now that he's even more nites. Once they're inside the metal they will replicate themselves."

"How many do you need to make it work?" Itoh asked.

"I had over a million," she said. "Losing them was a colossal blow for the both of us."

"I have over a million now," I said. "Take what you need. It will work now, right?"

"Let's hope so," she said.

"I guess." Balsy let out a breath. "It's worth another try." He paused, chewing some food. "There's a lot of us with nites too. They've been replicating inside all of us. Maybe we all can spare some?"

"Would that work?" I asked the room.

A sigh came through. "I think that would work, if they were willing."

Balsy spooned in pie, gravy dribbling down his face. "Let's get everyone in the forge then. See if we can get this pot of metal cooking properly."

I tried my best to finish the pie on my plate, it suddenly tasted really off, making me feel sick.

"Oto, come to my office." Geo's voice came through and we all exchanged glances.

I looked out the open doors toward his office. The tone of his voice worried me. A lot. "I'll be back as soon as I can," I said to the room, and I slipped away.

From across the track, I could see Geo watched me approach.

I took the stairs two at a time and knocked slightly before I walked in.

Geo turned from the outside walkway toward me and indicated for me to join him. He nursed a coffee. "Help yourself," he said.

I poured a cup and then joined him, watching the antics on the track.

"Everything okay?" I asked and sipped the cooling drink.

"Taryn wants to ask you over for the holidays," he said.

I paused, my mind turning. "It's not something I've ever done before," I said honestly.

"She wants you to meet her family," he said.

"Really?"

Geo smiled. "Yes, really."

"So they're coming here?"

I saw him look up. "No," he said. "We're to go to Halara Prime."

"You want to take me off planet?" I swallowed the coffee, still too hot; it burned down my throat. "Ezra?"

"Ezra, Alek, and Tatsuno may accompany us."

"Wow, how long will it take?" I asked. "What about Ivori?"

"It's not usually custom to leave your Icarian behind." He shook his head. "It's a lot to ask of you, I know. She's not fit for any kind of off-planet transport."

"No," I said. I clenched my fists together, that stung, even if I knew she wasn't. "She will be one day, though. I'd like to see all the other planets, but the timing is wrong. Everyone else needs to do what their family is used to." I side glanced at him. "I need to do what's best for Ivori and I. Right now, I have to be here with her. We need to figure out and get her running once again."

Geo let out a sigh. "We'll see what we can organize for us, but I will be away for a while."

"We'll be okay without you," I replied. Then felt terrible. "Oh, I don't mean it . . ."

"It's okay, I understand. This will be your first holidays with Alek and the others. It should be special."

"You don't want to go to Halara, do you?"

"It's a very powerful planet—even I feel out of place there."

I almost laughed but stopped myself. "I don't understand?"

"I may have been born on Tikinia, one planet below Halara on the scale, but I still had to work my way up, just like everyone else has. I came here eventually, after I learned my place in the world. My heart, like my brothers, is here, with the racers. Those on Halara are leagues above me. Rank-wise. Spirit-wise. Everything-wise."

"What levels?"

He looked at me, held my eyes with his. "What do you think happens here as you level and then move up the races?"

"Just that," I said. "You get the opportunity to move off planet and race on their tracks."

Geo nodded, then with a flourish of his hand, he brought up six little rotating fireballs. "Isla is the lowest planet. What most would call the 'mortal' realm. Here there's true death. Levels within the Azris system, even with the Icarian and upgrades, never go above Master into King; their progress usually stalls, and they get sick. Feeling really uncomfortable till they move to the next planet, Copter."

I slapped the railing. "I'm an idiot, aren't I?"

"No." Geo sighed. "We are. We keep expecting you to know everything, how everything works. How it all stays sane."

"But the Councilors, Pete, Lena?"

"We're visitors only. We can't be here without guards. They're allowed for protection, but also slightly more than that. With someone we trust, the uncomfortable feeling is lighter. Councilor Koh and Mason are both Immortal rank; they need several guards like Pete to dampen their sickness."

"So Halara Prime has Immortals. Many Immortals?"

"Not that many, no. But it's run very differently. It's hard for me to even be around them, their planet."

I understood a little more now. I hoped I wasn't going to start feeling sick as I grew stronger. I needed history. I wanted to study, all of it. "Will you send all history, all the things you think I need down to the garage? I need all of this to move up, to understand what might be coming."

"Ivori hasn't given you much, has she?"

I shook my head, fisted my hands together. "I get so frustrated because I don't fully understand how all of this works. I should know. I should have had a better upbringing."

"Forgive us all," Geo said, lowering his head, and his eyes. "We're the ones failing you, not the other way around."

"It's not you," I said.

Zero Light

"No, it really is. I'll make sure you get everything I have on our system's history. Our planets."

"Thank you." At this, I smiled. "I want to do the best for all of us. With more knowledge I will, I know I will."

"Yes, I have no doubt."

Silence stretched before us.

"So," I pushed gently. "Taryn?"

I could see there was lots going on, so I waited for him to speak again. "You brought something else to our world," he said. "My world. My place is here too. I'm going to tell Taryn that."

There was a cough behind us, and we both spun.

Taryn stood before us, her face scrunched slightly. I was quite surprised. For the first time ever, she was not immaculately dressed. She wore slacks, thick socks, and a thick sweater that stretched out over her growing stomach rather oddly.

"I-I . . ." Geo stuttered a little.

"You should have just said. My family is stressful." Taryn tried to smile. "I don't think I could travel anyway," she said, her face paling before us. "I feel awful."

Geo moved to her side and helped her over to his couch.

"I can call the doc," I said, moving to his desk.

Geo nodded at me, and I called through. "It's Taryn, Doc."

"We've been monitoring her closely. We're already on our way."

"If my family wants to see me, they're going to have to come here," she said. "Pretty simple. I'm not fit enough, and I'm not putting our baby at any more risk."

"You're sure? You were really looking forward to seeing my home."

She looked at me and took his hand in hers. Gently, she placed it on her stomach and I saw Geo's eyes light up. His Azris shimmered down his arm, but he pulled away.

"No," I said.

"What?"

I moved to kneel before them. "Touch him," I said. "You're drawn to him as much as he is to you."

"You think so?" Taryn asked and reached for Geo's hand once more.

I watched as he struggled with his emotions around his child. "Geo, trust me, I've felt it. He wants to be closer to you."

Geo let Taryn place his hand on her stomach once more, and I could see the Azris exchange this time. Slow but nice and steady.

"You need to stay close," I said. "It looks like it will help."

Doctor Styx and Beata came in, and I moved out of the way. Settling back to the desk, I noted Geo's schedule, and messages from Luca. The doctor helped Taryn back into Geo's suite with all of them in tow and I sat staring it the blinking icons.

I knew I shouldn't, but I did.

I clicked open, reading quickly up till I saw.

Geo - Taryn wants us to go to her home for the holidays.
Luca - You don't want to?
Geo - No, Halara always makes me sick. You know that.
Luca - You're close to breaking through. It's just Azris sickness.
Geo - They hate me.
Luca - They love her. You need to face this.
Geo - Ugh, why do you always make sense?
Luca - I'm your "older brother."
Geo - I can't do it.

There were days between the next message, and one he hadn't opened since yesterday.

Luca - We're coming to Isala for the holidays. It's not going so well here. Something's wrong. I can't get them to open up to me either. We'll be there in a few days and stay at the track if you clear out the "shack." Been a while, but we'll be good in there. You okay with Mira, the kids, and the team instead?

Geo hadn't answered.

Luca - We really need to set off if you want us there? Thoughts?

Luca - Geo? Damnit! I'm worried about them. They need this. I need to see you.

The blinking icon in the box needed me to answer it. I tapped out.

Geo - Sorry, baby issues, everything is fine, but we're not going to make it to Halara. I'd never deny you coming home. Come. We'll work out what's going on when you're here.
Luca - Oh, phew, good. We're already on our way, see you soon.

Geo stood in the doorway looking at me with a shake of his head. "You answered him?"

I swallowed yet nodded. "You were unsure because of Halara. You're not going now. So . . ."

"I think I should have gone to Halara. Luca's wife is worse than Taryn's family."

I laughed at that. "Damned if you do, damned if you don't?"

Geo edged over and sat on the edge of the desk. He leaned over and pulled up several files. Then he fired them over to the garage, and clicking on some others, forwarded them too. "These should help."

"Thanks," I said.

"Go, study. I need to get ready for the holidays. Make this place somewhat available for them to stay."

"We can get accommodation set up. There're enough buildings."

"Inside the track itself?"

"Move out all the old parts around the back, yeah. It's called the 'shack' but used to be a really nice place. One of the old track managers used to live there. It's decorated beyond just being storage."

He runs a hand through his hair. "You're right. As kids, we'd spend all our time here. We stayed here. It did used to be nice up there."

"What happened?"

"Time." He sighed. "Things changed."

"Well, we've some time before they arrive. Let me get the teams on it. It can be clean and ready then. Sound good?"

"You have brought so much to our lives, Oto." Geo smiled. "Thank you."

I stood and made my way to the door. "Thank you."

I made my way over to the garage. Entering it, I said simply before anyone had chance to ask, "Luca's bringing Camran and Amalia in for the holidays, plus his family. We need to shift the parts out in storage and make this place habitable."

"Damn," Balsy said. "That place is a mess."

"Yeah." Nishi put her hands together though, cracked her knuckles.

"Come on, then." I waved at them. "*You've* got a lot of work to do."

They all looked at Balsy and Itoh, who both simultaneously pointed at Ivori.

Everyone piled out, and I turned to both Ivori and Balsy. "Let's see if we can get some of these nites transferred and working."

Balsy stood. "We've some ideas."

"Good." I followed them both out of the garage, through the break room and out to the shack.

3

Tuesday, December 22nd *Lunch*
Year - 27514

It was hot out in the forge and subsequently that heat drifted through into Balsy's paint studio.

Ivori's parts were spread out everywhere, almost reminding me of the time I'd first seen his graying paint job.

I moved around, giving them the once over. They looked nice and molded, ready for his paint. So far, I'd not seen him do a bad job. Always perfect, at least in my eyes.

"Talk to me," I said. "Tell me more. What and how can we do this?"

"Some of that's down to Ivori," Itoh said.

"I don't have the strength to manifest all the time." Her voice drifted through to us from the comms. "As much as I know I can, it takes great amounts of Azris from both myself and from you."

"Oh," I said, staring toward where her voice came from. Then I shook my head. She wasn't really there or anywhere. I moved back to the metal at my side, touched it. "I can control the nites in me pretty well just by asking. Just need to get them to go back, right?"

"Not quite that simple." Ivori said. "But let's try."

"Forge," Itoh said. "We've been trying to infuse the nites with the paint, but they were fresh nites, not established ones."

"I didn't even know that was possible."

"I guess it isn't," Itoh said. "None of what we tried has been working."

"Even Ivori wasn't sure what would work. But it seemed easier than extraction."

I frowned at those words. "Extraction—yeah, that sounds painful."

"It will not be easy," Ivori said. "They're a part of you now. You might control them, and have some sway with what they do, but they are yours. Not mine. I lost all of mine."

"All of them?"

"That device almost killed me, Oto."

I recalled back to feeling her life ebbing, and emotion flooded through me. I wobbled on my feet.

Itoh came to my side. "We all saw it. We're going to make sure no one ever gets a chance to do anything like that to her ever again."

"You can't say that," Balsy said. "We have no idea the power or the people they've going to be facing in the future."

"I do," I said. "Those much more powerful and knowing than we are. We must think past anything we ever have. We're going to have to use resources and invent things we could never have dreamed of to do everything this team needs to . . ."

"Invent?" Itoh said.

Fazel's face appeared at the door. "Someone mention invent?"

I turned and looked at him. Not having seen him for a while. The door opened, and Fazel swung in a steaming pot first.

Balsy's face dropped. "I thought you went with Camran?"

"I did, and I was for some time. There were some issues here I had to fix. My father called me back. Geo asked me to look everything over. I've been studying your findings, progress, and working on a little something myself."

Balsy moved to take the pot off him. "This isn't, is it?"

"A pot full of live nites, yes, it is."

Itoh's face lit up. "How?"

Fazel grinned from ear to ear. "We have to have better control over some of the other planets."

"Who are you?"

I asked. I recalled our conversation what seemed like ages ago. Fazel held his hand out. "Fazel Rochenko," he said. "Bit of an enigma when it came to Camran's team. Hara took the lead, and I just stuck in the background went where I was needed any time of the day."

"Highly skilled," Itoh said. "Genius on many levels."

"I'm glad you're here, especially if you think you've got the answer in that pot."

"That will be something to be seen. I've never lost every nite on a car before. There was usually someone still hanging around to take control of the newer ones."

"They're not stupid," I said. "If—"

I held my tongue slightly. Fazel had no idea what we'd done already. Itoh looked to the pot, then to me "If I may speak a few truths . . ."

I nodded. "He's here to help, right?"

"O'course I am."

"Then you need to know there's a lot of us here that took in several billion origin nites."

"Origin nites?" Fazel's face paled. "How?"

"Long story." I motioned him in. "But if we can get some of our nites to mesh with these, I think we've a real chance of getting Ivori's stock and systems up and running properly."

"Let's not keep them waiting, then. They've been losing some of the temp while I've been transferring it here. Get it back to optimal and let's get it cooking."

I followed them all out into the real heat of the forge and, standing by the doorway, watched everything they did even if I didn't understand it.

"Come here," Itoh said, and beckoned me with a hand. "We're ready for you."

I sucked in a breath, the sweat already dripping down my back. "I'm not so sure about this." My whole body itched already, and I scratched my arm. The nites inside me were as unsure of stepping forward as I was.

"We're not going to hurt you. Just ask that you direct them into the pot with the others."

On the inside I was screaming—no, *they* were screaming. "They don't really like heat."

Balsy slapped the side of his head. "You're right, they don't. Remember they were turning when you gave them to us."

"What are you saying?" I asked.

"He's saying . . ." Ivori said. "That to get the nites to cooperate, you're going to have to cool this forge right down."

"We can just move elsewhere?" Itoh said. He turned to the temperature gauges behind him. "We've not turned the forge off in weeks."

"Moving them again from here won't do down well either," Fazel said. "They're—"

"Then it looks like I will," I said, moving over to the gauges.

Itoh stepped into my side, then to the control panel. He tapped in commands and then slid the main gauge all the way down. "It will take hours, days to cool."

"We don't have that," I said. I knew how to balance it. I'd been balancing everything—fire, steam, water related—on the inside of myself for months now. "Let me."

Itoh put his hand on my arm. "Don't hurt her," he said.

I looked into his eyes, understanding some of what he was going through. To him, this place, this space, was his. He worked within these walls to create masterpieces. I smiled at him. "I wouldn't dream of it."

"You're sure you can do this safely?" Fazel asked. "Artificially cooling a forge?"

I was already pulling Azris to me, though. "I'm not sure I can cool the whole thing, but I can sure speed its process up."

"Need me to get Geo?"

"No," I said. "We've got this."

Itoh watched the gauges. "Just not too fast, you'll crack her."

"Very easy," Ivori said.

"I will," I pulled forward from my water Azris, covering my arms and hands with the wonderful coolness from inside me. Then I balanced it with fire.

Itoh took a step back, yet Balsy and Fazel stepped in closer. "I've never seen anyone manage dual elements like that before."

"Fascinating indeed. I knew he could, but this, this is out of anyone else's league here."

"Even the council?" I asked.

"Maybe not. Some of them are really powerful."

I focused out their chatter, had to; I matched the heat from the forge and then started to introduce the cooling effect of my water energies. The heat from the forge dropped and dropped fast.

"It'll crack!" Itoh said.

I pushed more heat through, steadying it off. "It's easier than I thought. I guess managing my own core's come in handy for this. The balance is super important, but it's not life threatening."

"How cold do we need to be?" Fazel asked.

"The main room where we got them from was cold. Winter cold. I don't think we need to get that chilly."

"But I think you'll know when the nites react opposite to what you've been used to seeing them do."

"I'm keeping a close eye on them. So far they're okay."

"Why do both sets work so different?" Balsy asked.

"Because the ones in the hot pot aren't Icarian made. They're man made. They do a programmed job, of course. They work the car's systems and upgrades, but the Icarian nites—"

"Are almost alive," Itoh said. "Even I feel that much."

"Yes," Ivori said. "Almost alive, that's how you'd see them. To the nites, they are very much their own species, and alive in how they see themselves."

"Pot's squirming," Fazel said. "They're core temp's dropping a lot. I don't know how much more mine are going to take."

"A few more minutes," I said. "Just a few."

I tried to stabilize the forge; we couldn't do without it.

Itoh tried his best to help with the readouts, the balance of energy dropping.

"Hairline crack, fuck," he swore, and I almost lost control of the temperature.

"Focus," Ivori said, and within a moment, she was at my side. "You're stronger than you think, but you are also much weaker than you need to do this quickly. Slow it down."

I swallowed. "How's the pot?" I asked.

"Settled somewhat," Fazel said. "Give them a little more time like that. They're adjusting."

"You got this?" Itoh said.

My heart pounded in my chest. Comms went off to the side of the room. "What's going on in there?" Hara asked.

"Breaking boundaries," Balsy replied. "We've a solution, but it's a struggle."

"I can see that. The whole track's shaking. If you don't calm it down in there, the whole city will know something's going on under here."

"Crap," Itoh said.

I met my eyes with his. "I can't stop now. It would do more damage than anything else." My hands started to shake. This had been too much, too hard. I was putting all of us at risk. Even if we needed those nites to work together, it wasn't worth this.

Balsy stepped up behind me. "Don't doubt yourself now." He put his hand on my back. I felt something then. A deep connection between us.

"That's fantastic," Fazel said. "Origin nites."

"Nites without an Icarian host. A body," Itoh said.

"No." I looked at him, and reached for his hand. "There's a host, there's a body for them, and they all share it. We just didn't understand it." I turned to Ivori. "They're scared, scared in case we put them in danger like the last. They saw it, they felt it."

Ivori's eyes turned away, and she stepped toward Fazel who had never seen her before, her ghost-like figure. She met his gaze, and he stepped forward, protective of his pot. "I won't hurt you or them."

"Ivori, you can't," I said.

She glanced at me the once, and I could see her form solidifying before all of us. Gently, she reached out and took hold of the pot. The sheer amount of Azris in this room alone was tremendous. I had no words for it, but even I felt the floor shaking even more.

"We don't have a lot of time," she said. "Balsy, take my hand, and then Itoh's."

Balsy moved to step in just a bit closer, and he held his hand out for her. More than likely, he expected his hand to pass through her apparition, but it didn't. He paled, but then reached for Itoh. "Keep the heat from us for now. We've got this Oto."

Ivori gave Balsy's hand a squeeze. "Breathe," she said to him. "Oto, we need you to complete this."

My legs still shook, but I gave the temp one last look before I even dared to step away.

"Stable," Itoh said. "For now."

The swirling coolness followed me as I moved to them. I held out my hand for Itoh. Ivori took her hand from the side of the pot and, meeting Fazel's terrified eyes, put it into the liquid. "They need to know me; they need to understand me. I am the bridge between you and them."

Fazel's brows rose. He moved to the side to watch closer.

I looked inside myself. "You hear her? You're as much hers as you are to me. Go to her."

My nites had to cross over Itoh and Balsy, though, to get to her, and I could see the knock as they moved down my arm, then into his, and then through him. The few I'd thought to send started to grow in numbers and size. They were taking some of Itoh's with them. When they got to Balsy, they did the same. They grew in strength yet again. Seeing them cross over to Ivori was something else. Then they entered the pot.

Ivori struggled to keep her form, and she was gone. I tried to feel for her, but I had expended almost all my energy as well. At least the surrounding room had stopped shaking. That meant that at least we'd be okay.

Fazel was on his computer screen in front of the pot, shaking his head. "What did you do?"

"Hopefully we had the temperature right and held it out long enough that our nites could bridge the gap with yours."

"The whole temperature's falling. But they're all doing okay."

"All of them?"

"Yes, all of them."

That was it. My legs gave way, and I was a heap on the floor without even blinking. As much as I had a bit more weight on my bones, I still felt that floor under me. It hurt.

Itoh put his hand on my shoulder. I could see his legs wobbling too, but he held his ground. Balsy sat on the floor right next to me. "That was wild."

"You think they are okay?" I looked from him to Fazel.

"They are okay. I promise you, Balsy can spray them onto the panels whenever he's ready."

For that I was glad.

Check your stats, Ivori said. *You might not be able to train or work with me, but you can train your Azris and cultivation still. That was a hell of a workout.*

I pulled up my stats, noting the growth even in the last few months. She was right. As much as we weren't making major strides with her, I was still growing in leaps and bounds.

Ivori was right I'd hit Master Rank 3. I quickly put my points 1 to each: Strength, Dexterity, Constitution.

Name = Oto Benes
ID Number = 4188927
Age = 22
Species = Anodite
Sex = Male
Alignment = Neutral
Bloodline = Unknown
Health = 69%
Cultivation Level - **Master Rank 3**
Active Meridians = 12/12
Nanites = 1 million
Artefacts = 1
Chosen Specialist = Racer
First Chosen Affinity = Water

Zero Light

Second Chosen Affinity = Fire

Strength = 38/**104.12**
Dexterity = 26/**67.34**
Constitution = 36/**99**
Int/Wis/Spirit = 47

Affinities - Rank

Water - **Green**
Fire - **Yellow**
Earth - **Orange**
Air - **Orange**
Light - **Orange**
Darkness - **Orange**
Spirit - **Yellow**

Droll's Leg Pouch – three refillable containers hold the power of life or death. One use per origin user.

4

Wednesday, December 23rd *Evening*
Year - 27514

I slumped back in the garage chair. All of us had been working through since we fixed the nites yesterday. The paintwork had taken this time, with the nanites' layer coating every piece of her chassis in a beautiful rainbow of gray. I mean, I couldn't expect anything else.

Now she was almost back to perfection. Perfection of a very different level. She was an amalgamation of the whole track. Every single one of the amazing people here had given up something so that she could—no, *would*, race again.

"Last piece," Balsy said, holding out a badge.

"What's this?" I stood back up to take the piece off him.

"I made it," he said. "For the front."

I turned it over in my hand, the exquisite detail. It was perfect. I looked at the hood. There really wasn't anywhere to put it.

"It will just stick, Ivori assured me. It wouldn't move once it was there."

"Okay." I moved to her, placed my hand on her cool metal. Her engine sparked to life underneath me. Gently, I placed the Ocean Slayers emblem on the hood. It clicked, and the beautiful color of the ocean spread out from it like a ripple.

"You feel good?" I asked her.

"I feel wonderful," she said to the room. "Absolutely wonderful."

I put my other hand on her and felt the exchange of Azris pass through me to her, to the nites. I had a much better understanding of how they worked, how she worked now. The whole process for the nites was symbiotic, just as it was for her, and we needed each other.

"They feel like they're happy," I said.

"They are," she replied. Her engine started, roaring to life. The backfire had all of us flinch. The exhaust roared. Damn, that was loud.

"Get in," she said.

Those words were like music to my ears.

As much as time as I'd spent helping put things together, to help the others cover the seats, the interior, I had not seen her like this. So shiny. I ran my hand over the seat before I slid in. The soft leather, cut to fit. I sat, and my heart raced.

"Oto?" Alek said, kneeling at my side. "What is it?"

I let the belt tighten across my chest, stared at the dash. "I've never seen anything as beautiful."

Alek put his hand on my shoulder. "She deserved it. So did you."

I met his eyes with mine. "You coming?"

His eyes flickered, just the once. "Didn't think you'd ask. Give me a minute."

When Alek rushed off, Tatsuno was in my space. He tapped the steering wheel. "This is a lot more sensitive than what you were used to, there's no gear stic—"

I looked at the middle column. "What? How do I even—"

Tatsuno leaned over me, took my hand in his, placed it at the wheel. "You have column gear changes now. Downshift . . ." He moved my hand over the button. "Upshift here." Placing my other hand to the right, I felt it.

"You think this is easier?"

"Oh, it will be far easier than what you're used to."

"What is everything else for?" I asked, staring at the whole array of buttons and things staring back at me.

"We'll explain them as you're on the track will make more sense then."

Tatsuno spun around when he heard Ren fire up. "You better get your ass out there."

I nodded, feeling really odd with one fewer pedal and no gear stick to shift.

"You still control speed and brakes," Ivori said as Tatsuno shut the door.

Her screens lit up. I was tired; I could see my health was low. All my stats, her stats there were good though. Everything was green. I touched the gas lightly. The surge of power underneath me spread through every fiber of my being. "Engine's got quite the oomph."

She coughed. "You put points into the engine and shielding."

I closed my eyes, thought back to what and how much we'd grown, to what Alek had spent his on for Ren. We were both so close to ranking up in our Azris use, just not close enough, even though we'd spent lots of time around the track and had still been training with Geo, Lena, and the others.

Now with Alec and Ren at my side, I felt like this was my first time on the track again. That everything rode on this, on me getting Ivori to respond.

"Oto," she whispered. "Relax."

"Kinda hard with everyone watching."

"Everyone is no—"

She cut off as she realized, and I pointed. "The whole track's out."

"Oh," she said, and I felt her engine falter a little.

"Now who's nervous?" I asked.

Her energy draw, though, wow. She pulled in a little more from me. Her engine settled. "They all have a little piece of them with us. They want to see us nail this track."

"All in," she said.

"All in," I replied.

The dash flickered and all our systems turned from green to red. They'd hit green again when they were ready for that "all in."

I looked up at the lights. They counted us in.

Three.

Two.

One.

Alek sparked into the air, his wheel taking off.

We were right alongside him. The gear changes were smooth; I barely felt anything change on the inside.

"Careful," Ivori warned as we headed into the first bend. Alek was already way ahead of us, his line perfect, and I coaxed the wheel a little too much and had to ease off as we clipped the side curb.

"Responsive, isn't she?" Tatsuno asked over comms.

"Very," I replied, shifting down and into the next bend. Changing up as soon as we were able. The power under us, though, that floored me. If every upgrade, every decision we made had this kind of real change. Ivori . . .

"Yes, Oto. We are going places. This is not like the skin I had. The rusted, trussed-up old chassis. This may be parts from many other cars, but they are pristine. They are new."

"Then let's break them in some." I pushed the gas, making sure my tires and everything else started to reach optimum temperatures. "How are we looking, Tatsuno?"

"Next lap should have everything in sync, looking good. We're monitoring you both on every level."

"Good." I approached the next bend and our tires hit optimal, but then something sparked red in my view.

"Owwww," Ivori moaned.

Shit. I let go of the gas.

Down changed the gears fast. Ivori let out a groan. And she pulled to the side of the track, speed slowing gradually. It took a while, but we eventually stopped.

"What is it?" I asked. "What broke?"

I opened the door and got out. Steam billowed out from the back tires. Braking system something . . . ugh.

Ivori just groaned still.

"Tatsuno?" I asked. "What?"

"Brakes failed," came his reply. "We're sending the truck up."

Alek pulled alongside me. "Ouch," he said.

"Yeah." I put my hand on the side panel. I could feel the extra heat. Pulling energy to me, I fed cooling water down through her systems, where it was safe to do so. The steam billowed out, and I had to sidestep to not be scalded in the face with it. But I knew she felt better.

"We're going to get things sorted." I patted her roof. "Just takes a little time, a little tweaking."

"Of course," Alek said.

"When's the next race again?" Ivori asked, as if any of us could have forgotten.

"We're six weeks off."

"Is that all?"

"We need to be in that race," I said. "I don't think we can afford to forfeit any others. We have to be fit enough."

"I know," Alek said. "You will be, I'm sure."

I turned to watch the truck pulling up behind us. I hopped on the back of Ren to get a lift back.

It was tough to see Ivori put back on the ramps. Especially with only just getting out there.

Alek came in behind us, and parking Ren, settled in beside me as Tatsuno and the team ran more diagnostics.

"We'll have to strip them down again, rebuild." Jin appeared from the back end.

"It's not good," Stacie agreed. "They are expensive parts."

I sighed. "Nothing is cheap. I'm getting used to that."

Tatsuno was already searching through the vicenet. "Sadly, very correct."

35

The price flashed on the screen, and I cringed. I stepped to Ivori. "We'll sort it," I said. "I'm sure we will."

"I know," she replied. "I have full faith."

Thursday, December 24th *Evening*
Year - 27514

Taryn,, as pale as she was, glanced around the room, plonked down on the couch and laughed. "It's perfect." She patted the seat next to her and Geo obliged. "Luca and Mira . . ."

"Mira will hate it," Geo said with a sigh.

"Whether she hates it or not, you've all done your best. I can see that."

I locked my eyes with hers. "They really have. It almost looks habitable."

Hara's voice drifted over comms to us. "Tant is inbound. Track flights are opening."

The whole shack rumbled. "Flights?" I asked raising an eyebrow at Geo.

Taryn's eyes widened. "You've never seen Tant, have you?"

"Briefly, I think," I replied.

Geo stood, smoothing his suit. "No, no, you haven't. Tant never comes in like this, usually. But he has bigger cargo this time."

"Cargo?" I was super confused now. Geo held a hand for Taryn, and she took it. The rest of the team followed us out of the shack and to the edges of the track.

When everyone's eyes drifted upward, what I thought I saw was the track roof moving.

"Holy shit, no way?" I asked, looking to Alek.

Geo spoke low enough I could only just hear him. "Yeah. Tant never comes in like this. The whole city will have seen him."

Zero Light

I swallowed; my hands also suddenly sweaty. The large ceiling above us shook; the lights around us and the dust off them drifted down. A line up the middle split the ceiling in two. Then it spread. Through the widening gap, I could see the blackness of the skies above. The odd twinkling stars.

The whole thing split. The whole roof moved, opening up.

"What was above us?" I asked Alek.

"A lot," he said. "But mostly that's all front facing. Here out the back, the stretch of the track reached out, under fields, empty space."

I ran a hand down my side, my hands sweating. "That makes much more sense."

The stars vanished, and a gust of wind ripped through the whole track. Taryn held onto her dress, and Geo pulled her in close.

There I saw it. Tant.

The sleek black nose dropped down first. Two large and then two smaller, sleek, V-shaped wings started to close off as downward thrusters slowed their momentum. Lights flashed on the underside, and stripped paintwork shone on all sides.

I'd seen trains, short range travel copters, and other things. But this? Tant was phenomenal; there were no other words for him.

Approaching cautiously, the wings dipped even further down and then he was inside the track itself. With a clang, the roof started to close immediately. Tant hovered there for a moment then descended further, stopping about a meter off the center inner field.

"Beautiful, isn't he?" Geo asked me.

"They can all do that?"

"Eventually, if that's what you want."

Ivori? I asked.

We have a lot to do before we're ready for any of that.

You can—

Yes, I was space born before I drifted to your planet. Whatever form I take can be upgraded, changed. What's putting on a few hundred tons, right?

A drop-down ramp appeared under Tant's belly and five figures walked down it.

Geo and Taryn moved to intercept. I felt shy, more than shy. I wanted to see Camran and Amalia. Sure, I did. But Luca's wife and kids. I . . .

Alek bumped into me. "They're all just people."

"Very powerful people."

"Yes, yes, they are."

"His kids look older than me."

"They're not as far as I know, but careful, they're—"

"What?" My nerves were already shot.

"They're probably going to be as scared of you as you are of them."

I straightened out a bit as the two groups met in the middle, the wide light doors clunking closed, the cool temperature over the track dissipating.

I walked with Alek. Ezra and Nishi were already hugging and chatting incessantly to Amalia.

Amalia smiled my way, yet turned her eyes down. She couldn't look at me? Why?

I moved before her, and to my surprise, even with Ezra there, she threw her hands around my neck. "Oto," she whispered, her breath tickling.

I gave her a squeeze. "Hey," I said. "What's wrong?"

"Later," she whispered and pushed away from me. "For Ezra's sake," she added. Then she spoke to Ezra. "He's grown on you."

Ezra blushed and came to take my side, a little possessively. "Looks good, right?"

Amalia grinned, giving me the once over. "He does."

Camran moved in beside her. "It is good to see you," he said, holding out a hand.

I took hold and shook it tightly. The others seemed to have moved off already, the kids in tow.

I felt a little lost. These two amazing and talented racers were so subdued. Gone was the excitement, the ferocity within. They were almost shells of their former selves.

I needed to talk to them both, but I knew they wouldn't talk in front of Ezra, maybe even Tatsuno.

"Break room," I said. "Nishi and the others set up before they left. We've got drinks and snacks."

"That sounds good," Camran said. "Been a long trip."

I glanced at Tant. *I'd love to talk to him*, I said to Ivori.

I'm sure you'll get a chance, she replied.

When Alek coughed, I moved back in with them and headed to the break room.

Geo and Luca were gone.

5

Friday, December 25th *Early Morning*
Year - 27514

It had been a long night. Ezra and Tatsuno kept the conversations going forever. I never thought I'd get her away from Amalia. But eventually, Ezra poked me from my thoughts. "We should go," she'd said. "We'll be back early enough."

She also hadn't been kidding about that. I didn't think I'd barely gotten a wink of sleep when she was kissing the side of my neck.

I tried not to let her wake me fully, but who was I kidding. I looked up into her beautiful, sparkling eyes. "Morning," I said, kissing her.

"I let you sleep as long as I could. I just wanted to give you your present before anyone else was up."

I ran my hands up under her nightshirt, and she giggled. "Not that, silly." She then hopped off the bed and moved to our small dressing unit. I leaned up on one elbow and watched her. The sharp contrast of her mechanic implant still made me think of how much she'd been through the last few months. Heck, what all of us had.

When she turned to face me, though, her smile would have lit the world with the brightness in her eyes as she pulled a small box around for me to see. Then she bounced back over and plunked onto the bed.

"What is this?" I asked, my voice cracked slightly. From the dryness of the previous night's talking or the dry air.

She looked suddenly shy, resting a hand on the neatly wrapped box. "You've never had a present, have you?"

I reached for her hand, placed mine on top of hers. "No," I said.

"I shouldn't have, should I?"

She tried to pull away, but I held onto her.

"I've been so stupid, haven't I? I've seen you fussing around. But I've never understood the why, the reasons. I get it is a holiday for most. But . . ."

Ezra pulled back then. She went to her bedside drawer, and pulled out an old, tattered book. Then she wriggled back in bed with me, putting her present box on the nightstand.

"Let me tell you a story," she said. "This came from a planet and civilization much older than ours. Maybe even from where we originated."

She turned the book's pages over and I listened intently. I let her tell me of the origins of Christmas, and it was pretty fascinating. When she got to the last page, she ran a finger over the Christmas tree.

Short, spiky green flora covered in shiny silver and red bells which seemed to be lit with Azris from within. Then wrapped all around its circumference were long, silken, multicolored cloths.

"This helped you, didn't it?" I asked her, once more taking her hand in mine.

"We might never have had much, but we tried at Christmas to do something for each other." Ezra picked up the box once more and held it out to me.

I tried to swallow the emotions. The story was nice. The reasons were nice. But this woman, she was giving me a gift. She couldn't have given me anything that could surpass her love for me. That I was sure of.

"It took me a long time," she said. "A really long time. But I wanted you to have something which would remind you of the start of your journey."

I tugged the tiny yellow ribbon, and it slipped off. Then I sucked in a breath, about to open it. Ezra snuggled into my side.

I took the lid off carefully and looked inside. A ring. Her ring. I couldn't touch it. Or do anything. "Ez—" I started.

She reached over and pulled it out. "It took me a long time to get it reset. It's not just my ring." She held it out to me, her eyes shining. "It's part of Ivori too, and Ren."

"What?"

"I had to ask. Their metals are in short supply; even this amount is worth so much. But Ren and Ivori parted with enough to mix with the gold. The gems are new. All fully charged." She held it up to me, so it glinted in the lights from above us.

The detail around the outer ring, and then on the inside . . . "I—"

Ezra took my hand in hers and gently put the ring on it.

Its stats popped up then.

Ring of Light - A gift from Ezra
Adapted, so you may use it as you wish.
Boosts Azris circulation and usage, + 30 to all stats
Uses = 5

It had much more punch than hers had. "You need this," I said to her. "You shouldn't give these things away."

"No," she replied. "This is for you; you need it. It's meant for you. I'll find something when it's time. We are family—family looks out for each other. Look, it says so on the inside—"

I cut her off this time and read it. "Family isn't always blood."

My hands shook as I reached to pick it up. Ezra poked the box. "You don't need to wear it as a ring, only if you want to. There's a chain, just in case."

I didn't know how I felt about it, but I pulled the chain out and slipped the ring onto it. Ezra then helped me fasten it around my neck. I pulled her into my lap then and kissed her deeply.

The knock woke us both later. I let Ezra snuggle against me and I traced the skin of her naked form up her back of her thighs and ass before she giggled and pushed me off.

"We'd better get up. I have no doubt Tatsuno and Alek have spoiled you rotten, too."

I groaned. "Really?"

She laughed but moved to dress. I was sad to see her naked form covered up, but I pulled on clothes too. "You really never noticed any of our preparations the last few days, did you?"

I cringed. "I'm sorry."

She held out a hand. "Come on." And then she tugged me with her into the lounge.

All the lights were on, and right in front of us stood a rather large tree. It wasn't as decorated as the ones in her storybook. But it shone just like her face did. "Wow, I never saw it at all."

Ezra put a hand on her hip. "I told you he was one-track-minded."

I yanked her to me, nibbled her neck.

"Eeeew," Alek said.

I laughed at him and let her go. She bounced off into the melee around the tree then. I moved to the couch and sat, still feeling tired from the night before.

Lena sat next to me. "You look like I feel," she said and handed me a drink.

I sipped the fruity tasting liquid. "It's been a tough few days."

Lena nodded as Pete brought over a couple of trays of breakfast foods. He'd only got the tray down when Alek and Ezra's raised voices got all of our attention. "I told you not to," Ezra said, pouting.

She'd a box open in front of her, but her face told everyone she was thrilled. "It's not much," Tatsuno said. "Really? It's just because we love you."

Tears burst free from her eyes then, and I was about to stand, but Lena put a hand on my arm. "This is the first year they've had the opportunity to spoil each other."

I couldn't help but stare at the three of them, Alek in pajamas and Tatsuno in his finest slacks and shirt.

"They're amazing," I said.

Lena handed me a plate with toast on. "It's going to be awhile before we get lunch. Eat."

I looked at her. "I thought it was being delivered from Grovers?"

Pete shook his head. "With Mira here, not a chance. She had new orders out and delivered through the night. I have no doubt whatsoever that she's been working through the night for us."

That baffled me. I knew Ezra could cook to some degree, which was lovely, but most of our foods and all the extras now were supplied by Grovers. We'd become a small army to feed, and Geo made sure we were never without. Even Bodil brought extra in everyday just to be sure. I felt like I'd never stop eating. There was always so much food around.

I patted my stomach, though. I wasn't fat, not by any means, but I was a lot, lot heavier than I had been when they'd all first met me. I wanted to put the toast down. Lena gave me a side-eyed glance. "Eat."

I put it back in my mouth and chewed the crust off.

"Better," she said and ate her own.

Ezra and Alek spoke for just a moment longer before all eyes turned to me.

"Your turn."

"Guys," I mumbled.

Tatsuno moved in front of me, offering a hand. I put the toast down and wiped the crumbs off me before I let him pull me up.

Alek beamed at the tree just as much as his sister. "This is for you." He pulled out a rather gigantic bag, and when he handed it to me, I groaned at the sheer weight.

"It's taken us a lot of running about, but we never got that trip to the shops."

I pulled out item after item. "This is an entire wardrobe?"

Tatsuno nodded. "I've watched the kinds of clothes you picked out of Alek's. I think they're to suit and to the right size."

There was so much of it, and I felt terrible. "I haven't gotten anyone anything," I almost stammered out.

Alek put his hand on my arm. "We didn't expect you to. We wanted your first with us to be special."

I almost dropped the bag, Tatsuno whirled it all away before I could. I pulled Alek to me, and I held on tight. "It would have been special with just you around," I said.

"Well, at least now you won't look like a cast off at dinner." Tatsuno laughed.

I moved to hug him, and he squeezed me tight. "You're welcome."

While they gave Lena and a surprised Pete some gifts, I went to put the clothes away and to get changed into a nice pair of jeans, shirt, sweater and jacket. There were new boots, too, and I slipped them on before I checked myself out in the mirror.

Clean cut clothes, lines that my eyes traced down, I had fine form. This looked good, so good. I would have even taken myself to be in Geo's league, and that was saying something. He was smart.

I stepped out into the living room to their stares. "Damn," Alek said, and looked from Tatsuno to me. "Think I should have tried to turn him."

Ezra burst out laughing, and Tatsuno grinned. "If you couldn't," he said, "I'd sure as hell try!"

I held a hand out for Ezra, but she just spun around me, her hands roaming the silken clothes. "Eyes only for me, right, Oto?"

"Always," I said, then yanked her in for a kiss.

Friday, December 25th *Afternoon*
Year - 27514

The car had picked us all up and taken us to the track. I had no idea our track's 'shack' as they all called it, could look so good.

I followed all the others inside and had to do a double take. Geo and Luca stood out on the balcony sipping what looked like alcohol out of crystal tumblers. The three kids I'd not met yet were all playing a board game in the central lounge with lots of opened boxes and gifts to them.

I just stood watching, not knowing where or what to do with myself. Ezra talked excitedly with Amalia, Tatsuno and Alek made their way outside with the guys, and Lena and Pete made room on the couch before joining in with the kids.

I heard a cough from the kitchen and glanced over. The woman that looked back at me was well dressed. Her hair tied up and under a see-through net. I smiled at her, but didn't know what to say.

She waved me over. "Oto?" she asked, her voice smooth, warm.

"Yes, ma'am."

She held out a floured hand for me to shake. Then realized it, laughed, and wiped it on her apron. "Mira Gianetta."

I shook her hand gently, surprised at her strength. "Don't be surprised. I might look on the dainty side. But I'd show you a thing or two."

I almost choked on my own spit.

Mira laughed. "They've been filling your head with nonsense, haven't they?"

"I try not to listen and judge people for myself," I replied.

"Well then, let's leave them to it." She tugged me into the kitchen. "You can help me with some of this, right?"

I glanced down at my new clothes, cringed on the inside. But Mira was pulling out a fresh apron in seconds.

"Just follow my lead." She smiled.

"I've never spent any time in a kitchen," I admitted.

"You'll do fine. If I can teach my kids, I can teach you."

I did exactly as she said, and she was brilliant with her instructions. She told stories about Luca and Geo, and all of her four children, though Ray wasn't with the gaggle playing the game. Most of the stories were of the antics at Christmas for the whole family. Lots of stories about the tracks, and life in general. We veered off once or twice but they all drifted back to being about Ray. I didn't want to pry. I felt she had to tell these me these stories, and it felt good to be around her. More than good.

Luca came through once to refill his glass. He stood at the edge of the rather old-looking breakfast unit and put the glass down. I watched him for a moment. He lowered his eyes. "It's been a while since I've seen you like this, Mira."

Mira turned to him. She gasped, then her eyes bristled with tears. All of a sudden, this strong, amazing woman I'd just spent the last few hours with totally fell apart.

Luca came to her, wrapped her in his arms. "Hey, hey, you know you don't need to do all of this."

"I have to," she sobbed. "I need to."

Tears filled Luca's eyes too as he held onto his wife. I'd no idea what just happened, or why. She was full of stories, so many wonderful stories. Why did she turn so sad? I swallowed my own tears. Seeing her and Luca like this . . . hit me hard.

Taryn stepped in and came to me. She put her hand in mine and tugged me gently away.

"He's dead, isn't he?" I asked her as she made her way through to the balcony, Geo nowhere to be seen.

"You've been thrown in at the deep end. This"—she waved her arm around the track—"their lives, the track."

Taryn leaned on me. "Ray lost his life last year. It came as a shock for every one of us."

"What happened?" I asked.

"He was coming home from training, just a regular trip, nothing out of the ordinary. He had guards, just like Geo and Luca have, just not quite as up front as they were. They were ambushed, all died. We've been investigating for him, my family and some of my closest friends from Tikinia." Her eyes narrowed; lips pursed. "I believe the Sevran Vipers had a hit on the shuttle, but we can't prove it."

"You've not said anything to them, have you?"

Taryn shook her head, wiped a tear from her cheek. "There's always been this thing between them. Even I don't fully understand why they picked on the Frasers brothers."

"I do," I said.

She raised an eyebrow at me. "Oh?"

"They can see the potential of the family. They are a threat." I turned around to look into the living space. Lena was laughing at Pete and the kids were in fits of giggles. "Amalia and Camran are struggling out there? I bet it's because the other teams are literally throwing everything, they can at them, right?"

Geo appeared at the door with two fresh bottles in hand. He glanced at the kitchen and then out to us. He made his way over, a frown creasing his face.

"I think you are right," Taryn said. She then let me go, and moved to take the bottles off Geo. "I'll go help Mira. I'll send Luca back out here in a few, okay."

Geo moved to my side, handing me his glass. "Looks like you could do with this."

I took it off him, sniffed the liquid. "Strong?"

"Very," he replied. "We should have warned you."

"I'm learning, though you and your family are more—"

"Broken then you thought?"

I downed the alcohol, savoring the liquid as it stung the sides of my throat and down into the now pretty hungry pit of my stomach. "Yeah." I smiled slightly when I said it, reaching to put a hand on his arm. "Much more like me than I realized."

6

Friday, December 25th *Late Evening*
Year - 27514

Ezra curled into my side, and I wrapped her up tight. Mira and the others made their excuses and off they went to bed. Despite the earlier setback. Amalia, Alek, and Tatsuno had all helped Mira out with the rest of the work in the kitchen. The fifteen of us managed to squeeze around a table for eight—well, ten at most—and we ate, we laughed, we shared even more stories.

Bon was totally smitten with Amalia; the kid hung on every word. It was also obvious to see Amalia and Camran had grown closer. I didn't know their relationship status, but caught them holding hands, giving each other nice long glances.

I needed to get some time with her, though. I had questions. Questions for the both of them and I didn't want to have to wait.

Alek yawned. "Time to go," he said and patted Tatsuno's hand.

"Damn, it's not even 10 p.m.!" Tatsuno chided. "Thought we were going to go out dancing?"

Amalia's eyes lit up and she made puppy dog eyes at Camran. "Can we?"

"You really want to go out now?"

Amalia nodded enthusiastically and looked around the group. "Ezra?"

Ezra shook her head. So did Alek. "I'm exhausted."

I could either go home with them, it seemed, or out for the night. I was torn. Ezra prodded me. "Go. This is your first year to be able to enjoy it. I won't stop you."

I stared deep into her eyes. "You're sure?"

"I trust you, yes. Just sneak in quiet as you can. But make sure you come home."

I kissed her nose, then her lips. "I will."

Lena's eyes sparkled. "I love dancing!"

Crap, I couldn't shake my tail, though. I gave Pete an apologetic glance, but he just smiled back at me. "Bring her home safe," he then added.

They waited for the others to all leave, never making a move; the house, almost deadly quiet, spooked me.

Camran moved to the kitchen without saying a word and came back with a full bottle of booze and four shot glasses. Lena returned with a tray of nibbles, a bottle of lemonade, and a bucket with ice.

"No dancing?" Amalia asked, eyeing the bottle.

Camran sat and popped the cork. "You knew it was a ploy to get Oto on his own."

I threw Lena a glance. "Well, not quite on my own."

"No way I was missing this," she said. "These two better spill the beans, and fast. It's been driving me wild."

Amalia's face furrowed, she picked up a glass of the rich, red-looking liquid and downed it, slamming the glass down for one more. "Fill it."

Camran eyed her sideways but filled the glass again. When we'd all got one nestled in our grasp, Amalia lowered her eyes. "Luca doesn't know—"

"Yet," I added for her; they knew I'd tell him.

"It was easy to laugh off at first." Camran took Amalia's hand in his, entwining his fingers with hers. "I'd started to get threatening DMs on the vicenet."

Amalia squirmed, and it made my stomach churn, anger flooding my veins. Camran pulled her into his side. "I guess because they couldn't get any rise from him, they came to me instead. I've had my fair share of admirers." She cast him a glance. "It wasn't the usual, guys just looking to hook up, spammers, bots. It was nasty from the start. Not even the usual dick pics, but much more serious stuff. Pictures of what they said they wanted to do to me, while Camran watched."

"You couldn't trace the origin at all?" Lena asked. She slid off the couch next to me and moved before Amalia. "Do you still have some of them?"

Amalia's hands shook. She put her glass down, then obviously flicked through her system, her eyes glazed over—and not from the alcohol. I saw her eyes change again as she sent the files to Lena. "I didn't want to keep any of it. But once I knew you were here, I knew you'd be able to help us."

Lena put her hand on Amalia's knee. "Who is your guard on Copter?"

"We've been under the close protection detail of the family Sect Yijun Zhong. But the tracks at Praitar city are rougher than anything I ever expected."

I didn't have a clue, but Lena glanced my way. "I have some sway with Yijun's guards. It's been a while since I had any contact with my closest allies there. I will get word to one of the sects from Jomar, Duan maybe. No." She paused. "I'll go to Sawa, they're probably best."

"I've heard of them," Amalia replied. "I don't know much about the politics there though, or above us, we've both been—"

"We are so out of our depth," Camran said and sighed, nursing his drink.

"No," Lena said. "You're not; they are. They don't know who they're messing around with."

Amalia downed her next drink, but when she asked for more, Camran wouldn't pour her another. "The threats started coming more often," she admitted. "Then they got worse."

I wondered how much worse . . .

Amalia sat upright then, and with deft fingers she unbuttoned her shirt, and shrugged out of the left side. There were large, deep purple bruises across her forearm, shoulder, and back.

"What. The. Hell?" Lena asked. "When was this?"

"Two days ago," she said, her voice cracking.

"And that's with a healer's aid, I presume?" Lena moved to sit on the side of the couch, arm placing a hand on Amalia's bare shoulder.

Camran nodded. "She wouldn't let me help when we had to leave for here."

"I understand that," I said to them both, knowing all too well how energy transfer could tip you over the edge, if you weren't ready to commit.

"The connotations?" Amalia asked me, while I noted healing energy enter her body from Lena.

"Yeah," I said.

Amalia grinned then, and winked at Camran. "I already made him mine, in full."

Lena coughed. "Oh, but?"

"He's a race as soon as we get back from here. I can't have him risking anything. I'm healing, it's just—"

"Slowly," he said, the pain crossing his brows.

"Does Luca know you're bonded?" Lena asked.

Camran nodded. "Yes, I asked him first. I didn't want to put any of us at risk just because I was in love. I would have waited forever if I had to."

"I wouldn't," Amalia chided. "Besides, we spend so much time together, could you have kept your hands off me, if I flaunted my skin a bit more?"

It was the way she jiggled her shoulders—it made her chest bounce, and I had to look away. "Damn, girl. That's cruel." Lena laughed, her energy still seeping through into her. She indicated the glass on the table and Camran filled it and passed it to her. "Thanks."

I sipped mine while Camran told us how she got jumped, and then subsequently beaten. He knew she was injured because of their connection. Because Etol was going nuts in his DMs too. "It took me too long to find her, holed up in some bin at the back of the Jin-Jo hotel."

"You went into the Jin-Jo?"

Camran nodded. "The owner there is an avid racer. He let us stay in one of the high rolling suites till the following day. I wanted to keep her there for a while, but Luca wanted us to come home. Amalia said we should."

"Because?"

"There're some messages in my DMs that involve you," she said. "Both you and Alek."

I literally poured the rest of the liquid in my mouth and swallowed quick. "Let me see them."

Amalia glanced at Camran, and he sent them over.

I felt the file hit my system and, with a quick pull up, click, and flick through, I scanned the messages.

They were vile.

Not just Alek and me, but Ezra. Thick black bonds had her trussed up, naked. Her mechanical leg on show, her scars. Every tiny detail was perfect. They'd really mastered these. As fake as they were, they were awful, and it wrenched at my soul. The need to protect her vibrated through me, so very real.

"Oto," Lena said. "The pictures aren't fake."

I glanced back at her. "What do you mean, not fake?"

"They're real people," Camran said. "They're not fake at all."

I looked again at the Ezra look-alike. "Real?"

The picture moved, turned into a 3D video. A man approached her, something in his hand. Then he struck her with it, slicing deep into her flesh. The scream penetrated my mind, and I immediately put my hands to my ears.

Lena was sitting next to me then. I felt something pinprick the side of my skin. Then she was poking around inside my mind, my system. "They're gone," she said.

When I looked up, she gave Camran a glare. "He had no idea what you sent him. He's like a child on the inside."

"I'm sorry," Camran said. "I—"

I swallowed. "They used real people, they hurt real people to threaten you, to threaten me, us?"

Amalia nodded.

"That's why you've been off your game, the training, the races?"

She nodded again.

I couldn't blame her for it. Those images were burned into my mind now. I would never forget that.

Lena knelt back down before the three of us, taking another drink herself and then pouring Amalia another. "Message already received by Shuko Sawa, the sect lord. He said he has two men he trusts with his life. I asked him to send them to Luca, and you when you get back."

Amalia's face paled. "Luca will . . ."

"He won't do anything, sweetie. Oto's got me. You need to talk to him, and you need the protection at that level, on that planet."

"They're stronger?"

"Sawa's men are tremendously strong," Lena said. "The two he's sending, I trained with myself."

A cough at the door. Luca stood in blue silk pajamas. "What's this?"

Amalia covered herself quickly, but Luca was in front of her in a split second. "No, no, you don't." With an outstretched hand, he waited till she took it, then she stood in front of him. Even with the power inside him, the anger etched on his face, Amalia didn't shake. Though I would have. I was trembling here on the couch. His aura threatened to flatten all of us. Carefully, he eased her shirt off her shoulder, his eyes widened.

"Luca," Lena started.

He held up a finger. That was it, and she sat back down. "Camran." Luca glanced at him.

"We were going to tell you," he said, lowering his eyes.

"Come here." His finger pointed to Amalia's side.

Camran didn't hesitate and moved to her side.

Luca then reached out with that finger, touched it to the side of Camran's temple. "Release," he said.

I saw what happened, though I'd no idea the how, the logistics as Camran just opened his mind for him.

Luca's eyes darkened, his skin changing too. Amalia let out a gasp, and reached for Luca's hand, but he didn't let go. The healing energy that flooded her also flooded the room. The feeling of alcohol that was buzzing through my veins, gone in a split second.

Luca let his finger drop, and Camran reached for Amalia. "Don't ever be afraid of what I'm going to say to you. Ever."

Camran's face lowered, but Luca lifted his chin so their eyes could meet. "Never. If anyone hurts either of you, they're hurting me. Understand?"

Camran nodded.

"You're family. You might not be blood, but you are mine."

Amalia threw her arms around him, and Luca pulled Camran to him as well. "Okay," Camran said. "Okay. I promise."

Luca turned to the both of us, yet his eyes glazed. Did he just wobble too? "What's the plan?" he asked.

"Sawa will coordinate with Copter and have men with you as soon as you land. Tell them everything, hold nothing back. At all. I mean that."

"You'd trust Sawa with my life?" Luca asked.

"Yes, I spent a good few years with them on Copter. They're good people."

Luca finally eased off Camran. When their eyes met again, he shook his head. "Kids, you'll be the dang death of me for stress. I knew something was wrong. I left you both *all* the opportunities possible to come to me, yet I had to come here to get you to talk."

"Kids?" Amalia asked. Her face had at least stopped flushing.

Luca eased off her, then with soft hands, pulled her shirt back over her shoulders, looping in the top few buttons. "Yes, you're not much older than mine, as much as you don't think you are. You really are still children."

She rolled her eyes, but then her face beamed at him. "Can I call you Dad?"

Luca's face fell, and I saw him struggle with his words. "If you promise me you'll never keep anything from me, you can call me anything you like when we're on our own, when there is just us."

"You're serious?" She put a hand to her mouth, mumbled out, "Really serious?"

57

I knew she'd been joking, but I had seen how he reacted over Raphael and Alek's abuse, and now how quickly he'd reacted to her being injured.

"Tell me here now, you've never thought of it?" he asked her. His shoulders fell, his eyes soft.

Amalia swallowed, and I saw her tremble. Camran held onto her. "You've always treated us like family," he said. "But those words mean more to us than anything."

"Good." Luca turned to us. "Get another bottle and let's make sure we're all on the same page. Because when we return to Copter, you need to nail those races. The both of you."

Lena moved to get the extra glass and another bottle from the kitchen. When she returned, Luca was sitting next to me. As much as we'd spent the day with them, seen his family and kids play, play up. Love each other. Right now with these wonderful people, I felt home. I loved being around Geo. His fire sparked mine and my water in ways I wanted to push every day. But Geo was on a whole other level. I wasn't saying it just because he was Emperor Rank 8, either. Wait. I looked at him. "You've moved up a level. While you healed Amalia?"

He glanced at me. "I might have tried to keep it as low key as possible, but with you around there's no real chance of that, is there?"

"You ranked up because of me?"

Luca raised his glass to her. "I did. It's not often I actually get to heal anyone, and you were hiding more than you were telling."

Camran shot her a glare. "Babe?"

"I didn't want anyone to worry. It would have healed."

"What if it didn't?"

Amalia fought her emotions. "Promise it won't happen again."

"Better." He winked at her.

"So," I said. "What does someone at your level do with their points?"

Camran almost spat his drink out, and Luca chuckled. "There's no etiquette whatsoever with this young man, is there?"

Lena started to laugh, too. "Not at all."

"What?" I asked. "I only asked what you were all thinking."

"Touché," Lena said, dipping her head at me.

Then all eyes turned to Luca.

"Okay, let me tell you a few things . . . then we'll sort out the plan for going home. Deal?"

"Deal!" all four of us said at once.

Luca poured himself another glass to sip. His shoulders sank, his whole posture changing. My eyes glanced to the others; we all felt that energy draw.

Luca pulled it to him from everywhere, and I watched in awe. It came from below, deep from the planet. His eyes darkened, even from the iris this time. His skin turned a deeper brown. I breathed in that scent, rich, sweet, and earthy.

It felt like home. All of it. I breathed out a large sigh. The effect of the alcohol, or something else?

Luca turned to me. "I don't often let anyone see me," he said. "You've all been part of something today that no one would be privileged to. My family. Because you are family. This is who I am."

"Protector," Lena said.

"Ambassador," Camran added.

"Father," Amalia almost whispered.

I couldn't put words to exactly what I felt. "You could kill us in a heartbeat," I managed.

"Not quite," he admitted. "The system doesn't alter for us, but it does make a much bigger difference when you rank up."

With the flick of his hand. All four of our stats displayed in front of us. Then to the side was his.

"A little more detail than *you* first saw."

He wasn't kidding. Tant's stats showed underneath, and his affinity rankings.

Name = Luca Giannetta
ID Number = 217717
Age = 37
Species = Altraision
Sex = Male
Alignment - Chaotic Neutral

Bloodline = Royal Seven
Health = 99%
Cultivation Level - Emperor Rank 9
Active Meridians = 12/12
Nanites = 891,621
Artefacts = 1
Chosen Specialist = Azris Racer
Chosen Affinity - Earth
Second Chosen Affinity - Fire

Statistic = Normal + Car + Cultivation
Strength = 69/390.54
Dexterity = 32/166.08
Constitution = 54/294.84
Int/Wis/Spirit = 63

Affinities - Rank
Water - Orange
Fire - Red
Earth - White
Air - White
Light - White
Darkness - White
Spirit - Red

Name - Tant
Icarian-WarLord
Model - X2217- MetalWalker
Year/Birth - 27416

Composition -
Solids - Silver
Liquid - Harilliom/Mercury
Nanites swarm - 2.3 million
Nanites detached - 1.3 million

Artefact - 1

Slots allocated - 57

Engine - Level 6
Outer Frame - Level 4
Tires - Level 5
Lights - Level 3
Steering - Level 5
Bumpers - Level 4
Windshield - Level 3
Mirrors - Level 1
Core Intelligence - Level 7
Chassis - Level 5
Shield - Level 8
Nitro - Level 6

Total =

STR - 21
DEX - 7
CON - 16

"One look, one lesson," he said. "I'll answer some questions at the end, okay?"

Everyone stared at the screens. There was no hiding who we all were, not at all. Lena looked a little embarrassed, and Luca spotted her blushing face.

"Do not be ashamed of what happened in defending the others. You broke an artifact, that is all. You are more valuable. Look what you've done already for these two; understand that's worth more than an artifact."

Lena sucked in a breath, nodded, and then looked at the sheets once more.

It was also nice to see where Camran and Amalia sat on the scale. I wasn't far behind. That gave me hope. Lots of it.

Luca spoke again. "I only get the same number of rewards you do, so still three points to assign per level. If I put them evenly, I grow pretty nicely on all sides. Balance is what I'm mostly going for now."

He placed them temporarily into the slots so we could see the bump up.

Strength = 390.54 to **406.7**
Dexterity = 166.08 to **174.9**
Constitution = 294.84 to **308.55**

The difference was nothing at all to sniff at; even the bumps already from Tant and whatever he'd been doing on Copter had made a difference, I recalled his first stats that I'd seen. He'd either taken place in four races himself, or been awarded something else. Racing, really? I wanted to see that.

"If I put all three into Strength, he said. It would go from—"

The numbers changed.

Strength = 390.54 to **419.76**

"Or the same for the other two—"

And changed again.

Dexterity = 166.08 to **186.2**
Constitution = 294.84 to **320.91**

"That's a hell of a change," I said.

"Yes, and for you, those three points would move only . . ."

My stats altered, though I cringed a bit like Lena had. The point was very clear.

Strength = 102.38 to **105.12**
Dexterity = 65.75 to **68.25**
Constitution = 97.95 to **99.95**

While it made a nice little difference to me, it made much more of a difference at his level.

Seeing it made it sink in much more.

"So what are you picking and why?" Lena asked.

His eyes twinkled, his brows furrowed. "Where I'm at, and where Amalia and Camran need them to be. Two to Constitution and one to Strength."

He moved the points back and clicked accept. They altered right in front of us permanently.

Strength = **70/406.7**
Dexterity = 32/**169.28**
Constitution = **56/314.72**
Int/Wis/Spirit = 63

When he faltered, his glass in his hand wobbling, I reached out to steady the glass.

"Still feels weird?"

Luca's eyes dimmed. "Yes, it really does." He waved his hand, and the stats vanished. "You get one question each, that's it. Then sleep."

7

Saturday, December 26th *Very Early*
Year - 27514

Luca bid the others goodnight and asked me to sit with him so the others wouldn't get to overhear my question.

Lena wasn't going to move, but he only had to look at her once more, and she dipped her head. "I'll wait outside."

The door clicked behind us, and Luca turned to me. "The others saw what I wanted them to see. You saw everything. Your question pertains to that."

"I didn't think they saw everything," I'd admitted. "Why me?" I asked. "That's not my question, though."

"Because I don't have a choice, Oto."

"I don't understand," I said. "Talk to me, don't hold it back. Please?"

Luca's eyes darkened, and I could feel his aura. Even if it didn't floor me, he was powerful, and it should have. It didn't make sense. "You're a lower cultivation rank. You're lower in body specs, too."

I frowned. He knew I was. Heck, I knew I was. Everyone did. That wasn't really an answer.

He raised an eyebrow at me. "But what are you stronger with?"

I thought, hard. "Oh," I replied. "My affinities. But wait, only some of them?"

"Yes, but those that matter, yes."

I brought up my stats, remembered what I'd just seen on his sheet. "Spirit, Light, and Darkness," I said.

He smiled. "You're an enigma for sure. The higher we get, we can slowly move our other affinities, barely. But you're advancing them almost as fast as your Azris levels in general."

"So that first time you shared your stats with me?"

He rubbed the stubble growing on his chin. "It was a struggle to keep you from catching I was hiding things." He chuckled. "Now, I can't hide at all."

"Anyone who shares themselves with someone like me, I can see everything?"

"I've only encountered one other person like you, and I know the other Immortals can't do it, either."

"One other?" I asked, suddenly scared. "Who?"

"Miklao Akamine. He's Taryn's uncle."

"On Halara? Where Geo wouldn't go . . . so he's . . .what?"

"Azris, Immortal, Rank 9, last I heard. But that was a very long time ago. He could be even higher now."

"God—" I said and knew. "No wonder Geo didn't want to go there."

Luca sipped from his glass and checked the time. "I understand his fears. Taryn's family is more than impressive."

"How did they meet?"

"You've had more than one question. We have many stories I could fill your head with all night long. But that pretty little lady of yours will wake and worry."

I looked at the time myself. "Crap."

"Be back here nice and early," Luca said as I moved to leave. "No slacking on training just because you've been here all night."

I dipped my head at him. "Of course. Thank you for today. It's been one of the most memorable in my life."

Luca stood. "I hope for many more. I know Mira does too. She likes you a lot." He waved me to the door and finding Lena where she said she would be, we both ran for it. She never once asked what Luca wanted me for.

I crawled into bed beside Ezra way too late—no, early. My questions to Luca bouncing around in my head. I was filled with even more I wanted to ask. Maybe one day.

Taryn though, I could ask her some more. If she'd talk to me. She might.

Ezra snuggled against my chest, and I slept, eventually.

Thursday, February 4th *Morning*
Year - 27515

Every day, we trained. Every day, the team sold or traded items to get Ivori the part she needed in time.

While Geo and I sparred in the outside parking lot, Hara rushed across the track. I faltered at seeing him running, and Geo got a nice crack to the side of my ribs.

"Ouch," Hara said.

"What is it?" Geo asked.

"Part's in, they did it."

Both Geo and I moved to follow him back across the track to the garage.

Once inside, we could both see the team working like crazy. I stood to the side and just watched.

It feels good, Ivori said to me.

You think this will work? We really don't have long to get ready.

Less than two weeks, Oto. This is it. We're either in, or we're out.

Out?

Out, totally. We have to be in this race come hell or high water. Even if we don't win it, we need it to be able to continue, and for that, we have to be in it.

I sucked in a breath as Jin and Itoh popped up from under her. "Done!"

Hara hit the drop button, and the ramp lowered her down. Ivori's engine roared.

"Well then," I said, and grinned. "Better test her out."

Nishi tapped the top of the cab. "Zero's all checked out. You're good to go. Track's clear."

"Now that sounds like a blast," Alek said, and was up, helmet on, kicking Ren off his stand in seconds.

I slid into my seat, my belt securing around me. I flexed my hands on the wheel, noting all the differences again, remembering each part of the process.

Finger flick to the right button and I never even felt her click into first. I hit for the gas, and I made her engine roar. *Bang!*

Even Alek flinched.

All eyes turned to the 3D screens.

No red lights. I held my hands up, "Sorry!"

Tatsuno laughed and pointed. "Get your asses out there."

Alek and Ren were ready before I even knew it.

Steady as I could, I eased her out the pits onto our track. Her gentle purr settled my soul in such a way I wasn't even watching the lights.

Alek tapped on our hood, "Good?" he asked.

"All green," Tatsuno said through comms.

I held up both thumbs to Alek and replied, "All green, let's do this!"

Everything purred and hummed as it should. Finally, everything was running.

We had this.

Warm-up lap around had both Alek and I passing each other in stages. I loved how he flew past me, jammed on, then let me pass him in return.

When the lights were ready to go for real, timing us, the track and Alek had my full attention. No games this round.

Alek didn't pop any wheelies out the gate, but he was so fast without. "They're getting better," I said, and flicked through the gears with ease, following him into the bends with a little more care than I did that first time around. I watched our temperatures, and our lines still waiting for confirmation from the team before I opened Ivori up properly.

"Don't forget how much stronger you both are," Ivori said. "You're outgrowing this track."

"When Amalia and Camran left, they weren't any higher levels than Alek and I, were they?"

"No, and you know that because you saw their full stats at Christmas."

"By the time we're ready to move on, we'll be past them." I eased into the next few bends, coming out strong, anticipating our end run and the possible Azris burn.

"Way past them," she said, and as I flicked from left to right and dropped down another gear to power out the last corner, Ivori simply said, "Hold on."

I held on, and when she tapped into my core, Azris, I felt her rip away from underneath me, forcing me back with tremendous power into my seat. "Easy," I said. "Don't want to blo—"

"Holy fuck." Tatsuno's voice broke apart, staticky.

We flew; it literally felt like flying.

The speed I couldn't even register.

We shot past the start, and the timer, knocking more off it than we ever had before. I hit the brakes and waited for it.

"We're still green," Tatsuno's voice came across the dash. "You can breathe."

I let the breath out, looking to the dash, then back to the track as we neared the finish line. Alek sat on Ren, waiting. I turned the wheel slightly. "Best not wipe my best mate out," I said.

"No, you best not," Tatsuno chided.

We stopped beside him, and he flipped his lid up with a huge grin plastered over his face. "You nailed that. You put my timing to shame."

"What?"

Alek pointed to the board.

Alek/Ren – 6.04
Oto/Ivori – 5.99

We'd shaved five seconds off his time, his time. He was on two wheels.

I hopped out and stood gawking at the time.

I laughed. "We need a bigger track."

Alek kicked the side stand down and stood beside me. "You've got this," he said.

"We've got this," I said.

Saturday, February 6th *Morning*
   Year - 27515

We spent every spare moment practicing. The night before the race, I didn't sleep a wink, tossing and turning. Today would reveal if that practice was enough. I just couldn't settle at all.

In the end, I slipped out of bed, hoping not to keep Ezra awake any longer. When she came into the living room rubbing her eyes, I went to make her a hot tea. "You look like I feel," she said.

"I'll be okay once we're city side."

"This trip's a lot different," she said. "I understand."

"Alek's been through it with me several times, especially while we loaded Ivori and Ren into the box."

"They'll be fine, just under the train's belly."

I nodded, but my stomach still churned.

The train was nothing like the one we'd gone to the city in. This was private run. Locked and loaded. Everything about it screamed money and lots of it.

Lena and Pete were on edge while waiting as everyone else loaded on and we were last.

"You nervous about anything specific?" I asked Lena as she sat next to me. Ezra sat across from us. It might have been a private car for our team. But something had her on edge more than anything else.

There was water and hot drinks on the table for us, and I managed to sip mine as the train set off.

"We're okay," Ezra said. "Lena's just doing her job."

"Making me nervous," I said.

"Sorry," she poured herself a hot drink. "I don't mean to. I'm not used to someone else worrying about us as much as I am. Stop worrying."

"It's been a while since you've had a target on your back," Pete said.

That didn't make me feel any better.

I settled back, and so did Ezra, her feet entwining with mine under the table. I liked this. It was comforting without being too much.

I rested my head back on the pillow on the seat and closed my eyes. "Rest if you can," Lena said. "We do have a long way to travel."

Several hours before we even hit the ocean, apparently. Okburg was on the other side of the planet. The furthest city away from Esrall. Once we hit the ocean, it was again a few hours out before we came to their lands, and then several hours in.

I could only pretend to sleep for so long, though. Some of the team rested here and there but the buzz of their chatter around the car was electric.

I glanced over at Geo and Taryn, who sat with Pete and Hara. I mean, could I expect any less? This wasn't just *a* race; this was *the* race. Geo asked those he could afford to take the time off to come, and although the others at the track still needed Hara around, he'd said there was no way he'd miss it. Everyone else would have to watch from the track itself, live if they could. There was a local time difference as well. I had never experienced another time zone.

This whole trip was bringing in all the experiences for me, and as much as I'd been overwhelmed with everything at the start. This . . . my stomach lurched with the train.

I moved to stand. "I need the bathroom."

Lena let me out and pointed me back the way we came.

I ran for it, hitting the door and making for the nearest toilet bowl. I just made it before I vomited my early breakfast everywhere.

I leaned back on the cool tiles. It made me feel better, the open door swinging behind me.

Taryn stood at the sink, rinsing her hands.

"This the ladies?" I asked, feeling heat flushing up my neck.

She glanced at me. "Communal, it's a private car." The rumble of the train's engine underneath shook the floor. Taryn turned, came and sat in front of me, crossing her legs slightly. She handed me a wet towel, her hand resting on her growing stomach. "Just nerves?" she asked.

I wiped off my lips, needing more water, but knew it would come straight back up now.

Taryn offered me a mint, and I took one. It would do for now. "This race means a lot to them," I said.

"And to you too."

"For all of us, yeah."

Taryn's hand bounced slightly, and she glanced down at it. "Baby likes this," she said. "I'm not so sure I like it with a baby."

"You could have stayed at the track," I said.

She looked up at me, her eyes twinkling. "I won't let my father baby me, let alone Geo. I am. We are fine."

"Who is your father?" I asked carefully. I'd dug some information up, but that was all I had.

Taryn's face paled. "You're asking something you shouldn't."

I was going to apologize, but I pulled it back. "No, these worlds, and these families, are more interconnected than Ezra should know. But Alek and I. We're all in for you. You understand that. Ivori is—"

"Very, very special, the fact you're linked to her even more so." She patted her stomach and her eyes met mine. "I've done some digging of my own. Geo and Luca think they can hide things, and that yes, maybe I shouldn't know. But we're already linked more than they know, more than we should be."

"Because of . . ." I didn't want to say it. "The accident?"

"Yes, that day I fell off Ren. Everything had gotten to me, to us, and I

Zero Light

let my guard down. You defended correctly. It was a mistake." She lowered her eyes, and I saw shame in them. Her cheeks flushed.

"Without it, would you have told Geo?"

Both hands rested on her stomach now. "I don't know, eventually."

I risked prodding again. "Who is he? Tell me why Geo is so scared. What does it mean?"

Taryn closed her eyes. "It will mean nothing to you, but my father's name is Quintin Tullius."

"Your last name is Tricoa, or no . . . your mother's maiden name, to trick the system here that you were someone else."

"Taryn is also my middle name," she admitted. "My full name is Sertoria Taryn Tullius."

None of it made any difference to me, to how I looked at her. But I could see she was nervous about telling me. "It's nice to meet you, Sertoria."

"Please, they all do call me Taryn."

"Okay," I said. I thought things were falling into place in my mind, at least a little. "Where is your father now?"

"Right now?" she fumbled. "Drakol."

"Let me get this straight," I said. "You are daughter to one of the most prestigious families in this universe, your father is on Drakol in an interplanetary face off with the Sevran Vipers, and we all just happened to be at the bottom of the pile, trying to make our way up, caught in all the crossfire."

"Pretty much," she agreed.

The fact she admitted it made my stomach churn all the more. Taryn was honest with me, all the time. I knew Geo and Luca were meant to be, but . . . I couldn't help myself, swallowing that sinking stomach churning feeling. "Where did you meet Geo?"

"Copter," she said. "I hated Halara; the schools there are so pretentious. I should have gone to one by our sect, where my brother went, but I made a run for some of the more underground cities the other side of our country, and eventually got off planet. I made my way to somewhere my money would last awhile, and I ended up at one of

73

Copter's gate races. Geo and Luca were both there with one of their opening teams. Fresh off Isala."

"You fell in love with racing and with Geo."

She nodded. "It took my father a long time to track me down. He was going to force me right on back to Halara. Geo stood up to him. He told my father things about me he never knew. Things he wanted to know. I've never seen him so angry and so sad before."

"I'm not one to understand family so much, but I can feel your emotions rolling off. It's still pretty raw for both Geo and your father. Does he know you're expecting?"

Taryn shook her head.

"That bad?"

"They'll want me home right away. They know I love Geo. They're pissed about the 'no wedding,' but they'd be furious till we were wed. They'd be right here, the whole family as fast as they could possibly be."

"Then tell them straight. You don't want them here till you are ready. Till you want that special day."

"I don't know if he still does."

"You're kidding me." I shook my head. "There's no way in hell that man out there wouldn't marry you, wouldn't be yours one thousand percent"

She let out a sigh. "I know, I'm just . . ."

"As nervous about that as I am about this race."

The bathroom went quiet. But I just let my head rest, calming my thoughts. My mind. So much to think about, so much that really was going on in this universe.

"If we don't get out there, they're going to knock that door in," I said.

"I think they know we're both in here. They'll be speculating."

I couldn't help but chuckle. "Do me one favor," I said to her. "Getting Geo to admit to you he didn't want to go to your home world was hard. Luca bringing his family back for the Christmas holiday was hard on them. I'm facing my fears every single day. Please talk to your family. I'm more than sure they will get you, they'll understand and support you, whatever you decide."

Tears brimmed in her eyes. "You're so good, Oto."

"Then do me one favor," I dared. "Look up my parents. They're working for someone. I have a feeling it was, or still is the Sevran Vipers. I just need to know for sure."

"You think your parents made you for the Vipers, don't you?" Her face fell. "That—"

"I don't just think it, I feel it." My gut twisted even more, and I tapped my chest. "I need you to confirm it before I address it. Them. Well, tell them anything. You understand that, right?"

"You can't know that for sure. Oto don't panic. Please." Her hand lazily traced over her stomach now, the act itself soothing her and me. Mesmerizing me too.

"I can't help but panic," I said.

"Because they'd be worried you'll turn on them?"

"I'd never." I shook my head and yet I also had to admit. "I am worried though."

8

Sunday, February 7th *Early morning*
Year - 27515

"It's massive," I said to Ezra, feeling rather lost in looking at what lay before us.

For the most part as we drew in closer, the outer city buildings were bathed in moonlight, their occupants still tucked in their beds.

Once inside the main city limits, skyscrapers graced the horizon as far as I could see. Tiny lights from underneath illuminated them in eerie, yet beautiful flickers of things I could see one moment, and then gone the next.

Ezra leaned over and pushed my jaw up. "This is the first time I've been here too," she said. "But I agree. It's beautiful, but it's so big. Everything about it is just . . ."

Lena pointed to the lights at several spots. "There's three tracks here you can see them. Two are training. They're out in the distance. First and Second. Then that's the one we're heading to." She moved her hand across in front of us, the view so vast.

I stared. It was so far away, yet we could clearly see the layout from here.

"We've downloaded all the info we can on the track," Alek said. "But we'll get a good look in the morning on our first run."

"We're allowed out on it tomorrow?"

"Each team gets one play per day till the race. Select few gets to come in and watch, usually VIPs from surrounding cities."

"That will be good. I'd like to get a feel for it. Before the actual day, and a few thousand people here."

Lena poked me in the back. "A few *hundred* thousand. This city has a population a hundred times that of Mote Lerate."

I linked Ezra's arm in mine, and she squeezed on tight. "As long as we get to settle in somewhere for the night, eat and rest up. It will be fun."

"We've got the rooms at the back of the track, specifically requested for easy guarding."

"Makes sense," I said. "I'll be happy wherever you all are, and where Ivori is."

My mind drifted as we drew in closer and closer to those lights. The neon signs pointing us toward our destination shone around our cabin and lit Lena's hair with purple highlights. It made her look kinda sinister. Even I'd be anxious if I didn't know she was on our side.

I never stopped looking out of the window on the way in. Ivori would be brought in at a later time, once off the train with Itoh and Balsy and Hosoke. I could deal with that, just about. I didn't need to be there a hundred percent of the time.

Just nerves, I kept telling myself.

Everything was just so new to me. This, a real race, my first in this category, specific fast laid-out courses. Of course, I'd been tested every single day. We'd trained, and I'd been the one that pushed them here today. I had said I was ready.

What if I wasn't?

We are, Ivori said.

The hotels around the track also stretched high, higher than I could see. When I stared up at them, they pushed in on me. I shook the feelings off and concentrated on everything else. The roads gleamed; not a stray pebble marred their surface. The streetlights provided an orange glow that illuminated the sidewalk. It was as if the city's construction had only just finished yesterday. Even the paint on the signs glistened. So very different from ours.

"How are they so spotless?" I asked.

"Bots come out as soon as something is needed. Nothing is ever left on the ground for longer than a min. If you drop something you risk a fine. They're really strict," Lena said.

"That's good to know." I glanced at her. "Anything else I should know?"

Lena rolled her eyes, thinking, then focused back on me. "There's a curfew, but you're not leaving my sight, anyway. So you'll be good there."

It took forever for us to disembark, to go through security, and to be herded out into a bus and taken to the track. Then we were escorted by several guards into the house at the back of the track. It well kitted out. Much nicer than our shack, but the track itself, from what I glanced at on the way in, was also a lot bigger than ours. They had the room.

"How many garages are here?" I asked.

"Tons," he said. "This city loves racing. They don't have any competitors themselves; they just want to host. This is all for us!"

"Really?" That just seemed weird to me. "They've spent so much money on building all this."

"Nope, not one driver," Tatsuno said behind us. "They just love racing and watching everyone else compete."

I turned to see Alek and him coming in behind us, making themselves at home right away in the kitchen.

It was more than a relief to settle in for a bit. The weight of the last few months shifted off my shoulders. I smiled. We were able to train, to learn here for a bit and do what we wanted.

Study, drive. Race.

Wednesday, February 8th *Lunch*
   Year – 27515

"All the food's gonna be cold," Berni moaned.

"Is that all you think about, your belly?" Andi asked.

"Drinks are on me tonight," Vral added.

"Sod the food, I need beer," Zac said.

Their conversation as we came into the last few bends disturbed me. Disturbed on such a level I missed my gear change.

"Are you okay?" Ivori asked.

"You're kidding me?" I downshifted into the corner, late, then powered out the bend. "They're all pally-pally going for drinks . . ."

"Would you go with them?"

I cringed. "No. You know I wouldn't."

"Then why are you worrying?"

"I just am," I said.

I pulled Ivori in off the track, and the team jumped at us as soon as I slid out of the cab.

Bren moved before me, eyes checking everywhere. Even though with the tech from the suits, the track they knew more than I did. "How you feeling?"

"Fine," I said. I held his eyes with mine, sighed, and added as I looked away, "Like I'm way out of my depth."

"Huh?" Alek asked, he waved around our garage, "We all saw how you've been performing out there. You're in top form, you and Ivori."

I glanced over to the other garages. Could see what they were doing. Getting ready to go for lunch. Together.

Why was it bothering me? I couldn't put my finger on it, not really.

Then they walked past us.

Andi laughed at Berni's joke. Don and Vral were talking close together about something, the track maybe, the race?

Stop worrying! Ivori said internally. *You're way better than this. Than them.*

But they're all . . .

What? she asked. *Friends?*

Well . . . I tried to put into words what I saw.

They're not friends—they're not anything. They're all pretending. You really think that out there they're going to be that pally. That on show?

No. I let my head hang.

Then stop worrying. We don't need that. What we need is right here. Look around you.

I couldn't.

Look around you, now.

I did.

The garage, Balsy, Itoh. Bren, Staci, Eryk, Hara, and Tatsuno.

They're all here for you; they are everything we need.

And Alek.

And Alek. Very much Alek, she said, warmth spreading through her.

Alek stood next to Bren, watching me close.

"You okay?" he asked.

My starts had suffered, and I just couldn't pinpoint why.

I sat in the garage inside Ivori while the team went over the latest details of our most recent run-through.

You're just panicked, Ivori said.

I don't mean to be, I replied, running my hands down my suit.

This is your first real race, she said. *Out there, everything matters.*

I rubbed my eyes. I was tired. "I need a nap," I said.

"You do," she replied. "You're exhausted."

I nodded and got out. "I'll catch you in the morning," I said, allowing a little of my Azris to surface for her.

She didn't take it, though. "Keep hold of it, rest, and I'll see you in the morning, refreshed, so you can nail that start."

"I'm heading back to the house," I said.

"Feeling okay?" Tatsuno asked.

"I'm okay, just need some extra sleep while I can."

Alek cast me a glance. "I'll come with," he said.

Tatsuno raised an eyebrow at him. "Yeah?"

I laughed. "I need sleep," I said. "Ain't no time or strength for any of your antics."

"Spoilsport." Alek laughed and then bumped me. "Come on, I'll get you something nice to eat on the way past the bakery quarter."

"I could do with that," I said. "Been a long time since breakfast."

"You had a snack?" Alek asked.

I shook my head. "I wasn't feeling it."

"You're on a strict diet," he said. "Just like I am. They're watching everything in and out . . ."

My eyes crossed. "They can't watch what comes out, right?"

He laughed. "Got you!"

I punched him.

The smell drifting over from the food hall made my mouth water. Different eateries stretched both sides. A nice safe space where we could all go to sit, walk, stand, drink, eat, anything that involved food. It was here. The last few days, I'd eaten more than I ever had from Grovers. Alek moved to a line of a fresh donut stand, his grin spreading as he patted his stomach.

"Don't you think we should get something healthy first, then the sweet stuff?"

He shook his head and moved when the line did. "Won't ever have time to eat these again," he said. "Not going to waste it."

I listened as he ordered several flavors, and we moved to wait for it to be boxed up. I turned, looking out into the crowds of the quarter.

Vral stood at the other side of the seating area, looking right on back at me. His eyes were calculated, cold. At his side stood Berni and Don.

Then I saw someone moving in behind them. "I thought he would have been in some kinda jail?"

Drei walked up to them, and they started talking.

Alek moved to my side. "Doesn't look like it but I never followed up with how things were going for them. Sorry."

"Not your fault," I said with a shrug. I'd try and not let it—or him —bother me.

But the sheer thought that he was here with Vral was making my stomach churn already. "Can't they like just keep him away from us?"

"I doubt it." He pointed toward a set of guards at the far side of the quarter. "It does look like they're aware, though."

I noted two of them had their hands on their sword hilts. "Good," I said. "Come on, I'm not sure I want to eat anything now."

When I moved to walk away, Alek grabbed my arm. "Nope, no way. You're getting your lunch. What did you want?"

"Beef thaita noodles," I said without hesitating.

Alek tugged my arm then. "The queue over there's not so bad."

I moved with him. "I am hungry," I said.

"I know. I can hear your stomach growl from here."

I let my nose take in the scent of onions and herbs. "Welcome back," the server said. "Same again?" he asked.

"No, can I try the beef thaita, with extra onions?"

The young man grinned. "Coming right up."

It was nice to watch him pull out and prepare all the fresh cooked ingredients and mixing it together, with sauce and noodles. "Damn," Alek said. "Make that two."

The young man grinned and pulled another carton out for him, to then copy the same ingredients out of the pans. He swirled and moved with the soft music playing around us.

"Forget Drei and Vral," Alek said.

"How can I?" I asked. "They caused the most damage ever to Ivori. How can I be sure they're not going to try anything like that again this time around?"

"I don't think any of us can ever be sure what is coming for us. We just have to presume that something is."

He made the most sense. "Thanks," I said, and picked up our cartons of food. Instead of making my way out of the quarter like I'd thought five minutes ago, I spotted an empty table. Heading over there, I parked my ass so I could still see Drei and Vral and opened the carton to the wonderful smell of onion and garlic, topped with what looked like hot chili flakes too. I pulled out the throwaway fork and just dug in. Twirling the noodles onto the fork, I took my first bite. It was hot, but hot and spicy. The flavor exploded on my tongue, and I grinned at Alek as he did the same.

"The meat's done to perfection," he said.

I could only nod and took a drink from my water bottle. I concentrated on eating, eating, and watching the others. They all seemed to gather around, then Drei kicked some youngsters off a table, and someone brought them food. I caught the tail end of some of the things they were talking about. The fact Ivori had survived that atrocious hit. The fact we'd forfeited and were still allowed here today.

It didn't matter if we didn't win; we had to be here to not be kicked out. Or we were just done before we started. I'd heard Geo and Luca go over the stats and the tracks' finances. We'd get something for just showing up today, ready or not. I'd done my best to convince everyone around me, even Ivori, that we were ready on the inside, though I wasn't. I knew I wasn't. I'd still give it my all, though.

It wasn't long before I finished eating the carton of noodles. I opened Alek's donut box and while his eyes widened; I picked one out and bit deep.

The jam on the inside was so fruity; it dribbled down my chin, and he laughed. "I thought you'd have gone for that one," he said. Then pointed to its twin. "Hence I got two. I wanted to try it."

"Thanks," I said. "This is some of the best food around. I wonder if we can get the recipe for Grovers."

"I doubt it." Alek frowned, then licked his fingers. "They guard these things like gold."

I sighed and moaned. "Will miss this, this really is some of the best food around."

"You've got many other cities you have yet to eat at," Alek said.

I caught his eyes with mine. "I've never dreamed of half of this. It's just fantastic being here."

"Yes, it is," he said. "I've never had so much fun, so much to look forward in my future, together, all of us."

"You think we've going places?" I asked, licking even more sugar and jam off my fingers then popped the last of the dough into my mouth in one rather big bite.

Alek laughed. "Now try to speak?"

I rolled my eyes at him.

"Yes," he said. "I've never felt more at home than I do with Ren. Even cars of the past weren't this good a fit."

"You trained for years driving, though," I did eventually say.

"I did, but it wasn't like this. We've got a good chance to get off this planet, to go to the next stage."

I watched as Drei got up from the far table, then left. Leaving the others. Berni was the one who met my eyes. I didn't look away as I finished my water off. "I need that sleep now," I said. "Let's go."

Alek finished his noodles. "I get it," he said. "I'll eat those later."

He took a swig of his water and stood. I followed him to throw the trays in for recycling and we moved to leave. "Just gonna use the toilet," he said and ducked inside the small building.

I waited for him on the outside. The crowds around carried on eating, drinking, and joking around.

Alek seemed to be taking a while. I'd not paid attention to who went in or if he'd come out.

I glanced around again. Vral and his friends, the rest of my opponents, had gone. "Alek?" I asked walking in, the stalls and urinals were set pretty much like any public bathroom. It was clean, mirrors at the far end. Alek stood leaning over the sink. I approached carefully. "You eat too much?"

When his eyes met mine, I saw his lip was split, and he spat blood into the running water. "What the hell?"

"They're not playing by any fair rules," he said.

I put my hand on his back. "Want me to get Ezra?"

"No, no way. No one's gonna know about this."

"Why? Who was it?" He turned and looked at me. I reached for him, took hold of his chin. "Let me see."

I held him gently. I could see he was in just a little pain. I allowed my Azris to flow through my arm, into my hand. "They broke your jaw," I said. My eyes searched his, looking for any other indication. Nothing.

"Bad?" he asked.

"Hairline crack, but you took some punch for that, especially with the nites in there."

He nodded, closed his eyes and sucked in a breath. I let my other hand gently trace over to where I saw the cracks. Alek flinched.

"Hurts?"

"Just a bit." His eyes met mine. His face flushed.

"Don't be embarrassed," I said. "This is not your fault."

"It is." He sighed. "I provoked him. It was just reaction."

"Drei?"

"I couldn't help myself." He went to push my hand away. But I cocked my head at him, letting more Azris in through my fingers.

"Oto," he said and swallowed. "As much as it's something we're okay with, it's still pretty intimate. This—close."

He wasn't wrong. I had him pinned against the sink, the warmth from his body crossing into mine. I could see every detail of his face, the tiny scars he'd done probably while first shaving, the bumps where the odd hair was a little ingrowing. I didn't like him like that at all. "Only eyes for your sister," I said with a slight smile. "I adore you, Alek. More than that and you know it. I can't hide things when I'm . . ." I coughed. "This close."

He laughed, and then cursed under his breath. "Fuck, that really does hurt."

"Let me do some more at home," I said. "You okay to walk outta here?"

"Just don't tell Ezra or Tatsuno."

"I won't, but we're going nowhere on our own, okay?"

"Deal," he said.

9

Friday, February 12th *Early Morning*
Year - 27515

Sleep evaded me, just like it had for some time. I didn't think I'd ever get past Lena, but I slipped out of the small setup at the track, my mind drifting partly awake, partly asleep.

The air here wasn't anywhere near as cold as Esrall City at this time of year, and it held a scent I couldn't work out at all. I stood outside the house wondering where I could go, what I could do. 2:21 a.m. No lights on anywhere, bar some emergency lights illuminating the outer track walkways.

At the far end, I could see track sweepers out. It would get the best treatment all night long, I'd presume, before they opened up for the big day.

I kept easing my thoughts away from what I should have been doing, sleeping next to the woman I loved, to the racing ahead.

My feet wandered off, and within a few moments I found myself out in on a nice flat piece of ground.

"Good a place as any," I whispered to myself.

I dropped to my knees, spread my feet shoulder width apart, and lowered my hands.

Softly, and very slowly, I began taking myself from the very first step of each stage, pulling Azris to me. I opened up my mind, cleaned out all thoughts and feelings. I was too tired, and though pulling in Azris was easy, it wasn't stable enough. I noted the imperfections in everything I did. I was too tired, too stressed.

It is pretty scary here on your own, Ivori said into my mind.

I looked out toward where I thought it had come from. Then, like a homing beacon, I wandered in that direction, following the threads of her energy.

It was easy to find her. *Think I could find you anywhere,* I sent back to her. Her presence alone guided me.

Then I stood before two double doors, locked. I stared at the screen. The system locks to get into the garage were something else. I'd had someone with me all week. Now, I stared at the panel, totally afraid I might set something off.

"Let me," a voice said behind me.

I jumped, whirling around to see a short man standing behind me. "I—"

"The drivers from out of the city never sleep properly. I'm the night guard, and I guess inside helper."

He held out a handheld device, flicked the scanner on. It made several clicking sounds. That clicking took me back a few years, to Tonis and Sta at the gate.

I swallowed the emotions threatening to choke me with a heavy cough.

"You check out," he said. "Drawn to your Icarian too, she's right inside. I'll let you in."

"Ahh, yeah, makes sense. Thanks," I said, stepping aside at least to let him in and closer to the panel. Within seconds, the side door opened.

"I won't lock you in. I'll be around, garages are mostly the same, just don't poke about too much, and stay with her, or you'll set the alarms off."

"I won't. Thanks again," I said and off he wandered, his scanner still lighting up the path before him in eerie green.

I slipped inside the garage then, using a tiny bit of Azris to light my way, finding Ivori sitting central with all the lights and systems blinking around her. Her lights flickered softly at me, and I wandered over, letting my hand trail over her hood.

"You doing okay?" I asked.

"Not really." I felt the rumble, and the door clicked open.

I pulled it and slid inside, settling into the seat, edging it backward to give my knees a little room. "I understand," I said and allowed my Azris to trickle down my arms, resting my hands on her wheel.

"Relax," she said. "Close your eyes. You need rest as much as I do."

I did close my eyes, let my head back, and slowed my breathing down. Within moments, I was gone.

The flicker of lights woke me.

"Told you he'd be in here." Alek's voice drifted to me.

I sat up, wiped at the drool on my chin, and then saw Ezra's blinking cute face at the glass. "Sorry," I said.

She smiled at me and opened the door, then was on my lap before I knew it, her arms wrapped around me. "Knew you weren't far, but you still worry me."

I snuggled against her, taking in the soft scent of her regular perfume. "I don't mean to," I replied, kissing the side of her neck.

Alek and Tatsuno walked in, flicking on more lights. The garage lit up around us. "Show time," Alek said with a wide grin. "Let's get 'em up and running."

I stretched slightly and climbed out, my back clicked and popped, and I let out a sigh.

"Come here." Itoh pointed to the chair. "We need you in top form."

"Food's coming in," Ezra said. "We've a bit of time before anything starts."

"I'm not sure I could eat anything," I said. "My nerves have my stomach in knots."

Ezra pulled my shoulders, so I sat straighter, then she gently massaged the knots out of my neck. Damn, that little sleep in the car broke me.

"That tight?" she asked, stretching the outside of my neck to my clavicle.

I groaned. "Yeah, really tight."

She continued to make sure the muscles got some expert attention, and I relaxed, watching the screens as things moved around us.

The entire world watched this track today, not just us. On the screen I could see people reporting on the day's events, the racing coming up, the leader board as it was. I sucked in a breath, knowing what was there, but seeing it today in person made my heart pound.

Our garage door's *click-click*ed as they moved back into their housing, letting in light and smells from the track itself. People were milling around everywhere.

I could literally do nothing but watch. The ground around would fill up soon, and the track's Zero cars would go out.

It didn't take long for the food and drinks to vanish, and the Zeroes' engines started up. I moved to the locker for my suit, and Ezra helped me into it.

"Seems you're growing quite a bit still," she said as I had to literally suck in a breath for her to fasten it.

"Too many bacon rolls." I sighed. "I'm going to have to curb those when I get home. I'm putting too much weight on."

Ezra pulled me to her, planting a kiss on my cheek. "No way, you're healthier and fitter than ever. This is all muscle. We'll have to get you a new suit."

Crap, more expense. We'd only just about gotten here in the first place. This, everything, moving up, was just beyond me.

"Don't worry about anything," Ezra said. "You're going to win."

I frowned at her. She'd kept me so positive, but right now I just wasn't feeling it.

I pulled her to me, kissed her. "I'm going for some air. I'll be back."

My hand in hers trailed off till she finally let me go, and I sneaked out the back door to literally get some fresh air.

This was my first actual race.

I looked up at the back end of the track doors for us. Still, so many people are around. I glanced down at one of the other doors. There stood one of our rivals. Berni Grogg stood out at the back end, just like I was. Except he leaned over the wall with someone rubbing his back.

A cough to my side made me spin around. Zac Memmot in person stood right before me, the smoke from an e-cigarette billowing out around him. "He was out too late. Should never drink before a race."

"He was drinking?"

"Looks that way." He sucked on his e-cig again. This time, when he blew it out, it drifted my way and made me cough.

Zac laughed. "It's got bonuses that help me concentrate on the track."

"Oh, that's a good thing, then." I patted my belly. "I just got shoved full of food instead."

"There's better means than food. If you'd been around the first few races, you might have picked some of the tips up by now."

I frowned, watching as Berni threw up again and then someone hit him with Azris. "Ouch," Zac said. "The hangover would have sucked, but that would have even more."

I watched for a moment longer as Berni came around. When I turned to see Zac, he'd gone.

That was fast. I caught sight of him wander over to . . . ugh, Vral. They might not be with a team, that was clear, however, the other drivers had all settled into this way of life already. Here now, with the lineups, the banter, out drinking and partying together at night, I was the outsider. I'd seen it the day we arrived just walking around.

I was an outcast, and one they wanted to get rid of by any means possible. The fact someone had taken Vral on had floored me as was. But the brothers were high-flying racers. No matter if Drei had been fired, the skill they had—and I'd watched, watched them racing at Mote Lerate, then Brotok City—it had been very impressive. I couldn't deny it.

Skilled. Very skilled.

I sucked in a breath and turned back to our garage. Alek waited for me. "You okay?"

"Yes," I said. "Just needed this."

"Forty minutes," he said. "Time to suck it up."

"I'm ready," I said and patted my legs. "Ready as I'm gonna be."

Everyone in the garage was ready, waiting for us, and I climbed into Ivori once more.

"I'm feeling a little funny," she said.

"Me too." I wasn't lying to her.

"We've got this, though," she pushed. "We've done everything we can."

"Everything."

Hosoke was in front of me then. "Follow me," he said.

I nodded at him and together with Bren, we started a good warmup for my body. All it would take was one wrong twist in the cab, and I'd injure or pull a shoulder or neck muscle with terrible consequences. I did not want that.

"Doing good," Hosoke said. "Follow me. Left, slow, stretch those muscles. Right, the same. Up and around, nice easy circles."

He knew how to treat me, how to get me to supple up all those tight muscles. Then I was truly ready. Ten minutes later, I was as limber as I was going to be. They knew how to push me in the right places.

The thirty minutes call went out.

It might be the warm-up lap first, but this was still something big.

Ivori's engine rumbled and I let the others take the leads. I waited, then when I was ready, five minutes or so later, I guided her out into the pit lane and then onto the track. One good lap was all we needed, and the others were at different places, ahead, behind me. I wasn't worried about them.

I watched our temperatures all over. Hairpin bend, round and out, nice and steady, twenty below optimal speeds. Sixty to one-fifty, then down again. Seventy into a nice straight up to two hundred, then dropping fast into the next bend. Picking up a lot more, 130, back down to 110, then well into the straights and up to 250. Couple more bends, three hundred. I was pushing it, but we were already at optimal temps. Green all across the board. This was a good track, and spending the time here the last few days had done me the world of good. Watching, listening and, more importantly, learning everything I could from every overheard conversation going. Back toward the start and pit, nice and steady to either do it once more or line up.

I took the opportunity to line up. We were lined up according to the list.

Zac, Vral, Don, Berni, Andi, and me. Last.

Only Berni went around again. "Something wrong?" I asked Hosoke and Tatsuno.

"He's still on the cold side. He's almost there."

We all waited for him to come back around.

Fifteen minutes lights went up. The pit was closed. This was it.

My stomach flipped, and we watched everyone around us do their jobs. Check everything. Tires were all good; everything was warm. I kept the gas burning, and as I was sure the other drivers were doing it too, allowed a little of my Azris to circulate, warming up just a touch.

Ten minutes. Green lights lit the top row.

Ivori's engine rumbled, and we made our way out onto the track.

It sucked being at the back, but I'd no choice. I'd not been in any other races. This was just how it would be.

Sixty laps, sixty. . . . This was a lot to concentrate on for approximately an hour thirty. I was ready.

I flexed my hands on the wheel, watching those lights.

The referees joined the lines, made one pass to look each driver in the eyes. When they got to me, I locked with them, nodded.

"Good to go," Hosoke said through comms.

"We're all watching," Tatsuno said. "You've got this."

I tapped the wheel, waiting.

Five minutes left, two red lights lit my view.

I checked over her stats, my stats.

Three minutes. Four red lights.

"Breathe." Geo's voice came through to me. I saw the line. Private. "Concentrate on my voice."

I closed my eyes then, not watching the lights. "That's it, in and out," he said. He reminded me so much of Ezra here. "In and out."

I stayed with him for a while. "Good," he said. "Much better. Trust yourself, Oto."

I opened my eyes.

One minute. Six red lights.

I touched the gas.

"Easy," Ivori said. "You've spent weeks practicing."

I let it go slightly.

Fifteen seconds. Eight lights.

Then we were going backward.

Eight.
Six.
Four.
Two.
GO!

Fuck, I fumbled it. Quick to recover, sure. I still didn't hit the lights dead on.

"Don't panic," Alek said. "You've plenty of time to take this back. Concentrate."

The others were well gone.

I shifted up through the gears in seconds. Belting it to over 150, then straight back down for our first hairpin bend. Right down to eighty.

I needed to catch them up, and I pushed myself forward. We'd plenty of time, sure, sixty laps. I'd shadow behind them for a while, watching, letting them find and make their own mistakes.

I needed to keep patient, time my advance right. Slow and steady, to be able to get in behind them, overtake at my leisure, then speed up to the next, and repeat.

So steady we went. Laps one through fifteen, so simple.

This was me warming up for real, getting used to everything at my own pace.

I found that nice steady drive enjoyable, and I relaxed into the race for the first time.

I was at the back . . . but I would get past them. I just had to hit my timing right. Wait for the opportunities.

Eighteen laps down.

The next few laps around, and I was sitting right behind Berni. He didn't seem to be doing so well. "There really is something wrong," I said to Alek. "Can't you see anything?"

"No, nothing is wrong here," Alek said. "We've got good views of all the cars. They're all looking spot on."

I frowned, dropped down and into the next straight, then quick with the flick of the steering, I was out and on the outside of him powering through and into the next corner. I cut him off dead, and I was ahead.

Twenty-two laps down.

My mind raced ahead of where I was, picturing the others, where they were, what opportunities I could get as I took each bend, each position.

Twenty-six laps down.

Then thirty-eight down.

The others were way ahead of me, but we kept pushing. Coming in on lap forty, this was going to be my chance.

Don was next ahead of me, but he was fighting Andi for the third place. I watched them for some time, taking each of their lines, their choices into consideration.

Andi was very good at faking her turns and gear changes. I watched with awe over the next few laps. They struggled, and the way they struggled just made it so I couldn't get past either of them.

Forty-five down.

Berni must have gotten over his whatever . . . he was behind me. Coming into the next set of bends, and into the real testers, the straights. Don and Andi were out right pushing it. "What speed are they at?" I asked.

I was hitting 270. They must have been at three hundred easy. "That's insane. We're not even a third done yet. They're goi—"

I never got to finish my sentence as I saw Azris spark ahead of me. Don wasn't taking any chances. He wasn't letting Andi keep that lead.

Then . . . he was in front. He'd done it. I knew he'd be celebrating. That was an awesome overtake.

Heading to the next bend, we all had to power down.

In slow motion, sparks lit the underside of Don's car.

No fucking way.

The car immediately reacted. The left wheel wobbled. He couldn't control it. Who could at this speed?

Ivori's panic flooded through me as his car snaked left, then right.

I glanced backward. If I hit the brakes now, Berni would ram me from behind. I had nowhere to go.

He was too close. It was a total disaster.

No, there it was. I had one way out of this.

My Azris flared in full, responding to my needs.

"Oto, you can't!" Ivori said. "We'll lose!"

Only survival was in my mind. What I saw coming was heading one way.

Time slowed even more. I could see the way things were going to go, the lines I needed. It was as if it was drawn in front of me.

"One chance," I said to her. "I have to try. If I don't, we're toast!"

Don's front end snaked left once more, and his tire exploded and bounced, right into my windshield.

There weren't enough fucks in the world for how screwed I was.

10

Friday, February 12th *Morning*
Year - 27515

My windshield and the tire flipped end over end, out of my field of view. My eyes never left the horrendous, slow motion view in front of me.

I should have thought about Berni. I should have done something else. I couldn't think about him or my actions right now. Only us, only getting us out of this mess.

Don's severely damaged front left tire hit the ground, sparks everywhere. It also veered left, straight into Andi's car.

With the both of them spinning out of control fast, I had one opening.

Ivori's systems flooded with Azris, and I dropped gears faster than the car could handle it. She clunked under my control. I felt the mechanics complain, then they fell into place.

I hit that gas, rocketing forward with such speed I knew what everyone out there would see this.

Pain erupted from my core. But I pushed through it.

Ivori squeezed through the opening in front of us as Don's car forced Andi into a wild spin that just ripped their cars apart. Debris sprayed everywhere, then flames. I may have been through the gap, but this was far from over.

Berni didn't stand a chance, either. His car plowed into Andi's, bounced over the top and came at me . . . even though we sped forward and away from them.

"Oto!" Mixed voices came over the comms. I flipped the wheel left, taking us over the next bend's marker bumps. We hit dirt, then the front end walloped the side barriers. Straps gave me a little room to bounce, digging into my shoulder, then pulling me back. Our left side was gone, my own tire blown into smithereens, with debris everywhere.

Fire threatened to take hold. I drew in as much Azris as I could from the surrounding areas and doused it. Then I threw the door open and got out, stretching my legs, then hitting the track at a jog.

"Alek?" I shouted, ripping my helmet off, throwing it to the ground. "We're okay. Get me what you can."

"Drones are out, lights red. Marshalls and recovery on their way!"

My shoulder and back were agony, but now in front of me lay the carnage of three Icarian. My stumble turned into a run.

"Life signs?"

"Two," Tatsuno said.

Two . . .

Just two, Ivori confirmed, *and two Icarian.*

Four out of six lives . . .

What the hell. This couldn't be happening, right?

Oto, it can easily happen. They're gone.

I pushed more and ran with everything I could. I didn't care who they were, rivals, opponents. They were not my enemies. They were just drivers, doing the best they could. Like I was. This wasn't open war. We . . . we . . .

Don helped Andi from the top of Berni's car. She slipped and fell into his arms. Then they hobbled out of the way, their cars in flames. I drew in closer, my breathing my heart so fast. I wasn't fast enough.

Berni was still in there. I reached Don and Andi, her helmet gone, her face cut to ribbons. I tried to sidestep them, but she caught my arm in hers. "Oto, no."

"What?" I asked, her strength confusing me. I tugged myself away.

"I said no." She grabbed hold of me once more. "He's gone."

Within seconds, drones surrounded the cars, putting any other signs of flames out. Then medics and others were with us, the track around us alive with vehicles.

"Come with me." A young woman in uniform took hold of my arm and guided me away from watching the cars. "Here." She sat me on the back of a truck. Then with deft fingers she took my chin in her hands, drawing my eyes to hers. "I've got you," she said. "Let the teams take the rest. I'm only interested in you."

"What?" I mumbled.

"I'm Denna," she said. Gently, she moved my chin from side to side. I couldn't help but wince.

"You're going to need a full check over," she said. "We can get you to the nearest hospital in moments. Don't panic."

"No," I said. "Track garage only. I'm fine."

She held her eyes with mine. "Let me be the judge of that."

Nice and deftly, she pulled a collar out of the back of the truck, securing it around my neck. Then picked up a hand scanner, and using it, she brought up a 3D image to her left. I could see my left shoulder had taken a battering. My neck showed in red too. My eyes danced over the image. Everything else looked fine. There were no broken bones. No other major injuries.

"This will help," she added. "Drink it all."

I took a small vial she held out, and popping the lid, drank it all in one. The liquid energy flooded through me, and my shoulder started to feel better, even if my neck didn't.

"Team truck is here," a voice said in my head.

"She's okay," Tatsuno confirmed. "Just banged up."

Banged up wasn't what I wanted to hear. The crew picked up pieces of debris around the track. I pushed myself up. "Thanks, Denna," I said. "I'll get looked after now."

"Keep the brace on for a couple of days," she said with a nod to my team's truck and everyone else running around. "Good luck, Oto."

When I stood next to Alek, he put his arm against mine.

"Careful!" Hosoke shouted. "I thought you were gunners." He directed them as Ivori was winched onto the back of the truck.

"So did I," I admitted, my head down. "The race?"

"Let's get you both back, we'll talk. Geo said he'll see us there."

"I blew it," I said.

"You're kidding." Alek nudged me. "This was nothing to do with you, your skill or anything. The track investigators will watch everything. This was—" He sighed. "Just a tragic, tragic accident."

I tried to turn to look at Alek. I couldn't. "Let's go," I said.

The truck took Ivori into a different garage this time, one at the back of the track. Out of the view and noise of everything else. Hopping out, I could see Geo's hand on his hip, his eyes looking Ivori over as the large image scanners flicker over her body on the truck.

Geo saw me and headed straight on over, pulling me into a gentle hug. "How are you doing?"

Emotion welled up, but I suppressed it. "How's Ivori doing?"

I'm okay, Oto, came her reply.

The images of the damage to her flashed up on the screen behind us and we both moved to see it, in all its glory.

"Going to take some fixing," Itoh said, standing with us. "Full side rebuild."

Tatsuno and Alek joined us next, and Ezra burst in, coming to my side. I put my arm around her, pulled her into me, holding on tight. She never said a word, just looked at the damage with the others. She knew; I knew nothing would help her. No amount of words could.

"Track news coming in," Balsy said as he moved to the other screen, flicking a few switches. The investigators could be seen in the background as the cars were pulled apart.

"Official news." Geo moved to the screen and pulled up something else. Balsy stepped back.

The picture flickered. An older woman stood with two others. Her eyes were raw, her face flushed, but when she looked at us through the camera lenses, she held herself with grace, poise.

"City administrator, Docheck," Alek whispered, and we listened to her words carefully.

"Fellow racers," she said. "Today, what should have been a wondrous day for all . . . was not. We stood and watched with all of you the tragic accident that took the life of twenty-one-year-old Berni Grogg. Okburg track teams will investigate thoroughly what happened here today, and report as soon as possible. It is decided there will be no other race. Get your Icarian home. Heal. You will hear from us soon, and we'll decide after the investigation placing for the next race. Okburg will need your full support going forward from here. Thank you for your patience."

The screen went black. "There's nothing we can do here," Geo said. Luca came in. "I've got us on the next fast-track train home. We'll fix her up there."

All eyes were on him. He was the eldest, the guy in charge, after all. He moved to stand before me, his eyes searching for something. I wasn't sure what. "With me," he said and turned. Then motioned to Geo.

I followed, head low. Would I get the telling off now? Was it over before I'd even gotten anywhere?

Luca led us out the back and to a waiting vehicle. "We'll meet the others at the station," he said. "I just need some . . ." He slid the door back and Geo jumped in. "Take your time," Luca said.

My body didn't want to step up. No matter what I wanted to do. Then, in a whir, Luca was behind me, and I was in.

I kinda flopped onto the seat. Geo held out another drink for me, this time a stiff one. I took it from him and downed it. Luca then sat next to me, placing his rather cold hand over the top of my other. The calm he had inside him washed over me with the alcohol and I let out a breath. "I—"

"Don't," Geo said. "We saw everything. We watched it again. We're going to get you home, then take it from there. Okay?"

Healing Azris came seeping into me then. "I just needed to get your levels up before you passed out," Luca said. "That was a lot of energy to lose in one go."

"I didn't have any other choice. Without that, Azris burn . . ."

"I know. Projections from the track teams say if you hadn't gotten out of the middle, it would have been worse. We may have lost you all."

I let that sink in for a while. All four of us.

Geo poured me some more, and I sipped it this time. "What happens now?" I asked.

"The race adjudicators will make the decisions on the lineup. I have no doubt, Donnaton's team will bring in the next best. Berni's loss will hit them all, but it won't mean the team's off the circuit."

"Us?"

"We competed. It wasn't your fault what happened. We'll be in the next race. We just have to get her back together again."

"Sounds like an old nursery rhyme." I sighed. The vehicle set off, and I let the motion relax me a little.

I watched and listened as Geo brought up files then sent them through to my system, then brought it up on the big screen at the back of the cab. "You've not seen any playbacks yet. Watch them."

I watched the screen. My nerves shot. Coming up to the accident point, I squeezed my fists. Felt the burn of Azris as anger welled.

It was a split second. Azris sparked, the tire blew, hit my windshield, bounced. Don's car veered off, and I was out the opening gap as it spun out of control and then Berni hit them from behind, Andi's car ending up on top of his.

I took the control and hit replay. Geo and Luca let me. They let me watch it another three times. Then Luca stopped it.

"There was nothing anyone could do," he said.

I looked into his deep brown eyes, closed mine for a brief second. "When they find out what happened, make sure you let me know."

"We will," Geo said.

"How do you—"

"Get back on the track?" Luca asked.

I nodded, watching Geo's face carefully to see if they'd even let me back on it. Geo tapped the screen, and a different view came up. "This was me, in Okburg many years ago," he said. "Dropping down from 280 into the first turn, I had the lead. Brakes failed, causing the car to basically stop. Accalt hit my rear end, spun me into the wall, just before the main straights. Axel and Vroni, behind us, also didn't have anywhere to go."

The screen turned into carnage. Just as he'd said, the lead car Vrolst suddenly jammed on at such a speed his back tires looked like they'd blow. Sparks everywhere. Then bang, walloped the barriers, the wall.

"Holy shit," I said, eyes wide.

"It takes a lot to watch these," Luca said. "This is Copter, the Reanola track."

"This was the worst start in Copter's history," Geo said, to Luca's frown. "One of their charity drives."

Twenty-four cars on the track. Their starts were perfect. I watched them all with envy. Then, as they dropped down into the first left-hand bend, one of the cars at the front caught the side of another. They hit the wall, taking two others out. Then three more hit from the back.

"Fourteen cars, damaged," Luca said.

"That was you in the front?"

He nodded. "Shamefully, yes. It was my fault too. I turned the wheel too fast. I have no explanation for it."

"Were you kicked off?" I asked, feeling suddenly like that might be the way this would go.

Luca shook his head. "No." He tapped the screen this time. "I got to be involved in this one."

The track this time was something I couldn't quite believe. "That's not a track," I said.

"Halara's first city track," he said. "And yes, this is in space."

I ran my hand down my trousers, watching as six space racers—no other way to say it—sped around a designated run.

"Trying for the double overtake," Luca said.

Three of them came out of some heavy chicanes, then a hairpin bend into a straight. I could see the Azris burn from the one at the back. It was going full out to take the both of them. Yet something popped, went wrong. The two in front stayed in front, and the back end of the third just exploded. The second car got the upper hand then on number one and sped over the finish line mere seconds later.

"What was it?" I asked.

"Faulty wiring. Something came loose through the laps; the scans missed it. He lucked out. I lost my concentration for just a split second and Rae got the win."

I saw the leader board flash up then. "Luca Gianetta, second place."

"You lost the race?"

"I lost the season," he said. "This was last year."

Ouch, that hurt him a lot. It spread across his face. "That sucks," I said.

Luca chuckled. "Yeah, it really does. I'll get another chance, but . . ."

"But," Geo said, "we took the time out for Isala."

That hit home. Really hit home. "For Alek and me?"

"It was one reason why." Luca looked away from me, and I actually felt his anger flare.

I glanced at Geo, who drank down his alcohol. "We've complicated lives," he said. "You were one reason we took some time out, but you're not the only one."

"How's your stats looking?" Geo asked, totally changing the subject.

I hadn't looked; I hadn't even thought about it, or wanted to. I'm sure there were lots of notifications going off with that race start and disaster.

To bring Luca back into the conversation and to at least show them how we were doing, I flicked through my screens and brought up onto the screen before us my stats. It at least replaced the view of space from here.

Nothing like being judged by the only two men I really looked up to. Luca especially. Everything Geo did for me, Taryn, every single one of the others with training with each and every single start we'd practiced. My log was there.

Open book. Still.

Geo squeezed in on the other side of me, making me feel even worse. He patted my knee with a laugh, and said, "Piggy in the middle."

"Hey," I said. "I know I've put some weight on, but not that much."

Geo laughed. "Oto, you're at least double the size you were when we first saw you."

I coughed and looked down at my thighs. "You're just mean." My stick-thin legs, though, now had muscle, weight. I couldn't deny it.

"He's done so well," Luca said, scanning down my list with his eyes.

I read my list too, the gift off of Ezra counted as an Artefact, the affinity changes. They were really good to see. I was proud of me, even with this fail. Finally, I felt like I was moving in a direction I wanted.

Name = Oto Benes
ID Number = 4188927
Age = 22
Species = Anodite
Sex = Male
Alignment = Neutral
Bloodline = Unknown
Health = 78%
Cultivation Level - Master Rank 3
Active Meridians = 12/12
Nanites = 1 million
Artefacts = 2
Chosen Specialist = Racer
First Chosen Affinity = Water
Second Chosen Affinity = Fire

Statistic = Body + Ivori + Cultivation
Strength = 38/104.5
Dexterity = 26/67.33
Constitution = 36/99.36
Int/Wis/Spirit = 47

Affinities - Rank

Water - Blue
Fire - Green
Earth - Orange
Air - Orange
Light - Orange
Darkness - Orange
Spirit - Yellow

Droll's Leg Pouch – three refillable containers hold the power of life or death. One use per origin user.

Ring of Light - A gift from Ezra
Adapted, so you may use it as you wish.
Boosts Azris circulation and usage, + 30 to all stats
Uses = 5

I really had moved in the right direction. "You kick my ass, the lot of you, every single day. For someone not to grow with that going on."

"Seriously deserves—" But Luca stopped speaking.

I looked to the both of them. "What?" I asked, worried.

Luca reached for me, pulling me into a hug and a pat. "Anything you want, just ask for it."

I pushed him away, but Geo joined in and I didn't have the strength, laughter bursting up from my belly. I gave in. "You two are killing me," I said. "I'm not used to any of this."

Geo grinned. "Good, because we don't want you to be, but we do want you to get used to it. You're family, Oto. Don't forget that."

The warmth spreading through me wasn't Fire from Geo this time. It was something else. Belonging.

11

Thursday, February 25th *Lunch*
Year - 27515

Itoh, Balsy, and Hosoke were literally knees deep in fixing and pulling Ivori apart again. Itoh turned to me, his face nothing but a scowl.

"You both are gonna be the death of me," he said. "I hope every race isn't going to be like this."

"You saw what we did on the track, right?"

"I don't think anyone missed it. That's your balls-out, no-hold-back display."

Hosoke turned to me, waving a little hammer in the air. "The whole universe is going to be talking about that, again."

"You think they'll know what I can do with that display?"

He shrugged. "I'm not sure. Either way, no one's ever shown that amount of power in one go. No matter what they think of the display, that alone is something that will get them talking."

Ivori let out a sigh. *It comes from within*, she said to them all. *It is and will not be missed by the Vipers*.

Even more a target, I replied.

They're going to throw everything they can at us either way. Their teams . . . their Icarian, they'll all be out for us.

The door opened and Alek came in with Tatsuno. "News is in," he said. "Track drivers have been placed. The next race is going ahead, if we can get her back running."

Itoh tapped the side of the chassis. "She'll run again, but I'm not sure to what specs, certainly not what we had."

Alek frowned. "No funds?"

"No, not unless we start selling off cars."

That was bad news. "I don't want anyone selling their cars. They've already done more than enough getting us the parts in the first place."

Tatsuno brought up the screen. "No foul play on the cars, nothing out of place. Andi and Don were checked out, top to bottom, and their Icarians. Fully up to all health checks."

The leader board read now . . . and of course we were last, but Alek was killing it. I was just the one dragging him down. "Alek, you never said you'd won the last race, too."

He blushed. Actually, really blushed.

"Why?" I asked.

"I didn't want, you know."

I cocked my head at him. "Man, never hide that shit from me, okay?"

"The only reason we have a stab at getting off this planet," Tatsuno said, "is you." He pulled Alek to him, and kissed the side of his cheek. Alek melted into him, and I smiled. Their affection was so genuine.

"What do we need to secure our spot?" I asked, now extremely worried.

Tatsuno turned back to the board. "Alek has to go six for six. You both have to go three for three. Sidmont, Vrance, and Isala."

That was a lot, lot of pressure. "Alek?"

He winked at me.

"You can really do six for six?"

"Hell yeah, you see that beast out there?"

I grinned, seeing his grin, ear to ear. "Seriously."

"Seriously, I'm not losing one race. Ren's the best there is, and we've got each other's back. The others don't stand a chance."

I glanced at Tatsuno, who beamed with pride. "If anyone can, my *man* can."

"Then we're going to match you, even if it's only three for three." I held out my hand for him, and we shook on it. I couldn't let any of them down now. At all.

I looked back at the scoreboards. "How do they even score everything?"

"It's easy to follow. The only reason we are where we are is that every other driver or rider has failed at least one or the other in terms of races."

Made sense. We were just lucky Alek was as skilled as he was. Or we'd no way have a chance to score enough points to get us to move up.

"First or second place moves us," Alek said. "But if we lose one of those races to the wrong person, they might take second place, leaving us here."

"I'll concentrate on the wins, don't you worry," I lied and turned back to the 3D image. My concentration was way off; my mind whirred. I winced as my neck hurt.

"You still need to see the doc some more, that neck still giving you trouble?" he asked.

I tried not to look at him. sideways out the side of my eyes was enough. "You've still not let Ezra see, have you?" I lowered my head, heat washing up my, yes, very sore neck. "Oto," he said. "Back office now."

Tatsuno pushed him away slightly, and he moved off. I looked around to the others for some kind of support, but I got nothing other than a few lowered heads. "Go," Tatsuno said. "You've been told."

"Ugh." I kicked the chair in front of me, then followed him into Geo's back office. He stood over one of the chairs, pointing at it. "Sit," he said.

I sat and waited for him to do something. It wasn't what I expected. He tugged at my shirt. "Off."

"What?" I complained, and was about to move out of the chair. Alek put pressure on my shoulder, and I gasped loudly.

"Take it off. Now. I *need* to see it." It was the way he'd said need—

he wasn't giving me a choice. "If you haven't let Ezra know how hurt you are, you're hiding it from all of us. Take your shirt off or I'll get Tatsuno in here and he'll drag it off."

I dropped my head, tucked my fingers under my shirt. "Alek, please don't tell her."

"I don't understand how you're keeping it from her if you share a bond," he said with furrowed brows. "She would help you; you know that. She'll play all hell with the both of us if she finds this out."

"Don't," I said. "Please, promise me."

"Why? We love you?"

"I feel like such a failure already, I . . . ." I struggled with the words. "I don't want her to see me as weak."

"Oto." He swore under his breath. "Gods, you're far from weak, but you are hurting, much more than just your shoulder." I felt his hand on my head then. "We're brothers," he said. "If you say it, it stays with me." His hand drifted to lift my chin so our eyes met. "But I need you to be one hundred percent honest with me over everything. We're what's gotta pull together. If I gotta lie, I need to understand the reasons. I need you to talk to me, always."

"Okay," I tugged my shirt up, and when he saw I couldn't even get it over my head, he helped. "Fuck me, you fool," he said. He came around the front of the chair, then knelt in front of me, putting both hands on my knees. Holding my eyes with his. "You need some real help."

I shook my head. "No, no, I don't. I need to get over this, heal myself."

His eyes traced down from my collarbone. I knew what he saw. The deep thick purple bruises, my left side even had a slice where the belt had been the only thing keeping me in my seat.

He reached out and gently let some of his Azris flow out. "This is—"

"Dark," I said. "I can see it perfectly, and your intention?"

"Let me show you," he said. The dark energy swirled over his arm, into his wrist, hand, then finger. He held it up so I could see it. "Remember when we made our way down into the museum the second time? How we worked together?"

I nodded, yet I still felt a little afraid. "I remember it. We did work really well together."

"Let your Azris surface, your Light. Meet mine with yours, then I'm going to touch you, okay?"

"Alek, I…"

"If you're not going to let Ezra or anyone else help you, then it's down to me. This is just for you," he said. "'Cause this is as intimate as it gets. Family, okay?"

I let my Azris pool. I wasn't as strong with Light use. Barely strong at all, but it met him, and it danced. So beautiful.

"Now you understand, right?" he asked.

"It's so pure," I said. "The Darkness . . . I never expected it."

"Fuck, you're gonna make me say it . . ." He blew out a breath, and it tickled my face. "You and I are meant to be. As much as Ezra is yours, so am I. So is Ren." He placed my hand on top of his, the energy moving fluidly all around us. Then he did what he said he would. Almost crossing my hand over my chest, he guided both our hands to my collarbone. Then, very, very gently, he put his hand to my skin. It felt cold at first, and though I hadn't wanted to, I flinched.

"Sorry," he said. "I'm being as gentle as I can."

"I know," I said. "It's easing already, thank you."

"This is more than sore, right?" His hand stopped just the inside of my nipple.

My hand twitched, pain ripping through me. "Okay," he said. "Hold there."

While he concentrated on me. I got the time to look at my best friend up close and really personal. "You're okay, right?"

Alek's eyes met mine, and they flickered. "Honestly, this has been a whirlwind of everything."

I agreed with him there, yet I waited. He wasn't finished.

"No," he said, and lowered his eyes from mine. "I'm not okay."

I gently squeezed his hand in mine. "I got you," I said. "I might—we might not be able to process it right now. To talk openly." His eyes met mine again. "We will."

"I want to talk to you about things," he said. "I want someone I can come to for everything. Tatsuno is amazing. I've never felt so much, but I need that confidant over him."

"Same," I said. On his raised eyebrow, I chuckled, then winced as my chest hurt. "You know, Ezra, not Tatsuno."

"You've come a long, long way," he said. "I couldn't be prouder of you."

"Even if I just lost Okburg race?"

"You didn't lose," he said. "You would have won. I'm more than sure you would have."

I swallowed my emotions. "Thanks," I said.

"That's what friends are for." He smiled.

When he wobbled slightly, I tugged his hand from my skin. "Enough," I said.

"You need more. Much more."

"I'm not taking it today. It will heal in time."

Alek's eyes scanned the deep bruising again, his face flushed. "You won't be able to keep it from Ezra for long if you're intimate with her."

I felt myself redden as he had. "She's better off not knowing just how bad. I'll do everything I can not to be." The thought of rejecting her, any kind of advance on me hurt.

"No." Alek moved to stand, then sat on the other chair. "Probably not."

A knock at the door roused us both. Alek threw me my shirt, and I slipped it on. "Geo and Luca want to see you, Alek," Tatsuno said.

"Coming." He stood and although Tatsuno didn't see him falter, I did. When he'd gone, I let out a sigh, and just sat there, looking around the room. There were old pictures on 2D image screens dotted around the room. Races I had no clues about. No matter how much I studied, how much I did . . .

I wasn't enough.

Alek might think I was; the others all might think I was. But inside it wasn't working.

I slipped across the gap to the main computer station and pulled up the map for Sidmont. To truly win this race, I needed to learn more. That meant I would watch everything I could.

I stayed in the office till Alek popped his head in much later. "We're heading back. You coming?"

"I'll stay a while longer," I said, knowing he knew it was, of course, to avoid Ezra.

"Okay," he said. "I'll make sure I come see how you're doing tomorrow."

I didn't want to agree to it, but he held my eyes with his till I nodded. "Can't avoid you and your sister," I said.

"No. No, you can't."

Then he was gone, and they left me looking at the screen still. I watched and watched other races until I heard the garage doors lock for the night. Everyone bar my shadow had gone. I moved into the garage and stroked the metal, feeling every bump over Ivori's broken body. "We'll be well again," she said. "Alek's found us some parts at the market in Esrall. You should be able to pick them up from the seller in a few days."

"That's good." I smiled. "How you feeling?"

I saw her form flicker before me then, and I looked into her face. "I can't do this too often," she said. "As much as it's nice, and I like to see you from these eyes. It takes a lot from me, from us at this level."

"Could you do it easier if I were stronger?"

She nodded. "Of course. It comes with a lot of practice."

"How strong would I have to be for you to stand with me every day?"

Her forehead crinkled, and she reached out to poke me. Poke gently because she knew I was very sore. "You'd need to be at the top."

"The top." I sighed. "Think we'll ever get there?"

"Yes," she said with a grin. "I'm not stopping till we are. Go, Lena's waiting for you. Poor woman never gets any time to herself."

"Ahh." I glanced their way. "My shadow. She is kinda relentless."

A cough at the door and Ivori vanished. "It's my job," Lena said. "Come on, I actually am exhausted."

I gave Ivori's chassis one more little pat, and she pushed my Azris back at me, though, again, she knew I needed it more than she did. "Thank you," I said to her.

Outside, the cool air misted before me. Light clouds hung overhead. There was maybe a little rain coming. I picked up my pace, making sure we'd be home before it did rain. It was lovely out, dark, normal. Lena kept her head down and did just what she was supposed to: her job. I liked that. She kept her distance when I needed it despite she had to be my shadow.

A message came through to my internal system and I almost stopped walking. "Meet me outside the house in twenty minutes." I tapped to find its origin. Of course. Trayk.

We were soon home, and Lena was heading to bed in less time than it took for me to pretend to be making a hot drink and curl up on the couch. I waited seconds and then went for the door, hoping I wouldn't have disturbed her at all. She was exhausted; I was too. But she was the best at making out when and where I was, and sneaking out wasn't usually on my agenda. I made my way back outside into the fresh air.

Across the road, a sleek blue car flicked its headlights so I could spot it. It hadn't been raining a moment ago; now it poured down. I pulled my shirt over my head and ran for it. I hit the passenger side door, and it opened for me.

"Trayk," I said, looking in.

"Get in," he said. "Everything's getting wet."

"Don't drive off now," I added, and did as he said. I slid into the seat and closed the door.

Trayk stopped the engine, and the car went dark.

"What do you want?" I asked him.

"We all saw your race. Everyone's analyzed it, top to bottom."

"And?" I crossed my arms, even though it hurt.

"I wanted to say personally that I know you didn't do this. Berni lost his life, and it truly was just a tragic accident."

I stared out the window at our block. Security cars stationed at each end of the street. "I never noticed those when we walked in."

"They're mine," he said. "There's been a few threats."

"To you?"

"Berni was . . ."

I sighed, already knowing where this was going then. "Sevran Vipers."

"He has a big family. They're very upset. Even with the result from the adjudicators."

"I don't get it," I said. "Why are you telling me any of this? How does it affect me, or us?"

"Berni came highly recommended after Drei was—" He looked away. "It wasn't what we wanted as a team, and I didn't want this either. There's some very high-end people watching—and insatiably after you."

Trayk's nose twitched. His Azris sparked, and I felt it really trying not to flinch. He looked at me. "You and the rest of your team are fully guarded, but I'm leaving the cars here."

I sat back. "What?"

"Everyone else can think we're rivals, Oto, but we're not. I have vested interests in the Ocean Slayers getting through the next few races, and in winning."

"Don't you dare," I said.

His eyes flared too then. "Dare what? Use my money, my sway in this community to help you? Why wouldn't I?"

I didn't understand any of this. The dashboard lit up. Red flashing lights.

Trayk swallowed, and a number ID flashed with the red then.

That ID. I knew it.

"Camran?" I asked.

"I need to get this," he said and swiped to accept.

Camran's face came on the screen then, flushed. No, not just flushed. "Tee," Camran said. "They got me outside Praitar's City limits. Vahid and Niqou are dead."

My stomach somersaulted, and I could see Trayk's face drop. "I'm with Oto," he said. "Cam. I'll ask—" I reached out to him, put my hand on his arm. It surprised me to feel him shiver. "I—" Trayk stalled, shaking.

"Are you safe?" I asked, breaking the sudden awkwardness.

Camran looked at me, his left eye bloodshot. "We're not safe here anymore without some serious backing. We need much more. I never expected this. They're out for blood, serious blood. Ours."

I glanced up to the building, and I tapped my internal comms. Trayk was about to stop me, but I shook my head. "Luca tried it his way. By the books. It's not working by the books. There's only one person I know who can turn this on its head." I then spoke clearly into my comms. "Lena, I'm outside, and we need you. Camran and Amalia have been attacked again. The guards we sent are dead."

"Fuck, fuck, fuck . . . fuuuck," her muffled voice said. "Idiots" came through first, then a thump. "I'll be down in thirty."

12

Friday, February 26th *Lunch*
   Year - 27514

Silence filled the cab, then Camran coughed, dipped his head at me. "I'm going to drive us to a hotel off beat for now. Comm me when you get settled, with a plan. This number will work for now."

"You're not going back to the track?"

"No, not yet, not till we've got someone else in place. It's just not safe for us. I'm not putting either Icarian or us at risk anymore."

Trayk put his hand to the screen. "We'll sort it, brother. We will." Camran vanished.

I locked eyes with Trayk. "I hoped it would be better, not worse. Why is Copter so easy for all of this . . ."

"The underground, the way it runs. There's a lot more politics when you get off Isala. This is a protected planet for a reason."

"Protected?" I didn't understand that. "Doesn't seem so protected with the attacks around already."

"Almost child's play to out there," he said. "It's our most basic planet in the system. That means there's people here who start out at rock bottom, with the most potential. They're protected because otherwise they'll never grow. On the other planets, when there are sects, or clans. There's protected schools."

Both back doors opened. I whirled around to see Pete slide in, as well as Lena. "Pete?" I asked.

"You bet." His frown was deep. He rubbed at tired, sticky eyes. "My girl wakes for a call in the middle of the night and rushes off, I'm going with her."

"We need somewhere to talk," Lena said, standing watching the street for a moment. "There's a safe bar around the block."

Lena slid in, then placed her hand on the back of my seat. The dash changed, and a map flagged up. Trayk glared at her. "You hacked my system in—"

"The fastest time possible. Just drive. We'll talk there." Trayk started the engine, and Lena took Pete's hand in hers.

We pulled up outside a small corner building with a sigh on the door. *Hard Day's Done.*

I smiled and watched Lena as she took point. Pete stayed behind us both. "They're—"

"—treating us as their guard," Trayk said. "Understandable. Especially since you shouldn't even be out of the building."

Once inside, it was much bigger than I expected. There weren't many people sitting around drinking, though. Lena walked directly to the bar.

Pete found us a table in the corner. "You think we're safe in here?" I asked him. The clientele didn't look so hot. The closer I looked around, the more I thought it was the worst place we could be.

"Lena's been coming in here often. You can see she knows everyone. I just don't know when she gets the time watching your ass."

Trayk laughed, but it was strained.

Lena placed a tray moments later on the table with four beers and eight shots.

"Planning on a long night?" I asked. Pete picked up one shot and downed it without question.

"Drink," she said and picked up a shot.

I took the drink, and Trayk and I, as she instructed, downed it. My body flooded with healing energies, and my eyes lit with fire. Lena smiled. "Now you get it. If I'm getting no sleep, I need this." She downed the other.

I couldn't argue with her logic.

Pete touched the side of the table and a nice privacy shield spread around us. "That good a place?" Trayk asked.

"A lot of business goes on here," Lena said. "Most of it, they don't want under prying eyes, or ears."

"The others in the bar know who you all are. We don't want anyone listening in." Pete added. "There's seriously no other place around here that's as safe."

Trayk nodded, and within thirty seconds, he'd filled them both in on the rest of the story for the last couple of months. Lena listened and so did I. Copter was horrific. Their racing, their lifestyle.

"I have people I can call in," Lena said, and looked at Pete. "But I'll have to go to Copter to do it."

"What? No way," Pete said.

"These guys don't use regular messaging services. It's the only way."

"What about Oto here?" Trayk asked.

"Just because Pete only trusts me, doesn't mean there aren't other favors I can call in." She took his hand in hers. "It just means that financially—"

Trayk coughed. "Don't worry about the finances, for any of it. I'll cover you."

Lena met his eyes with hers, and I could see her mind working. Her eyes sparkled. "This is not going to be cheap."

Trayk lowered his eyes. "Whatever it costs will not be an issue. Do it."

Lena kept tight hold of Pete's hand. She tapped the side of her head, then brought up a 3D image before us. We seemed to be in space, then no, we were bouncing around space. Connections after connections. Satellites, stations. Pete watched, his face paling. I risked a glare to Trayk, who couldn't take his eyes off her. Now there was something else I could see deep inside Lena. Her eye, it wasn't real. Both of them?

Mods. She was more tech than I had first thought. Perhaps than even Pete had thought.

Within seconds, we approached a planet. Absolutely stunning. Huge. We zoomed in.

"Halara?" Trayk asked.

"Yes, I'm going straight to Sawa."

Trayk swallowed. "You have connections within Sawa?"

She smiled, but the view kept us all focused. From here, all I could see was vast high-rise buildings, interspersed with water, greenery, and yes . . . race tracks. Not just one or two, this planet had many. Many *massive* tracks. Much larger than anything on Isala. They surrounded forests and lakes, deserts and fire pits, ice lands. I wanted to see more, so much more.

I had dreamed of places being so beautiful. I'd studied some of the lore, of course, surrounding the six. I'd still not fully understood the dynamics. This, this showed me the dynamics.

Rich, powerful.

Lena seemed to stall then, on an outside satellite. "Waiting on my connection," she said.

We all waited, and I held my breath. A man came on the viewer, looking at her. His dark hair, sharp jaw, and lines under his eyes told me he was around Luca's age. "Lena Scar," he said, not looking impressed. "A surprise. To what honor do I owe this time?"

This time?

"I need permission to use the underground security on Copter Prime," she said, then at his raised eyebrow, "All of it."

"Who is that?" I asked Trayk.

He glanced at me, swallowed. "That is Shuko Sawa. That isn't just access to Sawa; that is the core of Sawa."

I logged his facial details in my mind, watching his reaction to Lena. He moved slightly, his hands operating off screen. "You're one of our top agents. You don't need to ask permission. What is it? Taryn?"

"I can't comment on Taryn. That's not my place."

His face changed, slight anger there. Lena didn't flinch at that. "You honor your name, Scar. You have permission to use anyone with one condition."

"Name it."

"If I ask you to, you will bring her home."

Lena swallowed and looked at me. Why me? Why was this my decision? I thought fast to the tiniest details I knew of their family, their dynamics. Spending Christmas together, what we'd all shared, what Luca had lost. Connections over connections. I understood. I nodded at her.

"You have a deal, but Shuko," she said, "that is a last resort. You know that."

Pain crossed his face. "I know. Talk to her for me. For us."

"I will. I'm heading to Copter as soon as I can get the flights."

"That serious?" he asked.

"You need to talk to Miklao," she said. "Tell him I sent you."

"Be well, Lena Scar," he said and lowered his head to hers. Then cut the comms.

"You'd escort Taryn home?" Pete asked, pulling his hand away from hers. "After everything you've seen, been a part of here?"

"It's more complicated than you know," she said. "Don't judge me, please."

"You're an agent of Sawa?" Trayk asked.

Lena looked at him, her face scrunched. "I'm an agent for a lot of people. But Sawa is at the top." Her eyes misted for a few seconds. "I have to go." She then turned to Pete. "You understand that, right?"

Pete's face pinked. "We only just—"

Lena pulled him to her, kissed him deeply. "You'll be on Copter before you know it. With Geo, with Oto and Alek."

"You'll be okay, right?"

"Always. These guys got nothing on me."

"Your arm," I said.

"Fuck, Oto," Lena cursed.

I'd just revealed her weakness. She glanced down. "I'll be able to get it fixed there, if I have the funds." She then looked at Trayk again.

I saw Trayk consider her for a moment, then roll his eyes. He blew out a breath. "Whatever you need. Seriously."

"Thank you," she said. Then she downed her drink, pulled Pete up and out of the privacy shield. Both Trayk and I watched them leave the bar.

I picked up my other shot and downed it, too. "Everyone thinks a lot of Sawa's sect," I said.

"You don't get to the top without being both powerful and ruthless," Trayk said, drinking his own shot in one too.

When Pete returned, he sat, eyes on me. "You better hope you both know what you did."

Trayk lowered his head. "If Sawa gets involved, we'll all know about it if it goes wrong."

"Exactly," Pete said, holding Trayk's eyes with his. "But this is from me. If anything, anything at all happens to my girl, I'll come for you myself."

"Fair," he said. "I'll accept that."

Pete motioned to me. "Home, now. I've got some explaining to Geo and Luca tomorrow. We both need some sleep."

I moved to stand, and Trayk grabbed my arm. "Thank you," he said. "If you hear anything, anything at all, you let us both know, okay?"

Trayk nodded. "I will."

I left with Pete, and the walk home was not good. Silence wasn't in it. When he made to just enter the building, I snuck in front of him fast. "We okay?" I asked him.

"You'll have two escorts from tomorrow," he said.

"Okay." I frowned. "Us? Talk to me."

Pete closed his eyes, then met mine with his. Emotion flared. Sadness, anger. "I'm okay. We are okay. I just need a little time. I only just got her back. It's difficult to be so far away from her again, so soon."

"She's the best there is. You told me that. I trusted you, now trust her. She knows the best there is out there to help."

"Direct line to Shuko Sawa . . . I never expected that." Pete ran a hand over his tired face. "Yes, she really is the best, and I love her and hate her for it."

Pete sidestepped me and we went inside, him back to his bed alone, me to Ezra.

Zero Light

I hesitated outside the door. I should have gone to the spare bed. It was way too late. But I wanted to hold her, I needed her.

I undressed and then snuck inside, letting my Azris light the room only enough so I wouldn't bump myself on the edge of the bed.

Slowly I lifted the blanket, and slid inside, curling around her. I let out a sigh. She smelled so good. I squeezed her gently, but she stirred, and when she moved, my shoulder caught. I winced.

"Hey," she moaned, sleepy, so damned sexy. When her arms snaked around me, I kept still, not responding. Fuck, the not responding to her hurt more than my shoulder, but she was asleep again in seconds. I closed my eyes and followed her. Exhausted.

Ezra, Alek, and Tatsuno listened as we told them in the morning what was going on, then Pete and I went to see Geo at the track.

Taryn raised an eyebrow at me when Pete said she'd called Sawa. "I wish you'd called me first," she said.

Geo pulled her to him. "You would have called your father?"

"No." She sighed. "Maybe Miklao, or one of my uncle's wives."

"Then don't be worrying about the what ifs. The deals are done."

"That's not quite everything." Pete lowered his head. "Shuko made Lena promise if he asked her that she'd take you home."

"She wouldn't," Geo asked, "Right?"

"She would," I said. "And if it came to that, not one of us could stop her, even Taryn."

Taryn's breathing quickened, and she rubbed her stomach. "I don't want to go home," she said. "Please don't make me."

"No one's going to make you." I tried to add to ease her fears. "But you should talk to them. They're clearly worried."

"They just want me to marry someone else," she spat. "I won't."

Geo glanced at me, then hugged her some more. "Hey, hey, they both know this. We're not going to let anything happen to you."

"Geo." She wrapped her fists into his shirt. "Something's wrong."

"The baby?"

Taryn nodded again. "Who's here? Medical-wise?"

"Bren? Ezra?" I said.

"Get Ezra," Geo said, then when Taryn dropped to her knees with a howl, he shouted. "Now!"

"I'll call the doc," I heard Pete say as I ran for it.

The track was alive with cars, but I saw Ezra, comm'd for Tatsuno right away. "Red lights," I said. "Track's compromised!"

The whole place lit up with flashing red lights and sirens. Ezra made a run the rest of the way to me. "What's going on?"

"Taryn, needs a healer," I said. "You're it."

"Me? I can't. I'm not qualified for anything," she said. "Let alone anyone in line with Geo's standing!"

We raced back up the stairs to the office, the wail of Taryn echoing around the track now. There was no way that anyone in here wouldn't hear that. No way at all.

Ezra rushed the stairs, and I was right behind her.

"Doc's on his way," Pete said. "Help where you can. Even Geo's not touching the pain this time."

That said a lot to me. This was something other than their DNA connecting and bond. Pete and I watched Ezra enter the bedroom and Geo came out, his face pale. "She's bleeding," he said. "A lot. Ezra's doing what she can, talking to Doctor Styx."

"Hospital?"

"We can't move her," Geo said. Then he fell onto his couch. "This is all my fault. We should have known. We should have been more careful."

I moved to sit with him, put a hand on his arm. "This isn't your fault. This is mine," I said.

"The training?" I nodded, and he sighed. "That's not all on you either."

"Still feels like it," I said.

Geo put his hand on mine, and I held his. Waiting.

Doctor Styx came in and entered their back bedroom. Pete made us all coffee, and we drank.

The training outside carried on, the bikes and cars zipping in and out.

When it was their turns, I listened, tracked the gear changes, the tempo, the speeds.

It was the only thing I could do. Waiting was impossibly hard.

I moved to the window to look out, then went to stand and watch. Pete joined me a moment later. "Lena messaged me. She's all good. Will be on Copter in a day."

Honestly, I tried to smile at him, but couldn't. Everything here was my fault. Everything. From day one. This was all on me.

"Geo's right when he said we can worry about all those what ifs all the time, you know."

I nodded and leaned on the railing. "I know. It doesn't stop any of us thinking of them, though."

"No, it doesn't." He went quiet.

Geo joined us a while later. "Itoh and Balsy have located some more parts. We're going to head out the market to pick them up in a few days."

"That's good, right?"

"Of course, means with a little more luck on our side, you'll be ready for Sidmont."

Ready for Sidmont?

My stomach churned. I hoped he was kidding. But we really weren't that far out now. Six weeks. Six weeks to get my ass into gear, to win.

Winning was the only option.

13

Thursday, March 4th *Lunch*
   Year - 27514

Winning wasn't the only option. Epic failure was on the cards too.

Itoh and Balsy came back from not just one market, but several others without the parts we needed. "It's as if the market's fucked," Balsy said, slamming the door behind him.

I jumped. I had been studying with headphones in. Sidmont's track was much more complicated than any of the others in terms of bends and speeds.

"Sorry, Oto," Balsy said, slumping into a chair.

Hosoke came out from Ivori's back end. "No luck?"

Itoh shrugged. "It's like we see parts that would do, that would fit, then no sooner as we try to secure them, they're gone."

With a clunk, Hosoke came and sat with us. "Sounds like they're doing this on purpose?"

"That's my thoughts," Balsy said.

I let out a sigh. "They can't get to us in any other way than the parts we need," I said. "So that's exactly what they are doing."

Itoh nodded. "Yes, exactly."

"How can we get through to them?" I asked, "Get someone to actually sell to us?"

Hosoke spun his spanner. "I think if we really need to speak with someone in the city circuit, see why they're so scared. Dig in. This isn't just money."

"You think they're being threatened from outside Isala?"

"We've got less time than we think to get these parts. We have to make sure they're up and running; it could take a few days to do that. It doesn't matter what kinda threat there is, we need to stop someone fearing the consequences of selling to us."

"There's three parts at the market track near Sidmont. If we're first in the morning, I think we can talk to them."

"Okay," I said. "Sidmont's not too far. If we leave now, right?"

Hosoke glanced around at all of us. "Don't take all of us, I'd suggest, me, you, Tatsuno, and Alek, and we can take my car. There's no risk to anyone else then."

"What about Pete, or the other guards?" Tatsuno asked.

"We can't take everyone with us," he said. "I think we'd do better on our own. We'll have to be enough as your guards."

"I'll ask them to follow in their own car," I said, knowing full well Geo would flip if we went without guards. "They can hang around in the background."

Ezra bounced around fidgeting at the doorway.

"What is it?" I asked. Her face was so pale.

"Can I—"She looked at Alek first, who nodded at her, then she said, "Can we talk?"

"Of course." I stood and moved to her side, turning only to add. "Be back in a bit. Clear the trip with Geo and Luca and we'll leave soon as."

I walked out the back of the garage door, to the far road, way out of the ears of anyone else. She took my hand in hers, and though we'd spent many days and night together, and some apart, this felt off.

"What's going on?" I asked again.

"You know I've been spending a lot of time with Doctor Styx and his wife, right?"

"Helping Taryn and Geo, yeah."

"We've been doing a lot of research on the nites, and with Nishi and that little robot you found."

I stopped walking and leaned on the wall, pulling her to me, linking both her hands with mine. "What's that mean for me?"

"It means . . ." She paused, and stepped in close to me.

I wrapped my arms around her. This, whatever it was, was hard.

"It means I'm leaving tomorrow."

Her words hit me like a sledgehammer. "What? You're leaving me?"

She let out a small chuckle. Was she seriously laughing at me? At us? Had everything I'd felt from her, for her, been a lie?

I pulled away from her, my knees wobbling. She tried to reach for me, but I waved her off.

"Wait," she said. "Oto, I'm sorry. I didn't mean it like that at all."

"What did I do wrong?" I asked. "What am I doing wrong?"

"Oto," she said. "Look at me. I really didn't mean it to sound like that."

I turned back to her, trying to stop my emotions from rising. My eyes brimmed with tears. I couldn't help them. This was my worst nightmare. "Then what did you mean?"

"I've been offered a place at Mitaki Healing Centre for the gifted," she said with a partial smile.

I let out a sigh, brought her back to me, and kissed her. "To all the gods on Isla . . ."

"I still have to go tomorrow," she said. "I was planning on spending the time with you tonight, somewhere nice, just us."

When her fingers snaked up and under my shirt, I let out a tiny growl. "Everything around here timing-wise sucks."

She nodded at me. "I agree. I should have told you earlier. We could have done this sooner."

"It would hurt either way," I said. "I don't want to be apart from you at all. Where is this center? Is it far?"

"It's in Mitaki," she said and sighed.

I didn't know where it was, so she sent me the details through my internal system. "I guess I won't be visiting very often then," I said, looking it over on the map.

Ezra tucked herself into me. "Doctor Styx is amazing," she said. "You have no idea how smart that man really is."

"If he impresses you, then he must be really good," I replied. Her scent washing over me. I really didn't want her to go, but how could I stop her?

"What happens there?" I asked.

"We train specifically with Azris and healing," she said. "Councilor Troha has also backed me. I've everything I need if I want to go."

"If you want to go?" She was confusing me. "I love you, Ez. There's no way you're not going."

"But"—she looked up at me, her eyes filling with tears—"I'm just scared of being out on my own."

Fear flooded through me, the old home they had, the day we found Tonis and Sta dead after she'd been attacked. "There's security, right?" I asked.

"Geo say's it's fully secure within one of the council's safe spaces. It's one of the safest places on the planet."

"Then there are no buts. We both have to fulfil our potential. That means sometimes we have to spend time apart."

I watched her close her eyes, the tears spilling down her cheeks, "I know. I am doing this for all of us too," she said. "Having a fully skilled healer going forward, leaving Isala will be really good."

"You mean just so you can pick my ass up and shout at me?"

She dried her tears away with a laugh. "Of course, Alek too."

"Alek too—we could both do with a good healer around. I won't deny that."

"There are also good few double tag teams out there once we've left Isala. Copter runs some very different races. I want you to have the best chances, and Alek too. That means—"

"Both you and Tatsuno are very important," I replied, and also wiped another stray tear from her eyes.

"Yes," she said.

Hosoke poked his head around the corner. "We've got permission to go," he said. He glanced to Ezra and frowned, dipping his head. "I'm sorry."

Ezra stepped back, but I kept hold of her hand. "I love you too," she said, kissed me, squeezed tight and then without looking back, ran off.

I sucked in a deep breath, then went to join the others.

Friday, March 5th *Early Morning*
Year - 27514

Hosoke and Tatsuno took turns driving, and we all slept a little through the night. It was indeed a long way to go, but if this really helped us get the parts we needed, then it would be worth it. The city wasn't big, that quite shocked me. No sky scrapers, no neon fancy lights.

"This is the right place?" I asked as he pulled over and we got out.

"Yep, only has a small population. They can't support it otherwise from the river."

"River." I grinned. "You have to let me see it."

Alek laughed. "Water affinities."

"Never seen anything bigger than the lake outside our home," I said. "I'd like to even just for a minute."

"We've got time," Hosoke said. "There's a nice breakfast bar there. We can leave the car, walk down."

It was hard to walk anywhere. I wasn't made for not moving around. Once we were closer, though, I could hear it. I glanced at Hosoke, "There's a dam," he said, "that's what you can hear."

"The dam powers most of this city, and their track."

Then I saw it. The river itself was huge. It stretched out bigger than the small lake of ours. Boats passed each other, drifting in and out, but what drew my attention more than anything were the dam turbines.

"It runs in fast from the mountains," Hosoke said. It made sense for the local community here to hold it and let it through on their terms.

My eyes drifted to the structure that was the dam. It stretched higher than a skyscraper. Massive slits let the water out in literally millions of gallons. Underneath the river must have been such turbulence; on the surface all we could see was a rippling wave spreading outward.

Tatsuno moved away from where I just stood gawking, and eventually I followed him and my nose to breakfast.

We sat outside by the river's edge, overlooking a placid spot where wildlife gathered, hoping for bits of food to be dropped. Signs said everywhere, "Don't feed the ducks off your plate—ask and you'll receive something special for them."

Made more sense than giving up your food.

I let Tatsuno order, and then Alek gave him, nodding at me. He ordered for me too. "You'll love this," he said.

"With all the surrounding food, I'm never getting into my suit for the races." I sighed and patted my growing belly.

"Just up your training," Tatsuno said. When I shot him a glare, he coughed out a "Sorry."

The server brought out pancakes, bacon, and syrup, and it truly was delicious. Washed down with the finest coffee I'd had in a while. Not like on some of the mornings I'd rushed to make my own.

"What time does the market start?" I asked, pushing my empty plate away.

"Most of the vendors will be there now. Let's make our way back nice and slow and see if we can figure out who has what," Hosoke said.

Tatsuno covered the bill, and we made our way back up the slight incline to where we'd left the car.

There were a lot more people around. That wasn't a problem for me. I tracked everyone around me just as I had lots of other times. Alek, however, moved in closer to my side.

"What's up?" I asked.

"Just suddenly feeling a little vulnerable."

"Lena and Pete were sure amazing to have around."

"Yeah," he said.

Tatsuno stepped in beside him. "You have to learn to trust that we're going to be enough," he said.

"It's not that I don't want to," Alek replied, taking his hand in his. "I'm worried more about you than about myself."

Tatsuno leaned in and kissed him, then winked at me to say. "He's the worst. Never even asks me how I'm doing, or my levels."

Alek's face fell. "I—I . . ."

"Tat is training like a beast," Hosoke added. "We all have been, though. Sometimes you racers don't see everything we do." He paused, his eyes sparkling. "Well, we're out there with you every single morning. Every practice you are doing, we're doing, and we're most likely doing it at home, too. Some of us, you also gave the nites to, and they've had massive effects for all of us, especially boosting learning, energy, everything."

"They've really had an effect on you guys?" I asked.

"Ezra and Doctor Styx have been following us all very close."

"I should have paid more attention to all of you," I said. "I've let everyone drift."

"No," Hosoke said. "You're doing what we need you to, concentrating on the racing. We're just following you around. Hoping we get to be a part of your future."

"Really?" I asked.

"Not many of us can go to Copter, or farther, Bren . . . there are others at the track too," he said, and I saw genuine sadness in his eyes. "We've—well, we've become family. We're concentrating on the things we know you need. Like Ezra is."

"Tatsuno?" I asked.

"You need to fill us in on everything these guys are doing," Alek said. "If they want to come with us, we're not letting them go."

Tatsuno pulled him in tighter, and he struggled to walk, almost falling over. "You think I don't know that? I have everyone and everything logged. We're split the work, the team all has specific tasks and skills to learn, excel in."

I hadn't expected it, but it made the most sense. We needed them. When we got out there, they would become everything.

"Everything?" I asked.

"Everything, that means when we've had downtime, and you've been sleeping. We're still learning, studying."

"That sounds like a lot," Alek said, his eyes on his partner's. I watched their silent exchange.

"It is," Hosoke said. "When you leave this planet, you better believe we're all with you. You've your own personal track teams, no substitutes, no secret agents trying to get in on the inside."

We drew in closer and closer to what I could only see as the market. Stalls were fully kitted out now, with so much on display. I kinda wished I'd have more to spend. I could buy literally anything here. A new suit, any clothing item or . . . I noted a rather large display to the left, full of shiny potions and bottles. "That looks . . ."

Hosoke pulled me away. "No, you're not interested in any of those. The front loading stalls are just public pound shops, interested in only getting your funds and not providing much for it. We can do a lot better at the far end, when we've walked past some of these."

I had sticky fingers that kept stopping; I wanted to see everything. In the end, Alek linked my arm with his and Tatsuno got on my other side. "You're not fair," I said with a whine. "You've probably all seen these before. I haven't."

Then Hosoke pulled us to one side. "That's the stall we want," he said, giving it a sideways nod. "You stay around here. I want to speak with the owner first if I can. Then we'll take it from there."

"Okay, if you need anything, then please just knock."

The three of us watched him walk away, and I got to look over the stalls in the surrounding area. I did pick up an item: a dress, yellow, short, and very pretty. It had red etched flowers and parrots displayed all over the hem and arms. I loved it. I wanted to buy it.

"You think my sister will like that?" Alek asked, coming in up the side of me.

I turned it over in my hands, checking out the detail at the back, the soft silk delicate and hand woven. "Yes, actually. I think I've gotten to know her pretty well over the last few months. She likes to think she's not the kinda woman that wears these things. I know she'd kill it. Besides, we've a wedding to go to, and this would be perfect."

Alek shrugged, then called over to the stall owner. I listened then as he bartered to buy it. Compared to the price on the dress, he got it at a steal.

"Thanks!" I said when he handed it over, all neatly wrapped up.

"You can give it to her when she's home next time, then let me know if she'll wear it."

I tucked it in my backpack and grinned at him. "I will."

Tatsuno was standing on the other side of the stall. We moved to him. "How's he doing?"

"He's not letting go of the parts he wants," Tatsuno said. "I'm almost waiting for it to break out into a brawl."

My eyes focused on what they were doing. The woman at the stall was red faced, and serving another customer. Then she turned back to him.

I couldn't stop myself. My legs moved, and the next thing I knew, I was standing by Hosoke, my eyes meeting hers. "We can negotiate here," I said. "Or we can go elsewhere, but we're not leaving without those parts."

She struggled with her words, but then she shouted. "Tommi, mind the stall, I'm taking a break."

"Break!" A young voice said. "We're only just got going!"

"Get ya ass out here now," she said.

The young voice came out. A young man eyed the both of us, then nodded.

Hosoke kept tight hold of the parts, and when she walked away around the back of her stall and into a curtain, he followed. I glanced back to Alek and Tatsuno, who both nodded my way. I turned and rushed off after them.

14

Friday, March 5th *Early Morning*
   Year - 27514

The curtain revealed an old, battered truck which she climbed inside, then beckoned us both in. Hosoke hopped up, and I did the same. It was a home from home. I'd seen some like it before, traveling sales vans.

"What price we talking to take them home, Anna?" Hosoke asked.

"It's not the price that's the problem," Anna said.

I mean, I hadn't thought so. The parts had all been advertised at pretty much the going rates. By the time the team had got there, the sellers just refused to trade. According to all city states, you can't force someone to sell; it wasn't right. So they didn't. They had to walk away every time.

"If you're not selling, then why do you bring them out here?" I asked her.

"We are selling, we just can't sell to you."

"What? Why? Seriously. Who has something on you? What is it?"

She moved to a large screen and pushed a few buttons. "Not many allowed even to spy on these. We're part of the underground vicenet, but anyone caught selling you parts has been told we'll be boycotted city wide. That means—"

"And that means you can't survive," Hosoke said. "How would they even know?"

"They'll know. They're watching everything. They might not be able to send the assassins they want, but they're trying everything they can to stop you within the rules of our planet." Anna sat down and put her head in her hands. "I'm only just getting by as is. My husband's meds cost more than I earn some days." She looked to Hosoke. "Who am I kidding, most days? I'm done."

Hosoke sat across from her, putting the parts down, finally. I didn't want him to, but he took her hand in his. "Where's your husband?" he asked.

"Working out on the local fishing route," she said. "He earns a good wage when he can stand for long enough."

"How is the fishing?" I asked.

"It's honest hard work," Anna said. "But it pays well if they bring in a good catch."

"Sounds great, being out on the water," Hosoke said.

"It is. He loves it, was born on water. We're both from Malscrest."

"That sounds wonderful," I said. "There's an ocean?"

He smiled. "Yes, and the fishing out there is amazing."

"I really want to see the ocean," I said.

"We really need these parts," Hosoke said. "What would you be asking?"

"Clearly, money isn't much of an issue. But if I sell you these now that people have seen you around here, I'll be run off."

"Then you're not going to sell them to us," I said, and pulled my backpack around so she could see it. Hosoke's forehead scrunched. "You're going to swap them for the ones we have, go back out there, and put them back up for sale."

I unzipped my bag and then pulled out the parts we had, the ones that didn't work.

"What if someone else comes along to buy them?" She raised an eyebrow at me.

"You really think anyone will?"

Anna let out a sigh. "No, no one's been near in months."

"So we have a deal?" I asked.

"I can't take the funds, not today," she said. "They'd know."

"We can send it in increments?" Hosoke suggested.

Anna sighed, stood and paced her van's length. This was a big decision for her. She turned to face us. "Pay for my husband's meds for the next two years."

"I don't even know what he's taking," I said. "Or the cost."

"You had one of the biggest medical facility owners' brothers on your team. I'm sure you'll work it out. Deal or no deal?"

She held my eyes with hers.

"We need those parts. The race is in a just over a week. You need the practice."

I nodded at her, stood, and moved to hold out a hand. "You've a deal. No matter what I have to do, we'll sort it."

Anna smiled. "Now you need to get out of here, and out the back, before anyone else decides to come see what I've been doing."

Hosoke took the right parts, packed them in my rucksack, and we left out the back end of her truck. "I'll message Tat," I said, knocked for him. "We'll meet you back at the car in a few hours. Make it look like you're still enjoying the market. In fact, just enjoy it for real."

I disconnected and walked with Hosoke around the rest of the market. There were a few stalls he stopped at, mostly selling other car parts. He made sure there were lots of people around when he asked for the parts we needed to buy to fix Ivori. Everyone kept on shaking their heads at us, not knowing where we could buy them.

An hour later, we stood in a line for a drink and I yawned. "I'm ready for home," I said.

Hosoke waited to get the drinks, then moved us in the direction of his car.

We walked up the hill to the parking lot. The first thing I noticed was the crowd of people. I spotted Tatsuno coming our way, shaking his head. Alek was then right behind him, hurrying.

They reached us, and Alek linked my arm, spun me around, and started in the opposite direction. "Car's toast," he said to the both of us. "We're taking the next train or caravan out of here, but we're not going to be driving."

Hosoke tried to get past Tatsuno, but he held on strongly. "We got pictures before a crowd gathered. We'll let you see them when we're safe. We're not sticking around, though."

"Fuck," I said. "That bad?"

Alek squeezed my arm. "Just not taking any chances. The council will move it to a secure lockup. We'll find it when we come back."

Hosoke deflated before us, but resigned himself to walking with us, instead of trying to get us around.

The train home had three changes. Wasn't fast at all and we needed to buy more and more food at extortionate prices on the way.

By the time I crawled into bed, early hours of the next morning, I was beyond done.

The knock at my door at whatever time it was only seemed like thirty minutes had passed. "Ugh," I said. "Leave me be."

The bed shifted, and I groaned as I had to move to see who it was. "Alek," I said. "What time is it?"

"We all slept in. Tatsuno left for the track earlier, thought I'd make us something to eat while you got a shower."

"I feel rubbish," I said, and started coughing.

"Tatsuno said Hosoke messaged him with the same. Think we're all just exhausted."

I hoped so, didn't need any kind of sickness. I pushed off the covers, though, and froze. Alek let out an "Oh shit."

My legs were covered in thick black lines. "Is that my . . ."

Alek tapped the side of his head and brought up Tatsuno's comms on the house line. "Tat, is Hosoke with you?"

"Yeah, he's knee deep in putting the new parts in Ivori now."

"Do me a favor and ask him to drop his pants. Tell me what you see."

Tatsuno laughed. "I never thought I'd get that request today. Give me a minute."

Alek and I both waited. He stared at my legs, and so did I. I felt off, but nothing major.

Sound of a lot of swearing came over the comms, then Tatsuno came back. "Get one of the guards out to the local market, pick up some Isotop Simtra," he said. "It's not expensive, but you're going to itch for a few days."

"What is it?" Alek asked.

"This is something you ate or drank," Tatsuno said. "Seen it before. You'll be fine in a few days."

"I thought someone poisoned me," I said with a sigh, still watching as the black veins pulsated with my fast beating heart.

"Thanks, Tat, we'll see you soon," Alek said and disconnected. "Go get a shower. We'll have the drink and food ready for you in a bit."

Saturday, April 10th - *Lunch*
Year - 27515

Tatsuno had been right about the damn itch. My jeans especially made it worse. When we'd gotten to the track, I swapped out for some mechanic slacks and helped them all with the last of the parts swaps and upgrades.

Finally, Ivori's engine had started and everything on the 3D system was green. We were good to go, and that meant we had four days of solid training to get in before we headed back to Sidmont and the track.

I ran through any changes we'd accomplished with the team and listened to Alek as he did the same. Then, of course, we lined them up so we could all see.

"You're both learning to complement each other in some truly good ways," Ivori said.

Ren grumbled at the side of the garage, and I scratched my leg. Alek slapped my hand away.

"We've done the best we can for each other and the teams we're around. We have to think long term. We're going to be on the same track at some point, and it's not going to be easy then. Now is the time to do what we can, while we can."

"I wasn't arguing," Hara said. "I'm glad you've got support on all sides. Each team member is genuinely pulling out all stops."

I looked at him, dipped my head. "We've the best manager around, that's why. He kicks their ass—and mine—if I don't do as I'm told."

Hara laughed.

Now sitting in the transport with Alek and the crew around me. I felt elated and ready for this. Hara had let us work out amongst us what was best, but I'd seen how he'd been guiding Bren away from healing, to look more into race diagnostics, and problems, on the other planets. He knew we'd have Ezra eventually for any healing help we needed. What we didn't have, other than Tatsuno, was someone specific for now. Bren, Itoh, and Balsy were each specializing and learning for me, for us. On Alek's side, his team were doing the same. Though a lot of their instruction was, of course, coming from Ren.

On the inside, I wished Ivori helped us a bit more. Her instruction was rare and only when we'd struggled and exhausted all our own avenues. Mostly it was out of frustration with us then, and that got me down. Even if she didn't mean it.

Alek and Tatsuno talked about how his race was going to go. I'd listened to many of them, the rundowns, the after chatter. I hadn't yet watched any live. They usually ran the same times as ours. And that meant split focus for the teams. It was a good thing. It meant we couldn't get worked up before or after our own races. We just dealt with it as it came.

Being in the town helped. I already knew when we drew close, where we'd split off to the track, where the marketeers were setting up, and where the best place to eat was.

We sat, and I ate my fill of those wondrous pancakes once again. It felt good. Everything about this felt good.

Sidmont's track garage wasn't the best. There just wasn't the tech we were used to, but Tatsuno and Hara worked well to get everything they wanted on the main screens.

"That's what I want to see," I said as the green lights spread all around her chassis.

"It's a good sight to see," Tatsuno said.

Ivori responded with an engine roar.

"How's the lineup looking?" Hara asked.

I looked out to the main leader board. "You know I have to win this, and every race after it . . ."

Alek bumped into me. "You and me both . . . but you get off easy. This track's one of the best. I've gotta get out there in the wild."

I pulled him into me. "Go, you have another twenty minute ride to get there."

Alek patted my back and squeezed. "We got this, brother," he said.

When he and Tatsuno had gone, I focused on the screen. "He's more than super talented," Hara said. "I didn't even think he could ride, but he's gifted."

"Wasted as a driver," I said.

"Totally. I think if Trayk had known he was that good years ago, he'd have gone further than anyone on our planet. He'd already be reaching for Halara Prime."

I frowned. "Then they'd never have met me, or you, and things would be very different."

Hara tapped on the screen. "We've got less than an hour now. You can go meditate, do anything you want. I'll call when we're almost to the thirty points."

I moved to the back door and made my way out to find a nice spot to compose my mind, my thoughts.

Dropping my stance, I let my senses look all around me for the elements I found comfort in. Water . . . I found the local water source to be a great comfort. I could feel it here even though we were a few miles away. The gentle breeze moved my hair, and spots of rain spattered my face as I ran through from First Thought to Second Sentience and beyond.

"Don't stop." I heard a voice to my left.

I opened my eyes to see Andi. I kept my eyes on hers as I continued my moves, making sure everything inside me was aligned perfectly. I waited for her to get the courage to say what she was here for. Eventually, I brought my movements to a nice, rounded-out close.

"What?" I asked. "Spit it out. We don't have a lot of time for messing about before the race starts."

"I wanted to message you, to say something. I just didn't know what. Okburg . . ."

I stood in front of her, keeping my eyes locked with hers. She didn't stop fidgeting. "It was an accident," I said. "That's all."

"I wasn't so sure," she said. "But the ruling said so. I trust the council."

"As do I."

She sucked in a breath. "We all know what you need to win, and you are going for the win, yes?"

I nodded, and she pulled what looked like an old digital card out of her pocket. "This contains messages to both myself and Don. We've been asked to get you off the track via any means possible."

"What do you want me to do with it?" I moved to take it from her.

"I can't afford to not win this race," she said. "I can't afford to not get you off the track . . . I—"

I put my hands around hers and took the chip.

There was a cough to my side, and I glanced to see Don. "We're all in the same position," he said and moved to her side. "We're not throwing any race."

Andi let out a little sob. "We're standing for us, for what's right. No one should have the power these guys do on the inside."

"I agree."

"Out there," Don said. "Give it your all."

I held out a hand for him. "I will."

"Thirty min call in five," Hara shouted.

"That's for us all," Don said. "See you out there."

"Forty-four laps," Hara said. "They're longer. The bends are deceiving. But the speeds—"

"We'll be above every known record," I said.

Hara frowned, both his hands on my shoulders. I winced; it was a little sore, but nowhere near as bad as it was. He raised an eyebrow. "You got the *all* clear off the doc, right?"

"You know I did," I replied and stepped back.

"But it's still sore," he added. "I can see that. Why isn't anyone telling us this?"

"Because it hurts, but it's okay." I wasn't lying; the bruises had gone, the skin normal. "I'm not going to let it stop me. I'm managing it and the pain's within the race's legal limits."

Hara didn't look overly happy, but he moved out of my way so I could at least get into Ivori's cab.

I slid in and offered her a little Azris. This time, she took it and thanked me. "They're only looking out for you," she said.

"I know." I let her engine start properly and moved out onto the pit lane.

"Nice and steady," Balsy said. "We're watching."

I winked at him, and he gently slapped the top of the hood as we passed.

I wasn't at the back anymore. I was in fifth here. Four places to overtake. One per ten laps. That was my goal. I'd have to take the leader in the last couple. Or I could blow it if he got a chance to get around me again.

"Fastest time?" I asked Ivori.

"One hour, forty-four minutes," she replied.

"Okay, it's a fair bit longer than some of the others."

"Yes, it runs alongside the river, too. You'll like that."

The map came up on the screen. It did run alongside the river, and it was nice to see. Such a long straight. "Top speed hit?"

"327," she replied. Her engine shuddered. Strange.

"That's faster than anything we've gotten before," I said.

"I know, but we're not incapable."

All systems reset to red on our dash, so I could get them to optimum temps. Then we set off as steady as I could, hitting the first hairpin bend at minimum speed, eighty. Then heading out into this massive hit of straight roads. I eyed the river to my left; the boats lined up, watching us. It was something else to see water so close, so beautiful. Up through the gears, and up to 260. Everything moved through from red to orange, then back to green as we made it through our next right, left, and right turns. The gear changes were smooth, the ride itself and the landscape beautiful. It might not have been a rich track, or a big city, but it was somewhere I could see myself settling down. Somewhere I wanted to be.

We hit the last chicane into the starting area once more just as the pits closed off. Everyone lined up, and we waited for the all clear and the lights to change.

We were ready.

15

Saturday, April 10th *Late*
Year - 27515

Don and Vral were both off to a perfect start. However, Andi missed hers, and with her stalling even for a split second, I stalled too. Fuck.

She also wasn't recovering. Though she was in the green, I used her failure to my advantage to the gate into the first right-hand bend. I swung wide and, with some Azris use, powered out and into the straights.

"Careful!" Hara said through comms, but I'd already let loose the energy, and Ivori wasn't letting it go to waste. She and the nites fully used it to power us forward toward those ahead. I wouldn't risk getting too close now. I had to play this. I had to watch. We were way too early in this, and Andi would be back up behind me in no time, I was sure of it.

We hit the three hundred for speed, but I backed off way before the right, left, then right.

I watched Vral and Don as they power-played for the lead and kept up my speed and my tenacity.

They were pulling away with every bend, with every run through the gears.

"Don't let them," Ivori scolded.

I did, though. I had to time this so that we had enough of a chance to get past the both of them, and there was only one shot I had for this, the full straight. I needed to gather energy.

The next couple of laps were safe. Andi never even made a play for third again, though she had a couple of opportunities. She also wasn't ready. She'd be watching me as much as I was watching her.

Lap twenty-two, halfway.

"I have a plan," I said to Ivori, "but you're not going to like it."

She laughed. "You think I'm ever going to not like one of your ideas. . . . You have a lot, a lot to learn."

I frowned, coming into the next straight, lining us up. Instead of keeping my speed, I slowed down. "I'm trying."

I kept the pace for the next couple of laps, making sure I ran all the scenarios through my mind before I decided to act on it.

When I dropped my speed on lap thirty-eight, it was going to look like . . .

"Something wrong?" Tatsuno asked only a moment later.

"What's the slowest speed that we can keep a good distance between us all and not risk our place?" I asked, though I was already sure of my own calculations.

"I think I know what you're up to," Tatsuno said. "No lower than 280. Andi's gonna come up on you in a few laps, unless you pick it back up to silly speed after."

"Silly speed." I grinned. "We can do that."

We leveled with the river, and I asked the nites to drop the glass to my left side.

The wind whistled in, and I could smell the freshness of that open water. I sucked it in like I'd never breathed in years. Then I opened myself up, every meridian, every channel.

Ivori gasped as the purest form of Azris entered my system. *I had no idea you knew how to do that?* she said inside. *You're growing faster than I credit you for.*

I felt it the other day when we were here for the parts. There's more energy in this body of water than I've felt anywhere else.

Wait till you see the ocean, she said.

We reached the end of the straight, and I grinned. This energy filled me with such power, and yet fear too. I hoped I could do what I had planned. I—we—needed it.

"That's insane," Hara said. "Oto, you're taking in massive amounts of Azris."

"I've got this," I said.

"You better have it. We can't afford to lose this."

I kept my concentration on the lines I needed, the speeds I had to take the bends around the rest of the track to make sure when we hit that straight next to the river I could drop back down and take it all in.

With every pass, my levels were building.

Fire struggled to keep its place in my core. I had to vent it.

I'd never done this. Never thought I'd need to. I'd balanced my cores with both for so long. The thought filled me with a fear of what I was going to try.

But the next pass, lap forty, put me at risk of overloading. The balance was gone. Fire had to go.

Hitting danger point, I could see red flashing all over my system logs and the dashboard.

Hara's voice echoed in my mind, as did Alek's and the others. "Cut the comms," I said to Ivori. "I need to concentrate on this, and they're getting in the way, as much as I love 'em."

Done, she said a moment later. *It's just us here. They can't see anything.*

You think I'm crazy? I asked her.

The point is, are you ready? she asked.

It was the way she said it—I felt it on the inside, these connotations. They were pure Dark. This wasn't about just me, though; this was for the greater good, for all of us.

Is it wrong? I asked her.

The start line was coming back around.

Trust yourself, Oto. This is a choice, but it's your choice.

Ivori was right; it was, and this time, those watching were going to get a very different view.

You ready? I asked Ivori.

You bet I am, she said. Her excitement bounced around her in the cab. *Just don't set fire to the tires. We kinda need them.*

I laughed. We came out of the bend into the straight, and I let her hit for that Fire Azris inside me.

The cab instantly blazed, and we shot forward, the river calling to me, but I didn't let it calm me down this time. I needed the hit.

Temperature rising, Ivori said.

We've got this.

Speed rising, Ivori said. 310.

Hang in there.

320.

The far side was flying toward us. I harnessed the fear inside me and kept my foot on the gas.

330.

There wasn't much more room, but I still had Fire inside me.

340.

342.

I had to hit the brakes.

Fire dissipated fast, and I hit for Water, cooling everything off as we drew in far too close to that bend.

Ivori's brakes squealed, their new components complaining in every way. If we didn't blow something . . .

Holy shit, the bend was here.

I forced the wheel right, and my shoulder popped. Pain exploded within, and I almost let go. That would mean we'd hit the barrier at almost 240. We'd never survive.

Fuck!

I bit down and held on for everything I was worth.

220 into the next and then out into the next at 230. Flicking down the gears just in time to take the next at 140.

Each time I turned that wheel, my arm sent pain through to my core.

On the next small straight, I reached down, pulling one of the potions out of my pouch. I bit the top off, held it in between my teeth, and downed the liquid. It sent some relief flooding through my body in seconds; I tossed the vial behind me and held the top in between my teeth. With every bend I'd come across, I'd bite this instead of my cheek. I was going to hurt myself even more.

Vral and Don were right in front of me now. But everyone would think I just used my Azris stores to get over some complication. They had no idea I'd just filled myself in the last several laps to bursting.

This time we hit the straight, and I stuck behind them both at 335, they weren't holding back, their top speeds blooming everything else out. But I'd blown a new record. I was going to make sure the last lap I'd blow that even more out.

What's the goal? she asked me as we went into lap forty-two.

I'm taking everything I can and I'm going to hold on to it. We're taking them on the last one.

You're sure you don't want to do something now?

No, trust me. I'm going for a double pass. Vral will try to take Don's lead on the next run through; it's his only chance, and I have to take them both.

You're showing everyone everything you have with this.

I know. This is the only track I can do this.

The bends were at speeds that hurt my eyes and my shoulder. Every detail ripped past me in a split second. They kept their distance in front of me, and I noted Vral was hesitant. He feathered his brakes way too often. Nervous.

We approached the last few bends and into the next straight run.

Fuck! Vral hit for Azris, already!

He threw his Icarian around bend fifteen and into the bends at 280, then he was blasting away from Don.

I had to get past him. I couldn't use any Azris; instead I dropped the gear and hit the gas with only hope in my veins.

I also then flung wide, and with the world whizzing past me at 342 once again, I just overtook him before we had to both hit the brakes.

He's too close! Ivori screamed.

Don's left tire touched ours, and he spun. I fought the wheel. My shoulder really blew this time. On the screen, it turned black.

I'd never seen it turn black, but as I prepped to drop the gear, I realized I couldn't. I had no control over my fingers. My hand, though still attached to the wheel, wasn't responding.

The bend sped toward us, and my mind froze for just a second.

Then I ordered the nites, and they responded by flicking the gears for me.

I pulled my arm off the wheel. It was going to cause more problems if I couldn't do anything with it.

Right turn.

Left turn.

One handed

This would not work.

Instead, I let go of the wheel in full, cranking our speed back up again to head into the last lap.

Ivori never missed a beat. She didn't need to take control. Instead, I closed my eyes, picturing everything around us, and the Azris lines, the heat from Vral as he'd passed just moments before me. I'd follow his lines precisely if I had to. The bend approached, and the wheel turned.

I flicked Ivori out of the bend into our last straight, with Vral right in front of me.

He hit 357, and I followed. Right behind him. Except I hit 360!

I tailed him the whole way around the track, within an inch of his backside, threatening him at every bend. I feigned my attempts to overtake. He fought me every step of the way.

Right and then left. He missed his line, and I took it, flinging everything I ever had at my only shot to win.

Water Azris forced its way out of my core, and Ivori took every damn bit of me. I didn't gasp this time; I let out a scream, forced back into my seat with a thump on my shoulder. I couldn't take it. Consciousness was slipping from me.

We were, however, past Vral, and over the line in record time.

Ivori?! I said.

I've got this, she replied. *I've got this.*

She hit the brakes this time, and we snaked more than a few times around the bend. We were supposed to stop. . . . We weren't stopping.

She didn't have this. We were going to hit the barrier at 170.

With both hands, I took the wheel, reacting the only way I could, and I turned into the bend.

We just won that race, I said. *Points?*

Yes!

Shields, now!

The front end hit the curb, and we drifted wide, way too wide, the barrier looming in my view.

We were still going to hit far too fast; we were going far too fast!

Shield strengthened, Ivori said.

I saw it flicker with the extra power.

The left side hit the metal barrier and sparks ignited. The metal burning smell came in through the open window, and I grimaced.

We stopped, dead.

I let my head fall on the wheel, and Ivori seemed to wrap me up into her arms. Her spirit was all around me.

Take another potion, she said.

I looked at my pouch, the world graying around the edges.

Gently, I pulled one more potion out, and spitting the other lid out, took the top off the fresh one. I swallowed the liquid quickly. It dribbled down my chin, but I scooped the precious liquid in, licking my fingers.

The potion wasn't helping much, but it eased my mind back into focus.

Comms on, I said to her.

The slew of messages hit the dashboard, and the cab lit up.

"Guys, guys!" I wheezed. "I'm okay, I'm okay!"

"Med truck is on its way. We'll get you onboard as soon as we can." Alek's voice was the first one to come through again. His voice softened. "Are you okay?"

"No," I said, moving slightly, then wincing. "No, I'm not."

I closed my eyes, concentrated on my breathing.

One vial left.

I couldn't do it. Instead, I got out, and I walked. The river still very much called to me. I needed water. I couldn't get to it, but I was closer; I could see it. Smell it. It was beautiful.

This time, even though Dark was all around me, this would take me closer to that edge. I pulled for it.

No choice, I said to Ivori.

There in front of the metal barriers, I dropped my stance. Opened my channels once more and drew energy to me, energy from the river, energy from the ground itself. I glanced up to the sun, felt the wind in my hair.

I pulled all of it.

Fire tricked in once more and heated my muscles. Relief at everything I did. Every second that passed.

As the pain eased and things around me changed, the wind whistled around me, the sun beating down on me.

I dipped my stance even more, and without thinking, started from First Breath. Even without my arm, I managed, I adapted. Second Sentience. Third Awareness.

It all helped me.

Alek moved in beside me, extending his senses over me. "I'm right here," he said.

I glanced at him, nodded, and carried on. Alek joined me.

His Azris drifted my way though, his Fire, his Spirit, his Dark. I needed it all of it; I took it, and he let me.

When my knees wobbled and I could do no more, I stopped. Alek was right with me then and had his arms under mine. "I got you," he said.

I looked into his eyes. "It fucking hurts," I admitted.

"I know." Alek motioned behind him with a nod, and the next thing I knew, I was on my back on a stretcher, and I was being wheeled away. The sun above me, still so very bright.

I absorbed all of it.

Alek stayed with me, his hand on mine. Comforting. Brothers.

I eyed him with respect, with hope, with love.

"Hospital," Alek said.

"No, no hospital!" I insisted.

Now I was tucked up in the truck's cab, with the others around me. "Let me sleep for a bit," I said. "That's all I need."

"No," Geo said. "You need a lot more than sleep."

"At home," I said. "Please."

Geo's eyes narrowed at me, then he nodded to Alek. "Slow. Doesn't matter how long it takes, okay?"

"Okay, we've got him. We'll see you soon."

I don't recall the truck starting up. That Ivori was even with me, but I felt her.

I woke—or did I?—to find her staring at me.

"Hey," I said and tried to move.

"Hey," she replied.

"We home yet?"

"No, only just set off. I just wanted to see you before you drifted into real sleep."

"Ahh," I said, my stomach knotting. I was in for a telling off, I was sure.

"No," she replied. "You have to heal. There's no telling off, no training for a while. You have to get yourself better. I need you."

"I need you too," I said. I reached out for her, but my hand passed through her like a ghost.

She moved to me, though, kneeling. "We have eight weeks," she said. "You will rest. I swear if you don't, if you hurt yourself any more for this . . ."

"We have to win these races," I said.

"You don't have to lose your life."

"The points, the win, I had to . . . had to put them to shield."

"I'd be a mess again if you hadn't. Thank you."

"What about—how does that put us in the future?"

She let her Azris fill me this time. So different. So wonderful.

With a thought, she brought up our stats.

"What should we do?"

"You need strength," she said without hesitating.

I thought about it, watched my stats change, then energy spread through me. I felt better again.

Name = Oto Benes
ID Number = 4188927
Age = 22
Species = Anodite
Sex = Male
Alignment = Neutral
Bloodline = Unknown
Health = 87%
Cultivation Level - Master Rank 4
Active Meridians = 12/12
Nanites = 1 million
Artefacts = 2
Chosen Specialist = Racer
First Chosen Affinity = Water
Second Chosen Affinity = Fire

Strength = 42/**121.8**
Dexterity = 27/**72.9**
Constitution = 37/**106.19**
Int/Wis/Spirit = 47

Affinities - Rank

Water - Blue
Fire - Green
Earth - Yellow
Air - Yellow
Light - Orange
Darkness - Orange
Spirit - Green

Droll's Leg Pouch – three refillable containers hold the power of life or death. One use per origin user.

Ring of Light - A gift from Ezra
Adapted, so you may use it as you wish.
Boosts Azris circulation and usage, + 30 to all stats
Uses = 5

Core Intelligence
Name - Ivori
Model - A101
Year - 27188

Composition -
Solids - Silver
Liquid - Harilliom/Mercury
Nanites swarm - 2 billion
Nanites to Oto - 1 million

Slots

Engine - Level 4
Outer Frame - Level 1
tires - Level 4
Lights - Level 1
Steering - Level 4
Bumpers - Level 1
Windshield - Level 1
Mirrors - Level 1
Core Intelligence - Level 2
Chassis - Level 0
Shield - Level 5
Nitro - Level 1

STR = 8
DEX = 3
CON = 10

Then the world faded.
  "Rest, partner," she said. "Rest as long as it takes."
  I tried to fight it. I couldn't.
  Darkness, wonderful darkness.

16

Wednesday, April 14th *Lunch*
   Year - 27514

I woke with a start. It wasn't dark. Soft blankets covered me and there was soft skin, too. I reached for it, for her.

Ezra moved around me, pulling me gently to her. I let out a low moan as I moved. "Easy," I said.

"I'm sorry." I felt her Azris circulating, though. "I can't do much more to help."

"It's okay," I replied.

"No," she said. "You damaged your meridians, your channels. This is serious, Oto."

I swallowed and met her eyes with mine. I didn't think I'd done anything that bad. "Irreparable?"

"Ivori said you just need time. A good amount of time."

I struggled to move, but the pain. "I don't have it," I said.

Ezra put her lips to mine. "Shush," she whispered. "You have all the time you need."

"Vrance?"

"It's eight weeks away. You. Have. Time."

I let Ezra shush me, my thoughts wild but the pain so much worse. When I woke a few more times, she wasn't with me, then she was. I slept. I slept more than enough, then I slept some more.

The next time I woke, it was dark, and the stars twinkled through the window, our tri-moons glistening above.

I slipped out from under her even though it hurt and went into the kitchen. We weren't in the flat. We were in the shack on the track. I guess it was just nicer for me to be closer to Ivori. I slipped socks on one handed, struggled with my boots, and in the end just tucked my laces inside them and wobbled down the stairs and out onto the track to go see her.

Once in the garage, I felt better. I pulled up the race results, the 3D views, and I watched and watched what we'd done, the speed, the results, the speculation about the elements I could control. They'd witnessed it all, and then after the fact, it was clear at the side of the track I was using much more than even Fire and Water.

"I blew it, right?" I asked her.

Ivori formed beside me and put her hand on my good shoulder. "They were going to see you at some point. That was a hell of a stunt."

I let out a chuckle. "Yes, yes, it was."

"We're capable of so much more," she said. "I'm glad you trust your instincts. They're not wrong, you're just moving a little faster than you're capable of."

"But not faster than you're capable, that much is obvious."

"No." She moved away.

"Will you tell me?" I said, and I turned to see her.

Ivori looked away.

Then the screen pinged, and she vanished. I read the text.

Incoming comms from unknown. Accept Y/N

I didn't need to accept it from some unknown idiot.
I hit the N, and moved back to watch the race again.
The second ping came through.

Insistent.

Annoyed this time, I hit the accept.

Drei's face filled the screen. "Didn't think you'd accept," he said.

I rolled my eyes. "What do you want?"

"The rules might not say you're cheating, but you are. No one has ever had that amount of control on the tracks. It's not right."

"You think it's not right just because you can't do it. Doesn't mean it isn't. The races are to separate those who can rise to the top. Who can do things outside the box."

"You're so far outside the box, you're dangerous. You didn't even see what you were doing to everything around you, did you?"

I had no clue what he was on about, so I shook my head.

"You need stopping," Drei said. "I can't come anywhere near you, but you better believe someone is coming for you. Check the race after your last burst of Azris. Follow the draw. See what you're doing to this planet, this space?"

He cut off the communication.

That was it. All he wanted to tell me was that someone was coming for me, that I needed to check the race again.

I glanced at Ivori, but she was quiet. "Do you know what he's talking about?" I asked her.

Nothing.

"You're not sure what I'm doing to everything around me, or you just don't want to let me know? I'll see it in a minute if I look deeper, won't I?"

Nothing again.

Frustrated, I turned back to the screen.

I watched the end of the race, the draw from everywhere around me as it built.

I could see it, under the land, the skies, the air. Everywhere around me, I drained it, and in massive quantities that no one else would ever be able to manage.

I needed it to control the pain, to control Ivori. Everything in the area started to wither. Plants died. The ground itself that had been vibrant was no more.

When the race finished and I stood out, completing what I needed to heal somewhat, I saw it even more.

The waters, I drained it. Life, I drained it.

The fish that were in the area, that Anna's husband needed to catch. Their life gone, their everything gone.

I killed everything lower than me with just a thought.

On the inside, dread filled me.

I turned to Ivori.

"What did I do?" I asked her. "What the hell is that?"

She formed once more, sat on her own hood. Her eyes met mine with sadness. "You did what you had to, to win, to survive."

"What does it . . . I don't understand. I don't get it."

"Think, Oto." Her eyes flashed with anger. "Think who you are. What you are, what you are going to become."

She stood and spun around. The air moved with her, and I could see her Azris draw. All twelve meridians were open and connecting to me, all connecting to the elements around us. She was attached to everything, as was I.

Nausea washed over me. I didn't want this. I didn't want this. But I had done it; I had known I was doing it. I was a killer. What I'd done was beyond terrible.

With a heave, I leaned over and vomited. Sickening bile spurted out and I couldn't stop it. Then it was followed by thick black sickness.

Ivori was then beside me, her hand on my back, soothing.

"Oto," she asked. "I need to ask you this—" Her voice had a serious edge to it and I looked up into her eyes. They were full of emotion. "Would you do it again?"

I didn't hesitate, when I nodded. Though I still felt sick. "Yes," I said. "I would, but—"

"There's no buts," she said. "We can't think like that. Where we're going and what we're going to do, don't ever feel guilty. We can't afford to suffer because of the things we'll have to do."

"What are we going to have to do?" I asked her.

Ivori stood and moved away from me. "I can't . . ." she said. "I just can't."

I needed answers, now more than ever. I saw how much I could take. How much life it took to feed me, to sustain me. My eyes were drawn back to the video.

Messages started to come through once more to me then. This time, when I looked, there was one from Councilor Troha.

I flicked them all away, pulled my knees up to my chest, and watched the race video again and again.

The track woke early as it usually did. Everyone else came in, and I made to smile at them, though on the inside I was dying. Darkness swallowed me, and I couldn't see any way out of it. I couldn't train; I couldn't do anything.

Nishi brought Jin in, and to my shock she had the rotter with her. When he lunged straight for me, his tongue lolling out, his teeth on full display, I shrank back. Nishi yanked him back. "Brutus! Sit!"

The massive rotter did exactly what she said. "You think you're okay keeping him company While I take the Zeroes out?"

"He'll listen to me?" I asked.

"Oh, he'll listen, just let him see a little Azris and he'll be putty in your hands. I promise."

"Good, I can't afford for him to try taking off. I have to let this heal."

Jin frowned at me. "Hate seeing you like this," he said.

I looked at the floor while Hara shouted his orders. The Zeroes were racing around the track moments later, and then I could hear the bikes. I wanted to watch, to do something, but I just got more and more frustrated.

I watched Brutus as he sniffed around the break room. "Want to go for a walk?" I asked him, really not expecting the reaction I got. No sooner did I finish my words than did he have his leash in his mouth, and he sat in front of me, holding it out.

I took the slightly wet leash off him. "You're that desperate to get out of here?"

His eyes widened. "I guess so." I let my Azris pool in my hand. Both

163

Fire and Water were balanced once again inside me. He eased forward and stared at the swirling orb of energy. Forcing more Azris into the ball, I said, "You play fetch?"

Brutus then bounced up and down with excited yips.

"Let's go, then," I said, holding his leash with my good arm and making sure my duff one was tucked away inside my jacket.

I shouldn't have gone out, but my guard followed me, nice and slow behind. They were good guys, though nowhere near as swift as Lena. Or as stealthy.

Walking out in the open was nice. I made my way out into the city; I watched everyone around me. No one was coming near me with Brutus. In fact, everyone made sure they were going in the opposite direction. Brutus stuck to my heel; he never pulled on the leash once.

"Nishi's done a good job with training you," I said. "You're so well behaved."

He looked up at me, his deep yellow eyes glistening with Azris. It wasn't long before I reached my destination, and then we were playing in the open and I was lobbing Azris balls for him. Even one handed, this was the most fun I'd had in ages.

It was just good to be out. To feel some kinda normal.

Later, back in the break room with Brutus, I settled in, the noise and hustle of the track soothing. The exercise we'd both gotten had wiped us out.

When Brutus growled sometime later, I stirred to see Nishi and Ezra staring, laughing to each other. "What's up?" I asked.

Brutus had his head in my lap.

Nishi moved forward, put her finger to the ground. Brutus lowered his ears, his tail thwapping against the couch, then he hopped off and sat in front of her, head down.

"He was keeping me safe," I said.

"Yes, he looked like he would protect you with his life." Ezra grinned. "Come on." She held out a hand for me. "I've made us dinner back at the apartment. Just you and me tonight."

"Just you and me?"

I looked back to where my guards usually were—yep, still there.

"Well"—she rolled her eyes—"they can stand outside for a while tonight."

Nishi coughed. "See you tomorrow." And off she went.

Ezra took my hand in hers and tugged me out of the break room and into the streets once again. My guards must have felt like . . .

"Don't worry about them," she said, casting her eyes back only the once. "I want you and I to just enjoy tonight. Be us. I have to go back to the school tomorrow; I already missed a few important classes."

"You came for me?"

"Of course I would. Any time you need me, I will be there."

"Even to the detriment of your training?" I gave her hand a slight squeeze.

"No," she said. "I had permission for this one, but I might not get it all the time."

I pulled her hand to my lips, kissed it. "You have to do this course. You need it."

The smells coming from the apartment when we entered were divine. "You made all of this?" I looked to the table, the decorations, the love she'd put into it.

"Yes," she said. "I wanted you to see how much I miss you. I love you."

"It's perfect," I said.

Ezra ushered me over to the chair and helped me out of my jacket. When she saw me flinch at her touch, she eased my sling off, and then reluctantly my shirt with it.

When she touched the top of my head next, a shiver ran through me. There was something else there with her touch, healing energy. She trailed her fingers down the back of my neck, to my shoulders. Nice and steady, then she held her hands there. Radiating warmth and love trickled into me, and I leaned back against her stomach.

"I really love you," I said.

Ezra slid her hands down my shoulder to wrap her arms around me, kissing my cheek. "I love you too, more than I ever thought I could love someone."

My stomach growled, and she laughed. "Let me get you fed, and we'll curl up on the couch."

She slipped a fresh shirt over my head a moment later, and then busied herself in the kitchen. It was wonderful to watch her. I recalled us all around the table at Christmas, the family I never thought I'd have. It was perfect; *she* was perfect. I found my eyes drifting to her curves, and when she bent over, I had to look away. At least for now.

With the food served, and a nice bottle of wine poured. Ezra and I settled in to talk about everything but what was bothering me. I wanted to talk to her about after the race. I wanted to ask her some professional questions on my health, my goals.

It was wonderful to hear her talking about the school, the other talented students she was with. The sheer amount of knowledge she was gaining just in that short time there astounded me.

With my stomach full, she pulled a pie out the oven and set it aside. "We'll eat that later." She grinned.

I made my way over to the couch, taking the glasses and bottle with me. She then settled into my arms, and I held her without speaking. Just enjoying everything.

When she looked up into my eyes, she said the words I didn't want to hear. "Vicenet is talking about a lot of things," she said. "I know the track has been too. Geo's stayed away at the moment, but I've heard he and Taryn talking too. Are you okay?" she asked.

I tried to articulate what I wanted to, to talk to her properly, honestly.

I closed my eyes, terrible memories flooding through me.

"No hope for that one." Those words still echoed in my mind, every single day.

Ezra frowned. "I can see you're not okay," she said, her whole body deflating.

I pushed the memory aside. "Then why ask me?" I bit out, more frustrated than I thought I should have been, especially with her.

"Because I want you to talk to me, tell me."

"You saw what I did?"

She nodded.

"And you're not scared of me?"

"I couldn't ever be scared of you." She ran a finger through my hair, tugged me into a kiss. Her tongue flicked inside my mouth, tasting of the spices of dinner and the wine. "I do want to understand you though. How—or what I can do—to help you."

"I drained the life force of what was around me, in an almost devastating show of power. I killed animals and plants, anything I could get to keep me going, to get us through, to be safe."

"You did what you had to, to survive."

"No," I said. "I mean yes, I did."

"Then why all the sadness?"

"Ivori won't talk to me, not properly."

Ezra smiled. "I'm sure she will. You're still getting to know each other."

"We have to win every race going forward, to get us off this planet, to the future we all crave."

"You're worried she's something she's not telling you, that she's—"

"Dark," I said. "She never flinched with anything I suggested. Anything I want to do, she lets me. She doesn't guide me to anything other than the use of my powers."

"You think she's using you?"

I didn't know the answer to that, I didn't, and more important than that, I didn't want to know that answer.

To think Ivori had that dark side. I let out a deep sigh. I understood taking life to survive to live. I ate meat, I killed bugs; heck, I'd killed rotters. Then I thought about the rotter pups Nishi had raised. Things were different there; they were pets.

In amongst the life I'd taken were both flora and fauna, bugs, small creatures of the waters. More importantly, pets. Owners would return home to find them, just gone . . .

I'd felt it, every single soul I'd taken.

For Ivori to take life and not feel guilt, something. It hurt me inside on a very deep level.

For the first time since we'd connected, I realized how much I really didn't know. How much she might have been through, the decisions she'd made, the lives lost, the lives she'd saved.

Right now, this was the first time I wasn't sure I could trust her.

17

Friday, April 15th *Lunch*
Year – 27515

Bren and Itoh made sure as soon as they saw I was sitting down, they plied me with drinks and snacks. For the sheer amount of food, I could eat here, while I watched them . . . I worried I was going to stack the weight on. As much as I wanted to see what happened with that. I pushed the food away and watched Alek and the others outside doing first practice.

Ivori took my Azris, but wouldn't do much of anything else. The guys went about their work, and I was pretty much left alone again.

It was Ren that reached out across the garage to me while they trained. *May I speak frankly?* he said.

I stood and made myself go over to him, not really sure what to say, though my feelings were probably obvious to him. I let my Azris pool down my arm into my hand; he accepted it easily. Though he coughed. "Something wrong?" I asked.

Thank you for the trust, Oto. Thank you for the honor.

"You want to talk to me?" I asked, prompting him.

Take a seat, he said.

I hesitated, but then pulled one of the rolling chairs over, then sat. "Talk," I said. "It won't be long before they're back and you need to get out on the track."

We spent an entire weekend together before I even spoke to you about what I was going through on the inside, right?

"We did," I said.

You talked to me about a lot of things I don't even think you realize.

I swallowed and tried to recall all the things I had told him back then.

Ren filled me in. *From your first memories when your parents left you, the time on the streets with no one to turn to, no hope.*

The memories flooded me then, and I struggled a lot with how strong they still were.

You went through a lot, and you protect yourself by shutting them out most of the time. You and Ivori are so alike. Neither of you wants to admit the real you on the inside. I want you to know that even though I had all my walls up, your persistence, your love and care to me, to help me and Alek, was what got through to me.

"You heard things, saw me, where no one really does."

They do. Ezra, Alek, even the team. They see who you are, not where you came from. They see who you will be.

"There's a but, though, right?"

You need Ivori to trust you fully.

I knew that. I felt it on the inside.

"I just don't know what else I can do to get her to just talk, you know?"

I didn't say this, he said, then he whispered, *Take her away from here, from the track.*

I couldn't do that. They wouldn't let me.

Alek came in, and I gently shoved away from Ren. He grabbed his helmet and came over. "Coming to watch?"

I shook my head. "I think I'll take Brutus out again was nice to just walk, play."

Alek frowned, but then nodded and waited for Tatsuno and the others to come in before they started their run down to get him on the track.

I did exactly what I said. I found Brutus in the break room. He even had his friend with him. The other pup. Sass. I eyed the other rotter with care before I moved to the clothes rack at the back and picked up not just one leash, but two.

"You'd better behave together," I warned them.

It was even more fun with two of them out on the streets. There was only one person at the field who approached me carefully.

"Do you mind?" he asked cautiously. "I've seen them on reports, but never seen them this close."

Both Brutus and Sass sat down while the young man came closer, and they behaved perfectly. "Intriguing. There's so many bad rumors about them. If they can be this well looked after and tamed . . ."

"They make excellent guard dogs," I said.

He walked away, happy but muttering to himself.

I spent more than a few days with the rotters. I couldn't do any training. My only time out to actually do anything was to walk. With them, no one was going to mess with me, and it settled my guards, so the rotters went everywhere with me.

The next week went by, and the following one. Ivori's sadness spread through her as much as it did me.

Ezra called me every night before she went to sleep, no matter where I was. I frequented the bars, the park, my frustration growing every single day.

The more I thought about leaving, the nicer it was sounding. I wanted to take Ivori away from here.

I looked at the maps for surrounding cities, places to go. I looked at locations. Nothing felt right.

On the third week, I felt better. My no training had gone to pretending to be not training, out on the field. I let my arm out of its sling, and was using it.

The dark tonight was good; the rotters sniffed around where there were no people. This was the best time to be out. Where I could watch them, and they watched me.

The guards were behind me somewhere by the tree line. When I thought they weren't watching totally, I dropped my stance, and I ran through from First Thought. Really, really slow, gentle movements. My arm was super stiff, but feeling better the more I moved it, so steady I just moved it more.

When one guard coughed, I turned, put my sling on, and called the rotters to me. We wandered on back to the track. Though the guards didn't say anything, their judging looks had been enough to make me feel bad. I shouldn't have been trying to do anything.

Nishi took the rotters off me and grinned. "They adore coming here now," she said. "Your walks have been doing them wonders."

"They're good pups," I replied. "Well, not so much pups. Adults?"

"Not quite," she said.

Jin scuffed Brutus behind the ears. "I don't think anyone thought they'd settle in as they have. We've opened their eyes."

Nishi grinned more. "Good, maybe they'll realize they're just trying to survive, like any creature here. The Canillion, too."

I couldn't argue with that. My thoughts drifted to the Canillion though. I hadn't had much time to think about them. Now I did. I pulled up the vicenet. Actually, I wondered what kind of history I could find on them, their species.

What I got then was a shock.

As feared as the Canillion where, city Canillion were not originally city Canillion. They were caught due to their size, brought in originally as pets. Some didn't like to be pets; they escaped, they set up where they could. They bred everywhere they could. They hid, they were hunted, they were hated. Now they were pests. Pests that were all over Esrall and settled in Isala.

There was extensive history about the Canillion about their origins, and how powerful they were. I knew how powerful they were I'd seen that up close and personal.

What I didn't expect to find were several threads on the possible "artifacts" inside Canillion allies. I tried to follow the conversations, see who had been talking about it, where they were linked, but I wasn't

Lena. I had no tracking clues when it came to the vicenet. In the end, I made a note to ask Pete next time I saw him or Geo and rested my eyes.

Alek pulled in the garage a while later, he slipped off Ren and removed his helmet. "Just us tonight," he said while the others saw to Ren's comfort. "Fancy doing something, you know for your birthday?"

I coughed. "It's not my birthday yet!" But not like I could forget. Would have been my first one with Ezra, but she wasn't here. I sighed. I missed her.

"Can't do it Monday, today or nothing," Alek said.

I glanced at him. He dismounted and came over. "What? I'm not supposed to be doing much, remember?"

Alek rolled his eyes, came in closer to me. "Damn, I forget. What *do* you want to do?"

His face, so sullen. I didn't like that. I knew he was just trying to cheer me up as much as he was himself. He looked like he needed it, even though I didn't want to do anything. "Why don't we head to a few bars? There's some nice local one where the guys"—I threw my fingers behind me—"wouldn't mind being and we could grab some finger foods and just watch a show or something?"

His eyes lit up. "That sounds good," he said. "Local, and chilled."

We wandered home and both showered. I didn't put my sling on to go out, though Alek gave me the "you sure?" look as I stepped out of my bedroom.

"I feel bad enough as is," I stated. "I don't want to look bad, too."

"Ahh." He smirked. "Public appearances matter."

I nodded, and he grabbed his jacket. I picked mine up too on the way out.

The guards followed behind us, but far enough that I was sure they weren't listening in either.

Rain filtered through some of the clouds drifting above us, and I relished in its pitter patter on my skin.

Alek gave me a sideways glance. "Dang Water affinities, they just love being out in all weathers."

He pulled his jacket over his head, and I laughed. "Here, let me," I said. With a slight amount of Azris, I formed a small shield over his head instead.

"Showoff." His eyes lit with fire, and I loved it. I laughed so loud I think I scared the guards.

We walked around the back of our complex and into the streets at the back. I found my way back to the bar they used to frequent. It was nice when we walked in; that the barmaid was the same from months ago, too. It meant the job and the area were nice, stable.

She smiled at me and gave Alek the once over. "Nice to see you back, Oto," she said, using my name as though I frequented the place every week.

"Nice to be here." I returned her smile, then thumbed toward the dance floor. "You got something on later—" I was hinting at her name.

"Jessie," she said. "Yeah, there's a local band starting up in an hour or so. Usually give the guys time to eat and then either go home and get changed or get a little drunk before they start."

"That good." Alek laughed.

Jessie shot him a glare, but then held my eyes. "No trouble tonight, please."

"I don't want any trouble," I said. The bar had a couple of people sitting around, but not many. The older gent from last time was sitting with his granddaughter, who smiled at me as she carried on eating.

"You didn't want it to last time, but it seemed to find you, I recall."

"Can you bring us some beers over, and some good food?" I indicated the table in the far corner.

Jessie nodded, "Go sit. The rest of the staff aren't in just yet, but they won't be too far behind."

"Thanks," I said, and when she indicated the counter. I put my wrist to it, hitting a nice tip for her. Even if I didn't have much, I wanted to share it a little.

Alek pulled us two chairs, and we sat. "This where you had the brawl?" he asked.

I just nodded. "It was a long while ago. I doubt any of those same people still hand around."

"Sure, I think I came here once or twice, but not very often."

"Same," I said. "Never had the cash, but if I got enough, I'd come for the food. Not the beer. Sometimes I'd sit with Tonis and Sta. They were good guys."

"They were," he said, his eyes down.

Jessie brought the beers over first, and I held mine for Alek. "Tonis and Sta," I said.

Alek raised his glass to me, and I clinked mine against it.

It was nice to settle in here. Jessie actually kept the beer coming, which I was surprised about. "The tab's open till you leave," she said. "Computer knows, and well, if you're drinking, I'll serve." There was a ping behind the bar. "That will be some food for you. Be right back."

She winked at Alek, and I chuckled. Alek kicked me under the table. "Hey, I've got a partner, you know that."

"Won't ever stop anyone looking." On his frown, I had to add, "Alek, you're hot. People will notice you. There's no denying that."

He sucked his beer up the side of his glass and almost choked. "I'm getting used to the compliments, the looks," he said. "But it still feels weird. You know what I look like under here—" He waved down his shirt.

"Not going there," I said, and just in time, Jessie was placing hot food in front of us. It smelled great. Nothing like from Grovers, and it also looked the part. Real, just-homemade food on a budget.

"Enjoy," she said and turned on her heels to serve some more people as they came in.

While we ate mostly in silence, the act that was coming on later started to set up, and it was good to see them having fun with the other clientele in the bar.

I finally relaxed a little and sat back, stomach full, brain buzzing slightly.

Alek moved his chair around and sat beside me so he could watch better. "How's the training?" I asked.

Alek side glanced at me, then let out a sigh. His shoulders slump "Relentless. They never stop pushing me."

"You're okay though, right?"

He didn't answer at first, then he turned his whole body toward me. "This isn't your fault," he said.

Dread filled me. "But it is," I replied.

"No." He shook his head. "This isn't your fault. But there's a lot of pressure on us. Ren's . . . there's just no words for his patience, his trust."

Those words stung. Genuinely stung. The food in my stomach churning, round and around.

"I'm glad you have him," I said. "Really am."

Alek reached for my sore arm. Gently placed his on top. "I'm glad I have you. We're a team. But you are going to pull this out of your ass for the next race, right?"

I faked a smile. "Of course we are. We're getting off this planet."

His eyes lit up. "I can't wait to meet up with Amalia and Camran on Copter."

"Even if it's harder than here?"

"Hell yeah. I want to grow, learn, do more. I never wanted to stay on Isala."

"But Tatsuno?"

"Accepting I liked him more than I thought was tough. Seeing his face after the accident . . ."

"He kissed you, no hesitation?"

"Rather brave, right?"

I nodded, taking a swig of beer. "He never wanted to see you go through that again, and now . . . you're on one of the most dangerous pieces of blended alien tech known to man."

"I don't want any trouble!" Jessie said, her voice raised.

Alek and I traded glances before we both turned to the bar.

"Crap," I said. "What the hell are they doing here?"

Drei and Vral stood at the bar arguing with her. Our guards, at the back, both glanced our way. One shook his head; the other put his beer down.

"Could go either way," Alek said. "But I don't want the bar wrecked because of us."

"Yeah," I said. "Stay here. I'll go deal with it." He followed me after I pushed my chair back. I guess I should have expected it.

"Hey, guys," I said.

Drei and Vral turned to see me. "What?" Vral asked. "Not allowed to even get a drink anymore?"

"Depends," I said. "Why are you even around here?"

"We train not far. This is on the way to a friend's house," Drei spat. "If you really must know."

It was the way he stepped toward me that screamed threat, but I held my ground. I wasn't budging. "We're here for one night, and you happen to just be passing. Sorry, I'm not buying that at all. Just leave."

"You can't make us leave," Vral said and folded his arms across his chest.

I indicated to Jessie. "I'm not going to. Give them both a drink on me," I said. "Then go sit and enjoy the entertainment."

Jessie shot me a glare, but pulled two glasses out from under the counter.

"There's no way I'm taking any drinks off you." Drei shoved out from around Vral and bumped right into me walking out of the bar.

I winced as he'd hit my shoulder. Vral saw this. "We really were just visiting a friend," he said. "Thanks for the offer. Best go elsewhere, no hard feelings."

I dipped my head at him and watched as he left. "Could I have shots for us all," I said to Jessie, and indicated to my two guards who had followed sitting at a far table behind us.

"I'll bring them over," she said with a raised eyebrow.

I turned from her and made my way back toward our seats.

I didn't stop, though.

I couldn't, the pain in my shoulder worse than anything from before. I carried on past the dance floor to the toilets at the back. Alek followed me in, shut and locked the door. Panic set in his eyes. He stepped toward me, but I held up my other hand. "Don't," I said. "Please don't."

Alek took my hand in his. "I'm here," he said. "I'm not going anywhere."

I let him hold my hand, sucking in breath after breath.

With his other hand, he pointed to his eyes. "Watch me," he said, then he breathed in. "Nice and slow." He held it for a few seconds. "Then out."

"I . . . can't."

"Yes, you can. With me."

He repeated his breathing. I tried to copy him. At first I struggled, anger, frustration deep inside me, wanting to let loose. Then it worked. I could breathe slower.

"Good," he said, and took my hand with his other. "Keep focused on me."

18

*Friday, April 15th *Late Evening*
Year – 27515

I lowered my breathing more with Alek's help. We concentrated on letting my body and our Azris flow through me to feel it at least start to heal.

"He knew exactly what he was doing, then. He did that on purpose," I said.

Alek looked forlorn, his face pale, his Azris really low. "I should have just got us some takeaway and stayed in."

I shook my head, though it made the pain worse. "No way. I wouldn't trade anything we do together for something else, pain or not."

"Can I see?" he asked.

I rolled my eyes and chuckled. "Just because I said you were hot wasn't a come-on . . ."

He laughed with me. "Dick." His eyes, however, were not leaving mine.

"How?"

"I've been listening to Ezra, learning from Ren. Open your stat sheet, then take my hand. Show me your channels."

"You know this is getting more complicated every time we touch."

Alek didn't laugh this time. "I'm going to rely on you more and more out there. When we get to Copter, to the next planet and out into space. Things are not only going to be more serious, but we won't have the protection of the system like here. I need to know you inside and out. More so than Ezra ever will. I can't tell you how important that really is, only that you understand it . . . here." He tapped his heart.

"I'm joking," I said, and with a thought brought up my character sheet. "Kinda. This is just really hard for me. You found me, rescued me. I feel weird. I would have felt weird with none of that. I've just not had the upbringing or the surrounding family."

Alek accepted my stat sheet, and I felt him inside my mind, almost like that very first time he was poking about back in his garage.

"I understand," he said and opened a 3D image before us both. My shoulder lit in red, the Azris flow around it stalling. "I can help here, if you let me."

"You're asking if you can? Why?"

"Because this will hurt." He frowned and took my good hand in his. His Azris flowed through him and into me without him even altering his.

When I nodded, he didn't hesitate. With one short, sharp, quick pull, he yanked my sore arm down, and then fed through as fast as he could with his Azris. My knees buckled straight away, and he came down with me. He pulled me to him, holding on tight. "I gotta get you some more help."

"No," I said softly. "No. Do this for me, Alek. Please."

I knew it hurt him, but I felt him nod. "Okay, okay."

We returned to our table to find our drinks had gone. I motioned over to Jessie and she brought us fresh ones and then left a bottle of whiskey too. Which we slowly made our way through.

Out of the corner of his eyes, Alek watched me, but I just smiled. "Let's just enjoy the rest of the night. Head home soon," I said.

It was good. Mai actually came in, and she came straight for our table, settling in to talk about her life and the racing. Alek was totally charming, and when the old man and his granddaughter came over as well, we just let our table grow, enjoying both the company and the stories.

It was a good night. Alek walked us home, though we both wobbled a little. The guards wanted to call a car for us, but I needed the fresh air and the time to sober up a little.

Sleep came quickly but then so did waking up, in pain, probably not even twenty minutes later.

I'd only just moved slightly in my sleep and woke as soon as the stabbing pain started. I struggled to get on my other side, putting my weight on the sore arm. Then I just sat panting on the bed.

A knock at the door brought me around. "You decent?"

"I don't sleep naked," I shouted back.

Alek then came in, in his sleep shirt and shorts. "Heard you," he said and sat at Ezra's side of the bed. "I haven't had enough ale for this," he said. "Come on."

My mind protested, but my body just did as he asked. I would not get any relief without it. "It's a good thing Tatsuno isn't here," I said.

"He'd understand," he said.

"This is awkward." I just didn't know where to go, how to be that close.

"Pretend I'm Ezra," he said.

I tried to think like that and leaned back so he could put one arm over my neck. He laid his arm gently over mine, taking my hand in his, entwining my fingers. He put his other hand on my shoulder. "Close your eyes," he said. "You're going to sleep, and you're going to heal."

I let my eyes close, not feeling anything but Alek's warmth, and yeah, he was warm. Pretty hot, actually. His Fire was feeding into me at a tremendous rate. "Don't give me too much," I said.

"I can't," he said. "I'll get my ass kicked tomorrow if I do."

I let the healing Azris circulate and, feeling better, already sleep took me again. I woke once wondering who had hold of me.

"Shh, brother," Alek shushed me back down, and I let him.

Daylight filtered through the curtains, the fresh air too, when I woke next. I went to move. I cringed slightly. Alek had stayed with me all night. I edged away and stretched. My shoulder felt so much better.

"Fool," I said.

"Huh." Alek woke, wiping drool from his mouth. "Sorry."

"You okay?" I asked him.

He slid off the bed, stretched himself. "Stiff. Not exactly the easiest position to be sleeping in." He turned to me. "How are *you* feeling?"

"Much better, thank you. I'm glad you came in."

Alek dipped his head. "Anytime. I'm going for a shower. You're on breakfast duty."

I let out a groan. "Okay, I hope there's something in at least."

Monday, May 8th *Early Morning*
Year - 27515

The days had passed. My birthday had passed.

The weeks had passed.

It was the same, every, single day.

Sulking around.

Alek training.

Me nothing.

We got to the track and Alek went off to train with the others as usual.

I went to sit with Ivori. Instead of watching them. She at least welcomed me and was excited.

"Are you okay?" she asked, taking my Azris.

"I've been better," I replied, opening her door to sit in the main seat, running my hand over the wheel, clicking a few buttons. "If I take you away for a few weeks, would you mind?"

"Take me away?" she asked. I felt her engine rumble intermittently.

"Yes," I said, and I reached around to my shoulder. "I need to get away from here. I need to heal on my own somewhere special. I need water. Lots of water."

"The ocean," she said.

I smiled at that. The ocean sounded wonderful. "I'll—"

The comms went in the garage. "It's Geo," she said.

Damn, I didn't want to do this now either. I really didn't. "I'll be back soon."

As I went to leave, Ivori said, "Oto, I'm with you, even if you think I'm not. I'm right here. The ocean calls for us both."

There was no reply in me for her right now. The darkness that washed over me was for many things, and on the inside, deep inside, I was hurt more than ever. I didn't know how to fix anything, to move forward. With myself and with everyone around me. I couldn't let Alek risk himself helping me, and I couldn't let anyone else either. I had to work this out. Just me.

No, not just me. Ivori too.

My feet hit the track, and I walked, glancing only the once to make sure no lights or cars were out, even if the others were still in the training ground running through their stances, drawing in so much Azris. I was proud of them all. They'd come so far.

With a shiver at the top of the stairs, I ran my hand through my hair, breathed in, and knocked.

"Come in," Geo called.

He was sitting with his back to the door, looking over what seemed like charts, tables. I moved to stand at his desk and waited.

The wait, silent. I was in trouble.

Geo turned to me, his face pale, tiny lines creased his forehead. "How you doing?" he asked.

Three simple words.

The three words I didn't want to answer.

"Sit," he said.

I didn't want to sit either.

I wanted to bolt. Right now.

"Oto," he said. "Sit, please."

The chair seemed so far away. I couldn't reach it. My feet heavy, my mind with them.

Geo was up and had the chair by my side in a moment. "Why don't you want to sit? It's just right in front of you?"

Cold spread up from my core, ice cold. I shivered.

Geo sat in front of me, looking up, his eyes so deep. Beautiful flickers of fire danced on the inside. I could see his power, his core. Everything he was, was laid out for me. More so than when I looked at Luca. I didn't want to see that either. I turned my head.

"I don't need to say anything to you," Geo said, his voice soft. "You're doing more than I ever could in chastising yourself. I want to help you, but you won't let any one of us in. I had Alek call me earlier." I risked a glance at him. "He's worried about you. We all are."

I could only nod and try to deflect his real questions. "What's on the charts?"

"Finances," he replied. "I've been pooling my assets, selling things on."

"No hope for that one."

Dread filled me even more. This was all me, all my fault. "Because of me?"

"There's other things at play here," Geo said. "It isn't just you."

"But I'm part of it?"

"I won't lie to you. That wouldn't be fair to you or the team."

I noted something else. "You're selling the track?"

He reached for me, but I pulled away, moving to get a better look at the screen. "Not just selling it, you've already sold it?"

"No," he said. "The offers are there. We haven't accepted anything yet."

I looked back at him, fear so deep seated inside my soul. "You will though?"

"If we have to, yes, we'll sell the track." He moved in beside me. "Oto, things change."

Emotion flooded through me then, things I couldn't understand, pain and rage. "You can't sell it. What about their jobs, the area? You just can't!"

He held a hand up, and I could see the fire there. "Calm down," he said. "This is only the worst-case scenario. You'll win your races. I know you will."

Guilt then flooded through me, wave upon wave. What if I couldn't? What if Alek couldn't? This would all be lost. We'd, they'd never get another chance. This was bad, so bad.

"Good things also come with change." He tried to placate me. I wasn't taking it. "I'd sell the track only with the provision of our teams had places that they'd be looked after. There'd be conditions."

What about us, the future? His future, his babies. Luca's family, their legacy . . .

"I don't . . . I can't . . ." I moved to turn away, to run.

Geo caught hold of me. But I shrugged him off.

"I don't want to lie to you," he said. "We have only one way to go."

If only the ground could swallow me right now. That was the only way I could see myself going. Down further and further down.

I felt a hand on my shoulder. It almost dropped me to the floor. Geo let go, but our eyes never left each other. "We need you," he said. "All of you."

"I know," I admitted. "I know."

His eyes twinkled at me. "Those thoughts." He reached forward and tapped the side of my head. "Those that are from your past, they are not your future. Fight them."

I closed my eyes, pushed those thoughts away. "I'm really trying," I said.

"Good." He smiled. "The shoulder?"

"It will heal," I replied, reaching to stroke it. The pain was back almost as much as it had been the day before.

"Your core?"

"That is healing," I said.

"Whatever it takes, as long as it takes, right?"

It was a question. I glanced back at the charts, the sales page now blinking at me. "No," I said, straightening my back. "I won't let that happen. I promise you."

"Then rest, no more outings." His eyes looked me up and down.

"I will," I said. "I'll head home now. Some sleep would be good."

Geo moved and sat on the edge of his desk. "Okay, keep me posted, and I'll get the doctor to stop in now and then."

I agreed to it, but there was no way I was going to be there for it, not now. The seed planted in my mind had grown more and more.

I needed out.

My feet never rushed leaving the grounds; I walked with calm purpose. I didn't see Ivori, but I felt her presence. *I'll be back later tonight, when everyone has gone home.*

Okay, she replied. *I'll be waiting.*

It didn't take me long to get home. I left the guards outside, wondering, of course, how I was going to ditch them. But I was much more powerful than they; I knew how to do it. I just didn't want to do it. It would show them up. This was their jobs.

I packed a few bags, emptied quite a few bits of the dried goods from the cupboards. Filled some water bottles.

Was I ready to go, really? To just leave all my friends behind? Without letting them know anything?

I paced the apartment. Went to the fridge, got myself a drink. Drank it. Made a hot drink. Sat down and sipped it. I tried to let the thoughts settle, my mind ease. I couldn't.

With a flick of my wrist, I pulled up the vicenet on my HUD. I thought out some search terms, and I did some research. It would be quite some time before I could head back to the garage. When Alek and Tatsuno came in, I listened to his chatter about his day, his training.

Alek's eyes lazily wandered over Tatsuno as he headed off to their bedroom.

Then he carried on telling me how much he was learning off everyone around him. He made me laugh. He made me jealous. He made me feel better.

"I'm exhausted." He yawned.

It was a lot later than he should be up. Sadness washed over me again.

"You okay?" he asked.

"Yeah," I replied. "Tired."

"I'll come in if you need me," he said.

I shook my head. "I'll be fine. Geo's helped me this afternoon," I lied. It stung a little to do so, but I had to make sure he didn't come in and find my stuff all packed. I needed to get away. At least a good head start. I couldn't, didn't dare tell them.

The apartment went quiet. Outside went quiet. I dozed off a little, then when I came to, I pulled Azris to me, picked up my bag.

I couldn't do it. I couldn't sneak out.

I dropped the bag. Emotion threatened to swallow me.

Softly I crept to Alek's door, and knocked.

"Oto?" Tatsuno's sleepy voice asked. "What is it?"

"Can I come in?" My breath caught, and my hands shook.

I heard rustling. "Babe, Oto's at the door."

Then Alek shouted. "Come in."

Darkness swallowed me as I stepped inside, but then a tiny light flicked on. No, Tatsuno had lit the room with his Azris. Alek glanced me up and down, sighed, looked to Tatsuno, and then waved me in. My legs were as heavy as my heart, but I crawled onto their bed, between them, and buried my head in Alek's pillows.

Two sets of hands comforted me, and I could hear them talking, but not their words.

Soft fingers threaded through my hair. Gentle strokes, that made me sleepy.

The light went out and I drifted for a while, hearing soft murmurs, words of support, friendship, hope. A blanket covered me, tucked in around me. I was even warmer, sleepier.

A certain peace enveloped me, one I'd never experienced before, and the world faded for a while. A long while. Not knowing if I'd slept at all, it was a light touch to my cheek that stirred me some time later. I looked up into dark eyes. "I spoke to Ren," Alek whispered. "Ivori told him what you wanted to do."

"I couldn't do it," I admitted. I also couldn't keep my eyes locked with his, shame washed over me. "I couldn't just *leave* you."

"If you need to go," Alek said taking my chin in his hands. Meeting my eyes with his, his forehead scrunched. "Go."

Strong arms encased me, squeezed me from the other side, and I realized Tatsuno snored behind me. Heat flushed up my cheeks.

Alek let out a chuckle. "He's exhausted. Don't think anything of it."

I nodded at him, but on the inside, I needed his comfort too, their comfort. "You'll let me go?" Tentatively I asked, "Are you sure?"

"No." He sighed, tracing my cheek bones with a finger. "But you need to heal *your* way." Alek turned away from me then, onto his back, his eyes flashing Dark Azris in the dim light of early morning. "I understand that more than my need to have you by my side every day . . . suffering."

"But Geo, Ezra?"

"I'll talk to them," he said. "They might not understand at first, but they will."

I didn't want to say it, but I had to, if I went, I needed space. "Tell them not to contact me. I'll be in touch when I'm ready, when I can."

"I can do that, but I can't promise they won't."

"I'll ask Ivori to hide us."

"Don't," he said, turning back to me. "Please don't."

I let out a sigh, and I reached for him this time, putting my head on his shoulder. He touched my head, stroked down my hair again. I liked this; I needed it. Him. "Thank you," I said.

"I'm here always," he whispered. "Just promise me one thing."

"Anything," I replied.

"Come home." He tapped the top of my head with a finger lightly. "Come home, *right* up here."

Not sure I could keep that promise, I still made it, and then I slid out from Tatsuno's rather firm grip and out of our apartment.

My soul was heavy, but my heart felt lighter. I had permission. I could go. I could, for the first time in a long time, learn to be me.

19

Monday, May 8th *Morning*
   Year - 27515

It had taken me all of five minutes to tap in on the vicenet and find somewhere for us to stay for a few nights. The fact Alek had given me his blessing to leave had taken such a weight off my shoulders. I couldn't be here. I had to go, and we both knew it even if it was hard.

I made sure my links were as untraceable as they could be. That although communications could come in, Ivori would see them. I wouldn't.

Ivori's engine rumbled in the background. "You're sure you want to do this?" she asked over comms.

The sleek black shine of her new design shimmered in the lights of the garage. "Yes." I glanced around, the tools tucked away for the night. Everything had its place. I felt like I didn't, even if I knew it was stupid. I didn't belong here right now, and it hurt. Sucking in a breath, I pushed myself out of the office chair. No one else would be in right now. "I just need some time for me," I said. "For us."

"The open road sounds good to me," Ivori said, and the driver's door opened, inviting me all the more.

I did hesitate slightly, but I moved to climb in. The doors out to the track opened, the thought of just driving away opening with them, of driving with no destination, no worries, just Ivori and me.

The red lights flicked on the track as we made our way out. I closed Ivori's garage doors, making it look at least like nothing was out of place till someone stepped inside. Then would see we were gone. The main doors opened and then I paused to make sure they closed behind us.

"They'll try to contact you as soon as they know you've gone. Even though you said not to."

"I know." I tapped the side of my head. "All blocked."

I felt her sadness even though on the inside adrenaline flooded through me.

Once outside, Esrall City spread around me, the bustle just getting going for the early morning routines. Only the odd truck was out and about delivering its wares.

Watching it all, I didn't feel anything, just more of her sadness. I slowed for the main lights and picked the lane that would take us out of the city I'd grown up in. I'd never been out on my own, not like this. The lights changed, and within a few minutes, the city of Esrall vanished behind me.

"Any ideas?" Ivori asked.

"There were a few places," I said. "I want to see the ocean."

Ivori's screen changed, and a map appeared. "If we follow this route, it will take a few days. But I think you'll love the ocean. Being as strong with water as you are."

"That's one reason why I want to go," I said. "It's almost as if it's calling to me, like I have to. I really have to."

"I understand. I feel the call too," she said.

With nothing but the road ahead of us and all the pain behind me, I felt myself relaxing. Relaxing like I hadn't in weeks. I'd become something everyone else wanted. What they pushed me for, what I wanted to do for them. I wanted to be me, just me. For once.

My 3D image on Ivori's screen rotated like it always did, my high levels of anxiety and stress obvious. She'd pointed it out to me every single day without even meaning to.

Now, those red lines, the fast beat of my heart, started to settle. The more we drove, the further away we were, the easier it became.

I felt free.

We felt free.

There's a straight coming up ahead. Do you mind?

I don't mind at all, I replied.

The new system, the new gear changes, had all taken a little getting used to. From hands on her gear stick to fingers itching to flick her steering paddle. I noted the sun chink off a hood behind us as we entered the bend ahead. Just a little too fast, but I was ready. On the out, I flicked down and hit the gas.

Ivori's engine screamed, and she tapped my Azris at the perfect moment.

She didn't hold back at all.

I watched her speed increase.

Ninety.
One hundred.
Two hundred.
Two sixty.

Up ahead, I could see the road coming to an end. Shit.

Two eighty.
Two ninety-seven.

Holy crap!
I pushed every last bit of Azris I had into her.

Three-oh-three!

Ivori whoop whooped all around me! And I couldn't help but let my own out. This, right here, was freedom.

That corner, though . . .

I dropped the gears, hit the brakes. The speed dropped fast, the wheels threatening to lock. I eased off, feathering it till we were at a low enough speed to apply pressure.

Smoke billowed out from the back.

Did you see that? Ivori asked. *Did you?*

I saw it, I said. My heart pounded. My breathing ragged. I watched the details flash up on her screen.

305! That's faster than we've been on the track.

It felt amazing, right?

Yes, it did.

Another moment later, the rumble of another engine came up behind us. I turned and watched as the car moved closer, then eased onto the other side of the road. It pulled in alongside us and stopped.

"You okay, kid?" An old man hung out of the door shouting, graying hair and beard caught in the wind. His tanned skin glistened from the warm sun.

"I'm okay," I replied. "Thank you for stopping."

"That was some hellaburn you two just did. Don't think I've ever seen that on this stretch of road before. Thought I'd be picking pieces up for weeks."

I kept my hands on the wheel, flexing. I'd used so much Azris, we'd nothing left to fight with. First huge lesson learned. Never let go.

The old man's brows furrowed, and he looked up and out into the hills which surrounded us on all sides. "Friendly warning, kid." He looked back, and his eyes locked with mine. "Lot of people around here who would love that car of yours, especially with that kinda power behind her."

Ivori's engine flared to life. She'd try to run, but right now I don't think we'd have any chance.

The old man dipped his head. "No offense, my lady."

"None taken," Ivori replied through comms to him.

Zero Light

We both held our breath while the older man's hands moved off his wheel. "Good day to you both," he said. Then, in a split second, he'd gone.

I let my hands fall off the wheel into my lap. My fast-beating heart settled.

"Sorry," Ivori said. "I never thought."

"I don't think either of us did, but that was a good warning." I returned my hands to her wheel and clicked her into gear, then slowly moved off, following the old man's car.

The sun crept up higher and higher in the distance, and I settled in with the twists and turns of the road. The view changed. Rolling hills turned to small settlements, to towns, then into a city I hadn't even heard of. I drifted through, nice and slow.

Ahead, a dark building settled into my view. "Looks like a place I can get some food," I said.

"Looks dark," Ivori said. "I'm not so sure."

I moved in toward the building and the parking lot. There, sat on its own, was the old man's car from earlier. I swallowed. "I'm not turning around," I said. "I'm hungry."

"I'll be watching," she said.

I pulled alongside the cars, and with the spin of her wheel, reversed in beside the old man's car.

"You see how much effort he goes into maintaining that out here?"

"I see it," Ivori said. "He's got a lot of money."

I nodded, retracting my belt and then exiting.

Approaching the main area, I noted the guys sitting outside on the benches. They were talking and drinking, and they carried on, obviously deep in conversation. They paid me no attention whatsoever, or so I thought.

Any Azris in the area?

There're residual energies all around us, she replied. *I can't tell if it's from anyone in this specific area, though.*

Fair. I made my way closer toward the men sitting at the front. I was never going to get anywhere out here without growing some balls and just saying what I was thinking. "Hey there, any breakfast served in here?" I asked them.

One of the men turned his eyes to me, then looked up from my knees to meet my eyes with his cool, steely ones. "Marik has just got in, but the kitchen's been working a while. Should still be something for you. Not quite lunch yet."

"Thanks," I said and made to carry on into the establishment.

"Nice ride," the other guy commented. "Don't see many city racers out here."

I turned back to face him, suddenly. "Is it a problem?"

He stood with a smile that went from ear to ear. "Only if you don't show me when you've eaten."

"Lars, you can't say that!"

Lars laughed. "If I don't say anything now, this guy's gonna get fed and fuck off. I won't get another chance to see that beauty."

I nodded. He was right. I would have just gotten back on the road. "If you're still here when I get out, I'll let you meet her."

Lars turned to his friend. "See!"

I walked away, my stomach growling, and pushed the front door open, the smells drifting through. I really was hungrier than I thought.

You forget lunch and dinner on a regular basis. I'm not surprised. Let's concentrate out here in getting you into better habits, okay?

I can get behind that, I said and patted my belly.

The building on the inside was lit with dainty oval lanterns, a small fire crackled in the corner just ticking over, but the smell of burning wood drifted sweet, soothing tones my way, and I breathed it in deeply. My eyes were drawn to the dancing flames and the dog lying before it. Which didn't move, despite me being a stranger. The tail wagged, though, and a small not-so-much a growl escaped its lips.

"Roxy," a soft voice said from beside me. "Be nice."

I turned toward the voice, saw the woman behind it. Her graying hair and apron gave way that she might be the chef here. "Hi," I said. "The guys outside said I might get some breakfast?"

She looked at the digital display on the counter. "You're in luck," she said. "I have time. Or it would be lunch."

"Honestly," I replied. "I'd be glad for either."

Her eyes traced up and down my clothes. "Find a seat," she said. "I'll be out as soon as I can."

"Much appreciated." I dipped my head to her, and despite the dog's earlier warning, I made my way closer to the fire.

"Is she okay to approach?" I asked.

"Sure she is, softy at heart. She wouldn't be in here if she wasn't," the chef said, then vanished, leaving me with the dog and fire.

I sat in the chair beside Roxy. She lifted her head and glared at me. "What? Don't want to share the heat?"

Her tail wagged some more, and slowly, she got up, stiff or . . . no, I could see the gray hairs in her beard. She edged toward me, and I curled my fingers into my hand and held it out for her to sniff.

She didn't just sniff me; she nudged right in and licked me silly. "Ahh, you really are just a big old softy," I said, and rubbed her ears.

With a plop, she settled at my feet, and I stroked down her back, my eyes drifting to the fire, its soft crackling and flames mesmerizing.

A soft cough to my side brought me around, and Roxy moved away. "Look like you got the world on your shoulders," the familiar voice said, I turned and met the old man's eyes from earlier.

I looked him up and down the once—regular slacks, shirt, and boots. Nothing over-the-top special or rich. He moved to sit in front of me. Roxy plopped in front of him, and he fished a treat out of his pocket for her. I, however, remained silent, for now.

Breakfast consisted of large doorstop toast and butter. I'd never tasted bread like it, and that was saying something, coming from Grovers. I was spoiled.

"It's got enhancements," the old man added, pointing at the bread. "You looked like you needed that."

"I did," I said and patted my now-full belly.

"Lunch time lot will be in soon. As much as I'd love to pick your brain, you should move on."

I raised an eyebrow at him. "Really?"

He stroked Roxy, his eyes observing everything around him. "There are some unsavory guys around these parts. My earlier warning still stands."

"You own the place?" I asked.

"Been in my family many years, but it's changed, and sometimes I think not for the better."

I stood and moved to the bar. I ran my wrist over the 3D device and paid my bill, knowing I'd moved from one account to another and this transaction was safe from tracking. At least, I hoped.

I looked back at the old man, his eyes on the fire now. "Gramps was out on a call last night," the chef said. "He's tired."

"Thank you so much for the food," I added. "It was really good."

"You're welcome." She smiled. "I also chased Lars back to work. You're free to go without worrying about leaving."

I laughed at that. I mean, I would have stuck to my deal. I'd have shown him Ivori, but with Gramps being so super honest, Ivori opened up before I even got to her. I slid in.

"Time to go?" she asked.

"Yeah," I replied, clicking into gear and drawing out my space.

Leaving that village just seemed super creepy. We were on the open roads in seconds. Another car appeared in the distance, and we drew in closer.

"That's Icarian," Ivori said.

I kept our speed steady, and drove on past the first car, then the second. All six cars passed us.

"All Icarian?" I asked, though I already knew the answer.

"I'm searching the vicenet now," came her reply.

I let the sun drift in my window, then as the day drew later and later, it settled behind us.

"You never came back to me on who those guys were?" I asked eventually.

"Didn't want to worry you. Some things are better left unsaid."

I frowned. "We need to find somewhere for me to sleep."

"You can sleep," she said. "I'll keep us on a nice, steady course. I want to get us as far away from this side of our world as possible."

My seat slid back as far as it could and Ivori slipped my belt off. "I'm not so sure I should sleep and let you drive." I grinned. "You might just take me anywhere . . ."

"Wasn't that the plan?" she chuckled.

I reached for a blanket off the back seat, and Ivori upped the heating through my seat. "Temp's dropping," she said.

"Thanks," I replied and shut my eyes. The soothing hum of her engine and the silver twinkling of our moons soon had me snoring.

20

Tuesday, May 18th *Morning*
   Year - 27515

The sun rose ahead of us. This drive had taken us more than a couple of days—ten days, to be precise—I slept and stopped anywhere I wanted. The freedom was needed. Now, watching our sun in the distance rise above the one thing I wanted to see above anything else, my heart beat faster and faster in my chest.

"Why does this feel like coming home?" I asked her. I moved a hand from her wheel, ran it over my trousers.

"You feel the pull of energy, the body of water," she replied.

"It's so strong," I said. I wiped my other hand too, and then ran it through my hair, rubbed my growing beard.

"Road off to the left," she said. "Nice and easy. Been a while since I've driven on real sand."

Out of habit, I checked behind myself and noted no one else around. Then I eased the wheel off and onto the side road, which led out onto the sand. "How far can we drive?"

"I'll let you know when we need to stop."

It wasn't long, and she asked me to ease off. I would have agreed; the feel of sand under her wheels was very different from solid driving. Wet, soft, and slippery.

"I'll walk out with you," she said, and her form appeared outside, walking ahead, her soft threads glistening in the sun.

The glowing rays of the sun reached out, shimmering against the water ahead. I lowered the gears and stopped, opening the door to climb out.

The sand beneath my feet felt different, the hint of salt in the air, the promise of cool water ahead.

I closed the door and walked away. Feet squiggling in that sand, I paused and reached down, feeling how cool and even damp it was.

Ivori stopped before me. "Beautiful, isn't it?"

"I've seen nothing like it," I admitted. "It's more than beautiful."

"Walk with me," she said.

I moved in by her side. The soft clothes she wore moved around her frame as though there were wind down here. I smiled at her when she looked at me.

"You know what I'm going to ask. Can you tell me?" I held her eyes with mine. "I'd like to know."

Her brows deepened; her eyes flicked away from me. "From the beginning?"

"From anywhere you're comfortable," I said.

Ivori stopped walking and looked at me.

There was such emotion coming off her. Such pain. With a hand I reached out, tentative.

"I don't know if I can," she said, her voice cracking.

"I trust you," I said. "I'm here one hundred percent for you. Just like I know you are for me. Tell me the truth."

"All of it?"

"If you can," I replied. "All of it."

She swallowed, licked her lips. Even if she didn't need to drink, the action was clear. Her never were clear. The sun's rays changed the scene in front of us. "I'm not just an Icarian," she whispered. "I am *the* Icarian."

Her words hit me hard. I didn't know what it meant for her, or for that matter meant for me. "You're the first who ascended? More than royalty?" All I did know was how much I needed her, and I needed her to be okay.

She put her palm to mine, and I felt not only her energy, but her strength, her tenacity, and I pushed against her gently.

"You complement me in more ways than I think you could ever know."

"Why?" I asked.

"Because you are first of your line. Just like I was first of mine." Her eyes sought something from me, though I wasn't sure what. Understanding? I didn't understand it . . .

I thought, hard. I hadn't ascended, but she thought I could? Or I was going to? I coughed, ran my hands over my now-moist skin. "So starting out with me, like this, what does it mean for you?"

Ivori looked away, hearing something, I glanced the same way she did. Gentle waves crashed in the distance; birds flittered in and out the waves catching fish. "It means many things," she said, her voice low. "Our journey to the top is going to be fraught with so much more danger, with even more death."

"To the top?"

"My species has been floundering since I was locked away in that prison."

I swallowed, my mouth suddenly dry, the sun beating overhead. "It wasn't a museum?"

"No, it was not." Ivori's shoulders sank. "They knew exactly what they were doing to me. To us."

The overwhelming pain inside me dropped me to my knees.

Ivori fell with me, sinking into the sands. "If I show you this, all of this, of me," she said, holding my eyes with hers; tears streamed down her cheeks. "You'll understand. But you'll know there's no going back for me, for us."

"I'm not going to turn you away," I said, searching her face for anything but pain. There was nothing but pain. "I'd never turn you away. Please understand that."

Ivori reached for my other hand with hers. Instead of just palm to palm, she grasped tight hold of me, locking her fingers with mine. "I feel that," she said.

Within the next few seconds, I felt the surrounding breeze grow. Smelled the rich salt in the air, the hint of fresh fish. The ocean sounds, life, so much more alive. Everything here just . . . amazing.

"I'd never seen the ocean," I said to her. "But here now I can taste it. It's so alive. It's everything."

"When I brought my species here," she said. "I was drawn to the open lands, to the sheer amount of space you had outside of your cities. However, there was one place I was drawn to more: the ocean. It filled me with pure fascination, but such hope. When we first landed, it was hard. We felt so lost."

"You're talking about being inside the city, right? What happened over one of the auction houses?"

"Yes," she said.

"But that was over five hundred years ago. You're not that old, right?"

She shook her head. "I needed to keep it to myself. Forgive me."

"Oh, of course." I nodded at her. "How old are you?" Her chuckle spread up and infected me. "That old?"

"The year is what now?"

"27515."

"You can take the first two off."

I choked. "You're over seven thousand years old?"

Ivori looked away, though her pressure with our locked hands never left me. "I don't know what I expected when we landed. Just that the sheer amount of qi around your planet was heaven."

"Qi?"

"It has many names over the years. The species that can harness it use it. Qi was one of its original names. It sticks with some, especially in the higher realms. You called it Azris."

"Realms?"

"I'm sorry," she said. "This is a lot to take in. Your planets aren't just in one area of space; they cross into different realms."

"That's what brought you here." It might have been difficult to understand, but my mind was connecting the dots, slowly.

"Mostly, but we also needed your vehicles, the metals, the chance to live, to carry on. We'd been locked inside our ships for so long, traveling, searching. This was time for us to blossom again."

"You wanted to become a part of our culture?"

"Very much so. We needed a purpose. At first, I observed for many years. I needed to know you were a match despite the draw to the qi. Waiting, understanding—that's when I found the perfect place on Isala to integrate. To seed."

"Mote Lerate?"

"Yes, such a wonderful place."

She seemed to lose her trail of thought. Drifting in memories. I had to bring her back, even if poking those memories hurt. "So Roa?"

Her eyes met mine again, tears bubbled there. "Roa wasn't my first, no. But she was my last partner. The one they took from me before they took me away from the others."

Tears streamed down my face too. I couldn't even wipe at them; she held my hands so tight.

"My first was a mechanic at the track. His name was—" She paused, and I didn't push her. I had to let her tell me these things in her time. She eventually carried on. "His name was Mitch, though he never liked it, so he swapped it for a nickname his sister used to use."

I had so many questions, but she seemed to know this; she went there even without me asking now. The memories free flowing with ease, her emotions now unlocked for real, her story to tell.

"That day I showed him what we could really do. I blasted out the straight using his Azris and blew his mind. But yes, it was his sister that helped devise the system around the tech you already use, and integrated it around your world. She saw the ramifications of the upgrades to the vehicles and knew things had to change. The system was then born, and with our nites, easy to integrate to your world. Everyone was super happy seeing something they could quantify. The things they were rewarded for and, in general, the atmosphere around Isala and then the others shifted. They halted the races while they worked out some kinks with the other Icarian and my closest council."

"I don't get the rivalry between you all. What happened there?"

"I wasn't the only one to arrive that night, though it seemed we were the most prevalent in your histories. There were other factions from our initial journey across space."

That made more sense that there would be others, those with opposing thoughts, feelings toward us, or the way our society worked.

Ivori nodded; she'd heard my thoughts. "Yes, there really were. I fought as much as I could for those around me, and as far as my species goes, we did very well. But racing wasn't easy. It took us a long time to learn, to work out how we could help, enhance you, work with you."

"Others developed faster, even though you were personally stronger."

"It was hard to know. I'd lost my position over those years. Not only did they not trust me anymore, but I couldn't back up my claim as leader. What I had, the qi, my energies, to keep us all alive, I'd used all of it. I'd used all of them." Ivori moved to stand again, and she helped me. "The years we drifted, though we were alive. We're essentially a reset. Where we were once ascended, we were again mortal." I moved with her as she walked closer to the waters. "It almost broke me losing Mitch," she said. "But he'd taught me so much, and together we watched how the Icarian spread, learned how much joy they brought to your species as much as to themselves. I couldn't fault them for needing or wanting that."

"You spread throughout our universe then, racing?"

"Yes, it was amazing to see, to be a part of."

"But you wanted more from it?"

"I needed my place back at the top, as leader" she said. "As much as spreading across the galaxy was good for us, there was no governing body around you all, and you needed stability, guidance." She drifted a while again and we both listened to and watched the waves. "When I had moped around for long enough, I then found Roa."

"You planned on making it to the top with her? Off Isala, and wherever you needed to be?"

"I wanted to. There was so much that we had to hide. Including who she was."

"Wait," I said. It just made sense. Roa had been a woman even if her own people couldn't see that.

"Roa was—well, the name she was born with doesn't matter. A person of great import with great burdens upon her shoulders." Ivori said. "But they got to us, to her first. I was trapped by someone much more powerful. I had no idea how he'd gotten that powerful so quickly." Her face fell all the more this time. "They brought me into this place, locked my tires down, took parts of my engine away. Then when Roa found me, *he* dragged her away. I couldn't feel anything, I couldn't do anything. Eventually, they brought her back to me, beaten, hurting. Then he took her life."

My hands fisted, anger at her pain, their pain. "They killed her in front of you?"

"Drakol Viper did," she admitted, and then looked up at me. "For everything we'd lied about, for how powerful we were, what we could be. Because he didn't think we should rule. Because *he* wanted to. I didn't want to see it, to admit it was real. When her life was gone, I hid. I stayed away. I couldn't accept it. She was my chance, our chance for . . ."

"For what?" I had to ask. I had to know.

"Your Azris levels," she said. "What is at the top?"

"I understand that," I said, feeling every single one of her emotions. "I'm sorry. When you first asked for them, I thought you thought they were still alive."

She shook her head, her shoulders falling. "No, I knew. I just . . . I didn't want to accept it. The more awake I became because of you, because the nites kept asking for attention, the worse it felt. I—"

I reached over, put my arm around her. "I'm here," I said. When she turned into me, I felt her as solidly as I would have felt Ezra. I gripped tight onto her, and I let her cry against me.

"I don't want them to do that to you," she said. "Ever. But we're a bigger target than you think."

"Because of you?"

"Because of *you*," she said. "First of your line with the first of ours."

"You are still royalty," I said. "But what am I? First of my line? I don't get it . . ."

"You are *the* seven bloodlines." Her face softened. "You are more than royalty."

I let out a strained laugh. "I'm all seven bloodlines?"

"Yes," she said. "I don't know how they did it, or why. I am just glad they did."

"No hope for that one."

I pushed the thoughts away. Gods, immortality. Though the levels were clearly marked. All of this . . . it was too much. I couldn't be more than royalty; that freaked me out. I sucked in a breath, held my own fears in check. "We're rising fast. It's more obvious now where Sinclairs comes in. Even if Trayk wasn't the original owner. He's their manager now, and they're connected to the Vipers somewhere, right?"

"No," she said and eased back from me. "As far as I know, they aren't. But I never meant for things to be so complicated out of the gate."

"My life's been terribly complicated," I said, knowing it was the truth. "You made it easier though, not harder."

Hope sparked in her eyes, she wiped her cheeks. "You're sure?"

"I'm very sure. We can do anything with each other, right?" The tiniest smile tugged the corner of her lips, so I added, "When I'm with you, out there, there's nothing better."

Now she really was smiling. "Nothing fills my veins like the Fire you provide for me. Your Azris is pure, your heart"—she tapped my chest lightly—"your heart is so intense, but so alive."

I breathed in, felt the words we'd exchanged and the beauty of the day ahead. "Now all I want is to feel that water." Pure excitement rushed through my veins as I yanked my boots off, then my socks. I couldn't do it quick enough. As I ran for the ocean, sand squelched in-between my toes. It felt amazing.

The waves ahead drew me in, deeper, so much deeper. "Slow down," Ivori called to me.

I turned to watch her from almost just diving in. The sounds, the smell, everything here was so . . . I couldn't find the words. *Beautiful* just wasn't powerful enough. More importantly though, I felt different. I paused, watching her face, her joy at seeing me, and I smiled.

This was perfect.

I closed my eyes, listened to the waves. Dropping my stance, I began. I ran through all my training, my steps. Those taught to me, those I'd seen others completing when I shouldn't have been watching.

I moved with the sound of the ocean, felt water all around me. The wonderful rays of the sun tickling my face.

Energy built within, and I used it. I felt what it wanted me to do. Life in the ocean had a purpose for it, and without even thinking, I sent my Azris out to whatever requested it. I practiced till the sweat poured off me, and till the sun was high in the sky. Then and only then did I finish my set and open my eyes.

I couldn't hear anything. The ocean calmed around me; the waves moved on, and here I was just dancing on its surface. I panicked, not seeing land at all anymore, the concentration I'd had gone. My body dropped into the cool water. I'd swum, of course I had, but not in this. This was cold. So very cold.

"Don't panic," Ivori said at my side.

"Where am I?"

"You drifted where they wanted you to," she said.

"They?" Suddenly I realized I was surrounded by creatures. Large swimming creatures. From underneath me, something brushed against my side. I reached out, felt the thick hide. Then it surfaced; its long bottle nose almost poked me in the face. Two deep, dark eyes stared at me. It chittered at me, seeming happy.

"They are happy," she said. "They've enjoyed all the energy you brought out here with you."

The creature nudged me, swimming around me, its dorsal fin protruding out of the water. "Grasp hold," Ivori said.

I did so, and let out a little shriek as it then sped off with me in the water.

This, everything about it, thrilled me. Racing along in the water. Another of the creatures came in on my other side, and I reached out to take its fin too. Now I felt much more stable. With my Azris around me, I felt the water stiffen. I changed my angle and rose slightly out of the water.

"Surfing," Ivori said. "But you're best off not moving much further out. They just want to get you back to shore."

"Okay." I laughed, though. It was immense fun. The two creatures stopped a while later, and I could see the beach. I stroked down their backs once more, and they flipped out of the water, chittering excitedly in a great display of their own power.

I swam to the shore, my feet squelching in the sand. "Thirsty," I said. "All this water around and I'm suddenly so very dry."

"You've been out here several hours," Ivori said. "We have water and food in the car, remember."

"Thank goodness."

With soft steps, feeling weak, I walked over to where she was, sliding in and helping myself to the water.

"Easy," she replied. "We can go get more. There's a hotel that isn't far."

I wiped water spillage off my chin and looked to where we actually were. "You had to move?"

"The tide was coming in." She laughed, started her engine, and then backed us up and out.

"I want to come back," I said. "Every morning for the next week."

"Then we will. It was truly amazing to see you out there."

"It was amazing to be out there, the power of the ocean. It understands me, and I it."

"Check your stats," Ivori said.

I brought them up and almost choked. "What?"

"Exactly."

I swallowed. "My progression for Water . . . is . . . off the chart."

"This is what you needed, what we needed." I'd reached Master Rank 5 already. It was insane. I popped a point each to my stats, noting my Int/Wis/Spirit had gone up five points too.

I read through them carefully, noting the changes, more importantly Alignment, chaotic neutral, really? Royal Seven for bloodline?

Name = Oto Benes
ID Number = 4188927

Age = 23
Species = Anodite
Sex = Male
Alignment = **Chaotic Neutral**
Bloodline = **Royal Seven**
Health = 78%
Cultivation Level - **Master Rank 5**
Active Meridians = 12/12
Nanites = 1 Million
Artefacts = 2
Chosen Specialist = Racer
First Chosen Affinity = Water
Second Chosen Affinity = Fire

Strength = 43/**129.43**
Dexterity = 28/**78.68**
Constitution = 38/**113.24**
Int/Wis/Spirit = 52

Affinities - Rank
Water - Blue
Fire - Green
Earth - Yellow
Air - Yellow
Light - Yellow
Darkness - Yellow
Spirit - Blue

Droll's Leg Pouch – three refillable containers hold the power of life or death. One use per origin user.

21

Wednesday, May 19th *Morning*
Year - 27515

The days on the beach flew past me. I loved every minute of it. I got used to the times others started to drift in from the surrounding villages, and I was up early, practicing and learning everything I could about what was around.

My progress from that very first day had slowed a lot, though. Just like gaining ground on any level.

I sank to the wet sand, my hands sinking in deep. Frustrated. I wanted more so much more.

"It's not your fault," Ivori said. "I think we need to think about trying something else."

I looked up at her, but her form faded. Laughter in the distance, and four forms came into view, a third bouncing up ahead of them with four legs.

"I think we should leave," Ivori said.

The tiny critter drew in closer, bouncing around, sniffing everywhere, excitement even if she was graying. "Roxy?"

The old dog made a beeline for me, her tail wagging, and I held my hand out for her.

"I never expected to see you again," I said to her, patting her head gently. With a sigh, I pushed myself up and off the sand, allowing my Azris to flow through me in waves of warmth, drying off as best I could without chilling my bones.

Roxy parked her ass in the wet sand around me, and I waited while two of the figures ahead drew in closer. The other two hung back, watching.

When they were near, Roxy ran back to them and left me alone.

I noted the walk to the man, and the fact the one to his left was younger and yes. Marik and his granddaughter? The two behind them, I was guessing, would be Lars and his friend, whose name I wasn't sure of as yet.

The young woman clung to her grandfather with a smile. "I told you he would be out here. I sensed Water in him; it's a natural place to come."

"You came looking for me?" I asked.

"There's been some rumors," Marik said and held out his hand. "Marik Sinclair."

Ivori! I shouted at her on the inside.

I told you we should have gone. She shied away from me.

"You know who I am, then?" I didn't hesitate to take his hand to shake, though on the inside I was cursing myself.

He squeezed my hand hard, his strength showing. "From the moment I saw that Azris burn on the straights heading out of Esrall."

"You didn't—"

"Tracy, return to the others. We will follow shortly."

Tracy smiled at me. "Look after him," she said to me. "He's a bit wobbly on sand."

Both Marik and I watched as she walked away, back to the other guys. Marik sighed, then rolled his eyes and turned to me. "They worry too much," he said.

"Or not enough," I replied with a raised eyebrow.

"Exactly." He looked directly at me. "You look a lot better than you did that first morning. I saw you."

I glanced down at my clothes. Though a little dirty, I'd filled them out some more. Muscle and probably a bit of fat.

"I've had a really wonderful week," I said.

"Training?"

I glanced at the ocean. "Yes, it felt right here."

"As it should with an affinity for Water as strong as yours."

"And you?" I asked.

"Never had the skill," he said to my complete surprise. "My family has every single one. Yet it skipped me. Even my granddaughter has a strong Spirit."

"Ahh." I glanced her way. "Why were you looking for me?"

He wobbled in the sand, and I reached for him, but he held his hand out. "Don't be babying me like she does."

I stepped back, winced.

"I don't mean to grouch. It bugged me, you bugged me," he said. "So when I got the chance, I went looking, digging. Frasers have been an opposing team of mine for many years, but the rivalry is also what spurs us to become greater. It didn't take me long to figure out you'd taken off."

"You're not trying to poach me, right?"

"Gods, no." He laughed. "I wanted to talk to you, to listen properly to what you want, and if I may, offer a little guidance that someone offered me many years ago."

My throat felt so very dry. "I'll talk," I said. "If you find us a nice bar, a fire, and somewhere for some food out of the way of others. The beach fills up pretty quickly as the sun reaches toward noon."

"I would imagine so. This whole place is brimming with your Azris right now. It would attract anyone wanting to make the most of it."

"So that's why it's been getting busier around here?"

Marik laughed. "Your Icarian's not been teaching you much, has she?"

I glanced over to where Ivori sat on dry sand. "It's complicated," I said.

"Mind if I ride with you?" He started walking, albeit slow.

"It's kind of like letting the snake into the baby bird's nest—" I replied. "No?"

Ivori, however, opened the passenger door for him. "Seems you have a friend nonetheless."

"I wouldn't say friend. But maybe she's open to talking." Marik said.

"Seems so." I indicated for him to get in, and I followed, sitting beside him.

"This vehicle is something else," he said. "You've been working on prototype tech?"

"Not so much," I said, her engine starting, and I gently moved off the sands. "If you've followed my progress with Frasers at all, you'll know she was battered to an inch of her life at the Derby."

"Yes." He lowered his head. "They're not the best of races, but they are if you need the funds."

"You watched the Canillion run too?"

"Yes, I did." He was nodding thoughtfully. "And those you came out with were fantastic riders. I now have them on one of my special teams."

I raised an eyebrow at him. "Eula and Bessie now work for you?"

"They *race* for me." He grinned.

"Wow." I steadied my hands on the wheel.

"If you take a left up ahead, and out onto the county lanes to the next city, you'll see a small gate eventually to the left. We'll take that."

Should I trust him?

I'm not sure. He doesn't give off any bad vibes. He's sitting here . . .

She was right. He felt just normal. I liked it.

It wasn't long before another car was settled in behind us and the sand changed to road, then to rockier roads. There was no sign of a gate, till Ivori spoke clearly. "It's here now?"

"Correct," Marik said.

"How far are we from the city?"

"Considering you've only been gone a couple of weeks, I would have thought so, or you've broken every speed record going." Marik stared at the map.

"I never thought about how far. I just trusted Ivori; she said we'd get here."

"You're over fifteen thousand miles from your home city," Marik said.

We really had traveled, and I was way out of my comfort zone. No, I thought. No, I wasn't.

Getting back might be a bit of a problem though, if we're out here too much longer.

Unless we can get a train.

The large gate before us started to move and then open.

"The car behind has the key," Marik said.

Ivori moved us in as I just watched, taken aback by the property's sheer size. This was bigger than the council estate in Mote Lerate.

"What did bring you out so far?" Marik asked.

I didn't want to answer; I didn't really know myself. The injury, the need to learn, to be me. Everything. In the end, I sighed. "Complications brought me out here, the need to—"

"The need to be yourself?" Marik asked, but he was nodding. He carried on without letting me say anything else, even if I had wanted to. "I was brought up in a big house, with a family that already owned one of the most notorious racetracks and teams going. We stretch out now into the stars, into the universe, and some of it was not what I wanted growing up. I've no Azris. I've no drive to race cars."

"But you're still here," Ivori said. "Why stay?"

"Family," he answered her. "As much as I hated it, I also owed them a lot."

"So what did you do if you couldn't race?"

The view before me spread out as he waved a hand. "I managed."

"You managed . . ."

"There's a track here," Ivori said.

"Yes," Marik said. "This is Sinclair's elite training grounds."

"What?"

"In your own words," he said. "Welcome, baby bird, to the snake's nest." Then he pointed. "Follow the road around to the left, then out past the main house. You'll see the stands and the start to the track."

"Why bring us here?" My heart rate sped up. It showed on the dashboard.

Marik kept his face calm and opened the windows. "I love my family," he said. "I also liked what I saw the other morning. Just come in, let me show you around. Meet some of the teams."

"You want me to meet *your* teams?"

"They're amazing young people. I'd like you to stay here for a while, if you would."

"I'm not swapping sides," I said, my hands gripping the wheel tighter.

"I know." His eyes seemed to twinkle at me. "I'm hoping you'll help push them further, just that little bit further, though."

Ivori? I asked. *Do you think we should take him up on his offer?*

Take a look around you, she said. *A really deep, deep look.*

I did. Then what I saw on the grounds astounded me. "The energy around here is amazing."

"So you will stay?" Marik asked, his eyes searching for my answer.

"Yes," I said. "This is better than the beach."

"If you look far enough out into the distance, you will see the beach is still here."

I tried to squint and look out into the far distance. I couldn't see it.

Ivori brought it up on the screen, much closer for us. "They have their own private side to the beach."

I felt my eyes light up. "Can I?"

"Any time you want," he said.

It felt too good to be true, and I wanted to run off right now. I didn't, of course.

Ivori pulled up where Marik pointed, and we could hear the whir of tires on the track. The sound ahead as his racers used the track and the surrounding Azris to its full potential.

Marik pointed up to the box above. "You climb. I'll be in the lift."

I did exactly as he said. And made my way up to the top of the watchers' boxes. I could see the other car pull in behind us, and Tracey and the guys exited.

I went to the front of the box and leaned over, watching the track. A large screen to my right tracked the cars with drones. Six cars raced down the far side of the property, perfectly in their positions, perfectly tracked. They were really moving, though. Cars like I'd never seen before. Huge thick wheels, one central seating area, whale's tail, and wow. They were so sleek, so fast.

I heard a ping behind me but didn't turn as my eyes watched what was playing out before me.

I was joined on one side by Tracey. "They're amazing, right?" she asked.

This close to her I could feel her Azris, yet it was no way near strong enough to race, maybe for healing like Ez—in that moment I felt my heart flutter. She would be going nuts over me leaving, even if Alek had explained. I let out a breath, losing all concentration on the race going on before me.

"I'm sorry," Tracey said.

I shook my head. "For what?"

"I'm sensitive," she said. "To people's emotional needs. I never let up when you left, hounded him till he eventually did some digging and looking."

"So I'm here because of you?"

"You're here because of *you*," she said.

The shuffle behind us had Marik move in beside me. "She really is sensitive, I'm just receptive. I'm glad you're here."

"You might not think that if we get out on your track . . ."

"If?" he asked then winked at Tracey. "You mean *when,* right?"

The Azris burn from the far end of the track sparked, and I felt it on a very deep level. My knees wobbled, and I leaned harder on the railing.

When the cars blasted past us, my head whipped to the side with them.

"They're fantastic," I said. My eyes met Tracey's, and she grinned.

"Come on," she said, and waved back down toward the stairs. "They do want to meet you. They hoped the rumors were true, that you were here."

Nerves twisted in my gut. But I nodded and followed her.

We walked down toward the cars as they settled in their respective garages. I could feel the Azris everywhere. The draw was superb. *This place is beyond amazing, Ivori.*

Marik stepped slightly in front of us as we approached the first garage. Several sets of eyes drifted his way, their laughter and chatter dying off a bit. Eyes lowered, none of them would meet his gaze. They were scared, or just . . .

In awe, Ivori said. *Though he owns the place, I highly doubt he comes down here very often.*

Makes sense.

Then their eyes fell on me, and there was more than a raised eyebrow. A young man in a slick black leather suit smiled at me. He stood straight and then moved to intercept us, bowing over low. "Master Sinclair, it's good to see you. You brought him to join the team?"

Marik laughed. "You know he won't."

The young man was just that, much younger than me, much thinner, and I couldn't get even a hint of his aura. That worried me. Were they that much higher than me, even younger?

The young man came to stand before me. "Ellis," he said and held a hand out for me. "Number one here *at the moment.*"

I took his hand and shook gently. "Oto," he said. "Just a visitor."

"He will come on the track, though, right?" Ellis glanced at Marik. "Please, let him?"

All eyes were on me then. "I'm not sure, your cars are—"

"Why don't you bring Ivori in?" Ellis said, his eyes glowing with Azris. "We've some time to look her over, run some upgrades. Smooth her out a bit, right, boss?"

"Oto?" Marik lowered his head to me. "This decision is yours. Not mine."

"I'd like to see more, learn from you," I said. "Trust goes both ways."

Ellis grinned from ear to ear. "Come, I'll show you Shah. She's beautiful, inside and out. You'll love her."

He rushed off back into the garage. I glanced to Marik. "They all hold that ability to hide everything?" I asked him.

"Everything," he said. "Yes."

"Can I learn that?"

"I'm sure they'll show you how," Tracey said. "Go, I need to take my grandfather back to the house to rest."

"Shush," he said to her, his head shaking gently from side to side.

"What's going on?"

"He's just tired," Tracey said.

Marik rolled his eyes and moved away with Tracey, though, and they both never said another word. I watched them walk away, albeit slowly. Then turned to where Ellis had gone. I must admit, heading into their garage, I really did feel like I'd stepped into their nest. The systems were, of course, very similar to ours. Shah's stats and the results of the race displayed before everyone. I stepped up to it. My jaw dropped, eyes reading the stats as quick as I could.

"You like?" Ellis asked.

Before me were stats that would rival Geo. "You match her?"

Ellis grinned from ear to ear. "You bet ya!"

He turned and moved toward his Icarian, and my eyes drifted to her side. Sleek matte black paintwork. There was no number, just the Sinclairs' logo on her side. Chrome wheels and golden discs shone in the garage lights. Ellis offered her some Azris, and I watched her take it.

I moved to her side. "It's nice to meet you, Shah." I pulled from my core and touched her door gently.

"It is I who is honored to meet you, Oto."

I noticed no real doors. "How do you . . ."

Ellis grinned even more. "You've never seen anything off planet, have you?"

I shook my head. "No, but seriously?"

Shah's side glimmered, and the whole side vanished, allowing me to see inside.

I'd never seen anything like it. Of course, our steering wheel had altered. Everything I needed to touch with my hands, or move my hands, was within finger access now. But this . . . this was . . . wow.

"Get in," Ellis said.

"Wait, you're sure?"

He nodded, and I moved to the seating, not knowing the how. But he patted the side, and said, "Hop up and just slide in. The nanites will form back over the top; you'll find they're intuitive."

I followed his instructions, and jumping up, glanced down into the soft, leather-looking seating. Then, putting my hands on either side, I dropped down into the cockpit. There was no other word for it, really. It was phenomenal.

Shah's engine flared to life underneath me. "You have a lot of untapped potential," she said. "Ivori is taking it very easy on you."

"You think?" I didn't think she was. She was pushing me, but maybe . . . maybe just not pushing me hard enough.

"Here," Shah said. A 3D image of my body came up. "This is where you are now, correct?"

I could only stare at it. I was laid out. Everything.

I coughed.

"You're an open book," she said. "There's not one person here who wouldn't be able to see this."

I scrunched my hands together. I felt bad. Like I kept trying, but everything I did, even with the Councilors' help, was wiped out with every person I met that was higher levels than me. I had to fix this. As soon as possible.

"This is how you should look." The image flickered before me, and I stared at it.

Name = Oto Benes
ID Number = 4188927
Age = 23
Species = Anodite
Sex = Male
Alignment = **Chaotic**
Bloodline = ???
Health = 98%
Cultivation Level - **Master Rank 7**
Active Meridians = 12/12
Nanites = 1 Million
Artefacts = 2

Chosen Specialist = Racer
First Chosen Affinity = Water
Second Chosen Affinity = Fire

Statistic = Body + Ivori + Cultivation
Strength = 51/**167.79**
Dexterity = 56/**188.16**
Constitution = 49/**161.21**
Int/Wis/Spirit = 65

Affinities - Rank

Water - Indigo
Fire - Blue
Earth - Green
Air - Blue
Light - Green
Darkness - Blue
Spirit - Blue

Fascinating. *Ivori?*

Marik has some heavy blocking systems in here, so no one else can get access to us, Shah said. *She's probably freaking out, not being able to contact you right now.*

I could only imagine, but I stared at the truth before me, wondering about all the other secrets and things she was keeping from me. I knew she had to. I knew it was taking time for us to get to know each other, but I felt like I should have known this.

This was the kind of secret I didn't want between us.

I sucked in a breath and asked the pertinent question. "You think I can get to this?"

Shah's engine chuckled, like a real chuckle and she answered for both of us. "There's no way *she* would be with you if you couldn't."

"So you know who she is?"

"Yes," Shah said.

"Does every Icarian she comes into contact know?"

"Yes. We may not have known what happened to her, or where she's been, but there's no mistaking her lineage."

At that, I smiled. "Do you see mine?"

"No," Shah said. "I can't see anything but what you are capable of. Most Icarian could see that."

Arla had, and I have no doubt about every other Icarian in the show lot.

This was me seeing me for how *they* saw me for the first time. It was interesting and scary.

22

Wednesday, May 19th *Lunch*
Year - 27515

It had been tough for me to leave the garage; I wanted to chastise Ivori, but I just couldn't. She meant more to me than anything or anyone I ever thought could, and yes, even to some degree, even a lot more than Ezra.

I sucked in a breath and went to the car lot outside. No sooner had I cleared the compound did her messages hit me, along with her emotion.

Stepping up beside her, I reached out with my hand and put it to her cool metal, my Azris in full open display for her.

Ivori reached for me, and I let her take it. Whatever she needed, I'd never deny her. I couldn't.

What happened?

"I saw myself," I replied, my throat dry.

I felt deep inside her the embarrassment. "I . . ." she started.

"It's okay," I said. "I wasn't ready to really see that."

"No, you weren't," she said. "They shouldn't have."

"You kept me from advancing that fast?" I needed to know.

"I did," she admitted, and her embarrassment faded. "If you'd grown that fast, do you think you could have controlled yourself?"

I shook my head. "What are we doing?" I asked her. "What do you want here?"

"This is all for you," she said. "Learning who you are. What you are. What we can be."

"It's a lot to take in," I replied. "But I need to see it for real. Can you guide me just a little more. Out here?"

"I know I've let you down," she said. "I'm sorry. It's one of the reasons I haven't overwhelmed you, that we're not only growing within the system we set, but that we're growing at a pace you're okay with."

"I want to go to the beach," I said. "Think we can get around there together?"

"Yes," she said. "We have permission to go there now, before dinner. Marik and Tracey want you at the house later, though."

I looked toward the house. "Sounds good."

Then I let her take us around the side of the property. The beach itself stretched on for some time, and she drove down with ease. Almost as if it were built. Not just created by the land and seas around us.

Ivori pulled into a small alcove, parking in the shade. "I think this is off the beaten track a little."

I opened the door. The sands were perfect, the sea out in the distance, bluey green. I moved into the sun, and let it warm my face.

The wind caught me slightly in surprise, and I glanced left to see tiny sand storms racing down toward us; they petered out.

With a laugh, I undid my shirt, pulled it off, then kicked off my shoes and socks.

"Planning a swim?" Ivori asked.

"Not today. Maybe in the next week or so. I want to test some things out while I'm here, with you, alone."

"You really think we're alone?" she asked. "This does belong to Sinclair."

I nodded and yet walked away from her.

When I stopped walking and dropped to my stance, she appeared before me and did the same.

"I need to finally stop everyone, everything, looking at me."

"You want to see you, but you don't want anyone else?"

I let my palms, though a little sweaty, face the heavens. I waited.

"You need to master and constantly use all affinities," she finally said.

"How?" I asked, meeting her eyes with mine.

"You are decent enough level in all of them; you need to combine them."

"Combine them," I repeated.

"The Icarian I meet knows me by feel. I cannot hide that. But they cannot see me."

"So they don't know your levels, if you're stronger than you are?"

"No, they can't and are rightly wary."

"But not on a racetrack?"

"That's professional, not personal."

"Show me," I said.

Ivori dipped her head and faced one palm up, one down.

I watched her carefully.

"The elements of our world are all around us," she said. "Most who use Azris develop one strong affinity, and a secondary. Over time, the strongest of all can develop slight uses of the others, but not maximum use. We have the ability to use all of them, and to their full potential. It still takes time. It still takes a lot of concentration. Follow me."

When she started to move, her movements were similar to First Breath, then they rapidly changed. When she stopped, though, she seemed to flick her wrist up toward the sky, then twist it and force it downward.

The beach lit up with orbs. I stared at them, awed. There for me to see were her open meridians, all twelve of them, and her affinities between them, the wind that whistled, the fire that burned, the darkness of the storm inside. "Can everyone see it like this?" I asked.

"No," Ivory said. "Look around you. See the strength of the world. What makes it what it is today. I don't expect this will be anything you will ever get to see at this level ever again."

I looked around me, to the winds and tiny sand storms still around me. The water spray as the sea came into the beach. The fire of the sun above us and the darkness of the earth. Its display of prowess, so much larger than ours.

"You see what each of them are doing?" Ivori asked at my side.

I looked at her. "They're connecting with their opposites?"

"Yes, but more than that."

I turned back to watch them. The wind and the sands danced together; the fiery reds of the sun mixed with the spray of water. The shadows and darkness behind us flirted as well. "They're wonderful," I said. "All of them."

I then watched her. With an upturned hand, she moved it higher toward the skies and the down-turned one around and then up to the skies too. The orbs moved with her, then she sped up, faster and faster. Till she brought her hands together, and they merged as one.

"What did you do?" I asked her.

"This is not what I have done. This is you." She lowered her head to me and opened her hands to reveal one orb. "You incite everything here with who you are."

"A bumbling idiot half the time," I said.

"No, look deeper."

I stared into the swirling orb before us, and she let go. It floated then, swirling around and around. "All the elements are inside here?"

"Yes." She nodded. "You combined them, all of them. You just need to shield yourself with it. No one else will ever see what you are, or what you control then anymore."

"I can just take it? Use it like I would any other single affinity?"

"Try it." Ivori stepped back as I stepped to the floating orb.

I reached out, and I took hold of it. "It feels very strange," I said. "It feels just like . . . home." Tears welled up inside me. I missed Ezra, Alek, everyone. Yet I needed this. I needed to learn to be me. I sucked in a breath, steadied my emotions, and I focused on this swirling ball of energy that was me, that was mine.

Gently, I guided it up, just like she had all of them, and I passed it from one hand to the other, essentially juggling just it, the one orb. Then,

I began to move, First Thought, Second Sentience, Third Awareness, Fourth Consciousness. Faster and faster.

"You've got it," Ivori said. "All of it. All of them, they're yours."

I didn't hesitate and went straight through into Fifth Understanding.

"I might have them in my mind," I said to her, moving softly, still enticing the memories, the feelings. "I'm not at the level to use them, though."

Steady, I recalled every moment I'd had with Councilor Troha. Then I took the next plunge, Sixth Acceptance, but I struggled. It didn't feel right.

I heard Ivori gasp, "One moment." Instead of standing and watching, she moved in next to me. I felt her presence, her draw to my push, and vice versa. "Together."

These were far more complicated movements, and though I'd seen them only once, they were also engrained in my mind. Angle of the feet, the turn, the hip dipped, the foot slip, then into Sixth Determination. We pushed through it. Sixth Initiative, we held on. Sixth Flight, my legs gave way, and my knees hit wet sand, but I laughed. I laughed so hard my ribs hurt.

Ivori stood above me. "You look silly," she said in the end, her own knees hitting the sand, hand on my shoulder. "But amazing."

"Again," I said, staring into her eyes. "I'm not leaving till we've gone through one full set."

"Even if it takes all night?"

"Even if it takes all night."

Monday, May 20th *Very Early Morning*
Year - 27515

Of course, I wouldn't get left alone out here all night. It was late, though, by the time Marik and Roxy showed up.

"You missed dinner," he said, approaching, and held up a small basket.

I stopped my practice, and with sweat dripping off my back even in the chilly night air. "This was the best time and place to do what I needed," I replied.

Marik set the basket down and looked out at the ocean. The waves, though I couldn't see them properly now, crashed into the distance. "You're a fast learner. I'm glad you came here."

I frowned. I'd technically still not done what I set out to. Sixth Flight still had me stuck. But I felt better about it.

"Eat," he said. "Then we'll walk back, you'll get some rest, and tomorrow morning, you're going to slot in with the team. I'll rotate one of the cars out with every race so they each get to be up against you."

"You really want me to have a go against your elite team?"

"What else would you sooner do? Sulk?"

I laughed, opening the basket to pull out the pack of sandwiches and fluids. When I bit into one, I realized how starving I was. "This is good," I mumbled through chewing. "Thank you."

"You're welcome."

"Do you look after all your team like this?" I asked, sitting down.

Marik eased down to sit near me, Roxy mooching around before she sat, eyes on me, begging.

"Personal treatment like this?" he said. "No, not at all."

"That position of pure leadership, right?" I took a sip out of the flask. It was warming, healing tea. Sweet and fruity.

"I have spoken to Luca," Marik admitted.

I stopped chewing, feeling nausea wash over me. "Why?"

"He's my friend," he said. "I wanted him to know you were indeed safe. I told them you were. You're with me, and when you're ready to leave, you will go with my blessings."

"What if I never want to leave?" I asked.

Oto, don't say that, Ivori whispered.

It's a legitimate question, I replied to her.

"If you don't want to leave, then I wouldn't force you." Marik held my eyes with his, coughed. "You will want to return. What you have"—

he tapped his chest—"is drive and determination to prove to yourself and to Ivori what you are. You wouldn't have come out here tonight otherwise. Correct?"

I tucked back into the sandwich. "Correct."

Marik moved to his knees, and he pushed himself up, though rather slowly. "Ivori is safe anywhere here on the grounds. My chief in the house will show you to your room. Get some rest. The track is awake early."

I smiled at him. "Wouldn't have it any other way," I replied. "I'll see you there."

"After lunch." He turned and started to walk away, Roxy at his heels.

I continued to eat, and only when I'd finished everything in the basket did I clear it up, put it on my passenger seat, and head back to his house.

Ivori sighed as I parked up, about to go inside. *You do realize Luca will be on his way.*

"I know," I said. "Rest. We've got some fun ahead in the next few days."

Ivori laughed. *Fun? I'm not so sure you're going to think that for long.*

She really hadn't been kidding. My mind was mushed from the night before when I woke and grabbed something to eat. The track was very much alive.

The night guard let me through and into the back run of the tracks. I followed him till we found a garage to pull into from this side. It looked different till I was inside. "Ellis," I said.

"Morning to you both," he said, dipping his head to Ivori. "We're first out, but I can't wait to get on the track with you later."

His team directed us onto the ramp, and within seconds, I was out of Ivori, and they were literally going over her with a fine-toothed comb.

They're tickling me. She laughed inside my head. *But they're very thorough.*

"What are you doing to her?"

"They're just making sure she's got some chance against the team," Ellis said.

"A chance?" I asked, stepping to put a hand on her tire. I spun it. "You better believe we've got a chance."

Ellis pointed to the screens behind us. "Quick rundown. Three of the top teams from Halara," he said.

I swallowed. Maybe I'd expected them to be from Copter, or Altrol, but to actually come from the same planet as Taryn? I sucked in a breath. "Give it to me."

"Pole is Apollos with Vaan. Second, Sass with Moo. Third, Jessia with Knight. Fourth, Mase with Pola. Fifth, Rohan with Denitx."

"So I'm last."

"Better you see how it runs before you try to even think about getting any other positions. They may swap you about if you can handle yourself."

"Fair," I said. "They're used to racing against each other?"

"They're used to being top of their races. This is a place to test their mettle against each other. Where it's safe to do so, without danger to them or their Icarian."

"What can I expect?"

"Not to win," he fired back at me.

I frowned; I wasn't having that. "I don't think I can go out there without at least some hope."

Ellis glanced over to Shah. "Just have some fun."

"Can we get a run through on our own first?" I asked.

"I think they'll be okay with that. I'll fire over the request."

I watched as Ivori eased back to the floor from the ramp.

I ran my finger over her hood. *You good?*

Excited to get out there, she admitted.

I grinned. As much as Ellis had probably served all my details on a platter to them, pitting them against me, I was, too. *Fun,* I said to her. *We could do with some of that.*

Yes, she replied. *I would like that, fun.*

"You're good to go," Ellis said. "Track's yours."

I moved to get inside Ivori, the feel of everything still so new, so fresh that any practice on a track I didn't know was good.

Ellis stepped in beside me as the front double doors opened. He leaned down. "I've seen what you can do. You're made for this. Good luck."

We were.

I flicked into gear and steadily made my way out onto the track. "Dash will show all the usual. Do you want to see the track?" Ivori asked.

"Yes," I replied to her.

A map of the track covered the screen. There were a lot more turns than I was used to, but the straights were longer as well. Excitement welled up inside me; this really looked fun. There were tiny numbers at the turns. I could only guess at suggested speeds. *Suggested* . . . 'cause holy crap, it was fast.

"Let's take it nice and steady," I said aloud. "I'm not blowing any parts here."

"Parts can be replaced," Ellis said through the dash.

I laughed. "For a price. And a price I can't pay right now."

"No," Ellis added. "Track's covered by the owner. No one pays anything here. This is their time. No pressure."

"You're telling me if I popped something, I'd get it replaced, no questions asked?"

"Exactly," he replied.

Why doesn't that make me feel any better? I asked Ivori.

Probably because we're used to paying for everything and everything having a price that's out of reach.

Out of reach meant strings attached. Or did it? I could only hope not. For our sake.

I tightened my grip on the wheel and watched the lights.

They hit the gas.

I'll break it down as we're heading in, Ivori said. *First time and all.*

You been here before? I asked.

No, she replied. *First turn ahead, ease to the left, power out, then into a right, left, sweeping right.*

I wasn't sure how to check any temps with the map there. How?

Don't worry about that. I'll let you know if there're any issues. You just feel as you need to, expand your reach around the chassis properly.

Steering here was fantastic, no resistance at all from the track. We slid around nice and easy. Though forty kilometers per hour less than it said on the map as the lowest speed.

We'll get it on the next pass, she said.

The gear changes were quick though, the next three bends quite fast without the speed. I couldn't imagine doing it at even their lowest.

We can do it, Ivori said. *Straight up to the next chicane, then another and out into two lefts.*

I hit the gas and got my speed up. Feeling the warmth around the car in general increasing with every twist and turn, I did reach out with my Azris and felt every change within her system. *This is so much easier. Fluid.*

You changed a lot last night, Ivori said.

That made the difference today?

Big sweep, then hot into another chicane.

They really like the sweeping bends. How big is this track?

Three times the size of Frasers.

Made sense, then, at least with all the turns.

"Come on," Ellis's voice came through the comms. "You must get that speed up."

I glanced to the map. Ahead of me were only a few more turns, one massive straight, and then back to the line.

I dropped the gears into the bends. Ivori let out a little squeal. *Not yet!*

I pulled back from letting my Azris go, heading into the straight at below par.

Past the finish line with the timing flashing in red.

"That's not a good score, I guess?" I asked Ellis.

"No, they'll slaughter you alive out there if you do that with them. Straight through into the second lap."

I didn't drop my gears down too much into the bend this time, my speed hitting eighty kilometers per hour more than earlier.

One hundred kilometers per hour into the next set.

Oto? Ivori asked in a rather sarcastic tone, as we started to come into the next sweeping bend.

Don't like the speed?

You're trying to break their record?

Would you expect anything else?

The map vanished. *By skill alone,* she said.

I winked at the dashboard, and she chuckled.

23

Thursday, May 20th *Lunch*
Year – 27515

The steering responded to my commands, but the speed pulled me close to the line. I couldn't touch the brakes. If I did, I'd not get that momentum back up.

I held tight.

Then I hit for more gas.

Ellis's next words across the comms came through. "You're not going to hold back, are you?"

The next chicane came into view. I feathered the brakes, dropping our speed and down the gears. Then we powered into the first bend. "Would you?"

I didn't hear a reply from him as our engine roared on the exit.

Don't hold back, I said to Ivori. *Take everything you need to nail that time.*

Why? she asked.

Because they underestimate both of us. I don't want anyone to underestimate us ever again.

The next bend, our tires bumped the curb, but I didn't let go. Down into the next gear. Then I floored it.

I'd never felt actual pain since the first time Akia showed off.

This hurt.

The pain ripped at my core.

Oto, Ivori spat.

Keep going!

She pulled even more.

332.

That frigging finish line was approaching way too fast.

I hit the brakes. I felt something in the back-end pop. Red flashed up on the dash.

Shit, shit, shit.

The wheel pulled heavily to one side, but I held it. I focused on my Water, letting its calm, its cooling flow out into her, and then out the back.

Holding, Ivori said. *Hot! Hot! Cool them down!*

On it!

Temp dropping.

We stopped dead on the line.

The time above us flashed, then stopped.

I took my hands off the wheel, resting them in my lap.

Breathe in and out, I said to myself.

Ivori's dash illuminated all the internal systems, all green. "What did we pop?" I asked.

Valve. Nothing major. If it had been, we wouldn't have stopped for anything.

In front of us, people appeared. Staring. Chattering to each other, hands waving.

What do you think they made of that? I asked her.

By the looks of it . . . I don't think they can process it.

I clicked into gear and hit the gas then stopped in front of them. Got out while they were all preoccupied in their very animated conversations. I sat on the hood and watched. Then all eyes turned to me.

One man stepped forward. "You just blew my record away, and you've never even been to this track before?"

I shook my head once and stood up straight. "Nope."

He turned to everyone behind him and barked. "Get your asses on the line." When his eyes came back to mine, he held his hand out. "Apollos," he said. "That was some of the best driving I've seen in a while and in a vehicle that's not usually up to par."

I shook his hand. "I showed you something," I said. "Now you show me something."

"My pleasure." He slapped my arm. "When these lot have gone home, we'll talk too, yeah. I have some tips for you."

"Really? Aren't you worried about when I advance against your own team?"

"Out there we do our best," he said seriously. Then he chuckled. "If we don't bring the best, what's the point?"

"Agreed," I said and turned to Ivori. "Ready to go again?"

Soon as that valve's fixed, yes.

Friday, 21st May *Afternoon*
Year - 27514

It was not anywhere as easy for others on the track, and they swapped us in and out at different places.

It was, however, so much fun.

Apollos not only was a great racer who I could show a thing or two about lines and gut instinct, but he taught me a lot too. Even when I'd gone wrong, I could pull it back, I could improve with my gear changes and acceleration.

Everything we did out there we could let it break us, or we could pick ourselves back up again and make it work.

It wasn't till two days later when we all sat in the break room after lunch, and chatted about the performances of the cars, when he said, "There's a call for you."

"For me?"

Apollos pointed to the office at the back. "You can take it in there."

I was curious, but stood and made my way to it, shutting the door behind me. Just didn't want anyone else to hear if it was who I thought it was. As an office, it was just like any other. Deck, hybrid connecting system to the net.

I sat, finger hesitating over the button. Then I sucked in a breath and faced him. Luca.

"I wasn't sure you were going to take this," he said.

"I wasn't sure either," I replied.

"I'll be landing on the beach in about thirty minutes. But we're not stopping. Have Ivori on standby."

"I'm not going back," I said and held his eyes with mine.

"Calm down, I'm not taking you back." His hands were busy. "Trust me, please, Oto."

His eyes never gave anything else away, but I could see his flicker of Azris. They darkened.

I closed my eyes, let out a breath.

I did trust him.

Luca didn't need to try to reach me, to calm me. Nothing I thought would do any good, any more than being here was, than being around the Elite, learning from them, seeing how good they all were, even against each other. Apollos was hot shit as a driver; his Icarian, Vaan, reminded me of the stats that Ivori used to have. We might be able to nail his score without anyone else on the track, but with them there, we never came close. I just didn't have what it takes. "Yet," he kept telling me. "You don't have what it takes *yet*."

Every single time we went out, though, I was improving; we were all improving. They'd all forgotten what it was like to have that ferocity from the bottom. This was more than fun. It was good for my soul and for theirs too. I honestly didn't want to leave. I liked the freedom.

When I opened my eyes and met Luca's once more, he was clearly very worried. "I trust you," I said. "We'll be at the beach in thirty."

He cut the comms, and I moved out of the office. Marik stood with Apollos. He stepped toward me and handed me a bag. "I gotta go," I said.

Marik reached into his pocket, pulled out a pin. "I won't get to see you for a while, but I want you to know, having you here has been a pleasure. Even if you kicked my team's numbers into the dirt." He undid the back of the pin and I saw the emblem on it, Sinclairs. "If you ever, ever need my ear again, don't hesitate."

On the inside, I was elated. I'd made other friends. People I liked and could trust. Even as much as my mind was telling me they were an opposing team, my heart was telling me otherwise. I trusted them, all of them.

"I guess I'll see you out there?" I said to Apollos.

We shook hands. "Been a real pleasure. If we see you out there, make sure you bring it."

I laughed, and promised I would. Then I left.

It didn't give me a lot of time to get to the beach.

Ivori drove while I drank deeply from a bottle of water. I got myself into a tizzy over seeing *him*. The consequences, the connotations. I took the steering wheel from Ivori when we hit the beach.

"He's coming in Tant?" I asked her. "Doesn't that attract a lot of attention?"

"It would seem so, and yes, more than likely it will attract a lot of attention."

We pulled up to the beach, and I could see the ship ahead of us. It wasn't as big as the time I saw it dropping down into Frasers' track. How many designs could he have? Shapeshifting?

"Metal Walking," Ivori said. "Level up high enough. It's more than possible."

"You could do that?"

She didn't answer, just sighed.

We approached slowly. Luca stood out from the ship. He nodded my way and pointed to the drop-down bay doors.

"You sure?" she asked me.

"He won't take us back to Frasers," I said. I moved faster to get up the small ramp. "Looks like we'll fit?"

There was a thunk when her wheels hit the metal, and I stopped. "Easy," I said with a chuckle.

There was just enough room for me to open the door inside and slip out. Which I did so as the hatch closed behind Luca.

I swallowed as he stepped to me and just stared. I felt like I was looking into the eyes of a father who wanted to chastise me, but couldn't. Who wanted to say so much, but didn't want to risk the fallout.

"Say it," I said. "You'll feel better."

"You knew they'd—" he started, then stopped himself. "I was worried."

"I asked Alek to trust me too," I said. "I said I'd come home in my own time."

"You really think even though he let you go, they haven't been trying to find you? That they wouldn't worry at all?"

"Are they okay?"

"They are worried, Oto. Just like I have been."

"You've left Lena . . ."

"With Amalia and Camran, yes. I trust her." He pointed to the front of the bay. "Come on, we have a fair way to travel, and I want you to talk. Not me."

I walked after him through a tight doorway and into a cockpit. There were two seats. "Meet Tant," he said. "Tant, this is Oto and Ivori."

"My pleasure," Tant's voice came back. He had a soft yet commanding tone. "Please sit."

"Is Ivori okay?" I asked and took a seat.

Luca sat next to me, and immediately started with the controls.

"I am perfectly fine," she said. "Tant's a pure gentleman."

"Good to hear."

Several clunks had me reaching for a belt, or something, anything.

"Left side," Luca said.

What was the beach and ocean laid out before us started to drop then.

I couldn't feel anything, nothing at all. We were suddenly hundreds of feet above the planet's surface, then thousands.

"Fuck," I swore, nausea threatening to swallow me.

"Breathe," Ivori said. "You've got this."

I hadn't "got" this. My heart raced. "You're taking me into space?" I asked.

"Tant is a fully capable spaceship," Luca said, "But yes. We're going on a small tour."

"Tour?" Ivori asked.

"Forgive me," Luca said. "There are a few things I need the both of you to see."

"That sounds pretty ominous," Ivory said.

"I agree," I added.

The sands and the giant track of Marik's below us now were just a pinprick. I couldn't look up, to see . . .

My eyes drifted up, and locking in on the clouds, the difference as we shot up yet still even higher. I gripped onto the cold, metallic arm rests. I had thrills being inside Ivori and getting to the next level, the next speed. This . . . was out of this world, literally.

"How does Azris work here?" I asked immediately, regretting it.

"We're in orbit," Tant announced. "Azris burn in three."

Oh shit.

"Two," he counted down.

My knuckles couldn't get any whiter. I stared at Luca, who never even batted an eye.

"One."

When that Azris burn took. Luca closed his eyes, and I couldn't do anything but watch the screen ahead.

The black seemed to melt into what I could only describe as fog. White, swirling, misty-looking rain clouds? Out here, in space.

I tried to focus on the screen, but the white moved fast, so fast. My stomach, if I'd been planet side, would have been all over the deck.

Instead, I closed my eyes like Luca had and tried to breathe in and out. Tried my best to settle what was really racing through my mind.

"You can open your eyes," Luca said. "We're in the deep now."

"The deep?" I asked without opening my eyes.

"Open your eyes, you'll see."

I did as he said, opening my eyes to see deep darkness. Tiny stars twinkled all around us. "It's beautiful," I said.

Oto, Ivori said to me, *they need to get us home, now.*

I couldn't understand her, but her panic was evident. *What? Why?*

"Some Icarian hate the feeling of space," she said over comms.

"I can understand that." I wanted to stand up to see more.

"Go for it, the screen is 3D. You're not really that close to the front of the ship."

I unclipped the belt, tested the gravity even though it felt lighter underfoot, and moved to the screen. "Where are we?"

I jumped back as the screen changed slightly. Ahead of us, a planet loomed. Grays, greens, and blues swirled below us. The cities were massive; you could see them from space.

"Drakol," Ivori said. Her voice thick, angry? What? "It's dangerous for me to be here. You must return us to Isala. Now."

Luca turned toward where she was manifesting. Her form he'd never seen; only the others on our track had. Or had it been recordable?

"Oh," he said, his face paled. "What's this?"

"I'm not strong enough to defend myself," she said to him. "If they come for me, they will kill me."

"They don't know we're here," Luca said. He gave her a side glance and asked me, "I've known Tant to manifest only once in my lifetime. He doesn't like it, and it takes a hundred times the energy than it does for a space jump."

"You make it look easy," Tant said to her.

Ivori put a hand on her hip. "We're built different," she said an obvious attempt to hide it.

"No, you're very different," Tant said. "I can feel the power, but I can't see anything else. Off either of you."

"Nothing off Oto either?" Luca said.

"Nothing at all," Tant said.

Luca unbuckled himself and moved to my side. He was trying to see inside me. But his brows furrowed. "I can't see anything now either. What did you do?"

"I did what I needed to protect myself properly from anyone, and I mean anyone. No matter who they are, or their levels."

"There's not been anyone for a long time who could hold their stats out against Tant."

"Even Councilor Troha?"

"They're lower levels than most in my circles," Luca said.

"You should be resting, moving to the next stage on Halara," Ivori said. "Why bring us here?"

It wasn't just a question; this was a demand. Her anger rolled off her.

"I could never abandon my duties to my track, to my father or my family."

Ivori muttered under her breath, moved to Tant's main computer system. She completely solidified before us. Her hand sparked, and within seconds, code after code flashed over the screen before us.

"You can't do that!" Luca spat as he tried to step forward. With only a glance, he stopped dead. She had stopped him like he was a rank zero.

But she was, she was rewriting Tant's code. I saw the nanite transfer as well. She glanced at me.

"He doesn't have the energy to return us to Isala. Neither of them does."

She tried to give Azris to Tant. I felt the draw from me. Then I felt the pain.

"Ivori," I said and my knees wobbled. "I can't do that. Stop."

It was as if she didn't hear me. My knees gave way, and I fell. "Ivori," I shouted. "Stop, please!"

She whirled to me, dropped to her knees, grasping a tight hold. Her eyes were wild. She was absolutely terrified. That made my stomach churn all the more. "I'm sorry," she said. "I can't get us home. I can't do it."

Luca's face paled. "What's going on?"

I reached for her. Took a hand in mine. She was solid. "I didn't mean to hurt you," she said. "I didn't."

"Breathe," I said. I took her other hand in mine. "Breathe steady." I pulled air into my lungs, showing her. "In, three, two, one. Out."

Ivori copied me for a few breaths. Luca moved; she'd relented her hold.

"Oto?" he asked. "Talk to me."

"The Sevran Vipers knew I was on Isala," Ivori said. "They know eventually I'd make a move to Copter, to Altrol, and above. They would track me. We need to leave. Now."

She might have been calmer, but the panic was still there.

"You need to talk to me," Luca said. "Both of you."

"I didn't want to," Ivori said, her eyes dropped. "I didn't want to show my . . . Oto's hand to anyone."

"I'm not just anyone," Luca said softly. He moved before us, held a hand out to me. "Neither is Geo."

"No," Ivori said, and she moved to let me stand with his help. "You have all seen where I came from, what I was. You do not know who, though."

"Who?" Tant asked, his voice cracked. "Who are you?"

She looked at Luca and then at the planet. Her eyes narrowed, her fists clenched, her breath hitched. She let it out slow. *Good*, I said. *I'm right here. Tell him.*

Only then did she speak. "I am the least of their expectations," she said. Her words held such emotion, such power. Goosebumps spread up my back, down my neck, and down my arms. I saw Luca struggle again. Was she . . . oh shit, she was. Ivori's aura spread out from her, suppressing everything around us. "I will take everything they stole from those lower than them and give it back. I will not stop till the Sevran Vipers are on their knees, and still I will not stop. I will take everything they are and rip out their cores. Death will be a mercy. I will not deliver mercy."

Luca's knees buckled beneath him, and he just caught the arm of his chair before he hit the deck. "Oto, what—"

"Ivori is . . ."

Her face fell, and she moved to sit in Luca's chair. "I am a failure." She shook her head, put it in her hands, emotion washing over me.

"Ivori," I said.

She looked up at me. Then she reached to help Luca. "I am nothing I used to be," she admitted.

"You are *something*, though," Luca said.

"If I could bow down before you, I would." Tant's voice came over the comms. "But it's kinda hard for you inside me."

Ivori looked up to the screen as a face formed there, then a body, and he did bow to her.

"Oh, Tant." Ivori laughed. "Thank you."

Luca's brows furrowed. "What are you saying, Tant?"

"Ivori is our first," he said, to her sigh. "The closest translation I believe would be Matriarch? Leader of all?"

"I've only ever heard rumors." Luca's face fell. "I shouldn't have brought you out here, I—"

"You didn't know," I said. I looked back at the darkness of space. "It would have come out, eventually. Better to be out here than with everyone else around us. Better to be you than . . ."

"My brother already knows. I'm sure of it," Luca said. "I just don't—"

"If he did, he's not said anything," Ivori said. "For that, I am thankful." She looked up at Tant's screens. "How long till we can get out of here?"

"To jump back to Isala, twenty-four hours."

Ivori sighed.

"Could we reach Halara?" Luca said. "I have good friends there with—"

"Taryn's family, and the Sawa Sect," I added.

Luca raised an eyebrow at me, but nodded.

"Possibly," Tant said. "But Copter is the closest."

"Without escort?" Luca asked. "That's a bit much."

"We've no choice," Tant said. "The Sawa Sect have homes on both—you know it."

"Where are they now?"

"Unluckily," Tant said, "Halara."

"Then set a course, please, Tant, for Halara. I fear we've already been spotted," Ivori added for us. He complied without waiting for Luca to confirm.

24

Friday, 21st May *Late Evening*
   Year - 27514

Ivori's form flickered. "Go," I said to her. "Use the comms."

She didn't hesitate, and I moved to sit in the other chair. Luca sat next to me and stared out into the dark.

"Course plotted," Tant said. "We'll be there in a few hours with minimal, shorter jumps. I'm jumping right away out of this area."

Luca sat back in his chair. "Keep scanning the area. If anything looks or feels out of place—"

"I'll let you know," he said. "First jump in, three, two, one."

I never felt this one at all, though the view on the screen changed slightly. Just looked like we faced a different direction.

Luca spun his chair to look at me. "There's two bunks," he said. "If you want to rest, you can."

"No," I said. "We need to sort this out first. There's not time to rest until we're on Halara."

He stood and moved to the back of the room, tapping a panel to get us both a drink. "Good a time as any," he said. "It's from Taryn's family."

I swirled the liquid around, savoring the flavor. I was getting a little too used to drinking.

"Ask," I said.

He contemplated his drink, then said, "I don't know where to start."

"Do you want me to leave?" I asked.

His eyes shot up to mine. "What? No."

"Then talk."

He contemplated for a moment, studying his glass.

"I believe very much like my father did. He wanted to make a decent place in the universe," he said. "One where his kids, my kids, could grow up not wanting for anything, where I could provide for anyone who wanted to be in our 'umbrella.' But it's been an uphill struggle from the" —pain crossed his face—"from the day my father died."

I took a swig of my drink. I didn't understand everything they'd been through then, or what he'd been through since.

"That was the Sevran Vipers back then, wasn't it?"

"I tried for many years to . . . to find someone responsible." He downed his drink and poured some more. "I did eventually track it to the Sevran Vipers. But I couldn't ever prove it, but we knew then, like we know now. The case would never make it to court, here or any planet. We just didn't have the evidence."

My heart hurt for my next words, but I needed to know. "And Ray?"

Luca's face darkened. Ivori might have been able to hold him back. There was no way I could. I cringed when he flexed his Azris my way.

"For what they did," he whispered, "I won't back down. I can't. I will get justice."

"*We* won't back down," I said. "Seems the Sevran Vipers need one hell of a wake-up call."

Luca nodded, then went silent. Eventually, he finished his drink, locked eyes with me, and said, "What can we do to help?"

"Keep who she is—who we are *together*—under wraps. We need to do everything we're supposed to. We need to rise up the ranks properly, so that her people and ours see it for real. I might have gotten a slight leg up at the start, but we've not been gifted anything special. It's just as hard for me as it is for anyone else. It's a very different hard."

You're right, Ivori said. *It is very different, and now you know the why.*

"But you're royalty," Luca said aloud. Those words, those real words. Fuck. He shook his head, poured another drink and downed it. "I'm not sure I can ignore you're even higher up than Sawa ever could be."

Red lights flashed. "We've several craft on the outer edge of my tracking."

My stomach flipped.

"Direction?"

"They don't seem to be coming in any closer. I would say they're curious, though."

"Can they tell what's on board?"

"They'll not see me, us," I said. "But they might not be happy if they can see you are out here."

"Good point," Luca said.

Ivori? I asked.

It took a lot out of me manifesting for so long. I'm here though.

You okay?

We will be, with a little time on Halara.

Luca and I drifted to talking about many things. He told me stories of Ray, even though I'd heard some from Mira it was good to hear his side. The jumps came and went, and eventually the alcohol settled the both of us.

A short while later, we were in the outer space of the planet Halara. Once again I was in awe. The screen before us lit up, and though I couldn't make out what was going on in front of us, many light years away, no doubt, Luca was on the edge of his seat.

Can we—

You've learned well. No one on Halara will see inside of us. We're safe.

I let out a sigh of relief.

"Incoming comms from Halara," Tant said. "They're sending in an escort for us."

"Good." Luca eased back in his chair, and I did the same.

"Anything I need to know when we get down there?" I asked.

"Shuko Sawa and his sect are interesting. You'll see many differences in our culture right away. They're very dedicated to family, and they show it off very well to visitors."

I was a little confused, but just nodded. "They spend time split between here and Copter, why?"

"It's one of the richest planets. Even if it attracts all the wrong people because of it. Rich means there's greed, and a lot of infighting."

"So it's ripe with energy, fighting an—"

"You'll learn," Luca said. "But yes."

On the screen in front of us came two other ships. Tant leveled off with them. Luca took our glasses away and sat back down while we were guided in. This planet was very different from Isala.

I sat forward on the edge of my seat watching, seeing as much as I could.

"You remind me of him," Luca said, his voice thick, eyes watery. I had to do a double take then, and lowering my head, I understood. "Ray," Luca added.

"Thank you," I said. "That's a great compliment."

Getting down was much worse than going up. I didn't think the alcohol had been such a good idea. By the time my stomach stopped flipping, we were on the planet's surface and I could let go of the chair's arms.

"It takes some getting used to," Luca said. "Straighten yourself up as best you can. We will be checked and escorted to Sawa."

"They're still cautious, even though they know you?"

"Of course," he said, standing, fingering through his hair. "They don't know you."

When the ramp lowered, there were several people waiting for us. Luca stepped off with confidence, not showing an ounce of what we'd been through on our way here. I copied him as best I could, though I was so far out of my depth I shivered.

"Strange," Luca said as the crowd before us moved in. "That really is Shuko Sawa. He doesn't usually meet people off the runways."

I looked at the man he'd indicated. He was taller than Luca, similar age, I would have guessed.

"They're both here. Fascinating. What's going on?" Luca spoke clearly so I could hear him. "To his right is Quintin Tullius."

"Taryn's father, who is her mother?"

"His first, Tofa, is to his right."

"Her mother?" I noted Tofa's features then, smooth skin, muscular frame. "Would pass for her sister. First?"

"I mentioned customs were different. They have many wives here, called a Taharri."

"Oh." That was different. I couldn't help but ask. "So Taryn was expected to share her husband with other women?"

"I have no doubt they already had a family set out for her to join. Being with my brother threw all of their work away." His face flushed. "Either way, to Shuko's left is his first, Portia and Umeko. Behind them are their first guards, and most trusted."

Luca moved away from me to meet them, and I followed, then almost fell over. He caught me and instantly apologized. "I should have mentioned there was a slight gravity difference."

"Ya think?" I picked myself up, dusted my trousers down from the wet grass, then stood to meet the entourage.

"First time off planet?" Quintin asked, his eyes meeting mine with curiosity. I'd spent so much time with Geo and Taryn that I couldn't miss those eyes. Taryn had the beauty from her mother and the fire from her father. I liked that. I could see how their son might look just off the familiarities of their family traits.

"Y-y-es," I stammered, and tried my best not to pale before them.

"Your presence is a little unusual without ample warning," Shuko said, but he stepped forward and offered a hand.

"Thank you for taking us in. It was unexpected." Luca took his arm in a solid embrace. "This is Oto Benes." Luca then formally introduced me to all of them, and I politely nodded in turn to their names, trying my best to make sure I didn't mix anyone up.

"We have heard about him quite a lot lately," Shuko stated with a raised eyebrow. "On one hand, I'm excited you're here, on the other—" He didn't continue his thoughts. His control impeccable, but I could see it. Worry.

I glanced between both men, yet my eyes settled with Quintin's. "Don't scare the lad," Quintin said. "Come, let's get inside where he can sit and not worry about him falling over."

"You can use Earth Azris to steady yourself," Luca said. "Just gently circulate it around your feet."

They turned as one to move away, and I could do nothing but try my best to follow, steadily, on very shaky feet. It was like walking on air. It was much lighter than Isala.

By the time we reached a building at the far end of our landing zone. I finally looked up to see where we were.

The building stretched up forever. Miles? To the stars?

I quickly glanced back to see where we'd come from and felt my jaw drop.

"Beautiful, isn't it?" Portia said, her voice soft, warm.

"I thought Isala was pretty in places. But this is amazing."

"This is our private grounds," Portia said as the others had moved inside. She waved a hand over the land before me, then the skies. "Our sect lands stretch as far and as high as the eye can see. Do not worry, you are safe in here."

When she moved inside, she walked slightly ahead of me, and I noted Quintin waited. Crap. Everyone else had moved along, so did Portia. She dipped her head to Quintin as she made her way past.

I held his gaze as I leveled with him. "Feeling better in here?" he asked.

"Yes," I said. I actually did, and didn't need to circulate Azris anymore. That was good. I needed to recharge. Ivori had kicked the stuffing out of me, taking that much earlier.

"I've heard quite a lot about you coming from Isala," he said, then his questions came fast, needy. "You're directly under Geo Fraser. Is Taryn with him now? Is she okay, her well-being good?"

I coughed. "Her well-being?"

"She left in such a hurry," he admitted, his eyes lowered. "I . . . we've all been worried about her, especially her mother."

On the inside, I sighed. I'd just done this to my friends, my family. But she still hadn't spoken to them, told them anything. Anything at all. Crap. I had to fix this. Now.

"You should really talk to her," I said. "She's doing extremely well."

"Oh." He let out a sigh. "She's refusing to come home," he added. "After Geo left, and said their wedding plans had changed, we'd presumed it all fell apart. We'd planned a wonderful union with her and a close family friend. He was willing to take her into his Taharri, but . . . she just took off."

I didn't want to say too much. I didn't want to betray her, or Geo. I thought carefully about how to word it. He was a father, worried. I could see that. "Apologies for not understanding your terms, your rank, or anything here as yet. Trust a stranger when I say . . . *you* need to *talk* to her. Put your differences aside, see her for who she is. You have a very skilled, strong-willed, and beautiful daughter."

His eyes narrowed at me. "You're not telling me something."

"No," I replied, there was no point in me lying to him. "And though I stand before you and you could more than likely just blink and I'd spill the story. You won't."

"Brave, or stupid?" I watched his forehead crease, his emotions in check. He lowered his head. "You are not wrong though."

"I respect Taryn." His eyes flickered with a tiny bit of anger. Wasn't I allowed to use her name? I stumbled. "Y-y-our daughter a lot. I adore Geo and Luca, and I know it is returned by many or I wouldn't be here right now." He glanced to where they'd obviously all disappeared. "I want you to respect your daughter as the strong woman she is. Speak to her, please. As soon as you can."

"You're worrying me," he said.

"I don't mean to," I replied, trying to smile.

He moved away. "Go," he said with a wave of his hand. "I will do as you ask now and comm for her. Tell my brother I will be in as soon as I can."

"Where do I go?" The corridor stretched on for a while, then split.

"Straight ahead, then left. There's an open lounge where they are. You can't miss it."

"Thanks," I said, and I watched him walk away, then dip into a side room.

I walked down the corridor and followed his instructions to the left. Though I wanted to go off and explore on my own, I wasn't sure it would go down so well.

Laughter drew me into the living space ahead and I paused at the doorway to watch for just a moment.

Shuko sat between Portia, and Umenko and Luca had everyone laughing. He noticed me. "Come on in," he said. "Luca was telling us how your first experience in space was."

I stepped inside and went to sit with them.

"My brother?" Shuko asked.

"He'll be along soon," he said. "He's just making a call."

Shuko's face fell. "Taryn?"

Luca's face paled. "I should have known he'd seek you out for that right away. I shouldn't have left you alone."

"Not often I get to tell someone at the Immortal rank what to do, and they listen, right?"

It was, of course, directed at all of them in this room. I didn't want anyone questioning my prowess. Or charm. I was also guessing their actual cultivation levels. No one sniffed at my use of Immortal; in fact, Portia started to laugh. "Oh Luca, I adore him already. If I hadn't already married off my own daughters, they'd be trying to steal him from you."

I swallowed my spit the wrong way and choked. Luca patted my back, while I gathered myself. That made them laugh even more.

At least it diffused the tension in the room at Taryn's name being mentioned.

"I should go to him," Tofa said. She lowered her head to Shuko and waited for him to speak.

"Go," he said, and she then rushed away without looking back.

Shuko paced around the room then, looked from his wife to me.

"Oh dear," Shuko said. "I fear there is bad news, such feelings around here."

Luca and I traded glances. "That's why you met us as fast as you did, for Quintin?" Luca asked.

"Yes," Shuko said. "We've all been very worried."

Portia moved off the couch and poured us all a drink. When she came to me, I took the glass from her with a smile, waiting on Luca to say something else, anything.

Nothing came.

We waited.

And waited.

I drank my fluids slowly, staring out of the window to my left.

Quintin eventually came back into the room. "I've left Tofa talking to her." He moved to a bar on the other side of the room. Poured himself a drink, then downed it in one.

Shuko stood to go to him. "What is it?"

Quintin faced us, his face flushed. "Thank you," he said to me, then announced with a grin, "I'm going to be a grandfather."

Portia and Umenko squealed, then jumped up to run to him, throwing their arms around him in delight.

Shuko managed to get between his wives to hug him, then they all turned to us. "You knew?"

I nodded. Luca stayed pretty stoic.

"Why didn't she say anything?" Shuko asked.

"My guess is, she wanted to tell Geo, and her father first," I said. "That's her right, not for me to take away."

Luca glanced my way. "No disrespect meant," he added for me.

"I'm aware Oto doesn't understand or know much about a different world or culture. None taken. In fact, having someone speak their mind is very refreshing," Quintin said.

Luca relaxed a little, and I asked, "What else did she say?"

Quintin stepped forward, and with only a hand gesture, asked me to stand. I glanced at Luca, who nodded for me to comply. When I did, Quintin once again stood before me, his eyes seeking much more than my mind or body was giving him. "She asked me to prepare you a gift. A very special gift that no one outside our family has *ever* received. Or would be able to use."

Oh crap. I swallowed, "Did she say why?"

Quintin looked across to his brother. "That she almost died, and so did my grandson."

The women both let out a gasp. They were truly in sync with each other and their emotions. Shuko moved to his side, placed a hand on his shoulder. "She is okay, though, right?"

Both men then stared at me. "She is," Quintin carried on, "because of Oto. Because of something he did that most would not have." Then Quintin did something I had never, ever expected. He got down on one knee and then the other, proceeding to bend over and kowtow to me. To *me*.

I knew my face flushed straight away. I didn't know where to look, what to do. "Please," I said. "Don't."

I looked at Shuko, who averted his gaze. Then to Luca, wondering what . . . how? Help?!

"It is his right as a father to show respect where it is deeply deserved," Luca said and dipped his head toward me. "Let him."

I waited for what seemed like a small eternity, then I spoke softly. "Thank you," I said. "Know that if I had to do it again, I would."

Quintin's eyes drifted up to mine then, and he held out a hand. "I'm not so used to being down here. Help an old man out."

"Of course." I bit my lip, reached for his hand, and the chuckle escaped still. "Sorry."

I gave him a little tug to his feet, and he embraced me tightly. Then he turned to Shuko. "I must fire the forge straight away. I have little time to get my gift ready to present to Oto at their wedding."

The women started to squeal once again, bouncing up and down. "You have permission to leave, brother," Shuko said.

I watched as Quintin lowered his head to Shuko, stepped back three times, turned on his heels, and fled.

25

Thursday, May 27th *Afternoon*
Year - 27515

Geo and I spent a lot more than a couple of days with Shuko and his sect. Halara was a wonderful planet, rich, forgiving. Considering how it had made me feel on our arrival, its overwhelming gravity and gathering Azris, I soon got used to the gravity and with schooling off Taryn's family in all aspects of life, I grew with it, so did Ivori.

Shuko took both Geo and I out into the grounds, showed us everything, how it worked, how he governed them all. I was floored. They really were very family oriented and their training for those in the sect, and their families second to none. On the inside, I wished I'd been born here instead of Isala, but then again, I'd never have met Ivori, Alek, Ezra, Geo, and Luca.

Quintin did come for me just the once. I felt a little odd going off and spending time with him, but he wanted to check my form, build, and gracefully taught me a lot more about the Kreeshon. He was patient and tentative with everything he asked and showed me. I could see where

Taryn got her skill and style from. He also took his sword creation to the extreme, and he explained why with every detail.

"I haven't created a sword like this since I made my first son's," he said, sighed, then added, "Adopted sons."

"Is he here?" I asked. "I'd like to meet him. See the blade?"

"No." I saw a little pain in his eyes then. "He's on a very important mission for the sect at the moment."

"Oh," I replied. "That's a shame. I'd have liked to see him. Taryn spoke very highly of him."

He raised an eyebrow at me, but didn't say anything else.

Their families were really complicated and big. He had an adopted son, and probably many more to the different women in his life. That kind of math threw me, along with all the possibilities.

I shook those thoughts off.

One woman was enough for me, and right now I missed her. Guilt did flood through me about leaving them all. I just had to. I needed all of this.

I stood and watched Quintin for a while, then in the end he chased me away. Didn't want me to see too much. He also said this would take till the wedding to be perfect. That was August . . . it seemed excessive to take so long to create something. But I didn't question him.

I wandered away feeling extremely happy, impressed with this whole planet, the way things ran, the way they looked out for each other. Shuko had said I would have needed to go to one of the lower training schools out closer to the cities. This here was way above my understanding. He was right. Most of the students were ranks above me, specializing in their training for a specific element. I toured them all, trying to see and pick up tips from them. Yes, I wanted to be here; no, I was not ready for it. Even some of their basics I fumbled, patient though they were.

Luca found me staring out into the distant fields of practicing students. "Are we good to head back now?"

I glanced at him. "You were waiting for me, weren't you?"

"I need you to be ready, yes."

"I'm ready," I said. "The deadline for the next race is looming. I need some practice in before we're there."

"And facing the others?"

"I can deal with it. I'll talk to them."

"Honestly?"

I looked back out at the students. "Yes," I said. "Honestly, and with heart. I need them to understand why I needed this. Why Ivori did."

"Then let us say our goodbyes and leave, even if you don't really want to."

"This place, this world, is something else." I scanned the horizon. I'd gotten so used to the Azris, the feel of it. "I feel at home, even if I'm not."

"I can see that. You're not ready, though. Not for this level of politics and skill. Not just yet. You've seen the good side to this planet; just like most others, there's a very bad side too."

"I know," I said. "I've spoken with the other wives quite often and they were much more willing to talk about their families, their sons."

That was a truth he didn't expect. Taryn's brother and some of his recent missions had been a topic they shouldn't have told me, but they had. I wondered why, till Luca explained it. It had been extremely eye opening for the things I might be dealing with out here. "Thank you for bringing me out here, though. As much as it scared the shit out of Ivori, and you know where we're heading, it was needed."

Shuko's wives—or their many daughters—didn't want me to go. Neither did Tofa. It was tough to say goodbye, but I knew I'd see them again and not too far off.

"Give this to Taryn for me for when you see her." Tofa handed me a rolled bag, and I promised her I would. Shuko and Quintin made sure to see us both off and, though Shuko wasn't sure he'd made it to the wedding, he said he would try. That was something from a busy man's perspective.

Luca made sure Tant was fully ready to get fly into space one last time before we boarded and, with an escort, were once again back out into the darkness of space. This time I was much more prepared for it, and the jump back to Isala.

It still took far too long to get home. My nerves frayed.

"I have Alek wishing to speak with you," Ivori said over comms as we approached the planet. "If you want to, of course."

"I'll take it. I'll come down." I turned to Luca. "Will be back in a bit." Meaning I'd have just that bit more privacy away from the both of them here.

"Take your time," Luca said, and I made my way down to sit inside Ivori.

I sat there for a little while thinking about how I'd talk to him, what I'd say. I wanted to see him. Even though he'd given me permission to know they'd still tried to contract me to talk to me. Ezra . . . no . . . fuck. I couldn't do this.

I flexed my fingers over the wheel, imagined myself on a track, then tapped the comms and Ivori put his image on the screen for me.

"Hey," he said.

I met his eyes with mine. "Hey."

Awkward silence followed.

"I'm glad you're coming home," he finally whispered. "I missed you. Ezra missed you too. We all have."

"I missed you all too," I said. It wasn't a lie. I really had.

"Good," he said with a genuine smile. "It means you want to come home."

"I do," I said.

"There're some things I need to warn you about," he said. His voice low, warning.

My stomach did a small flip. "What is it?"

"Bren's missing," he said. "The council have had investigators around. They've been looking everywhere."

"Nothing?"

Alek shook his head. "Not as yet."

"Everyone else okay?"

He hesitated at first, his eyes wandering around. "There's something else."

"Tell me," I said, expecting well anything.

"Your parents they showed up while you were away."

"What?"

"They got onto Isla using bum credentials, managed to get into the city. They approached us this week, as they'd not seen you anywhere."

"What did you say?"

"That you didn't want to see them, of course."

"They're not my parents," I said.

"I know. They want to talk to you about your bloodlines. They said there was something important, that your life was at risk without them to help you with something. They spouted all kinda of things. I couldn't follow, but Doctor Styx is worried."

I laughed, but if Doctor Styx was worried? "Oh, I'm sure they want back in my life. They want to know what triggered my Azris abilities, so they can work it out and do it again on some other experiment. No, no way."

"They know about the origin nites," he said.

"Wait, what? How?"

"I'm not so sure. But they do, and they know about the little robot."

My mind whirred, linking them to the museum, the building. Did they know Ivori was in there? Did they . . . everything spun, and I had to sit back.

"Oto, we'll talk more. Ezra doesn't know all this as yet. I wanted to tell you first, see what you wanted to do. Pete wanted to take them out. I wouldn't let him, not till we spoke to you, cleared things."

I swallowed a breath, sucked in another. "Don't do anything yet. We'll be there soon enough. Thank you."

"Just looking out for my brother," he said.

It was the almost casual mention of our friendship, our bond, that broke me. "I didn't think I'd be gone so long," I said. "I had to do it."

Alek put his palm to the screen. "I tried everything to help you, you knew that. I couldn't. I wasn't able to. I'm glad you went."

"You did more than anyone ever could. You listened to me. They just wanted to fix me. I just couldn't be fixed, not right then."

He nodded, his eyes brimmed with emotion, though. "Get here so I can hug you before my sister carts you off."

"That bad?" I cringed, feeling awkward.

"She was at first, just as upset as all of us for not being able to help, to help you or Ivori through this."

"It wasn't you, none of you. This was all me. I needed and had to break through my own barriers, to learn more about me, about Ivori."

"She opened up to you properly?"

"I'm right here," she said.

"I know, but I needed to ask." Alek blushed.

"Yes," I said, and ran my hands over the steering wheel. "We understand each other a lot more. We can *do* a lot more, together."

"Good. We got some shit to do when you're back. Seriously. Geo's been going full on with us training. I'm exhausted. Having you to pick on will give me a break."

Ivori laughed, and then so did I. "I actually think he'd like that," she said.

"Yes," I admitted. "I would."

Alek's eyes flickered off screen. "She's outside, waiting to speak with you. Can I send her in?"

I nodded, though I wanted to see her in person more than over comms like this.

Alek got up, moved away from the screen. Then I saw Ezra's face appear. She looked thinner, but she smiled at me and put her hand to the screen. I reciprocated.

"I love you," she said. "But please to all the gods out there, promise me you'll never do this again without talking to me too. I couldn't take it."

"I love you," I said, and honestly added, "I can't promise you that, though."

It hurt to see pain cross her face, her eyes misting. She closed them, and the nature of her lids closing forced the tears out.

"I'll talk to you more when I'm home, I promise you that. You'll understand why I had to, why I was so broken, and how I needed this."

"O-okay," she stuttered. "I'll try to listen. I can promise you that, too."

I ran a finger down her cheek, wishing I could chase the tears away. I never wanted to hurt her or Alek. But I had. I could see it.

"You're nearly here," she said. "I'll be waiting. We'll talk more then." She cut the comms.

"I'm sorry," Ivori said.

"It's not your fault," I replied.

"I couldn't talk to you about all the things that made me who I was. That is my fault. I love Ezra, and Alek too, I . . . will you be okay?"

"We'll be okay," I said and wiped tears from my eyes. "It's not like she'd ever break up with us, right?"

Ivori didn't answer me, because she didn't know. I didn't really know.

That thought alone, that my relationship with the one person I was meant for could be over before it really began, stung. I'd do anything to fix it. To take back the not talking. I only hoped I could. That we'd get through this and come out stronger.

The bay doors dropped open, and I backed Ivori out onto the track.

There were more than a few people waiting for us. I saw Geo and Luca exchange hugs and then walk off to the office. He wasn't sticking around to see me? Ouch.

I took Ivori straight into the garage and slipped her onto the ramp. Tatsuno nodded at me. "Glad you're back. Let me run this diagnostic and I'll let you know what, if anything, we need to do before you get on the track with her tomorrow."

"Thanks," I said.

Alek came straight to me and didn't hesitate to throw his arms around me. I squeezed him tight. "Hey, man," I said.

"You're bigger," he said, pulling back, then squeezing my biceps.

"Yes," I said. "A lot has changed."

"So I can see," Tatsuno said, and when we both looked over, he raised an eyebrow.

"Long, long story," I said.

"You best go to her." Alek slung a finger over his shoulder.

"Thanks, we'll talk soon."

I moved out to the back of the garage. Ezra leaned against the wall. I stopped tentatively in front of her, reached out to run a finger down her arm, not letting my eyes leave hers.

"You're an asshole," she said, and tears erupted from her eyes once more. "You know that."

"I know." I nodded, lowered my eyes. "I know I am."

"I want to hate you," she said. "I want to leave you so you understand what it's like to be left behind." Her breaths came out ragged, hurting. "I can't."

I looked up just in time to catch her as she threw herself into my arms. I wrapped her up tightly, nuzzled into her neck, and kissed her soft, scented skin. Then I put my lips to hers and kissed her deeply.

A cough behind us made me turn. Taryn stood, her rather rounded stomach totally on show now. Though she no longer wore the short skirts or high-heeled boots, she still wore very pretty long, flowing silk dresses and flat heels. I understood why because Ezra had explained how wobbly she'd felt and how she thought people would see her flaunting her rounded figure.

Ezra held onto me. "Everyone wants a piece of you, it seems."

I kissed her, yet didn't let go myself, holding her against my side as I faced Taryn.

"What did you think of my father?" she asked.

"You look like him, and your mother something wicked." I smiled. "They're crazy powerful. Thought I was a bit of a goner at one point."

"They're ecstatic about the baby," she said. "The wedding to Geo still, not so much."

"Still?"

"Different beliefs," she said. "It might take them a long time to come to terms with the fact that Geo just wants me, won't ever have any other wives to help with my household. So it's all on me."

When Taryn flinched and held her stomach, Ezra soon left my side to go to her. "You shouldn't be up and about."

Taryn waved her off. "I have enough people fussing over me. Please don't."

Ezra looked up at me. "There's been several complications with the baby, and she doesn't enjoy listening to anyone."

"Let's head to the offices. Seems Geo and Luca hid away from everyone else. I think I had best go see him, too."

Taryn turned and then with me at her side, we both stepped out the garages back across the track.

"Is he angry too?" I asked her as she slowly walked beside me.

"Everyone was at some points. But they've had some time for Alek to explain, and to understand why. When they finally tracked you, knowing you were at least safe helped them a lot."

"Alek tracked me from the get go, didn't he, even if I asked him not to?"

"Wasn't hard," Taryn said. "I believe Ivori stored all the messages they sent to you. Maybe you'll read them sometime."

"Damn," I said. "I will."

"Even if it hurts," Taryn said. "Read them."

"I will, I promise."

"All any of us can do is move forward," Taryn said.

She paused for a moment, while she rearranged herself a little. "I am thankful you told my father to call me. I wasn't sure I would have ever gotten up the courage to do so."

"He could have just forced me to tell him," I admitted. "I was way out of my depth on your home world."

"Yes," she said. "Just be glad my brother wasn't there."

"Kei?" I asked, recalling all the conversations about him. "Yeah, I heard a lot about him off your mothers. He's someone I really want to meet."

"You want to meet him? He wouldn't have hesitated in dragging any information out of you, kicking and screaming."

"I wouldn't have blamed him," I replied, though my heart beat faster at the thought. "I would have tried to resist."

Taryn laughed. "Oto, you are so fresh. I'm sure our families' ladies were totally besotted with you."

I felt the heat flush up my neck. "Yeah," I said. "About that . . ."

"I won't tell Ezra anything, but I'm sure she knows how attractive your traits are. She's the one who snared you, after all."

"She did that," I said with a grin.

I let Taryn take the stairs at her own pace. She didn't knock, just walked on in. I followed.

Geo moved to help her sit, fussing around like the expectant father I knew he was.

Then he looked at me. "Back outside," he said, pointing to the door, anger flared in his eyes.

I didn't hesitate and went back downstairs. Out in the lot, I don't know what I expected from him.

"Defense," he said taking off his jacket and throwing it to the floor. Crap. I was in trouble; he never treated his clothes like that. His eyes narrowed at me. When he dropped his stance and brought out his sword, I knew he wasn't kidding.

Geo struck out fast, yet I saw it and sidestepped. He didn't let up. With every strike he attempted, I parried perfectly. He swung around and tried a different tactic. Again and again.

I kept up with every single one.

He was intent on this punishment. That fact was pretty clear. Anger boiled inside him, and his Fire responded to it in every way possible. My energy levels were dropping, but not as fast as his.

I heard Luca and the others on the outskirts of my range. Even caught Taryn shouting at him to stop. But he didn't.

I understood.

I'd let them all down. I'd hurt him.

I had to take this.

So take it I did.

We fought for hours.

Sweat poured off me. With each passing wave of his attacks, he tried new ways to get inside my lines. I evaded them all.

Only when his legs wobbled, and I could see his energy was almost fatally low, did I pull back. "Stop," I said to him.

I held fast when he came at me this time, his sword aimed clearly at my throat.

Ezra let out a cry, but I held my position. Held his eyes with mine.

Geo stopped millimeters from slicing me in two. He lowered his sword and stepped back, panting. "What rank?" he asked.

I lowered my head. "King 1."

"Impossible." He shook his head. "Show me."

It was not just a question.

I held his eyes with mine. "Really?"

His eyes flickered just a little. He was worried.

"Please, Oto."

I smiled and brought up my stats, then sent them to him. At least some of it.

Name = Oto Benes
ID Number = 4188927
Age = 23
Species = Anodite
Sex = Male
Alignment = Chaotic
Bloodline = Royal Seven
Health = 99%
Cultivation Level - King 1
Active Meridians = 12/12
Nanites = **1.5 Million**
Artefacts = 2
Chosen Specialist = Racer
First Chosen Affinity = Water
Second Chosen Affinity = Fire

Statistic = Body + Ivori + Cultivation
Strength = 51/**189.72**
Dexterity = 56/**209.44**
Constitution = 49/**183.26**
Int/Wis/Spirit = 70

Affinities - Rank

Water - **Indigo**
Fire - **Blue**
Earth - **Green**
Air - Green
Light - **Green**
Darkness - **Blue**
Spirit - **Blue**

Droll's Leg Pouch – three refillable containers hold the power of life or death. One use per origin user.

Ring of Light - A gift from Ezra
Adapted, so you may use it as you wish.
Boosts Azris circulation and usage, + 30 to all stats
Uses = 5

"Halara did you wonders." Geo said.

He wasn't kidding. "It's rich with Azris and schooling." I let my sheet drop.

"Good, you needed it." Geo smiled then. "Sinclairs?"

"Also amazing teachers," I said with a slight wince, lowering my head.

"Rather brave of them taking you in. I expect they got a few secrets from you, too."

I didn't say anything else; he knew it, so did I.

"I'm glad you're back." He held his hand out for me. "I missed you too."

"I'm glad to be back," I said and took his hand in mine. "As nice as it was, as powerful as they all are, it showed me even more what I need to do to get to where I want—need—to be."

"You've done fantastic." He pulled me into a hug, and I was sure he got a sniff of me as I did him. He pushed me back. "Are you ready to get back on the track?"

"I'm used to a lot more than what they can give me," I said with a frown and a glance to our garages.

"I know," he said. "Luca and I have been discussing it. He's bringing Tant in for some extra and I'll get Vrolst on board as well."

"You want me to race against you?"

"What?" he said. His laugh was contagious. "Not scared, are you?"

I wanted to laugh, instead I grinned and looked ahead to the crowd of our friends who had gathered. Deep pride of how far I'd come filled me. I'd grown so much.

"I might have been at one point," I admitted. "Now? No way. Bring it."

26

Sunday, June 6th *Lunch*
Year - 27515

Luca had cleared the track of everyone not on our specific teams. That meant there were only a handful of us left. The next few words were going to be important it seemed.

"We've less than a week," Luca said. "I called in a few favors from Sinclairs. We needed an extra few to get Alek on the move. They'll be in for first practice in the next day or so."

"Bikes?" Alek asked curiously.

"A couple of them you know already. Bessie and Eula."

"They're coming here?" His eyes beamed.

"You've got a lot to prove out there, too. Some extra time with them would be good," Luca said at his side.

"Go home, rest, enjoy the night, be back here for first light," Geo said. "Got it?"

I checked Alek and Tatsuno. They both nodded, so of course I did. I checked Ivori before we left, and we walked home. Well, at least to what we called home. It was an apartment block in a rich area of our city. It didn't feel like home to me. The people who were with me, they were home. My guards followed behind us. Pete stayed at the track for now, and there were four other guards I'd noted at different sections on our way. It felt a little weird.

Ezra ordered takeaway food, and we sat talking. Well, mostly I was the one doing the talking. I had a lot to catch them up on. That meant every detail. Sinclairs to the Sawa Sect. None of them knew anything about other cultures or ways of life either, and Sawa's sect schools had them intrigued.

"It sounds so very organized compared to us here."

"Bit of a free-for-all at the bottom," Alek said.

When Tatsuno and Alek finally took off to bed, I sat feeling like the barrier which kinda protected me was gone. Ezra stared at the floor and looked as lost as I was. I took her hand in mine, gently pulled her up.

"I don't have to sleep with you," I said. "I can take the spare room."

The fact she didn't answer right away had my stomach flip. She reached for my shirt, wrapped her hand in it and tugged me to her. "No way," she said. "If you don't sleep with me, make love with me tonight, then you can stay in that room. Permanently."

Her voice cracked, even though she'd meant business. I leaned in and kissed her, then led her to the bedroom.

Saturday, June 12th *Lunch*
Year - 27515

I stood with Alek, leaning on Ivori's hood as the track doors opened.

Tru is here, Ren said.

Nerves filled me as a huge double truck dipped in, and then slowly made its way down to us with Hara and Tatsuno guiding it. The truck's entourage pulled in behind it. Several cars, bikes, and even a med van.

The passenger door swung open and Eula jumped down, stepping toward us. "Am I sorry for seeing you," she said, a hand outstretched. "But I am glad you called us."

I took her hand and shook. "Thanks for coming. We really need you." I looked around to the many people she'd brought with her. "All of you."

She dipped her head at Alek. "Ren doing okay?" she asked.

"Absolutely, really looking forward to seeing what you can help with."

"Don't you be worrying." Bessie joined Eula's side. "There's a good few things we can teach you boys, right, Oto?"

I nodded, thinking back to the time I spent with Marik and Apollos. "I can't wait," I said. "We're all willing to learn. Show us everything you can."

Show us they did. Alek and Ren raced with the others, every day. We stayed in the garage, watching, learning. Seeing how they timed things, what lines they took and why. What differences harder brakes, slower corners would make, firing Azris when no one expected it. What was left of the week just blew past. Bessie and Eula at our track brought more than enough crazy.

I loved all of it. So did the teams. They were energetic, charismatic, and skilled. What shocked me a little was that Bessie had her own with her. I almost expected her to not have an Icarian. The Canillion run was two man, no matter what. Now at least I knew where she got the biker sense from. Owning her own.

Motorcycle racing was something else entirely. Watching them with Alek all morning while in between bouts of ass-kicking off Geo, Pete, and the guards was great fun.

Today, though, once again with very little sleep, I faced one hell of an important moment in my life, in *our* lives: Vrance City.

Of course, each track was different. These were nothing like our practice track. Nothing at all. Vrance's circuit length was just under six kilometers, and we were to complete fifty-four laps. 324 kilometers.

These weren't just laps to figure out where we were in the race. This was a test of everything. The Icarian, the driver, and their Azris use, but also the team behind them. Without every one of us working together to nail this, we were out, just like we had been in Okburg.

Don't think about the failures, Ivori said. *Focus on there here and now. These are complicated races, but they're nothing we can't do.*

What's the record here? I asked her.

One hour, eighteen minutes, ninety-two seconds.

We'd traveled in Tant this time. There was no messing around, no trains, no trucks. Straight out into the planet's atmosphere and to where we needed to be within hours. I wished for a moment that we had access to Tant all the time, but then also knew that Amalia and Camran needed him and Luca out on Copter.

"You've studied as much as you can," Ezra whispered in my ear. I opened the garage doors, eyed Ivori sitting, waiting. "You're ready for this."

"I know," I said, giving her hand a squeeze. "I couldn't do any more than I have. We've put everything into this now. Two to go, that's all. If I lose this at all, if I don't pull this out of the bag. We're not going any further, at least not this year."

"Fastest timing, and the win," Geo prompted as we stepped inside.

"We have the speed," I said. I reached out to let Ivori take my Azris.

"Perfectly charged," she said.

"I'm a little more than that," I said.

"Yes, you are," she replied. "No matter what happens, these last six months—I'm so very proud of you."

That meant the most to me.

"They'll call in thirty," Tatsuno said.

Hara nodded. "Zeroes are out now. They'll be clear any minute."

"All green here," Itoh said.

I moved to the lockers and quickly slipped into my suit.

Nice. Heatproof—hopefully anything-proof.

My mind flooded of images back in Brotok. Berni's car, his death. Some of the races across Isala's tracks got really hairy; some of the competitors were not against using other means to try and knock you out. That meant, if they wielded any kind of affinity, they would come after you with a-vengeance. Deadly vengeance.

"Know the lineup?" Alek asked, leaning down to mouth it through the glass.

"Not going to be much different from Sidmont, right?"

He shook his head. "Last minute change." He tapped the window, pointing to my dash.

The names and positions flashed up.

There it was.

Zac Memmot had been in pole position for a few races now, clearly the guy to beat. This time, though, he was followed with Vral Lapplant. How the hell had he got in second? Ahead of Andi?

I didn't need to know the how. I knew it was coming. Somehow, by some god-only-knew means, they'd managed to get back on this track, and I had no doubt he was gunning for me.

"Get me anything else you can on Vral. We've been concentrating too much on Drei. I need to know what his damn brother is capable of."

"On it," Tatsuno said. "Will get you anything I can as soon as I can."

The fifteen minutes call went out. The team made all their last minute checks and triple checks again, and then I made my way out of the garage to the track and to the lineup.

This was it.

Andi's bright orange monstrosity sat slightly ahead of me, and I waited till the track bearer's check.

I felt like giving them all a piece of my mind. I usually found it semi-relaxing, watching what they were doing. How they were making sure we really were in the best condition. Today it just annoyed me. I wanted to chase them and just get out of there.

Time to warm up, then fifty-two laps to get us through this race; that's all we had. I had no chances to miss. I had to take every single one as it presented itself, and I would.

My fingers flexed on the steering, and I waited for the lights to change.

Then I hit the gas.

It was easy to see right away as sparks shot out from Andi's car that something was wrong. I sidelined her, swinging hard left to get up and around on the inside.

I passed, seeing the frustration on his face. She was out no doubt about that this was mechanical.

I wouldn't have been able to pass Andi on the warmup. She knew it; I knew it.

Sabotage?

I let my Azris seep out in Ivori's chassis, gently warming her components and mechanics all on instinct.

"Steady," Tatsuno said over the comms. "Don't let them know you've that extra energy to spare."

I eased back. "Good point. Thanks."

"We got you, you know that."

I did.

The first bends came up, and we swept around them, easing in and out, warming the tires the right way. The slow way.

They needed it; I needed it. I might well need that energy at the end of this race.

Hitting the straights at decent speeds, but keeping it under par was hard. I felt Ivori ready to let loose. She wanted this so badly.

"Racing with Sinclairs Elite spoiled us. Then Vrolst, and Tant . . ."

"It's been an amazing couple of months," she said. "Hard, but amazing."

I turned into a deadly sharp hairpin bend, catching the curb a little on the way out, even at this speed.

Tires are okay, Ivori said. *Don't worry.*

I kinda needed to worry a little, though.

The others had picked up a lot of speed. Here I was just bumbling around, making sure I fit everything. I tested everything. My plan seeded into my mind. I hung back a little more, knowing full well they were already warm and probably into their second lap. When I hit the start-up line this time, I put a lot more gas into it. The track was basically my own. There was no one to curb the speeds I wanted to take the corners at, no one behind me pushing me on.

Then just as my dash turned all green, and we were in top shape, did I see the last bend and the straight, just giving it enough Azris to enjoy it, then back off to hit the line in time so the others wouldn't be calling it for a false start.

"Andi's been really slow at the first couple of starts," Alek said. "As much as I want you to nail this, watch her, though she's sneaky as fuck. If she can run you off the track for trying to overtake, she will."

"Got it," I said.

The lights counted us in.

Two. Four. Six.

"I remember you telling me a story not long ago about that perfect start," I said, Watching those ticking lights. "I've never done it . . ." My hands were ready, my mind in full-on slow motion.

Eight.

When that last light flicked, I hit the gas at the right moment. "Until today," I said.

Ten.

Go!

I could hear the whoop-whoops of the team in the background. But Alek hadn't been kidding about Andi and her start. She sucked. I flicked up through the gears, settled into eight, and then I tried to get around her on the outside, but she moved out, trying to push me off the track and into the wall.

272 kilometers per hour.

The map in front of me said I could take the bends ahead at 290. I pushed harder.

I let my Azris burn, and a lot. Ivori shot forward, forcing me back in the seat.

As we drew in closer to those first important bends, Andi's Azris sparked.

"Oh, no, you fucking don't." With one hand off the wheel as we entered the first bend, I pulled all the energy I could and threw a shield up at the side. Andi's Air attack would have pushed us to collide with the wall if I hadn't. However, my shield and her attack pushed her out instead. The car hit the curb, bounced out and behind me, spinning to hit the wall instead.

The car shattered pieces all over, and flames erupted. Drones sped out above me, and I tried not to watch. Even after the last crash she'd not given up, now though with this one? I almost hoped she would. Would save us trying to keep beating her.

Lights flashed the track over.

All stop.

I hit the brakes, bringing us down as fast as possible.

"Focus ahead," Ivori said. "We're okay. Get going once again, and the next couple of bends coming up, nice and steady."

Waiting while the drones and the track was cleared seemed to take forever and yet it was less than a few minutes.

I circulated some of my Azris through the systems, keeping our tires, gears, and brakes at optimal temperatures.

When the lights changed, and we could hit for gas once more, I nailed that Zero Light.

Alek's voice came through to me. "You star! No one else hit it! Go. Go!"

His excitement thrilled me.

The next few bends were good. I hit the first just at the right speed, then dropped down to three to flick out the back end. Perfect into another shorter straight, ramping our speeds up to 180, then down again into fifth gear, around the bend and down to three for the next sweeping one.

I cranked up again to seven and followed the bends around, slight curve and into eight and then all the way up and over 310 kilometers per hour.

I was super glad we'd had that practice and finally hit some decent top speeds off any track. This didn't quite seem as fast now either, having practiced with the Elite.

I settled in at this speed and focused enough to let several laps pass me by. Getting used to every turn, bump, and condition in the road.

With a little luck, we'd be soon coming up on our next target. Don. His car was fast. I'd seen him hitting bends way faster than I'd have liked back in Vrance City, but now, after racing the elite, Geo, and Luca, this was child's play.

They don't have a clue how hard we've pushed it, I said to her. *Do they?*

No, and that's a good thing. You've got him on the next sweeping curve, just nice and steady.

It wasn't quite as nice and steady as she'd have liked when he laid down an ice patch for us to hit up ahead. I saw it and reacted, sparking my Azris and heat. I pushed everything I could into our tires, till I could almost feel the flames off of them.

"They'll pop!" Alek shouted through to me.

"We don't have a choice," I said. Our tires hit that ice patch. I sucked in a breath as I turned the wheel, hoping to any god around this would work.

We didn't skid. Instead, the fire melted the ice, and with another pull on my Azris, I sucked it away from under us before we had time to aqua plane instead.

The exploding wall of water behind me would have stopped anyone else. They wouldn't have been able to see. Let alone get through it.

We, however, passed Don like he'd stopped, and I waved at him.

Once we had a clear line again, I floored it. Lap eighteen. So many more to go. I had to settle back in again for some more hard earned grinding.

Round and around we went.

Forty minutes in.

Lap thirty-seven was coming up, and the others were at least a few seconds ahead now. I had to catch them up and take this from them.

We've got this, Ivori said. *They're already panicking ahead of you. Their team chatter is spreading through their ranks, and they're worried. You took out two of the top drivers.*

On the inside, I had hope. But I was coming up not only against Vral, but the leader of the last couple of races. Zac. I needed some kinda small miracle to pass him.

They were quite some ways ahead. Maybe half a kilometer.

Lap forty-three. We were almost on the next lap again before I saw them, and they were hooking it.

"They're not wasting any time at all," I said. "What speeds have they been clocking?" I asked the team.

"Averaging 275," came the reply.

"Us?"

"So far, 250."

I put the peddle to the floor. We needed at least 280 average to catch them and then be able to do anything about it.

We needed to settle in and bide our time. I knew where and how I had to do it. I just wasn't a hundred percent ready for it. Not yet.

I needed it to be before the last laps, or they could well have got the time to counter us.

Forty-nine.

Fifty.

On the next straight out, I put my foot down harder, allowing Azris to flow burst enough to catch them up.

I hit 340 before I backed off. Shit, shit.

I couldn't do anything. It was too close.

"There's time," Alek said through comms. But I didn't think so. I was fast running out of it.

"We've got rain coming in," Tatsuno said.

"Real rain, or their rain?"

I was right behind Val now. This was going to be good. He was so rubbish with his brakes. The more I watched him, the easier I could see that.

Getting closer to how I wanted to overtake him, he made his play for the lead, and I had to back off. I hadn't been thinking about how he was. He wanted the win just as much as I did. As the two of them danced around the next bend before me, Vral passed Zac on the inside line. But it was close, too close.

"Oh shit, oh shit!" Hara's voice said.

"They're gonna blow it!"

"Watch out!"

Vral's tires hit the track lines, spraying dust into the air.

Their speed and lines dropped all over the place. Heading into the next bend, they both were out. I held my line perfectly, dropped into gear, and held the fuck on tight.

Not yet, not yet!

I hit the gas as they drifted wide, then I downshifted and powered on past the both of them and out into the straight.

Now! Ivori screamed at me.

She tapped me when she needed it. This was all her.

That burst took us out well ahead and into the lead, but it didn't mean we were clear by any means.

Rain spattered on the windshield, and I could see it on the track ahead. It would make things a little different on the last few laps.

Vral might not be able to make another pass at Zac, but he sure as hell was gunning for me and stuck right up my rear end.

27

Saturday, June 12th *Evening*
Year - 27514

"Hold your lines," Alek said. "You've got this. He hasn't got the power to get him out of any bends ahead of you."

"Vral's also baiting him." Hara said. "They're pissed at each other for letting you get past."

The next lap told me that, between the two of them, they were still fighting it out.

"What points does Vral need to get his team up the board?"

I waited as we shot out the next corner and I powered up.

"Second," Hara said.

It made sense; Vral wasn't letting up. I was now a couple of seconds ahead of them again. Clear.

Fifty-four.

"You need to hit top speeds on all bends," Alek said. "These two ain't letting it go."

I could see it, and on every bend, it was closer and closer. If they got to me, baited me to panic anymore, I'd miss a line, even if slightly. One of them would get that upper hand.

Zac still had the spot behind me, and pushed in every corner trying to get around.

I'd never been in the lead before; this pressure was real.

Focus, in and out, downshift and back up. Easy on the lines, steady energy on the out.

"Keep a check on that speed!" Hara said.

I glanced as we approached the second to last straight, almost home.

344 approaching. I had to quick downshift, hitting the next bends at three hundred, down to 290, then 280. Still over.

We powered through back up to 348.

All I heard through comms then was silence. Nothing what so ever came through. We hit the speed trap, and I saw numbers flying past me, but didn't register them. Down once again to 260, 250 and into the sweep.

If Zac was going to go for it, he had one chance now.

Down into third gear, and sharp left, then right, change up into fourth. He couldn't do it. But Vral did manage to get past him. Into the last bend and I could only do what I had trained for, into fifth, then hit for Azris.

Ivori took the last I had, shooting us forward and up into more than a couple of seconds lead.

Vral and Zac tried to follow, but they'd used up more than they thought.

We'd done it. We flew over that finish line in first.

Fucking first!

The screen flashed red.

Oops, Ivori said. Her engine pop-popped and then all power went.

We still had so much momentum we chugged off the track. Now in the garage and up on the ramp, Tatsuno, Jin, and Itoh all stood shaking their heads.

I stared at the 3D image and her red flashing parts before me.

Eight weeks again to sort it out, rebuild if we had to.

The win would cover the parts, I knew it. But the time . . . time off the track and practicing.

Shit.

"She'll be okay," Alek said, bumping against me.

"I trust the team," I said.

"Better." He grinned. Then he threw his arm around me. "Pull your head out your backside, did you freaking see that! You nailed those last few laps . . . fucking awesome!"

Ezra whirred in with Geo, Luca, and Taryn.

I couldn't escape their excitement then. Their joy.

Infectious laughter, handshakes, and hugs were thrown around. Geo put the race on the big screen, and we all watched it.

"Vral really threw Zac off," I said. "He's usually confident and easy with his brakes; they were all over the place today."

"Gave you that opportunity to pass the two of them," Geo said. "Which was expertly done."

"Thanks to all the extra practice, and training both sides of the tracks."

"We've a car to take us out to celebrate in the public eye later, but for now, let's get Ivori patched up. There's some parts moving down from one of Vrance's top garages here. She'll be mobile to get to Tant."

"You push that steak around your plate anymore, the chef will think it's terrible."

I glanced up into Taryn's eyes, looked to Ezra, stabbed the piece of steak, and chewed. It really wasn't terrible. Far from it. My mind was just everywhere else but here.

Ezra leaned into me. "Give yourself a little bit of a break—you did amazing today."

I tried to smile at her. "You're leaving when we get back, right?"

Under the table, she took my hand in hers. "Yeah, exams early on Friday. I want to make sure I've got some more study time in there before."

I nodded, slipping my arm around her and eating some more. "Okay,

I've no doubt we'll be leaving early from here. This is all for show, right?"

"Yeah, can't just rush off. No matter how much you don't want to be in the spotlight, you earned it today."

I glanced around the room to see everyone was watching me, talking about me.

"I wanted it," I said. "I do want it, but all of this is a little more than I can cope with, still."

"That's why we're here," Alek said. When someone made their way to come up toward us, he headed them off.

It was good to have him and all of them on my side. It meant my exposure to any of the excitable groupies or press were minimal.

The commotion at the other side of the room, though, I couldn't ignore that.

All eyes trailed that way, and I saw Pete and our guards facing off against a couple. No, not just any couple. My parents. Donoto and Alice Benes.

My fork clattered to the plate, and I pushed my chair back. "Oto, what is it?" Geo asked.

Ezra scrambled to be at my side as I was about to bolt, but Luca stood in front of me.

"No," he said. "You knew they'd show up at some point."

"They?" Ezra looked back to the standoff.

"My parents," I said, watching them as they both tried to get my attention and sneak out around from two of the best guards on this planet.

There were a few people snapping photographs and filming all of this. My mind whirred.

"This is just what they wanted," Luca said. "Right here, right now, in front of everyone."

I shoved my chair under the table. Then strode toward them, Ezra at my heels.

Pete and our guards stepped aside.

"Oto." Alice. She was much older, gray hairs threaded through a braid to the side of her uniform, a uniform I didn't know. "We've been trying to reach you."

"I know," I replied curtly, and could do nothing but stare. Now was not the time to be bringing this into the front of everyone's minds.

"We need to talk, son," Donoto said and that was when Ezra lost it.

"Son. Son?! You have no right to call him that!" I was flabbergasted by her outburst. I mean, we'd talked a little of my childhood, but very little. Alek was the one who grabbed onto her, pulling her back. I nodded my thanks at him while she still carried on as he dragged her away. "He is nothing to you. You hear me? Nothing. You left him! You left him with no one. No mother, or father. You don't deserve that title at all!"

I blew out a breath. "This isn't the time or the place for this at all."

"We had no choice," Alice said. "We tried everything else. We were ignored."

"Rightly so," Geo said and stepped to my side. With both brothers either side of me, I felt not only comfort and presence and aura already flaring enough that they both flinched, but so did everyone else in the room.

"Please, let us talk to you in private." Donoto looked to Luca, who just held his gaze.

My mother held mine, but I didn't want to give in. I didn't want to listen to anything they said. Anything at all.

Luca's essence around me changed. Instead of the fire burning inside, the anger, resentment I felt, calm washed over me. I glanced at him, and he dipped his head to me. "This is your call, Oto. What do you really want to do?"

I found I struggled with the words I wanted, with everything.

Geo leaned in a little closer. "We've got your back, you know this."

I did, behind me, around me, although there were many other faces, my team were here for me.

"We'll see you at the track tomorrow," I said, then I turned and walked away. I'd had enough here; this night was over.

Outside, Ezra came to me with Alek and Tatsuno. "I'm sorry," she said. "I shouldn't have."

I pulled her into my side, "You said what I was thinking. For that, I'm grateful."

"Gave the press a good story for tomorrow's news," Alek added.

"Screw them, they know nothing."

"They'll have the full story by the time we're on our way home."

Geo and Luca stepped out the back of the club. "Ready to leave, then?" Geo asked.

I just shrugged, my heart and soul heavy. "If we can stay on the shuttle till we can leave, I'm okay with that."

"I've cleared it. They've swapped us to a slightly different model. We've some bunks to sleep in for the night, and even into the trip tomorrow morning."

Sleep, however, wouldn't come to me. Wouldn't be anything tonight. Ezra tried her best to keep me company, but when she eventually fell asleep, I slipped out. No one else was awake but Taryn. I found her in the main carriageway, standing and watching the world go by outside. I stepped to her side, making her jump.

"Oto, you're so quiet," she said.

"Not really," I added. "You're just in a world of your own."

"Seems we're both stuck in the 'what if' scenarios," she said, turning around, leaning her back on the railing. In this position, her baby bump prominently stood out.

"In what sense?" I asked her.

"I knew my father would take to providing you with something special. I just had no idea he'd take to it like he has."

"To making me a Kreeshon?"

"Yes. It's rare enough for anyone to not be able to take to one, let alone for a master as good as my father to gift one."

"Ahh, so when you said, *Perform well out there and my family will have a gift for you.* You weren't meaning that?"

"Not at all, maybe some extra parts for Ivori, but couple your performances with what you did? It's the greatest gift he could give."

"It's hand crafted and designed specifically for me. I think that's pretty special either way, without it being a family-only sword."

"For what you did"—her hand trailed down and settled on her belly —"I don't think any of us can repay it."

"Don't be silly. You have no need, really. Anyone would have." I thought to the life inside her, the baby growing, the baby I'd get to meet, get to watch grow up. Maybe even have kids of my own to play with him. I . . . I struggled with all of that. To think Ezra would really want kids.

"No, Oto, they really wouldn't," she said, her hand still lazily caressing over her son. "You are family. I hope one day you will really understand that, feel that."

I smiled at her. "I'm almost there," I said. "It's hard, seeing my parents, remembering they left me and I had nothing. Now that I have everything, it's still hard."

Monday, June 28th *Evening*
Year - 27514

I put it off, and put it off.
 I trained as much as I could. Every single day.
 When calls came in, I put them off too.
 I would not talk to them. I couldn't. Not yet. Not now.
 I wasn't ready.
 Wasn't ready to accept their reasons. Why they left me.
 How could they just leave me?
 Then Doctor Styx came to me and told me I needed to do this.
 Geo then gave me a choice who I could have with me to meet my parents. To "talk," as they put it. I thought a lot about the who, and decided it would be with Geo and Doctor Styx.
 "I need the medical opinions," I'd told Geo. "If they start on all kinds of technical or DNA jargon, I'm not going to understand any of it."
 So, now we waited. I had no doubts the others out on the track and practicing would be intrigued with the what and why. But this was for me to sort out. For me to talk on, decide. How could I do that, though? They really had left me.
 Rather than Geo's office, we'd decided the "shack" was better. There was less access to the track itself, and it had a more relaxed atmosphere.

Now all I did was stand, trying to get some fresh air out on the small balcony while I waited. Doctor Styx and Geo talked over things in the living space, and Pete made himself useful in making drinks.

He brought one out to me, and I took a sip. There was a little something *hard* in it, though it also wasn't as hot as his mug. "Thanks," I said.

"Just knew you might have needed some encouragement to, you know, speak your mind."

"I'm not sure I can," I added.

"You will when you're ready," Pete said. "Till then, we are all here, and we've got your back."

The door pinged to let us know there were visitors, and he moved to answer it, beckoning in both my parents. My father carried a rather large bag.

"Bag on the table," Pete said.

"We needed you to see it, so you might give us a little more time today than you'd planned."

I took another long swig of my drink, then moved into the room. I stepped toward them and the table, wondering what they'd brought.

"May I?" My mother was the one who unzipped it.

When she pulled the head of a pretty familiar-looking young robot girl, I saw Doctor Styx and Geo exchange looks. "What is this?" I asked.

"Please, sit, everyone," Donoto said. "I can't take back what was done, but we can explain some of it."

I didn't want to sit, but Doctor Styx and Geo did. My mother brought the little robot out even further. It really did look similar to the one we'd found. So eerily similar.

"Explain, then," I said. "What is all this?"

"We've worked with our technology and the Icarian since the first was discovered. My father was the one who created the first of these."

"You know we found it, don't you?" Doctor Styx asked.

"There's many things the vicenet is capable of finding out. We're not the only ones who have access to lots of info."

From behind the couch, Alice brought up a screen with all my details on. "We've had some pull in squashing them. But they pop up again in several other locations later."

"They've got everything?" I asked. "Literally everything I w . . . am, they can see it all." I almost let it slip that this wasn't who I was now. Not anymore. But I caught it.

"Is this through the racetrack logs? Or some other leak?"

"We're not sure. Every time we've tried to trace it, we've come up against several brick walls. Not just the regular ones."

"I'll track it," Pete said, and he moved away back to the kitchen. He accessed the vicenet and moved hella fast through the networking rings. When he looked at me, I smiled. After all he was still dating one of the best, Lena. He should know what he was doing.

I looked back to the robot. "What are they for?" I asked.

"Isn't it obvious?" Alice said. "The Icarian that don't want to race."

"Don't want to race?" I almost spat my next swig of drink out.

"Not everyone wants to or feels the need to be competitive. We had a couple of our friends over the years seeking out other answers."

"What am I, then?" I asked her. My anger burned up through me, pure Fire. Geo shot me a look, and I quickly calmed myself down with Water.

I hadn't wanted to know. Now I wanted to know, I needed to.

"What am I?" I asked again. "And why did you leave me?"

Alice hung her head. "You were a spark of my imagination."

"We can't have children," Donoto admitted. "Between the both of us, our genes never melded right. Every pregnancy we had, Alice couldn't carry to term."

"Once they discovered I was working on creating a child with specific bloodline traits, I had everyone interested. I couldn't carry to term at first either. We decided to try inside a pod. To grow outside of the womb. This was different, and again, many didn't take until—"

"Until you," Donoto said. "You were the miracle baby."

"Not just an experiment, then?" I asked. More than skeptical.

Alice's face reddened. "No, not at all."

"Then why did you leave me?" My hands shook. I could see the liquid sloshing around. I steadied myself on the back of the couch. "This is all lies . . ."

"This is the truth," Alice said. She stood and moved to me. I took a step back. "I know you don't want to believe anything. I don't blame you. I know nothing of you or your life anymore. Of growing up on the streets here."

"What we do know is somewhere along the lines, you're going to be imbalanced if you're not already." Donoto pointed to the little robot. "We've come a long way with what we were trying to achieve, but we used the technology from them, for you."

"Tech?" Doctor Styx asked.

"Oto's body has mineral compounds and nanites no one can trace because they're not in the known system. We . . ." Alice lowered her head again, not able to look me in the eyes. "We injected them while he was growing to help him grow; there were other instabilities as he aged."

"I already had nites in my system?" I thought for only a few moments about what that would mean. I looked at Geo.

"The nites, where were they from?" Styx asked.

"They had Ivori's nites. I already had her dormant nites in my system," I said. Drinking the rest of my mug and setting it aside, I then moved to the couch and sat opposite my father. "Is it alive?"

He shook his head. "We've had some success, but nowhere near what's happened with you and them together."

"What happened with me is a one off," I said. "You'll never get the Icarian and these genes to meld again."

"You can't know that," Alice said.

I took the little robot, looked deep into its sunken dead eyes. "Doctor, you know what I'm thinking."

"I do, but not here, not right now."

I nodded at him, then turned to Donoto. "What do you want? Why do you need me?"

"As much as we do want you to give us another chance, while we've been on Copter, we've been assigned more and more funding from others. We'd like to . . ."

Alice moved to sit before me, taking the little robot off me. "We know you have answers everyone needs. We'd like to work with you, and those you are with, instead of hiding on Copter. This needs to be taken elsewhere."

"I don't trust you," I said. "At all."

"We understand that," Donoto said. "That's why we've also brought this." He rummaged in the bag a bit more, then pulled out a data pad. "This has everything we have stored on it. Everything about you, the Icarian."

He handed it to Doctor Styx, who opened the filing system on it, eyes widening.

"This is incredible," he said. "I can do so much here. For you."

"You want to go with them?" I asked him.

"We need to do this," Styx said. "This isn't about your feelings. This is about your future. If you want one."

I closed my eyes. "Okay." My mind whirred. "Do it."

28

Tuesday, July 12th *Morning*
Year - 27514

Doctor Styx kept all of us informed with what was going on. They'd set up a small workspace at the hospital and up to now, I'd not been asked to do anything out of the ordinary. A whole month had passed. Practice, practice, and more practice.

Now, however, Doctor Styx was trying to message me while we were running through morning practice.

Vrolst stuck to my back end, and I couldn't shake him; we'd been bouncing around the track on and off for hours, me in the lead, him in the lead. Of course, Luca and Tant couldn't be here all the time, so this was down to Geo and me.

Most of the time it had been plain fun; now it was getting to me. I had to work out how to get rid of him properly.

When he managed to get around me on the next bend, I slammed my hand on the wheel with pure frustration.

"Garage." Geo's voice came over comms.

"We're getting a call from Doctor Styx," Ivori said. "You want to take it now?"

We pulled forward and backed into our garage, the roar of bikes out on the track instead of us filtering through.

The belt undid, and I slid out. "On the wall," I said to her.

Geo strode in a moment later as Doctor Styx's face appeared. "Oh," he said. "Full house?"

I glanced around the garage. "Is this private?"

He shook his head. Then I noticed something move behind him, something small.

Out stepped the small robot. I wasn't sure if it was the one we found—

Oh crap, out stepped the other.

I leaned forward on the chair. "Doc?" I asked.

"This"—he gestured to the one on his right—"is calling herself Roa."

I swallowed and felt Ivori on the inside of me twinge. "Roa?"

"Yes, Roa," Styx said. "She's asking to come to the track, to speak with Ivori."

I looked at Ivori. "What do you think?"

"I don't know. I don't know how that's possible."

Geo's hand was on my shoulder. "We should talk to them first. No one gets access to Ivori, let alone your parents."

I met his eyes with mine. "Okay," I said, then turned back to the screen. "We'll come by the lab now."

Had I expected any different when I got there? I don't know. Now I sat on a bed, with a tourniquet around my arm, and my mother standing near me with a needle . . .

Doctor Styx had been the one to convince me this was the best course of action. "You're sure they need to see all of this?" I asked him.

He took the needle off Alice, stepped toward me. "We need to know what's going on on the inside now. Especially with all the developments lately. I won't let them see anything till I've had a good look myself."

"The robot?" I asked him.

"Animating her takes a lot of Azris. Both your parents needed a break."

While the needle slipped into my arm, I thought. If my parents were supplying the robot with Azris, that meant they needed a bonded partner, pretty much like the Icarian did. "Ivori's not telling me everything," I said to him as he swapped one full vial of my blood out for another.

"Do you expect to know everything so soon? Ivori is what, hundreds of years old?"

"Thousands," I said without realizing it.

The doctor's hand trembled slightly, and the needle pulled in my arm. "Sorry," he said drawing two more vials before stopping.

"I need to talk to Roa," I said. "Alone." I motioned to both my parents as they puttered about the lab doing things.

"Can you supply enough Azris?" he asked.

"I'll do what I need to in order to talk to them."

"They're leaving soon, even if you're here I told them to go."

I forced a smile when my mother came over trying to make some kind of fuss. Eventually they left though, seeing the doctor had me all cared for.

"Do you think they're genuine?" I asked him.

"No," he answered honestly, without even looking at me. "I believe they think they did things for all the right reasons, but not what we'd call honorable ones."

When Doctor Styx moved away from this lab, he beckoned me to follow him, so I did.

The little robots were inside chambers much like the one I'd found the first in. I moved to look inside and stared into its empty eyes.

"It's really alive?" I asked him.

"I'd like Ivori's assessment of what she thinks is alive. From what I gather with the few moments it was awake, it maybe just has fleeting memories, perhaps stored in some of the nanites that were around at the time."

"Maybe she should come to the track," I said.

"Worried?"

"What if there's not a lot of her in there? Just enough for a message, or something? Like remnants . . ."

"You're talking about what happened with Amalia's car Etol?"

I nodded, the worry inside of me was true. What if there really was no time, if I woke her and that was it? I couldn't do it to Ivori.

Doctor Styx pulled a blanket out and walked toward us. "Then I guess we better get back to the track," he said.

"Really?"

"Who will be there now?"

"At most, Geo, Taryn—the others would have gone home now. It's late."

"Geo never goes home?"

"Sometimes." Ugh, who was I kidding? He'd made his home with Taryn at the back of the track. Though I hoped eventually we'd all get a nicer place to stay, something like Sinclairs retreat. That was wonderful.

I called for Geo on the way back to the track. Even if he'd been busy with Taryn, he would make sure we weren't left on our own for long. By the time we arrived at the gate and were inside with the little robot, he was walking across the track to meet us. "You're sure this is a good thing?" Geo asked. "Here?"

"You recall Etol, how much it took to get that last message out, right?"

"Yes." He lowered his head, then indicated the garage. "I think between us we should be able to power this op without causing you major harm."

"Hopefully," Doctor Styx said.

Ivori's trepidation came through to me as soon as we stepped into the garage with the robot.

"I don't know if I can do this," she said.

"I'm right here," I said to her.

"*We're* right here," Geo said with emphasis. He looked to me as Doctor Styx placed the little robot in the middle of the floor.

"What do you—"

"Sit." Geo motioned and then did exactly that on the other side of the robot. I followed his example and crossed my legs even if it hurt a little.

"Stiff," I said. "You've been training us solidly since I got here."

Geo smiled. "Wouldn't have it any other way." With a flick of his wrist, he called Fire down his arm and held a hand out to me. "Mirror me," he said with the flick of his other wrist. Water flowed down his other arm.

I raised an eyebrow. "You've been practicing both?"

"I've a good teacher to be around. Seeing what you do, I want to have that."

"Err." I closed my eyes for one moment, then pulled both elements from my core and around me. I couldn't mirror him exactly, and he knew it. Instead, Fire and Water flowed down both arms in a whirl of blue and red, snakes chasing after one another.

"I don't think I'll ever get used to seeing how amazing that is," he said.

"When I can do it without breaking a sweat, or feeling like I'm going to destabilize something around me, then you can fawn."

Ivori let out a chuckle. "When you can do that," she said. "Even I'll fawn over you."

I rolled my eyes at her, and then concentrated before I really did burn my clothes off.

"Good," Geo said. "You felt what Etol had before, so you lead. You're connected to Ivori; I'm just here as backup battery."

As much as I wanted to laugh, I kept it back, concentrating on what I could feel before me, around me.

What had attracted me to the robot in the first place, there had been so much more going on in that half-destroyed building.

I could feel the twinges of a consciousness. "There is someone here," I said. "She is very weak though." I tried to reach in deeper and deeper to find her. The world around me went black.

"What is this?" I asked into the darkness.

"This is the confines of the space I've been held in," a voice said. I couldn't tell if the voice was male or female, and I wondered.

"I am pleased to finally meet you."

A flicker of light around me and I could see someone. She stepped forward and into the light. It illuminated her face just enough that I could see it was indeed Roa. "You want to speak with Ivori?" I asked.

Aurelio stepped to me, put both hands on my chest. The contact sent a jolt of electric through me. "I need to show you first, before I speak to her. I will not show her this; you need to guard this from her, okay?"

I then witnessed everything from her eyes. The abuse, the pain, the torture.

The fact she had kept it all from Ivori and how much she loved her.

"You were stronger than you made out?" I asked. "So much stronger."

I felt her emotion inside me. "I knew it was coming. I understood everything we were, everything we could be, and no matter what I did, I wasn't enough."

Those words stung. "How could you not be enough?" I'd seen their combined stats, the strength they had without anything she'd been hiding.

"I wasn't." She looked into my eyes, her soul on fire, yet I couldn't see the other elements in there and I understood why she wasn't enough. "You have to be," she said. "You have to get her to the top."

"Drakol?"

"Yes, by any means necessary."

I swallowed. "Any means necessary?"

"They're not messing around, Oto. They will come for everyone you care about. They would take out this whole planet if they thought it would stop you."

"This is all very complicated," I said.

"More than you know," she replied and turned away. "I don't have any more time. May I please talk to her?"

I reached out and put a hand on Roa's shoulder. Light then illuminated everything around me, and I saw the robot before me start to glow. Fire and Water moved all around the tiny frame.

"I never saw it do anything like this in the lab," Doctor Styx said.

"We're giving her more energy than she needs to last," I said, and I reached forward with both my hands. To Geo's shock, I took both of his in mine. There was that connection I felt back the first time we'd been a part of something like this.

Geo was an open book right now, just as much as I was for him.

"Oto." His voice cracked slightly.

"It's okay. You can see everything I am." I winked at him. "Just the once."

"Ha," he laughed.

The little robot wobbled to its feet, then it stood, and with ease, dipped under out connecting hands. It went to Ivori and Doctor Styx moved with it.

"Keep your eyes on me," I said to him. "This is for them."

Geo nodded, and held my eyes, and I watched his life flicker on past me. Not just his childhood, his teenage years, but I saw something else here too.

Pictures, moving pictures, though from his view, as if I were Geo. It felt weird, so weird.

Taryn's family, here for their wedding.

How much he really loved her. Damn, it was beautiful.

The largest baby bump I'd ever seen.

The happiness in her eyes as she gave birth looking straight at him.

Then the pain in her eyes as he said goodbye to her, and kissed her, their baby.

What? The way he looked at me as we left her, and I left Ezra behind.

I swallowed. "You're watching this too?" I asked him.

"Yes," he said, his voice thick.

We board Tant, with Luca, Alek, Eula, and Marik.

"This is our future," I said. "This is where we're heading."

"Alone," he said. "I don't think I can do it like this."

"No," I replied. "We're not alone."

Pain struck my core, and I focused deeper to the connection to Roa. It was failing; we just weren't powerful enough.

"A little longer," Ivori gasped. "Please. Just a little more time."

Geo gripped my hands tighter. "We've got this," he said, though his hands and his whole body were shaking.

A shiver ran through me as my energy dwindled. He was still pretty full, but he needed me, and I needed him.

I reached even deeper then, and I pulled from the Earth, the skies. Saw the stars twinkle in his eyes, from memories past, the hot sunny days he'd spent by beaches I'd never dreamed of. I pulled everything I could, and I let Roa have it.

The last minute hurt me on such a deep level, yet I didn't care. I saw notifications flicking past my eyes. I ignored all of them.

Doctor Styx was at my side then. "Oto, you need to pull back," he said. "Now."

I closed my eyes. I could feel everything on the inside bouncing off each other in ways they weren't meant to. I could feel the energy bubbling like a volcano—no, worse, like something no one would ever have seen before.

I couldn't let this go; I couldn't let any of this go. This internal effort gave them the most precious gift in the universe, a chance to talk through everything and anything they needed to. They needed it.

I had to hold on.

Geo tried to pull back, and when he did, I held everything together. I didn't need him. Doctor Styx helped him out of the way.

"What's he doing?" Geo asked him, his breath in ragged gasps.

"He's giving up one of his saves," Styx said.

"What? Oto, no!"

"It's too late," I said. Tears from the pain streamed down my face, red fire tears, etched with every element burning to get out. Hurting to get out.

Pete had taught me on the cliff top that the energy could be used, redirected if you needed to. I didn't have anything I needed to do other than give them time. But that time was at my cost.

The elements finally hit combustion point.

The little robot turned to me, and I swear I could see a smile on her face. "Thank you," she said, then collapsed.

There was nothing left.

I had nothing left.

The whirling energy on my inside hit critical mass.

Zero Light

Then it imploded.

―――

Friday, July 30th *Evening*
Year - 27514

I wasn't sure what or where I was when I woke. Soft, heavy blankets covered me, and I pulled back from them, from the slumber that had taken me.

My mind flashed with many different notifications, things I wasn't sure I really wanted to see.

I clicked it, and brought up my log.

I already knew what I'd done, what I'd lost. I'd still do it again in a heartbeat.

This message was different from the first time. But it still had those same connotations.

System Failure - System Error

The code squirmed around and around, but it wasn't math I saw this time. It wasn't changing for the better. This was bad.

I saw it in clear writing then.

Death Thwarted - Used x 2

Yet again you performed something no one else could have. You gave everything of your life essence for another, but more than that, you channeled everything you were, and you gave it away like it was nothing. This has not gone unnoticed.

I only had one save left. One save, for whatever I needed it for. I hoped to all the gods I never would.

I knew I would.

My life was full of twists and turns I never thought possible.

The system knew it too.

My stats clearly sat in front of me now, and I read over them, the changes. The growth. Huge growth. Was it just because of my DNA? Was it Ivori?

Both, she said to me. *Both have made you who you are.*

Name = Oto Benes
ID Number = 4188927
Age = 23
Species = Anodite
Sex = Male
Alignment = Chaotic
Bloodline = Royal Seven
Health = 99%
Cultivation Level - King 2
Active Meridians = 12/12
Nanites = **1.5 Million**
Artefacts = 2
Chosen Specialist = Racer
First Chosen Affinity = Water
Second Chosen Affinity = Fire

Strength = 53/**208.44**
Dexterity = 58/**228.33**
Constitution = 51/**201.24**
Int/Wis/Spirit = **77**

Affinities - Rank
Water - Indigo
Fire - Blue
Earth - **Blue**
Air - Yellow
Light - Blue
Darkness - Yellow

Spirit - Blue

Droll's Leg Pouch – 1 potion left

Ring of Light - A gift from Ezra
Adapted, so you may use it as you wish.
Boosts Azris circulation and usage, + 30 to all stats
Uses = 5

Death Thwarted - Used x 2

Yet again you performed something no one else could have. You gave everything of your life essence for another, but more than that, you channeled everything you were, and you gave it away like it was nothing. This has not gone unnoticed.

> I swallowed.
> *Oto,* Ivori said into my mind softly.
> *It's okay,* I said. *It's all going to be okay.*

29

Monday, August 2nd *Morning*
Year - 27514

I met our guards on the way out of the building as usual.

"Bacon?" I asked.

They both frowned at me "You're killing us," one said. The other grinned.

Neither of them were big talkers, and I liked that. They, like Lena, got me. The need for social stuff was never a big part of me as a scrub. I didn't need it. I liked the quiet.

This time of the morning was exactly what I needed and reveled in every single day. I needed this.

The bacon breakfast wrap was on the way in. I'd not only gotten too used to it, but it fueled my day with the extras I knew Pa was packing on it.

The guards flanked the wall waiting for the bakery doors to open. Pa didn't look happy though, his face flushed.

"What's wrong?" I asked.

He ushered me inside. "Bodil didn't come home last night."

The bakery was a mess. Literally stuff everywhere. My guards stayed, staring through the open door.

"What?" My heart sank. The young girl had been quite a part of the track's regime. Everyone loved her, especially Geo and Taryn.

"I can't leave the bakery," he said, throwing his hands around the space, flour dust everywhere.

I stared at everything around us. "Only one answer to this," I said and tapped my comms.

"Oto?" Geo's voice came through all sleepy. "What is it?"

"Bodil's not come home and . . ." I turned from Pa, whispered. "No one's found Bren yet, either, have they?"

"No," he replied.

"Pa needs help at the bakery. We're going to go track her, but the scrubs and those around here need this place running. Anyone that comes in early who can help, redirect them here."

I heard Taryn's voice over his. "I helped around our kitchen a lot. I'll be right there. Pete can stay with us."

"Oh, okay," I said.

"We'll be there as soon as I can. Get all the info you can from Pa."

"Geo on his way?" The guards stepped inside.

I turned to see one washing off in the sink. "Yes, there's a few at the track that will help here. We need to go a-hunting."

The larger guard stepped to me. "You need to practice," he said. "You head back to the track. Pete will escort you back. Geo and Taryn will have got this."

Seeing me about to complain, he just held his hands up. "For now, let's get all of this a little more organized."

I sighed, moved to wash my hands, and then I joined them, taking direction off Pa.

When the others turned up, I listened as Taryn explained to the others what and where Bodil had been. Then I watched them leave.

"We'll find her," Pete said.

"I know," I said. "They've got this." It was more for Pa than anything else. Who was I kidding? I wanted to be a part of everything. I just couldn't.

"Delegation is half of leadership," Pete said. He handed me a breakfast roll and I took it, not even realizing we'd still not eaten.

Alek was on the track when we arrived, and together, we took to practice with some of the others even if my mind was on the missing kid. We had to do what we had to do.

That meant putting Ivori and Ren through their paces.

We practiced more on starts. Although I still had timing down really well, I could always improve. The new gears and the changes within me altered how I saw or did things every time.

When I failed to get going perfectly three out of five times, Ivory stopped me and pulled me off the track.

"You have to learn to focus through the hard times," she said. "As much as it upsets me that the young woman is missing, we have much more at stake here."

I let out a sigh. "I didn't think everyone associated with me would come under so much scrutiny."

"We can't guard everyone either," she said. "No matter how much the council step in, there's not enough to go around. Those who are around you, around the track mostly can protect themselves."

"Mostly," I said, running a hand through my hair. I opened the door and got out. Moved to settle into practicing my control.

Lunch came, they brought food from Grover's, and we carried on.

One day moved into the next and then the next.

Then almost a week had gone by.

Pete stayed with us. He spoke with the guards, Luca, Lena, and the council daily and came home in the mornings. The track had mostly returned to normal practice. We had no choice. It wasn't that we didn't care; we just couldn't let this be a setback.

Pa and Geo spoke daily. Taryn helped a little first thing, but the baby took all of her energy, so Geo sourced a couple of other bakers, putting them on the payroll and giving Pa time to go out with Taryn and to be around us at the track if he needed to.

He didn't want to be alone, so he'd stayed a few nights with us, and with Geo and Taryn in the shack.

Ezra had called through daily, never missing me in the morning, or at lunch if she could. Then last thing at night. I'd fallen asleep to her talking about her day, and I loved that. I missed her greatly. But we both needed to do these things. Every time I spoke with her, her stories about medical training fascinated me; she was growing in ways only she could. Pride filled me every time she said she'd done something with perfect precision.

Ezra came home just the once, but it was a stressful night. She paced the small living space; she'd not slept at all, and though we'd talked, held each other, and tried, it wasn't happening. She'd gotten up for a hot drink, and I tried to pull her attention away from her pacing by stepping in front of her.

"You should come to the track with us," I said. "Spend the day with family."

"I'd be no use to anyone." She sighed. "I have to get this out of the way. It's one exam, then I'll be back."

"I know," I said. "Worrying isn't helping any of us. This, the racing, the wedding. So much . . ."

Ezra threw herself on the couch and I sat with her, pulling her to me.

"You've doing amazing things," I said. "This will just show everyone what you're made of."

"They test everything," she said, holding my eyes with hers. "Not just your knowledge and history, but your use of Azris."

"They have to, right?"

"No, this is different. This is schooling beyond anything here on Isala."

I swallowed. I knew what was coming, I'd struggled with being apart from her through the last few weeks, watching her go away for weeks at a time, when she came home, exhausted beyond belief, she slept, and slept more than I thought anyone would.

With a finger, I reached out, traced down the side of her jawline. She leaned into me. "I love you," she said. "But this is taking me away from everything I do want."

"Really?" I asked her. "Be honest. I love you too, Ezra—that is never ever going to change. "But be honest. You want this."

Ezra closed her eyes, and I leaned into kiss her forehead.

"Don't be afraid of what you want," I said to her.

"I am, if it takes me away from you."

"Only in person." I tapped her chest. "Not from in here. No matter where you are, I'm in here. So is Ivori. You will be with me, when I need you."

"Always," she said. "You need me, just let me know."

"Back at you," I said.

Ezra checked the time. "You need to go. They'll be waiting on you at the track."

I frowned. Everything was getting more and more serious, and I knew we all had to take it that way. Each practice more important than the last, and no matter how much I wanted to skip it and see Ezra off, she wouldn't have it, and neither would Alek or Geo.

I kissed her once more, holding her tight. "Nail that exam," I said. "Come back to us, and we'll celebrate all weekend."

"I promise." She forced a smile, but I let her off. "I will."

Ezra had to pass that exam today just as much as we needed to win the races afterward.

"You know we're going to need all of her in the future," Ivori said. "This training is for you as much as her, and she knows that."

"We've a long way to go yet," I replied. "But I need those with me I trust more than I trust myself. That means the seven of us."

"Ten," she chided.

"Yes, I guess. Vrolsh, Ren, and you too. The ten of us will be moving on up without the others?"

"We have to keep this close," Ivori said. "Close as in the least possible people to get hurt."

I swallowed, my thoughts going back Bodil.

"There's nothing else we can do to help find her?"

"Lena and the council have everyone they can looking for them both," Ivori said.

I lay my head down, let the darkness around me do its best. I struggled with sleep every night I didn't fall off with Ezra talking to me.

Yet I still got up the next morning with Alek's knock.

We practiced with my starts most mornings, and I gave myself lots of time on my own, and then with Geo; he never let me take a real break, pushing me in every single way possible, and I him. The gap between us was closing, the gap between Alek and I increasing. So I made sure every moment I got to put Alek through his paces, I did. Despite his complaining at the time, he thanked me more often than not over dinner.

Today, almost a week from her going missing I'd paused, sweating at the side of the track.

I watched Alek leave Geo's office. He joined me a few minutes later, and his face . . . oh, fuck.

I pulled back my energy and stood before him waiting for his words. The words I knew were going to come. I hoped they hadn't.

"They f-found them," he stuttered. "They found—two bodies."

"Both of them?" I reached out and pulled him to me.

"They were just kids," he said. Alek shivered in my arms.

"W-w-wh-at?" I stammered a bit. "W-whe-re?"

"They've taken her to Mote Lerate's main hospital. Doctor Styx and the council want to—"

"I get it," I said. "I do."

"Geo's going to see Pa now." Alek pushed back from me.

My heart sank. *Ivori,* I said.

I'm here, she replied. *I'm so sorry, Oto.*

Geo stepped out of the office with Taryn; she clung to him. Alek and I walked over. "Do you need us?"

"No," he said. "I'll take the news to Pa and Bren's family. We'll make sure everything is . . ." His words faltered, his eyes brimming with emotion.

"We can't get away from it," I said. "All of it. But we can and we will find out who did this."

"My parents are almost here," Taryn said and held my eyes with hers. "I hate to ask this now. But I need you. Will you come with me to meet them?"

Geo gave her a squeeze. "Of course. Oto, please?"

"Yes," I said. "Anything you need. Both of you."

"I'll be back as soon as I can from the council."

"We're all ready for tomorrow, every one of us." Geo kissed her, straightened his suit, and then we watched him and Pete walk away.

"When are they landing?" I asked. "Where?"

Taryn rubbed her stomach. "I've never been so nervous," she said. "Their shuttle is on the way in now."

"Right now?" I glanced to the garage. "Ivori can take us. She's totally comfortable, with—"

"Pregnant hormones," Taryn said.

"I was going to say—"

Ivori coughed inside of my head. *Don't.*

So I didn't.

Ivori was nice and steady all the way there, but Taryn struggled anyway. "What's going on?" I asked as I pulled into the parking lot.

"Doc says there's some incompatible DNA between us, that I'm struggling to carry to term. My body just isn't so happy."

She rubbed her stomach some more. "What are they going to do?"

"Ezra and Doctor Styx say they're going to deliver after the wedding."

"That's early?"

"Not too much, but a little."

"They're not worried though?"

"Only if I decide to drop at the wedding." She laughed and I laughed with her.

We both felt the vibrations as the main shuttle came in, and she pushed Ivori's door open.

"You're ready to meet my family again?" she asked.

I frowned, watching the shuttle dip in from the clouds above. "To see such powerful people on this planet? Doesn't happen very often, right?"

"Not at all. They'll be heavily guarded despite the power they have."

"Understandable," I said and offered her an arm.

Taryn took it, and we walked through all the security going to get inside the station.

When the familiar faces of her family appeared, she shivered lightly. "You've got this," I said. "Don't forget why you're here."

"I love Geo," she said with a grin that lit my heart.

"Good. That will get you through anything that happens here now."

We waited for the group to step off the platform then spot us. Taryn led the way, down the ramps and toward them.

Their security detail was tight. All eyes on me.

Quintin Tullius radiated power, just like he had on Halara I strengthened the Azris that flowed around me.

"You learned a lot already from them," Taryn said. "But you haven't met my brother, have you?"

I shook my head. "The younger guy on the left?"

Taryn nodded. "Kei. I didn't think he was going to come. He's been on a super sensitive mission." I didn't let on I knew exactly what he'd been doing. We walked straight for them all. Taryn dipped her head to them. "Father, Mother, Kei."

Tofa stepped forward and took her daughter from me, wrapping her up in a big hug. "I missed you," she said.

Quintin looked around, but my eyes were stuck with Kei's. "Geo?" Quintin asked.

I dipped my head to him. "Forgive him, we had some bad news just before your arrival. He's gone to give the bad news to the family."

"The young girl I messaged you about," Taryn said. "They found her body this morning, along with another."

Tofa let out a gasp and turned to her husband, who took her into his arms. "We had no idea that it was so bad down here."

"You're on the first planet, Father," Taryn said. "You shouldn't expect anything else."

Several guards moved around us as Quintin then moved away from the landing zone. "There are others from our family in the next shuttle. They'll join us in the hotel first. We wanted to see you, talk with you."

"You're all right with Oto here?" Taryn looked from me to her father, concern flashing over her eyes.

"There's been some developments I wished to talk to Geo about beforehand, but Oto is a valued member of our family. I trust him. But let's get somewhere we can talk."

Quintin moved away with Tofa and Taryn, but Kei stood stiff. Three women flanked him, and I didn't need to see they were higher levels than me; I felt it. They didn't have the same elemental control though, and all stared with bright curiosity. Kei motioned to them. "Go," he said simply.

I stood and waited then when he walked. I followed. "My father and family speak very highly of you."

"I admit to not knowing very much about you," I said. I was older than him, I thought, maybe just a little.

"We're not really a talking family, honestly. I'm surprised Taryn's chosen such a different life."

"She's an amazing woman," I said to his raised eyebrow. "I mean, she is. I'm already committed, and well, I class Geo as family."

"So we'll be family then, too, in a roundabout way."

I nodded slowly. The daunting size of how things were progressing around me flickered over my face.

"Not a bad thing, Oto."

"You know what they're going to be talking about?" I asked.

"Yes." His brows furrowed. "Though I wish I didn't."

I focused on him, saw the glint of metal tech over his arm. It brought memories forward of things I'd studied about Halara, their other planet, Taryn's family life. A Taharri. What all these things could mean to someone in that position. "You're modified?"

He ran a finger over the metal and smiled. "Yes, recent. It's still a little too new."

"No Icarian?"

"Not as yet. I mean, I never thought about it, racing. I'm first son; I have family obligations. Which then makes me one sought-after new sect leader."

"Sect leader? So, with your three partners and the mods."

"It makes me one very sought-after young man in general."

"The Sevran Vipers?"

Kei nodded. "My father wants me to stay on Halara, but Shuko's sending me to—"

"Copter," I said with a nod. "To help with Camran and Amalia."

"How'd you know?"

"I'm good at guessing, and you're here to befriend me, and secure backing on Copter. Why? What's there for you?"

"I want Copter," he said.

I swallowed. "You want the whole planet?"

"There's a war coming," he said, letting his sleeve back over his arm. "It seems you're at the heart of it. I'm glad I've seen you to understand the why. Copter is our family's largest resource. The issues we've been having on Halara, ones I've sorted out these last few months, have all stemmed from Copter. We need to take Copter, and soon."

I turned away from him, looking to the building before us. "Working my way up," I said. "However, your sister needs this wedding. Then she needs to have her baby. I need to win my last race, and then I'll be coming to Copter."

"You know my father has made a gift for you." Kei stopped walking, "They are going to formally accept you into our family as well as Geo at the wedding. Expect it."

"What?" His words blew my mind.

"After Geo and my sister become man and wife. My father will take the stage and accept you formally into our family."

"That's taking their—"

"No, it will enhance their wedding. Everyone will see that through them, and you, our strength not only grows, but is becoming a force no one should mess with."

Did I want that? To be a part of something I didn't quite understand? I eyed him carefully. There was something else I needed to know. Taryn held him with massive respect.

"What about you?" I asked him, suddenly nervous. I knew what Taryn had said about him. He would not hesitate to do anything needed to protect his family. "Are you ready to accept me as family?"

"If my sister and father think that highly of you, then yes. But show me how you fight with our sword after the wedding, and on Copter you will want for nothing."

I held my hand out to him. "Deal. If you fight anything like your sister, I'm in. I could do with a good ass kicking."

Kei laughed and shook my hand. I could feel the Azris flowing around him, but I had no clues at all to what levels he was. He had amazing control over himself. That was a man I wanted on my side.

30

Sunday, August 8th *Lunch*
Year - 27515

I was not getting used to sleeping in strange beds. Hotels, other rooms, with other people all around us. I rubbed my eyes, and ugh . . . damn.

The more I tried to fiddle with my tie, the worse it looked. I couldn't do this, but I wanted to do it by myself. That's why I was now presently locked in the bathroom.

Everyone was waiting on me. I knew they were.

The door banged once more. "You okay in there?" Ezra's concern came through. "I'll help if you need."

I gave it one last attempt, then tucked it inside the jacket, smoothed over my hair, and went for the door.

I would like to say opening it to see Ezra was always going to be good. Her smile faded as soon as she saw me.

"Don't look so terrified," she teased and also tried to straighten the tie.

When she moved back into the bedroom, I got a glimpse of her and could do nothing but stare.

She glanced back to me, stopping in her tracks. "What is it?"

I swallowed, my mouth suddenly so dry.

"Spit it out," she said glancing down.

My eyes ran down her body. The pale yellow dress she wore had tiny red flowers all over it, cut to perfection around her curves.

"Do I—er—look okay?" she managed to stammer out.

I stepped to her, took her hands in mine. "You look perfect," I said. "Absolutely perfect."

"The leg?" Her eyes wandered all over my face, seeking any sign I was lying.

I could never lie to her. Ever. I put a finger to her lips. "Your leg is perfect too."

"You might not tell me any lies, but it's not perfect." Ezra sighed. "Come on, or we're going to be late."

"I don't want that." Everything had been working up to this, for Geo and the crew. A public display of not only his standing now, with Taryn's family at her side.

"Considering where we're going, no, none of us want that."

I checked the time again.

"Cars are all out front!" Alek shouted.

"Coming," Ezra and I replied.

The small lounge we'd gotten between us had been private. Now though, Alek, Tatsuno, and Pete waited.

I whistled. "You guys . . ." I turned to Ezra, still trying to get the tie to sit right. "You sure this looks good?"

"No." Alek laughed and stepped toward me. "You look like an idiot."

I shook my head as he undid it once more. Then, deftly, much like he had for Lazarus's funeral, he had it done and sitting right in a minute.

"You make that look so easy," Ezra said. "How?"

"Maybe I'll show you one day," he said. Grinning, he added, "But we need to go."

I thought with Ezra by my side I could do anything. Picture perfect to me, even if she hid at my side sometimes.

The cars out front was something I would never forget.

"Ivori," I said. "Dang."

At the front of the procession, she looked immaculate. "The guys polished them all, decked them out," Ezra said as we stepped to the curb, and Ivori's door opened for us. "You like?"

I reached out, feeling my Azris deep inside, pooling it into my hand, then I offered it to her.

Ivori accepted. "She looks amazing. She matches your dress."

"We thought it would be a nice touch," Ivori said through her speakers.

"You both look amazing," I said. "I'm—"

"Speechless." Ezra smiled. "A first."

I helped Ezra inside, then closed the door, moving to my side. Once in, we all made sure the others were ready behind us. Ren and Trix had a wonderful banner between them. As we set off, then they did, they kept a perfect distance, so it was an easy read. Behind them, the rest of our teams flanked us.

"It's not far, but we have eyes on all of us today," Ivori said.

"Rightly so." Ezra smiled. "Not every day you get to a wedding at the Council's Chambers."

"I'm glad we're here," I said.

Ezra's eyebrows furrowed at me.

"What?" I asked.

"You're wanting more from this visit, right?"

"Am I that obvious?" I reached for her hand and held it lightly over the gear stick.

"I can see the excitement in your eyes."

"I have a couple of questions for our esteemed councilors."

"What questions?" Ivori asked.

"Hopefully I'll get chance to ask them, and then I'll let you know."

The car ride was short, but I couldn't help sit with Ezra in awe. The council buildings had blown me away the first time I'd seen them, but now driving around the back opened up a whole new level of being blown away.

Ezra leaned into me, "Do you think we can get married like this someday?"

I coughed, held her hand tightly in mine, never wanting to let go. "When we get married, I want to blow today out the water." I stared up at the stone buildings, the wonderful stained-glass windows. "That might be tough though."

"As long as everyone is there, I don't mind where we do it."

"We're already bonded," I said. "But if you want something official, I'll do anything you ask."

Ezra leaned forward, ever so much closer, putting her lips to mine. She's put gloss over them, and she tasted of fruit and mint.

When the car finally stopped and we got out, I think my jaw hit the floor. Ezra took my arm in hers and guided us in following Alek and Tatsuno.

The huge, hand-carved wooden doors opened up into a large, open gathering area. Benches sat at each side, and once again stained-glass windows glittered stunning colors everywhere. Tapestries like those they had in their personal chambers adored walls between the windows. I could see protective barriers stopping the sunlight from damaging them.

The benches were full. Were we last in? "Crap, I really did make us late?"

"Don't worry about it. No one else is here just yet."

"Oh," I sighed. "Thank the gods."

Sitting with Ezra on one side, Alek on the other, I found myself enamored by everything.

Light music played in the background. Geo and Luca stood at the front. He met my eyes, and I couldn't help but beam at him. I was so proud. He looked amazing. Not only rich, but so powerful.

There was not one dry eye in the house as Taryn walked down the large central aisle with her father in arm, toward the man I had grown to respect and, well, much more than that. Love.

Alek nudged me and I looked at him. "Are you okay?"

I sucked in a shallow breath, feeling the aura of those around me, the energy in general. "It's overwhelming," I said. "All of it."

He nodded at me, lowered his eyes. "Makes you think of—" I saw him reach across to Tatsuno's hand.

I smiled at the both of them and pulled Ezra to me. "Yes, it does."

"Shh," Ezra said. "I can't hear."

I shied away from Alek a little to get in closer and listen with her as the ceremony got underway.

Geo and Taryn were the perfect couple, no doubt about it. They complemented each other in every single way. Right now, you could really tell she was pregnant, the large roundness to her stomach obvious. Everyone would know now. She didn't look worried; her hand as I'd grown accustomed to was stroking over her stomach.

Councilor Troha gave us all a welcome speech, especially to Taryn's family. I glanced across to them. Not knowing everyone, I had seen a lot of them when we'd visited Halara.

Geo and Taryn gave their own vows, and I found Ezra with tears streaming down her face. I tugged her to me, holding her tight.

When the councilor pronounced under House Duletoa's laws they were man and wife, the room around us erupted into claps, whoops, and everyone jumped to their feet.

Geo kissed Taryn passionately, and I even heard, "get a room" shouted out from the back. Geo glanced their way once, but then kissed his wife once more.

"Are you ready?" Ezra asked me, giving my hand a squeeze. "They're going to ask for you any minute."

Geo turned to me then, his face beaming. I mean literally, he shone like a beacon. His voice carried over all of the chatter toward me then, and I heard his words with crystal clarity, "It is with great honor that I—"

Everyone quieted down then, not knowing what was happening.

"That we—" Taryn said.

"That we"—Geo smiled at her—"would like to not only join our two lines together, that we ask you witness the young man about to step this way, join us as family also."

I stood to the gasps and looks of everyone in the church then. Ezra let go of my hand and I stepped out. Then, straightening my back, I moved to join them at the front of the aisle.

Taryn held her hands out for me, and I tentatively took them, looking to Councilor Koh and his wife, dressed in all their finery.

"Don't be nervous," Councilor Troha said.

I risked a glance back at the rather full area behind me. "It's all family," Geo said. "Not one stranger is under this roof."

I nodded. "Thanks."

"No," Taryn said. "Thank you. Thank you for everything."

"Today you not only witnessed the joining of man and wife under the Giannetta House banner, but their acceptance to bring Oto Benes in under their name."

I swallowed. I'd accepted their offer only a few days ago, but to be right here in front of everyone, it was almost too real.

"What do I need to do, anything?"

Troha moved to look out to the crowd. "You just need to listen, and accept what I am about to ask of you."

Troha stepped forward to the left side of the aisle, palms out facing upward. "For those who are blood-born Giannetta, Fraser, and Sawa, please stand."

I had no idea to what she was going to do, but I could feel the energy around her. So intense. I watched as not only several men on one side—strong-looking men—stood but several women too. Then they did so on the other side of the room too. Various colors, and ages, and more to the point, various auras.

Quintin and Kei stepped forward, then Luca and I could only presume another relative, much older, yet who looked nothing like him. His gray hair, and beard attested to that. I'd never seen him.

Luca took the man's arm in his and moved before us. He dipped his head to the councilor, but then she reciprocated. I wondered if they were in fact similar level. When she turned to the older man, she bowed over much, much lower. "Elder Sawa, it is a great honor to see you once more."

"My great grandfather," Taryn whispered to me.

"As it is for me." The Elder grasped her hands and then looked directly at me. "So this is the young man who has you all fawning over him."

My mouth was dry, but I bowed to him and introduced myself. "I am Oto Ben—"

He coughed over me. "Today, Oto Benes is no more." He turned to the room. "Today we all accept you as Oto Giannetta, Oto Fraser, and as one of our own. Oto Sawa."

Luca held the Elder's hand out, with his. I could only look at him. "Go on," he said.

I reached forward and put my hand to the older man's.

A short, sharp shock hit me like a bolt of electricity. His eyes sparked with Fire, and he actually tested me. My skin burned, and I quickly covered it with my Water affinity to counter it. He'd tested me in front of the councilor and everyone in this room. Why? Didn't they trust me, after everything we'd been through?

I felt wronged.

"See what I mean?" Luca said, bringing us both out of our connection.

"Yes." Elder Sawa looked to Luca, the Fire in his eyes fading. "Yes, indeed. How fascinating."

He looked at Taryn, and beckoned her to him. She took hold of his other hand. Turning to the rest of the church, he raised both our hands up to the ceiling. "Today, we become family. Welcome, welcome all."

Then as slow as he was, as we could walk together, he walked the both of us up the aisle with Geo and Luca in tow, followed by both councilors.

We stopped at every row, and I shook hands, met people, heard names I probably—realistically—would never remember.

I also soon noted we were heading out of the church. I guess that was a good thing.

Finally inside a room, with just the seven of us, the older man turned to me. "Come," he said. "I know you have some questions. I will answer them, while I get to know you."

"Eld—" Luca started.

"Shush, I will not have you"—he looked at Taryn also—"or you babying me any more today."

Luca looked at Geo, then Taryn, but he shook his head, and gestured I move forward. "Go, he will not hurt you."

The old man turned to him, chuckled and added. "Much."

I followed him out of the room, noting where he was indeed taking me. On the inside, I smiled.

"You'd never not remember being out here," he said as he turned to me. The sunlight lit his eyes in a way I hadn't expected. "And yes, Troha informed me of your previous session here. They don't often bring anyone here, especially an unknown. You not only impressed them then, but they let you in here, once again for today's ceremony."

I recalled the huge leaps in my cultivation and progress here. The twenty-six points. So many gains. Now here, would it happen again? *Could* it happen again? It seemed that he was walking better just being here, so I guessed the same could happen. I could gain once again. This sacred place was more than sacred. I swallowed, fear twisting in my stomach.

"I shouldn't be here a second time, should I?" I asked.

Elder Sawa removed his outer jacket at the side of the garden, placing it lightly and very neatly by the bench. He then stepped out to the center of the grass, turning to me. "No, you should not."

"I'm honored, Elder Sawa."

"Honor me." He actually bowed low to me. "By joining me. Please."

This was an open invitation back into the training circle of the ancients. By someone so powerful it oozed off him even more so than I'd seen it off Kei, Quintin, or Shuko. I steadied my hands, and stepped inside the circle.

This time everything felt very different. "What is that?" I asked him.

"You were here with Troha last time. Not someone of my standing. The circle expands to allow everyone to grow; that includes me."

When he dropped into a fighting stance, I really wasn't happy. My stomach flipped.

"Lazarus and Taryn have both taught you. Do not be so afraid of an old man."

"Forgive me for being so open, but I'd be stupid if I wasn't, Elder Sawa."

"My name is Atar," he said. Then, focusing, he brought forth a blade, a Kreeshon.

I couldn't match that, and I knew it.

"This," he said, then motioned to his sword, "this I forged with my own hands. He motioned to the side of the garden. There stood Quintin, a smile on his face and another sword held out in his arms. "That was forged by my son's hands, and etched with mine, and contains elements from all of us."

"From all of you?" I asked. "Elder, I—"

"Take her," Elder Sawa said. "She is yours. For everything you did for our family. For the unborn child that awaits his own adventure in the world."

I didn't hesitate then, and stepping to Quintin, I placed my hand alongside his. The connection between us for those brief seconds once again was something else. I felt a change in the aura surrounding the sword.

"She has a bite." He let go and left me with her.

The sword hummed under my grip. "She feels so very different, even from Taryn's. Why is that?"

Atar stepped back. "Try her."

I strengthened my grip, focusing into defense maneuvers. The blade cut through the air like nothing I'd held before. I moved from defense into attack.

"That's it, you're understanding each other. Now I see how complicated you are on the inside—why don't you show me what else you can do?"

I recalled Taryn's teachings, and how she led me. I put myself in her position and I went with what the blade wanted of me. Feeling Fire burning on the inside, wishing to escape, I let it, turning the air around me into a spinning whirlwind of death. The strength grew, and I was surprised to see and feel the vibrations within the circle around me growing with it.

The Air whistling around me took on a tune to itself, and I let it and the Fire dance with me.

"Can you bring forward Water?" Atar called to me. I almost couldn't hear him. I wasn't sure if I could add Water into the mix. The focus on these two elements not to actually tear myself apart was hard enough. On the inside, I could see my strongest affinity did want to let loose, but I wasn't sure how. The moves here now that I was completing, again and again, weren't what it needed.

"Listen to your instincts," Atar guided me.

I moved from the training I'd had to what I'd seen instead. Geo had moved up from King 6, and I'd seen him struggle with any new training to push himself. I'd practiced the moves for King in here, learned to stand with Geo, and it had been fantastic. Something else called to me now though, and my moves changed.

I could hear in the distant regions of my mind. "Consciousness, Drive, Trajectory, Opinion, Cause, Sentinel, Confrontation, Repair."

"Truly fascinating," another voice said, but I couldn't even look to see who it was. My concentration was full on, bringing Water now to the surface of the blade. The air was alight with Fire and Air. So I began to spin Water into the mix, keeping all three under control and in almost in perfect harmony.

Water hit Air, and then it all fell apart. I collapsed with it to the grass, Water from the area drenching me in one fell swoop.

I let all my energy dissipate, then I felt a hand on my back. "Wonderful display of control, and excellent skill with steps you never tried before, right?"

I looked up into Atar's eyes. "Yes," I panted out. "I've never felt anything like that before."

"Where you are kneeling is very sacred ground, powered by one of the strongest artifacts ever created. You got insight into what you will become, and how it feels to advance to that level. You're a ways off yet, but to see it all working together around you, I understand why there are so many people talking about you." He moved to offer me a hand. "Come, sit with me for a short while."

I took his hand, surprised by his strength to pull me up. "Who else was here?" I asked.

He cocked his head sideways at me, "Who else was here? Just me," he said and sat down.

"There's no one else?" I sat with him. I knew there had been someone else. "I swore I heard another voice."

Atar faced me. "Now, let me see the real you. I have a couple of pointers for your newfound skills, then I'm going to sit and watch you some more, while the others stress inside what I'm doing to you."

"I'm not as much an open book as I used to be." I smiled. "I can hide things now, but not from someone like you. I have no idea how strong you are."

"Stronger than Geo, Luca, and Taryn combined." He laughed. "But I am old. I am strong, but I am also weak."

I took his hands in mine, and my character sheet flashed up before us. To my surprise, my name hadn't fully changed, but was accompanied with theirs. I'd also blown past all my other attempts to gain levels in my affinities, just by being here. This place was amazing.

"I have points already," I said.

"Yes, where are you putting them now?"

"One to Strength, one to Dexterity, and one to Constitution, so I can move better, for longer."

I did so, watching myself grow, fascinated.

Name = Oto Benes - Giannetta/Fraser/Sawa
ID Number = 4188927
Age = 22
Species = Anodite
Sex = Male
Alignment = Chaotic
Bloodline = Royal Seven
Health = 99%
Cultivation Level - King 2
Active Meridians = 12/12
Nanites = 1.5 Million
Artefacts = 2
Chosen Specialist = Racer
First Chosen Affinity = Water
Second Chosen affinity = Fire

Statistic = Body + Ivori + Cultivation
Strength = 54/**208.44**
Dexterity = 59/**228.33**
Constitution = 52/**201.24**
Int/Wis/Spirit = 77

Affinities - Rank

Water - Violet
Fire - Indigo
Earth - Green
Air - Green
Light - Green
Darkness - Yellow
Spirit - Blue

Droll's Leg Pouch – 1 potion left

"This time," Atar said and motioned once again for me to look outside the circle, "you will be fighting Kei."

I faced him, my pulse racing, my heart pounding. "Of course."

31

Monday, August 9th *Lunch*
Year - 27515

Two hours became four.

I didn't feel anything like the exhaustion I had before, though I knew Atar watched the time. Kei was a superb fighter, almost as if he could tell exactly what and where I was trying to move, to hit him.

The more we parried, the more I questioned my sanity. He did know exactly where I was going to strike. Every single move, he caught.

We practiced for quite some time, and Kei tested me in every way possible. As soon as the hour had passed, he stopped to give me the time to put my points into place, because he needed me to be fully on form, and that meant to use every advantage I had the opportunity of using.

Four hours became six.

I was excited because I knew my points. Well, I hoped my points would be racking up like they were the first time I was here. Did Kei know this as well? How much would it alter his stats?

Excitement at the possibilities rushed through me. When I felt tired, I pushed even more. I wondered once—no, much more than that—if Kei was growing tired too. He didn't seem to be. His lunges, his counters to my attacks were just too perfect.

It was dark once again.

Kei never let me drop my stance, my guard, or his level of fighting. He was astounding.

Nine hours later.

Ten hours later.

I heard something at the edge of my consciousness.

Kei stepped back out of my range, and although I almost fell, I stopped myself.

"What is it?" I asked.

Geo and Alek stood at the edge of the circle. They both kowtowed really low, and I sheathed my new sword.

"Apologies for disturbing you, Elder Sawa," Geo said.

"Rise," Atar said, also moving to the edge of the circle. "You would not have come if it was not urgent, correct?"

Alek nodded, glancing at Geo.

"The truth's out about the artifacts," Geo said. "The Canillion nest's been outed over vicenet."

"That means—" Alek started.

"It means the ones we saved are at grave risk," I replied. "They'll go for the nest. Kill everything inside it to get to those artifacts."

Geo ran a hand through his hair. "We don't have time for heroics, Oto."

I looked at Atar, then to Kei. "I helped save a clan of Canillion, and they helped save me." I grinned back at Geo, then Alek. "Since when do we ever have time for anything?" I tapped the side of my head, thinking. "We can't leave them. I won't leave them."

Ezra and the others appeared at the door. "We should head inside. This is not the place for meetings of this caliber," Atar said.

I dipped my head to Kei. "Thank you for your instruction and your patience."

Kei dipped back. "You are very welcome. May it prove useful in the coming months, and when you come to Copter, I have your back."

I was about to move away, when Atar raised a hand and stopped me dead, waving the others away. They left us for a few moments.

I waited for him to say something, anything. His voice kept, calm, his face stoic. "Don't let anyone tell you you're wrong here. Trust your instincts."

"Oh," I said. "You believe the Canillion are in trouble?"

"If they get what's in those caves, everyone will be in trouble. The Canillion protect our future as well as our past." His eyes drifted back to my friends who waited on me. "Go," he said. "The time you've spent here will be worth it. Those extra points, spend them well. Go and do what you must."

"Always," I replied, bowing low to him once more. "Thank you."

I moved away to catch up with Geo and Alek. Councilor Troha and Elder Sawa stayed outside. We walked back inside, then to one of the council chambers.

"What are you thinking?" Ezra asked reaching for my hand "You can't go back. It's a free-for-all at this time of year. All clans, all species —the run happens at the safest possible time. When they are occupied at least for most of it."

"Ren's in contact with Tru, right?" I directed to Alek, but squeezed Ezra's hand softly.

"Yes. I think they spoke the other day," Alek said.

"Good. They're on the planet, right?"

"What made you think they wouldn't be?" Alek asked.

"They're with Sinclairs, just a feeling they were going places. I'm surprised is all."

"They've been swapping notes on some of the bikes' racing meets." Alek smiled. "I'm not sure where we're going next, but they do want us to team up again."

"We will be teaming up," I said. "Eula and Bessie and the others will have friends. Thalis too. Contact anyone who made the Canillion run with us and survived," I said with pure conviction. "We are going back. We have to move them."

"Oto," Geo said. "Move them? You're crazy."

I looked at him, then Taryn. "We should be celebrating. Today was—"

"Today is over," Taryn said. "We celebrated, we ate, we danced, we also grabbed some sleep."

"The baby?"

"I'll be heading the hospital soon. It will be okay."

I caught the moon still shining outside and yawned suddenly. "Sleep," I said. "What's that?"

"Something you'll be doing on the way back to the track." Geo smiled. "Come on. We can talk some more on the way. I'll take Taryn the hospital and then we'll make sure everyone we want is with us."

I didn't have time to rest. No sooner had we sat in a car to return to the track than Eula's call came in.

I tapped the side of the car to bring her face up on a screen before us.

"What's going on?" she asked. "Not pushing Alek enough?"

"It's not that." I shook my head.

Her face paled. "What is it?"

"We need to take a crew and several large wagons into the Canillion's run, to the nest we went to. Anyone you know, get them to Frasers."

She almost choked. "What?"

I wasn't going to lie to them. But I worried.

"The channel's secure," she said. "I'll call Marik, he's been messaging me weird texts about you and Alek. I thought he was just being cautious, but . . ."

"He knew this call was coming?"

"He's been watching vicenet, asking me to check on local gangs' messages."

"You can do that?"

"I've history," she said.

"With Lena?"

She didn't deny it, but she also didn't say anything else.

"The Canillions' young are going to be in grave danger. They'll keep the adults outside, locked in combat, and kill anything on the inside."

"Do you have any idea what it would be like trying to get across their territory now?"

Zero Light

"No," I said. "But I know we can't leave them there. Those coming in would do everything possible to get to them, and if that meant killing every Canillion on the way in, they would."

Eula turned her head. She spoke off screen for a moment. Then Bessie joined her, her face grave. "Oto, it is good to see you. Tru's sent through recordings from some of the other clans. They really are planning to go in big. What got them so excited?"

"I don't know," I said, and I meant it. I didn't. "We'll be back at the track soon. Call anyone you can, please." I cut the call.

We'd never told anyone what happened, but something had gotten around. Maybe our detour, something. I even thought about Trayk, and the item we didn't get. Did he think it was still out there? Was it something to do with him?

I shoved those thoughts aside, hoping everything inside my heart wasn't the truth.

I closed my eyes then, needing the rest.

You have points to spend, Ivori said. *You any thoughts to it?*

At this level, I really need to think on it, I said. *What do you think?*

It's your choice, she replied. *I've got the drive. Take a look; play with it like Luca showed you. I trust you.*

She might have trusted me, but I wasn't sure I trusted me. Ten hours, another twenty points to spend. It was truthfully amazing. I'd seen the effects with Luca at his level, this... blew my mind.

10 to Strength
5 to Dexterity
5 to Constitution

I felt good about it, so I hit the accept.
Now my main stats read:

Strength = 64/**253.44**
Dexterity = 64/**250.88**
Constitution = 57/**223.44**
Int/Wis/Spirit = 77

After I'd made my choices the lull of the drive was enough to let me sleep.

At the track, the others started to make their way to the shack. Ezra hung back. "I won't be long," I said. "I need to check something out."

She hesitated, then kissed me. "Okay."

I went to the garage for Ivori; she was ready revved up and waiting. "Where we going?" she asked.

"Other side of town, Trayk's estate."

"You're wanting to speak to him about the nest?"

"I need to make sure," I replied, hands on the wheel as I flicked through the gears out the track doors and onto the highway.

It didn't take long. Once at the gates, I pushed the comms panel.

Trayk answered himself. "Little late for a house call, isn't it?"

"I need to talk to you," I said.

"Go home, Oto. You've got a race to prepare for."

He wasn't going to let me in. I had to bring him around; I had to ask him outright. "I really need to talk to you, Trayk, For Lazarus, for Camran."

I heard him mumble.

Then the gates moved slowly, but they moved. "Make your way up to the house, then to the back garage. I'll meet you there."

When the gates were open enough, I edged Ivori through, and up toward the house.

I backed Ivori up to the doors, then got out. Rain spattered in my face, but I wiped it off.

Trayk stood in the open doorway, he stepped aside to let me in. Once inside I just spat it out. "Someone's organizing a raid on the Canillion. I thought it was you, but . . . you're—" I looked around the garage, noting several cars, and a bike. Wow, a really massive, bright green bike. *Sica,* a voice said to me, female. *It is an honor to have you here, Oto.* I heard her? *The honor's mine, I'm sure,* I replied. Then to Trayk, "Nothing is going on here at all?"

I watched his eyes narrow. His face held its usual stoic expression, then it fell apart.

"No." He shook his head. Then he turned and moved to a computer station at the back of the garage. His car was there, slick matte black with bright pink sparkles down one side. This wasn't the car I'd seen him in the night he tried to pick Ezra up.

"I've been getting blocked messages across the usual channels on the vicenet that I can see." He swallowed, his lips pressed tight into a frown. "I knew something was going on, just didn't expect this."

"You're telling me you've nothing at all to do with organizing several clans around here? At all?"

"No," he said. "We've been concentrating on the racing. The only reason I wasn't at Geo's wedding is because my team needed more time. More practice."

"He invited you to the wedding?"

That made me look at him sideways.

"Despite what you think of me, Oto, Geo and I have a pretty open talking relationship."

"Because of Camran?" I asked, then realized it really was the truth.

"Yes, because of my brother." He leaned back on the table and pointed to the lines of code scrolling on by.

"Send that to Alek," I said. "We'll get it broken down. Anything you can will help here."

"What are you going to do?"

"I've called in all the favors I can. Everyone who has something to lose."

"We all have something to lose if they get in there and take whatever the hell they want."

"The council can't stop them?" I asked.

"If they've got as many clans together as it sounds? I'll contact them, but by the time they mobilize anything, it could be too late."

"So it's just us, then," I said, feeling suddenly so overwhelmed by this task.

"Do you have a plan you think will work?" he asked.

"I think so. We have good numbers and fighters."

"You're wanting what? More?"

"I need to talk to the Canillion," I admitted.

"Talk to them?" He took a slight step back.

"They're going to have to move," I said. "We're going to have to move them. Trucks, cars, anything that can help. I'll bring that mountain down around me if I have to. No one will get those artifacts. No one."

Trayk tapped his screens, then I saw Alek's code. "The information's gone," he said. "I'm sure they'll be able to do something with it. I can't. I never trained in code."

"You didn't get a choice for training," I said. When his face pained, I added, "Sorry."

"Lazarus told you a few things, didn't he?"

"Your grandfather? Yes, he did. He told me how you came to be what you are. That everything you did was for Camran."

He fiddled with his buttons then crossed his arms. "I did the best I could. I'm not proud of everything. But I tried."

"Can you come and help us out there? You're one of the strongest people around."

"I can't. When you all move on, I'm the one left behind. I have to keep things as they are for Sinclairs, for the teams."

"They rely on you for a lot."

"Yes," he said. "I can't change that."

"They all expect a lot from us," I said.

He laughed, low, emotional. "Yes, they do. But you wouldn't change anything of it would you?"

I shook my head. Leaned on the wall beside him. "No, not at all. I never thought I'd say that."

Trayk moved to his car. "Many years ago, I found an artifact that helped me rise to this position. Then I found Teakan. I understood a lot more about the Icarian and racing, then. When Camran wanted it so much. Why our families had fought for everything we had."

"Instead of supporting him, you just kept pushing. Why?"

"Because I'm stupid," he said. "Because I couldn't say the things I wanted to him."

"He knows," I said. "I've heard him speak about you, your powers, your prowess."

"He did?"

"Yes, before I connected with Ivori, he was the one that convinced me to take that gamble on you. He trusted you."

Trayk's eyes misted. "You need to go," he said. "You have a lot to do and a long way to go."

By the time I got back to our place, everyone had gone to sleep. I parked Ivori up and the guards walked back with me, then I went to bed and slept, fitfully. Dreams of the Canillion, burning fire, death, so much death.

The others got the artifacts. It was bad. Really bad.

War broke out on Isala. Those who couldn't have power now had more power than they could handle. It ended badly, so badly.

My heart pounded, my breathing so erratic. I woke with a start, sweat dripping off me.

I rushed to the window, throwing it open, sucking in cool fresh air.

When my heart settled and my wet clothes went cold, I moved to the kitchen, pulling a bottle of juice out the fridge.

I sat on the couch in the dark, drinking, thinking, hoping.

It was Alek that came through to me. "You okay?" he asked and sat next to me. He stole my bottle off me and drank deep, then offered it me back.

I took it, and made extra sure I wiped the top. "Lurgies, ya know."

He punched me, then silence stretched for a while. "You really think we can save the Canillion?"

"We have to."

A knock at the door roused me. I went to answer it.

Bessie, Eula, and Thalis stood there. "Heard this is where the big guns hide."

I smiled and ushered them all in. "We've got a lot of people willing to help out," she said. "Marik's even sending down some of the elite."

"What? Aren't they supposed to never leave the training grounds?"

"No, they're not. But they're also some of the best and fastest drivers we could ever have on our side. They also have some Metal Walkers."

I swallowed. "Like Tant?"

Eula grinned. "Exactly. Now, let's get the 3D system in here up and running properly and lay out how it's best we counter their attack on your nest."

"Nest?" Thalis asked. "Can you tell me what's going on? I'm here because I'm getting paid, but—"

"We hid inside the Canillion's main nest," I said "The others are at heading in because of the rumors. Artifact rumors."

Thalis laughed. "They've been rumors ever since I've been racing."

Alek brought up a large 3D image of the Canillion run.

"But you did go off the grid for a while. We've all watched the play backs from afterward."

"Where did you go? Thalis asked.

I pulled out the little leather book the councilor had given me, and I passed it to him. "There's a lot of things in here that make no sense to me. But it does tell me one location—"

Thalis stopped on a page, and he read some of the notes I had so long ago. "This is the location of a nest?"

"Not just any nest," I said. "It is a very special nest, one that the Canillion not only protect and raise their young, but is filled with artifacts taken from the riders through all of the races."

"You found what most would consider the holy grail of cave systems."

"We did, and they're going hunting for it. With some obvious intention of taking it all."

"You really found it?" he asked.

I pointed to the leather attachment to my suit at the door. "We did, and they can't get hold of those artifacts. It would—"

"It would upset the balance of power on the whole planet," he said.

"Exactly," Eula added. "Now, tell us everything you know on your race."

We went around all of us, noting sections of the ally that we'd personally ridden through. The animals, the state of the ground. Things were a lot different when you were out there. We could have the best plan in the world, but we knew how unpredictable that area and the species that lived there were. We made a solid plan, a plan that would see the Canillion relocated, relocated with minimal consequences. I hoped.

32

Friday, August 13th *Late Evening*
   Year - 27515

The closer we got to the Canillion's nest, the more I worried. Not only for any of them that would fight who would get hurt. But for my friends and family too. These creatures were unpredictable, thousands of years old. We'd treated them and their breeding season as a game. I knew it wasn't.

What lay in their caves was a veritable wealth of powerful artifacts. So powerful others were willing now to risk it all, to head on in, in numbers that even I'd never seen. Vartoth and three others we'd tracked conversations between. They were all in; that meant many losses on both sides.

I wasn't sure how to do this, how to approach the caves. Ivori pulled up alongside Ren.

"You have a plan on getting in there?" Alek asked me.

I shook my head. Noting the large Canillion on the front just like previously, I watched as the old girl bent her head and looked in our direction.

"You need to stay here with the trucks," I said to Alek. I tapped the steering wheel, nerves spreading up through my belly. "I need to speak to them on my own first. Then we can start the extraction properly."

"You're never on your own," Ivori said.

Those words lit my insides with warmth. "Get me in as close as you can," I said.

"Good luck," Alek said. "Keep us updated."

I slipped into gear, and we set off nice and low. "Lights down," I said. "Low as you can, not like we can't see her."

The lights dimmed and though there were a few bumps in the road we negotiated in as close as possible.

I stopped her, then opened the door, sliding out.

The Canillion lowered her body, but fire escaped from her throat, snaking around her whole face, framing it in an eerie display of power.

We were opposites, even if my use of Fire was growing. I had more pull on Water, and the rain clouds had followed us out from the city.

I raised a hand, allowing my energies to surface. The Canillion lowered her head even more and settled it on the ground before me. I kept walking in closer, and closer. Trying my best not to be nervous, to even feel it. The ground rumbled with her growl. But she didn't make any other move. Her eyes locked with mine the whole way.

I could smell her musty scent from the recent rains. The water in the ground calling to me as much as the skies, I drew up from beneath too.

I slowed my walking, and I stood about ten feet from her, my hand still outstretched. She moved then, and I almost jumped back.

Slowly, she put her large head right in front of me.

Did she really want me to?

I think she does, Ivori said. *Touch her.*

I reached forward and placed my hand to the Canillion's rough scales.

"Hello," I said to her. "I mean you no harm."

"Hello, Oto."

"You know my name?"

"Of course. I am Etheera."

"It is good to meet you, Etheera."

"We knew you'd come back," she rumbled. The roughness of her scales scratched at my hand, but I didn't pull it back. "We did not expect you to return for many years."

"There's some bad people coming." I waved out to the desert, glancing in the direction I knew they were coming from. "I've come with friends, to move the youngsters."

"Move them?" she asked, moving her large head off the ground and looking out to the others. The trucks in the distance had their lights low, but still there.

"Yes, if the others come in and we've not moved them, they'll kill everything in their path with no remorse."

"They want the items off your dead," she said, and I didn't need to see anger. I felt it; it oozed from every pour of hers.

I nodded. "Yes, they do. There are some very powerful artifacts."

"Where would we go?" Etheera asked. "Our young are too small to be out there yet."

"I know. It's why we're here. I have somewhere we can take you, but you'll have to trust all of us."

"That will be difficult, since our queen's passing. There's been quite the unrest amongst the other elders."

I felt her sadness, it resonated through her to me. "Do you think they'd speak to me?"

She was silent a while. "I will ask for you," she answered, "but I fear to do so."

"Thank you," I answered honestly.

Her eyes glazed over, and I waited.

"The council will see you in the inner chamber," she said a few moments later.

I replied, "Do I just go in?"

Her large head bobbed up and down. "They'll be waiting for you."

I moved to walk inside the cave.

"Oto."

I glanced back at her.

"Go easy on them. Change is difficult, and our young prince will want to—"

"He's okay, right?" I worried instantly.

She chuckled. "He is growing; you will see. Go. Do not keep them waiting if time is the essence."

I nodded. "I'll see you again soon."

I made my way inside their caving system, recalling the last time we were here, what it was like. I started to sweat already, and bringing the cooling effects of my Water forward, and Air, I managed to cool off some. I was glad I was much stronger. When I got closer to the main cave, I brought up my Fire to match the heat of their center cavern.

What I saw when I entered the main cave threw me. Several large Canillion surrounded a much smaller one. Was that . . . crap, they were going to hurt him, kill him. My instincts kicked in, and without thinking I rushed forward.

There was no way at all I could protect him or myself from those teeth dominating the skies above him. But I blanket covered us both with Azris.

"Oto," a voice said to me. "You shouldn't have come."

The other Canillion backed off a little.

"You are?"

"Adeesa," he said. "You knew my mother."

One of the Canillion stepped forward, its dark blue scales glinting with my Azris use. "He protects himself with both Fire and Water."

"Using Air to cool himself while the others internally fight for dominance."

They were reading me?

"The council are strong," Adeesa said. "They will not listen to me."

"You knew we were coming?"

"It was only a matter of time. As young as I am I cannot sway them."

I turned to the massive creatures now circling the both of us.

"He is not strong enough," a yellow scaled Canillion said. "He's too weak for anything. We cannot trust him."

"Do you not see that internal battle? The affinities own him. He might not be strong enough now, but he will be everything Atire said he would."

Zero Light

"I didn't know her name." I spoke out to them. "But I knew how she felt."

Searching for the Spirit I knew was nestled in between my other affinities, I pulled it forward, thinking of her, what we shared in the brief moments we had together. Why she had come to my rescue.

The Canillions' voices around me grew louder, then in another breath while I held my rather small shielding around us, they lowered their heads down to my level.

"Atire sensed in you what we do now. Though you are still fairly weak, you have grown. You stand with our prince. Would you stand with him against us?"

I looked to the young Canillion next to me. He was the size of a gotong, much larger than Ivori, our trucks, but not as big as those surrounding us.

I let my Azris shielding drop; it was no use holding that against them. I thought about my word choices here. This was a different species; would my words here mean life or death for him? For them?

I licked my dry lips, then spoke from my heart. "I stand with you."

The dark blue Canillion edged his long nose forward. "I am Tonta, brother to Atire."

I stepped to him, placed my hand on his nose. Felt the heat from within. "I'm sorry for your loss," I said lowering my head to him. "I do not presume to understand all of your customs, your species, but I'm willing to try. If we can be friends."

"Friends?" he asked.

I looked to one of his large eyes, seeing the swirling Fire Azris inside them. Drawn to it in ways I couldn't describe. "Friends." I looked to the others around me. "And friends help each other out. You're about to be invaded."

"We know," the yellow Canillion said. "We have scouts at the edges of our territory. We saw them enter the area, and yourselves."

"Rellis is our Battle Chief," Tonta said.

"You have many other people with you. Why?" Rellis asked.

"We want you to move," I said. "We have a place you can be safe."

"Nowhere but this cave is safe," Tonta said.

"It's not safe anymore," I said. I looked around the cave, seeing the ground still littered with the remnants of our artifacts. "They will not stop till they get what they want, and that's everything in here."

"They will not get past our guard." Rellis spat, anger seething through his every pore.

"They will," I said. "They're stronger than you think, and they're coming with only one intention: annihilation."

"We have some young not capable of being moved. They are too weak. They need the heat, the fire."

I smiled, though on the inside I knew they were right. The young needed so much heat it was scary. "I have Fire affinities with us, many. They're willing to do whatever it takes to get them to safety."

"Your people would help us, relocate us?"

"Out by my city there's an old cavern system, the surrounding area was almost destroyed by tectonic movements a while back. But it is safe now, and there is access down to the planet's core."

"Heat?"

"Yes," I said. "Lots of heat."

Adeesa came up behind me; his large head then crested over my shoulder. "We need to move," he said. "Now."

"I do not know how some of our clan will respond to your people being amongst them," Tonta said, raising his head.

"Then you will keep them in line," I said. "Where are the youngest?"

"The chamber you first saw me in," Adeesa said to me. "I will take you there."

"I need to call my people, get the trucks in closer. Maybe the cars?"

"You will have to carry them," Adeesa said. "They're too fragile for vehicles right now."

I didn't recall any of the Canillion being that young back when we were here. "Okay," I said and I reached out for Ivori.

"Send in Eula, and those who have extra strong Fire affinities. No vehicles. On foot." My mind blanked to their names.

"They're on their way," she replied.

I carried on and followed Adeesa through the cave system. It was so hot. I'd forgotten how much so. I pulled more Azris around me, and then we were in the thick of it. The round nests were mostly empty, but there in the middle were several with babies. They were really small, barely able to be seen over the nests built up side. "Why are they so tiny?" I asked. We drew in closer and I could see the parents nestled in with their young. I realized. "There're city Canillions out here?"

"Our clan has two lines. This is our oldest; they only breed when we're older and have moved out of the nest space."

There were two adults in this nest with their young. They were huddled against each other. Once at the side, I noted Adeesa moving to the parents. He nuzzled against them both. I decided to climb in as they seemed to talk to each other. The young Canillion here were indeed very young. No bigger than a dog? Well, a good-sized dog. A few days old?

I knelt next to the squirming pile of skin. There were no scales yet. The creatures started squeaking and squealing right away toward me and I risked a glance back to their parents, who were glaring me down.

"Just nervous," I said, and held out both my hands in a show of—I hoped—"I mean no harm."

Gently, I turned to the pile of squirming bodies, and slowly I reached for one of the Canillion. With quick action, I scooped it up and into my arms. It squealed a lot, but wrapped its two front legs over my shoulders, and its back legs around my waist. Holding on tight, its wings curled behind, its tail almost trailing the floor. With a hand, I scooped up the tail and tucked it in around my neck. "I've got you," I said. "Don't be scared."

I could feel on the inside though it was, and already its skin was cooling around me. With a thought, I ignited my Azris around my body, trying not to set fire to my clothes. I guess if I lost them it would hurt, but not as much as losing these tiny mites.

I stepped toward Adeesa. "They're not too hard to carry. But they do require a lot of Azris."

"Yes," he said.

There were several other Canillion looking out over from the nests to me. Some young from Adeesa's clan and some city parents.

"We've got this," I said. "Let me head out. While the others come in,

I'll coordinate with them to make sure all of these guys are moved safely."

One of the city Canillions growled my way, and the baby squirmed in my arms. "What is it?" I asked Adeesa.

"They're just scared," he said.

Carefully, I made my way out with this baby. My steps were sure, my control of my Azris pure. I meant to keep this little one safe, warm, happy. I felt her then, yes, her. She reached for my mind with hers. "Brother," she said. "Feel. Sad."

I stroked down her back, letting heat trickle into her. "I know, I feel sad too," I replied.

Drawing into the cave system that led us back out to Etheera, I saw lights from my friends as they came in, the clear heat signatures strong. I saw the face of someone familiar.

"Eula," I said as we drew in closer together.

Her face fell, and she reached out right away. "Oh gosh, she's so tiny!"

"She is. There are more, maybe a few dozen. Take her to the truck get that temp up. They're going to need all the heat they can get, without melting the metals. Get them out of here, now, fast."

Eula sparked her Fire, and then reached out for the baby. She didn't want to detach from me. "Eula will look after you. She's warm, safe," I said. "Your brothers and sisters will be with you soon."

I let her go, even though I pined a little for the baby. "Come on," I said to the others, they're this way."

I showed them to the nest, and within several more minutes, together they were moving the babies. The trucks moved in closer, but on my third trip out, Etheera's low growling caught my attention.

"Pete?" I asked through comms

"We've got about twenty minutes before they get here."

Fuck.

Alek came in at my side. "Trucks are almost full. We need to move them as soon as possible."

"Send those out that are full ahead. We'll fill the last one and join you."

He put his hand on mine. "Get the Canillion adults out. They're going to have to fight."

"I know," I said.

Etheera's grumbling grew louder, and I could see the sheer amount of energy she was pulling to her. The whole area was full of Fire. Like . . .

No way.

I heard Ezra to the side, caught her eye. "We're full," she said running to me.

I kissed her quickly. "Go, get them out of here."

"You're coming, right?"

"We'll be right behind you. I promise."

She turned and fled, jumping into a truck.

I noted lights to my left as Etheera growled lower.

"That's a bike?" I tried to focus in on it, to see more. The lights were bright; nothing stood out.

"I have incoming comms for you," Ivori said.

"What? Who?"

"It's Trayk," she said.

"What? He said he—" He wanted the artifacts, didn't he? No, I'd trusted him before. I could. I could trust him now. Of all the things we'd been through, Sinclair's Elite track, knowing how much he loved his brother. Taking the artifacts himself . . . no that made no sense at all. He wasn't here for the artifacts. Not at all.

Alek's voice came through. "You accept comms and he'll know exactly where we are. He could tell the others."

I shook my head. "No," I said to him and moved to Ivori's side, it was the weirdest words that would ever come out of my mouth. "I trust him." To Ivori, I said, "Okay. Accept it."

"Is that you, Oto?"

I slipped into Ivori's seat. Though I could just about see his face, I could also see the desert planes slipping past his screen, way fast.

"You're on that bike, coming here, to us?"

"I'm in the middle of nowhere right now, where are you?" he asked.

I hesitated to send the location just for a moment. Tapped in the coordinates and then hit send.

"Locating now. I'm too far away," he said, paused, then added. "Get the Canillion adults in the air. Get everyone else out of that mountainside as fast as you can."

"You can't tell them or me what to do," I said.

He seemed to look directly at me then. "Oto, you have no idea who it is behind me. The Canillion need to buy me some time. I need to get to you."

I scoffed. "Time, time for what? To loot the caves before they get here?"

"No," he spat back. "I'm here to help you destroy them."

I swallowed.

"If we don't bring that whole area down, they'll get those artifacts, and this planet. This side of the universe will become a warzone faster than your wildest nightmares."

"We have explosives," I said.

"It's not enough," Trayk admitted.

I knew he was right. It wasn't enough. We'd done everything we could to get people together. My friends were in there setting it all up, but it wasn't ever going to be enough.

You've only got one other option, Ivori said to me.

I have only one life left to do this, I replied. *If I choose to overload and let loose in there, I have no more chances.*

I know, she said. *I'm one hundred percent with you.*

I swallowed and stared ahead. *There's no other choice. I'm doing it.*

33

Saturday, August 14th *Very Early*
Year - 27515

My heart sank. I could see the lights from Trayk's bike. I could hear the roar of the engine underneath him. He was moving faster than anyone I'd seen out here.
He's rushing to beat them; Vartoth and the others are right behind him.
Right behind me, I knew the last of our team were doing everything they could to get the last few babies out. Hosoke and Pete, our guards, were deep in the system setting up charges, much like those ones the Vipers had set, those that took her artifact off her. It had taken promises to get them. Not money. She'd had to owe favors to some of her top informants for this.
I watched out into the dark skies. My stomach churned. They were coming.
Even the smaller main Canillion clan were with this land. Adeesa too.

Etheera's head whirled around toward me. "Tonta orders the others to the skies."

I reached for her, put my hand on her flank. "I'm sorry."

"I may not have the wings I used to, but I will defend this entrance with everything I have."

The bike came in closer, and she was about to breathe fire on—no way, Trayk!

"Whoa, whoa," I said to her. "Friend. Let him closer."

She stepped to the side, and the bike stopped before me. Trayk was off and in front of me in a split second. Trayk glanced at Ivori. "Make sure she is safe," he said to her. "Please."

I felt emotion wash off Ivori. "Sica will be safe with the Canillion babies," Ivori returned to him.

Alek and Tatsuno were exiting as we were heading in. Alek took one look at Trayk, but I just shook my head. "Trust me," I said.

"I'm here to help. Lead the way," Trayk said, and pointed back down the system.

Alek dipped his head and reported. "We're nearly clear. We've got one more trip, but hurry."

So we did, my feet rushing as fast as I could, sweat pouring off me.

"All explosives are in place," Hosoke said through comms. "We're all making our way out through the cave system now."

As we grew deeper into the dark, I felt the mountain shaking. "Canillion fire," I said as Trayk glanced my way, his eyes nervously twitching with his Azris.

"They're here," he said. "I didn't think I'd be far off beating them."

"You've taken a hell of a risk. This is going down, hard."

"Oto, you've shown me a lot of things this last year. Mostly that there's change coming. I can't sit back anymore. I can't protect those I love without stepping up."

"Come on," I said, my feet never stopping. "We've got some of the smaller ones to move. You even seen Canillion this close?"

He shook his head.

I took Trayk to the center cavern, where all the artifacts literally lay out on the floor to see. His eyes widened at the sheer expanse of the cave, the nesting holes. "I never expected it to be so . . ."

"So full?"

"So dangerous," he said. "When I asked you to come here for that one piece, I never thought you'd find it. But you did."

"How did you know we did?" I asked him.

"Long story," he said. "It doesn't matter now. What matters is we finish it here, now."

He spun in the center of the cave, his eyes widening even more. I also saw something else from him. Power draw. I felt it.

He was something else.

"Trayk? We can't do this just yet—"

"They can't get their hands on any of this this, none of it. You need to get those babies out of here, and I need to make sure this goes nowhere else. At all."

"I'm more than sure my team have snuck a few things in their pockets."

He nodded. "I would have too. But I'm—"

The floor underneath my feet grew hotter. He was doing all of this. He was drawing the heat. I had to counter it the only way I knew how.

I brought forth Water, running it over my body. My feet steamed. The sheer heat in here was hotter than anything I'd ever encountered.

Trayk pulled in yet even more. His eyes burned with such pure energy.

"How are you even doing that?" I asked.

He tapped the side of his ear. And I noticed then. Two studs. Two gems. "Artifacts?"

"The smallest anyone's ever come across, and powerful. I've never used them."

"So why now?"

"This is what they were made for. One chance to do the right thing."

If only Geo or Luca were here. We could have done this easy, we could have brought down the whole mountain without the need for explosives.

The metal objects to my left were actually melting. I couldn't protect myself and bring in more heat. I couldn't.

"One minute," Alek shouted through my ears. "We've almost got them."

"I don't have the energy," I gasped. My knees wobbled and I struggled to hold me own. I was losing all strength. "We don't have time."

"No." Trayk's eyes flashed brilliant hues of red and blue around the cave. "You don't. You have to go."

"What?" I tried to keep standing.

Trayk reached into his pocket and took out a small book. I could see it start to singe already. He threw it at me, and I caught it, protecting it instantly.

"For Camran," he said. "You have to go. You have to win at Esrall City tomorrow. If you don't—" He swallowed, and I saw into his soul, his real emotion there.

I understood as Trayk began to let out even more energy, starting on our left side. He let out his colossal strength, everything he had, super heating everything around us, melting everything in his path. I cringed. The wealth of all of this, the power that could be gained. He was right. It had to be destroyed at all costs. That cost wasn't me, or my life. Watching him struggle, though, I had to help. I forced myself to do more.

"No," he shouted at me. "You need to leave. Now! If you don't win that race, if you don't join Amalia and Camran on Copter—"

I held on tightly to that book. "Everything you've ever done is for your family," I said. "Everything."

I knew I had to go. There was no more time.

"Thirty seconds," Alek yelled at me. "Get the hell out of there, Oto!"

I had to go now, and I had to win.

I had no choice, but at the moment I wasn't fit for anything.

Alek shouted for me again. This wasn't through comms; the cave in here was getting so, so hot.

Alek was then with me, pulling at me. "Come on, can't you see what he's doing?"

I glanced at Trayk, none the wiser. Trayk's suit was on actually on fire. He . . . the temperature in here. It was hotter than any fire I'd ever come across, ever would come across.

Fuck, I had to help him and myself.

Alek dragged me backward as Trayk concentrated harder, his whole body, his clothes, burning.

"We can't leave him," I said. "We can't—"

"Yes," he said. Alek's face softened. "Yes, we can."

When he dragged me this time, I didn't protest. My boots were sticking, melting to the cave's floor. Burning metals, flesh, leather—everything assaulted my nose.

Tatsuno met us on the outside of the cave. Ren's engine roared to life. "This whole place is going to go."

I looked back. The mountain, the volcano underneath.

"Trayk?" Tatsuno asked.

"He'll get out if he can," I said, though it was a lie, there was no chance of it. "I'm sure he will."

"Move before my tires melt!" Ivori screamed.

I jumped in, her engine roared, and she shot off with the door still open. My belt secured around me as the door slammed.

I turned as best I could in the seat to watch the explosions.

The ground thump-thumped as the charges we set went off in the deep caverns. Large dust clouds burst high into the atmosphere.

Then with one massive crack, light exploded into the night sky. I closed my eyes, and Ivori was thrust forward moments later by the force of energy as the whole underground and mountain dropped, then shot out into the skies as massive chunks of molten lava.

My mind whirled, I slammed the window, the nites obeying my command to drop. Then I leaned out and vomited over the side wing.

"Water's in the back," Ivori said. "I—"

I wiped my mouth, and stared at the horrendous dust cloud growing behind us.

Ezra's face appeared on the dash before me. "Alek says Trayk was in there?"

"He was," I replied.

"What are you saying?" Her face paled. "He got out, right?"

I met her eyes with mine, and shook my head. "He didn't make it," I said.

He forehead creased. "No," she said, tears streaming down her cheeks. "Oh gods, no."

"Ezra," I said. "I'm so sorry. I'm really sorry."

"You and Alek left him on purpose," she said.

I was about to say more, to defend her brother, myself. Her words reverberating around in my head, she cut the feed.

I glanced to the truck with the last of the babies in. Overhead, a shadow graced our flank. Then another and another.

"Tanto, and Rellis," Ivori said. "Rellis is injured."

I tapped the side of my head. Brought up Ezra's internal comms, and I tapped her. This wasn't time for games.

She didn't answer as a call, so I quickly thought out.

Me - One of the Canillion is hurt. You're in charge of healing when they get there. I have to split off, and you know it. I'll see you there, right?

Under my breath, I cursed. I needed her right now.

Nothing came in return. I waited till we were almost about to cut away from our small convoy and closed the comms.

"No hope for that one."

Her message came back to me as soon as Ivori turned us away from their direction, back to the city.

Ezra - I'll be there as soon as I can, we all will. Tatsuno's already gone ahead. Some of the other team members are there waiting for us.

"I'll show you no hope."

I tapped the wheel. Pure relief flooded through me; at least she'd messaged me. Ivori turned the wheel and we headed back toward Esrall and our final race.

"You know this city, this track," Ivori said. "You've got this."

"So do you," I countered. "Doesn't make me feel any less nervous."

"Without nerves we'd have no fuel to force us to be better," she said.

Zero Light

The city lights illuminated out path in, yet my mind could only be on Trayk, our losses. The Canillions' losses. I wanted to be there, to see to them all, to help. But my friends had this. I had to trust that together we made that difference, that things would be okay.

"How long until it starts?" I asked.

"We're first up. An hour."

I took the wheel back, slowed us down. Then turned away from the track route, and made my way to Grovers. It was super early still. But Pa would be there. We pulled up, and Ivori dipped her lights. I sat there for a moment, then got out, taking in the chill of the night air. You couldn't see the Canillion run from here. No one would even know what happened out there.

But I . . . I couldn't race without speaking to Camran. As hard as my words—if I found any—could be, I had to tell him.

I just couldn't.

I sat and let the emotions of the day wash over me ever more.

Then I tapped the dash and comms for Vrolsh. When he understood my request, he helped Ivori navigate through the vicenet. I watched as her signal, our signal, bounced over different feeds, satellites, and then our connection was speeding across the vast distance between Isala and Copter.

When she found the ID needed, I took a breath.

"Are you ready?" she asked. "I've got Lena at the moment. She's wanting to make sure you're really okay to do this, today of all days."

There was no other day to do this; it had to be now. "Do it," I said.

She knocked on Camran's personal code.

It took him a moment to answer.

"Oto?" he asked. "You any idea what time it is here. We've a race today." He paused. I heard noise in the background—was that Amalia? When his voice came through next, a video link came with it. His face was flushed, but sullen. "What is it?"

I held out the book Trayk had given to me, and I opened it up. I had no idea what was inside, or if I should read it, but I didn't know how to tell him. I didn't have the words. I hoped Trayk had.

"Cam, there's many things I wanted to tell you," I read even though my voice cracked. "Many things in this life that I shared with you as a father, but not a brother. I pushed you because I knew you'd go far. You're going to go far. If you're reading this now, know that I am no more. But that everything I've done is for you, for our family, and it will live on because of you, because of how truly good you are. This tiny book contains all of the best moments in my life, some without you, most of them with you. Hold onto it, hold onto everything that's good of me. You have access to everything I had, I am. Forget the pain, the trouble, the fighting. Brothers, forever. Race like I know you can, reach for those stars. Yours always, Trayk."

I looked up from the book and met his eyes with mine. Tears streamed from my face, as they did his.

"You need that race win," he said to me, swallowing his emotions. "As do I. We have to do this, today. The both of us."

"I'll win," I said, and I held my hand up to the screen for him to see my Azris. "I've a little time. I'm just going to grab some good food, and we're ready. You?"

Arms snaked around him, and Amalia clung to his side, kissing his neck. "We're ready," she said. "Thank you."

"Win that race," Camran said. "I'll talk to you in more detail later, when you hand that book to me in person on Copter."

I closed it, placed it against my heart. "I will win that race," I said. "And we will be coming to Copter."

"Good," Amalia said. "We kinda really need you here. Lena's driving us both crazy. A friendly face or two won't go amiss at all."

Camran wiped his eye, squeezed her tight to him. "Thanks for letting me know. Cam out."

As he cut the comms, I saw him bury his face in Amalia's stomach. Heard the pain as he cried out.

I threw open the door and fell out into the dripping rain, letting it cool me down, ease everything that was going on inside me.

And I cried. I cried because I didn't know what else to do.

I hadn't expected any of this. Trayk? The family complications, their dynamics, mixing so close with Frasers? Sinclairs, friendly . . . it not only shocked me, it shook me to my core.

A light cough, a hand on my back. I turned to look up into Pa's eyes. His bakery staff members stood in the doorway.

"Oto, what? What are you doing here. You're getting soaked." He held a hand out for me, but when I took it and he pulled me up, the physical contact broke me even more.

"Oh, Oto, my boy." He pulled me to him, and I couldn't help myself. I let out everything that was inside of me. I cried even more.

I cried for loss, for pain. For the many things we'd all hurt for.

Pa cried then as well. For his loss, for everything. He held me, until we'd nothing else left to give. Then wiping his eyes he beckoned me inside and into the back office. He brought me a towel, and guided me to the shower. "I'll have fresh clothes and food for you when you're done," he said.

I nodded at him and went in, stripping off, my suit, my boots melted beyond recognition. I turned the tap and stepped inside, washing the dust, the blood, the hurt, all of it away with the water.

My mind focused on the one thing I needed now. That win.

I stepped out, clean and ready.

Pa looked at me as I entered his office. "You okay?" he asked.

I sat before him, helped myself to the plate of food. I really was starving. "Loaded it fully with extras so you'd more to give in the race," he said. "The drink's been a special of ours for a while, you know that."

I nodded and picked up the hot mug, sipping slowly. The combination of savory and sweet was odd, but I needed everything this food gave me.

Outside I could hear the city was bustling again. "Everyone is out early," he said. "This is a big race."

"I know," I said, then I smiled at him. With everything going on around me, with how exhausted I did feel on the inside, everyone had confidence in me. I had confidence. I'd done everything I could to be ready for this race and more.

I could do this. I would do this. For Trayk and Bodil, and everyone else.

34

Saturday, August 14th *Lunch*
Year - 27515

Ivori's engine slowly rumbled beneath me. Vibrating, comforting. The roads were busy. We couldn't get away from that, but there must have been someone who spotted us, because the next thing I knew we had a security escort to the new track. This was Esrall's second track, not the same as the one where Amalia or Camran had raced, or I'd taken part in the tryouts. This was their best track. I didn't know what had made them pick this one for us today. Someone had said there was damage to the other; we couldn't get anyone to confirm.

The bikes slipped in before us. They dipped their heads, and two moved in behind. I admit I liked it when they flipped sirens and everyone moved out of the way.

"Very official," Ivori said.

"Agreed, a little overwhelming, though." I kept my hands supple on the steering, taking her in nice and steady to the back of the track I knew so well.

The garage doors opened, and the bikes pulled up on one side to allow us through.

Then they closed behind us. Everyone was waiting.

"Thirty-minute call is in ten," Tatsuno said.

"Where were you?" Alek asked.

"Refueling," I said, sliding out.

The team soon had Ivori hooked up and were running fast checks. "She's been through a lot," Itoh said. "Could really do with changing some other parts out."

"We don't have the time," Tatsuno added.

"Tires, and fuel," Balsy said.

I agreed. "Fresh tires are very needed after that run. We won't get far without them today."

The hiss and humming of the automated tire swaps filled the room. I covered my ears for a moment.

"Sensitive?" Alek asked.

I could only nod. "The noise in the cave was just . . ."

"I know," he agreed. "New suit's waiting. Get dressed fast."

I went out back and slid into the new suit. It fit perfectly. Much better than the other. This time, it had the Ocean Slayers logo stitched into it, and up the sides were amazing blue ocean swirls to go with it.

"You look good," Alek said.

"I've been working on this," Ezra said. She held up a leather belt with the containers from the Canillions' cavern. "It's not the same as the ring I've given you, but these potions are yours, and are with the suit now. If you ever need them, they're there."

She wrapped her arms around me and settled it on my waist. "You're never going anywhere without these. You use up too many other lives, otherwise."

I lowered my head. "I know. But I'd do it all again, and you know I would."

"Kill it out there," Hosoke said.

"You've totally got this!" Ezra leaned in and kissed me. "Love you so much."

My hand drifted to the small of her back while I entwined my fingers with her other. "I love you too," I said. "I—"

She put a finger to my lips. "Race," she said. "Then we'll talk. We have a lot to talk about."

I nodded. "Just don't leave me," I said.

"I'm not leaving you, ever."

"Thirty minutes call, gotta go," Tatsuno said.

"Ready." I moved away from her and slid back into Ivori, making sure I checked everything over before we even got the engine going.

"All green," she said.

"Let's get you all nice and toasty," I said. Firing her engines, she purred into life and we eased out onto Isala's main track.

"We made it," she said.

"So far, so good. We've a long way to go."

"Seventy laps, 4.38 kilometers—"

"Fastest time in 1:10:101," I added for her.

"Correct."

"Let's nail it," I said. "New lap record."

She laughed. "If I know you, and what you're capable of, we'll do it in 105."

"Oh, really?"

"You taking bets?" Hara's voice came through to us.

"Crap, boss is listening."

"I'll take that bet," Hosoke said.

"I'm not listening," I said. We came up to the first right-hand bend.

"Minimum speed 105," Tatsuno said.

I dropped down to third gear and took it nice and steady, making sure I bounced on the tires to get going. Sweeping bend right, then lefts all the way up through the gears again, topping speed to 150, then right back down for the fifth bend and fourth in the selector. The next few bends were easy, the tires warming the gearbox and clutch reaching optimum temps. We were good to go by the time we reached bend ten and hit out max speed on the track 250.

"Not got the distance to reach higher?" I asked through comms.

"No," Alek said, "This is more snaked and sneakier."

"How's she feeling?" Tatsuno asked.

"Responsive, ready, all good here."

"Check your readout again?"

I looked at the dash. Nothing was showing off here. "What is it?"

"We're not communicating with the second brake system."

"At all?"

"No," he said. "Pull in."

Fuck, we couldn't deal with this now. I checked the time and pulled back into the pits. Tatsuno, Itoh, and Balsy were out and around the back of Ivori in seconds. Itoh and Hosoke both were under the rear end.

"How's she looking?"

The track would call pit lanes' closing in mere minutes.

"We've a chip out," Itoh said, sliding out and rushing for the garage.

He wasn't coming back.

"Itoh!" Hara screamed through main comms. I flinched at his pitch.

Itoh was pelting it back to us seconds later. He slid, and miraculously didn't decapitate himself from the back end of the car. Then I felt a couple of taps on the underside, and the dash flickered and lit up again.

"Still showing everything is green," I said. Fifteen seconds till pits were closed

Itoh slid back out, banging on the rear chassis. "Go!"

I didn't hesitate. He said it; I was off, hitting the gas, nice and steady out of the lane. Back to my position in on the main track.

"Fifteen minute call. Pits closed."

"Once more around," I said to Ivori.

"You're sure?"

I tapped the wheel and hit the gas, then took my time around the track. Making every single second count, and keeping us in a top condition without supplementing with Azris.

"Good call," Ivori said. "Being more than safe."

"I have to be. This has everything riding on it."

"Yes, it does."

We lined back up as the last of our counters ticked over.

Then it was just waiting for that start.

Zero Light

I had my eyes on that prize, my mind fully focused, my skills and my breathing better than it ever had been.

"Got it," I said.

The lights counted us in.

Two. Four. Six.

"You're going for the perfect start again?"

Eight.

When that last light flicked, I hit the gas at the right moment.

Ten.

I hit the gas perfectly on that mark again. This time, though, I did one thing different. I let my Azris flare, and Ivori's gray chassis burst with colors.

"You didn't." She laughed.

"Oh yes, I did. I want them to know we're meaning business here today."

"Damn, Oto, you're on fire already!" Hara said.

I let the flames die off with the swoosh of water over us.

"Warning," I said. "Just a show of something I learned and they'll never learn."

"You think that will get them on edge?"

We came up to the first bend, and I was at way more than minimum speed. "Is there a max speed?" I asked, suddenly dropping down and as fast as I could.

"Well," Tatsuno said. "I don't think anyone's taken it at that speed!"

I pressed the brakes a little harder, hoping that dang chip was communicating right.

The brakes spread on nicely and even, slowing us just enough. I turned the wheel in time and hit my lines perfect.

Well on our way to a great start and right up the back side of our next overtake, Andi. I stuck with her all the way around. She didn't want me to get past at all. Her lines were good, her control even better. It was no wonder she'd given Vral a race for his life.

I backed off. Instead, I'd have to wait her out. This was endurance as much as perfection.

As we reached lap eighteen, Hara's voice came through. "You're going to have to take her. The leaders are going to be too far ahead for you to catch up otherwise."

I tapped the wheel, nerves finally kicking in. I did have to take her, and now.

Into lap nineteen and the first bend was coming up. Almost as if she knew there was something coming. She tried to stick the same lines she had before, but her brakes were off, her line just that bit shy. I gave more on the gas, and with the flick of my wheel, shot out around her.

We were lined up perfectly, as my line drifted off slightly. I needed more. So tentatively, I pushed Azris into the nitro boosters. Fire sparked around us, and we shot past in time for me to grab the line I wanted at the higher speed.

Then I tapped for more. "We're moving and shaking!" I shouted. "How many to catch up?"

"Safely!" Alek shot back. "You're going to be tight till the end."

"Screw safe." We hit the next right, slightly right, just that bit too fast, and I drifted. The front wheel caught the curb slightly, kicking up dust.

Dust? That wasn't supposed to be there . . .

"Alek?" I asked. "The Zero's been out, right?"

"Of course," his reply came back. "The track's professionally cleaned every day before a major race."

This isn't clean, Ivori said to me.

"Get the logs up. Check everything."

"On it!" Alek's voice came back.

"We need more speed," I said, gripping the wheel tight as we snaked into the next couple of bends. "I'm not holding back on this."

I know you can do both, she said. *But if I call the speeds, the line, will you follow them?*

"I trust you," I replied. *Frees me up to concentrate on what's in front of me. Deal.*

We hit the straight on past the start and out time. One minute, thirty-five seconds.

Consistency was key here.

Speeds logged through the track, the lines I met with pure precision on every single one. 140, 125, 265, 170, 135, 180, 185, 305, 260, 140, 150, 140, into the straight, top out 280, down to second . . .

The gears screamed at me. The changes were harsh. The temperature of the whole car soared.

"How much more can we take?"

"Enough," she said. "Trust me."

"You know I do."

"Four more laps to catch the leading two," Hara said. "You keep this up, you're going to push her too hard."

"No," I said and allowed my Azris inside to pool, spreading cooling energy all around us. "Not hard enough." I made sure we hit ten up on each over the next lap.

We touched the curb twice more. This time, there wasn't just dust.

"Alek?"

"No cleaning," he said. "Fuck!"

"The Zeroes?" I eased into the next bends, nice and steady this time. I needed to hear his words. Vral and Don were now up ahead enough I could see them.

"They went out. I'm watching their tracking now. They just show . . ." His voice trailed off. "No, no way."

"It's old feed, right?"

"Yes," he said. A shiver ran down my spine. "It's well hidden, but it's clearly not this morning."

Hara's voice in the background echoed through. "Red zone it, call it off."

"Don't you dare," I growled out.

Then his voice came clear as a bell. "You get any rain on that track, and it will be lethal if there's fuel spillages as well."

"Good job I'm all Water then, isn't it?" I spat back. "Don't you let them call it off. We've got one chance here now. I'm not losing it to bureaucracy."

"Oto, this is dangerous, seriously." Hara said.

"No fucking kidding, I need to hit speeds no one else ever has!"

I hit the gas, taking us into the straight and up to 315. The brakes squealed as we dropped down into the bend. I hit the speeds Ivori had wanted and then some.

"Careful," she said.

"Now you have to trust me," I replied. "Let me guide the both of us."

I felt her shiver. "You have full control."

"Alek," I begged. "Don't let him report it. I am going to get past these two in the next lap. I am going for it."

"I trust you too," Alek said. "Do it."

"Going dark," I said, and I cut the comms.

Watching the track around me on all levels, I began to notice all the other inconsistencies. The fact it hadn't been cleaned, debris here and there at the sides. Broken gates, holes in the side flagging. "There was no way this was a legality. They've moved this; everyone's been bought out."

"Something deeper than the council could track," Ivori agreed. "Lena would have seen all this."

"It was all a distraction," I said.

I felt her nod on the inside, then I felt a hand on my shoulder. My still-sore shoulder.

"It still hurts?" she asked. "Why? We fixed it. You healed, right?"

I shook my head. "It still hurts. It might always hurt."

I straightened my back up somewhat and focused on the track as we took bend number nine at 185. "I'm going to draw in everything around me," I said.

"Everything?"

"If I don't get those elements working for me here, you see what's coming, right? In the skies above us." I didn't let go of the wheel, but I knew she looked up.

"That's not just a storm," she said.

"No, that's coming for us. It's the biggest damn storm this city will have ever seen its existence."

"You feel it?" she asked.

"Anyone with *any* Azris affinity on this planet is going to feel it."

"The council will call this off before it gets any further. They can't let this happen."

"It's too late," I said. "That's not Vral in that car."

"Oto, I'm so sorry. We shouldn't be doing this at all."

The first few spots of rain hit the windshield. "This is going to get ugly fast," I said. "You're in, right?"

I felt her squeeze my shoulder gently. "Of course I am. Together."

The comms crackled as we caught up to Don and *Vral*. "Someone on comms, trying to get through?"

"Yes." She held off, as I made sure we got around the next bend. "Lena," she said.

"Open the line," I replied.

"Oto?" Lena asked.

"I'm here," I said. "Tell me straight. Who is in that car?"

"His name's Kidvek Rush. Call the race, Oto, you can't fight him."

"Fight? What?"

"He won't stop with just a race win, or lose. He's out for blood, and that means yours. Stop. The. Race."

"I'm not stopping. I have to show them all. This is my time."

With a swipe, I cut her off just as she cursed in a language I had never heard before.

I breathed in deep and then asked, "You recall anyone by that name?"

"Yes," she said. "Lena's right, we should stop."

"You're not stopping me," I said. "You're not."

"You know I could. All I have to do is back off take control."

I deflected her. "Tell me everything you know about Kidvec."

"He's Bratak's second hand man," she said. "He was right there when they took Roa's life from us. She said he'd been working on body mods and tech to be able to do exactly what he's done here. Hide himself."

"Slippery like the snakes they are, I guess."

"Yes," she sighed. "Oto, he's at least Emperor level …."

Fuuuck!

"No hope for that one."

My stats flashed on the screen. I was no where near enough to fight him. But I had to be. On the next straight, reaching up, I yanked on the chain holding Ezra's ring. I slipped it on.

The rush was intense. My stats changed before my eyes.

Name = Oto Benes - Giannetta/Fraser/SawaID Number = 4188927
Age = 23
Species = Anodite
Sex = Male
Alignment = Chaotic
Bloodline = Royal Seven
Health = 99%
Cultivation Level - King 2
Active Meridians = 12/12
Nanites = 1.5 Million
Artefacts = 2
Chosen Specialist = Racer
First Chosen Affinity = Water
Second Chosen affinity = Fire

Statistic = Body + **Ring** + Ivori + Cultivation
Strength = 94/**400.44**
Dexterity = 94/**396.68**
Constitution = 87/**367.14**
Int/Wis/Spirit = **167**

Affinities - Rank

Water - **Violet**
Fire - **Indigo**
Earth - **Green**
Air - Green
Light - **Green**
Darkness - **Yellow**
Spirit - **Blue**

Droll's Leg Pouch – 1 potion left

Ring of Light - A gift from Ezra
Adapted, so you may use it as you wish.

Boosts Azris circulation and usage, + 30 to all stats
Uses = 4

Death Thwarted - Used x 2

The rain on the screen got worse. I pushed the droplets away with a thought, letting us see better, but the track was getting damp. The debris that hadn't been swept up was going to get slippery fast.

"Watch the corners!" Ivori cried as I took the next bend and hit the wet slop and slid.

Then I heard another voice come through to me. "Ride it." Marik said. "You've done this. You spent time on the sands, in the wet. Nothing is worse than wet, sloppy sand."

I didn't try to counter the slide. I steered into it slightly, and we straightened up. "How'd you get through?"

"How do you think? You cut the comms to your team. We lost contact with Vral at the same time."

"It's not Vral," I said. "I'd presume he's dead."

"Drei found his body. The call went through to the council moments ago; oh he's very dead."

"Fuck," I said. I didn't want that. "Will they call the race?"

"Geo's talking to them now. I don't know. Oto, you need to stay safe. Don't worry about the race."

I laughed. "Don't worry about the race."

Lap sixty-six, Ivori said. *We've got four to go.*

"We're completing this race no matter what."

35

Saturday, August 14th *Lunch*
Year - 27515

We both hit the next few bends at over forty above our last top speeds. Ivori's tires screeched at every corner.

Bend eleven came up, and I hit it at almost 295. Kidvec never let up. Stuck like glue to my sides. I noted him inside his Icarian; the power oozing off him and the car was something else. When his eyes met mine, they were just as he was, as his Icarian was. Fire.

Fuck, I dropped gears fast. This was not a bend I needed to fumble over. We were going too fast even if I hammered the brakes. 170, still too fast. We started to drift toward him, and I fought to hold the steering wheel. My muscles shivered with overuse. I could not let go. Kidvec pushed out a fire shield—he wanted us out of the way. For good.

As we connected with the shield. I felt the heat from it, from him. It burned through anything I could put up, and I tried to cover it with Water. It just turned to steam. Instantly. His shield burned through anything that was Ivori and her nites too. The window beside me melted.

The smell hit my nostrils. Black, acrid. Tasted so bad, so very bad. It made me want to puke. I swallowed, again and again.

Panic hit me as we came out of the bend, ramping speeds back up again. I pushed in the opposite direction. Once we were away from him, I hit us with as much water and ice as I could. The metal around us creaked, and cracks spread through it.

The next bend I planned on keeping him at that distance, but he wasn't having any of it. I dropped another gear and eased into the sweeping left. The finish line wasn't far after this. Close, so close. Our timing was nothing they would ever see this side of Isala ever again. I knew it; they knew it.

Azris flickered above us; the fire storm took another turn.

"I've never seen anything like it," Alek said.

Fire swirled around and around, faster and faster. "Fire tornado? If that hits us, we might not survive," Ivori said.

"It won't hit us." I pulled deeper, stronger energies from the ground itself. Light and Dark came with it. Water from all around us, the wet track, even life itself, drifted to match that Fire tornado with water. Nothing was working.

The whole track around us sparked with Azris energy, and I tugged as much as I possibly could my way.

"There's far too much energy around here," Ivori said.

I hit the right bend and Kidvec's car drifted closer again. "Everything you've got, Ivori," I said. "Everything."

I caught Kidvec's eyes again as we exited the bend. He hit his Azris burn with such intensity I never thought we'd have a chance. But Ivori pulled on mine and we shot forward after him.

My shoulder complained, and the belts cut into my suit and my skin once more.

The world around me blurred, faded.

I saw it ahead of us then. The finish line flickered. Our time, stopped. Dead.

"What?"

Red enveloped us everywhere, Fire so hot, so . . .

"Something isn't right," I said. My voice echoed around the cab. It stretched as if time itself had stopped. No, not stopped, stretched.

I hit the brakes, pulled back, but we were going too fast, heading for that finish line.

No.

No, it wasn't there anymore. Darkness spread in front of me.

Pure darkness, like a brick wall.

"Ivori?"

She didn't respond.

We hurtled toward that darkness at speeds I couldn't comprehend.

Then we hit, everything exploded before me, and then we were out.

There really was darkness. I assessed what was before me in a moment. Skyscrapers spread above us, street lights, people. We hurtled into a city at breakneck speeds I could do nothing to stop.

"Oto!" Ivori cried.

Thank fuck she was back with me. "Where the fuck are we?" I asked her.

When she spoke, her words chilled me to the bone.

"Drakol Four. Reeka"

"We just what . . . teleported thousands of light years away? How in all hells is that even possible?"

"It's possible, but it takes much more Azris than I, than you have."

The dash flickered, everything for us flashed like those Christmas tree lights I'd seen months ago, greens and reds all over. Ezra's face flashed into my mind as my brakes weren't responding at all. Kidvec had already hit his brakes, and was now way behind us.

"There's people up ahead," Ivori said. "Thousands of people."

The city center was alive. So alive, even if their streets weren't. Maybe the cars barely ran on the ground. I didn't have time to think about it.

We were approaching the crowds with only one intent, plowing head into them.

Azris flooded from this planet in droves. I thought fast; harnessing it helped the both of us, the chassis, the damage we'd taken going through whatever portal that was, and it healed in a split second.

I hit our brakes, and we started to slide. People screamed. I heard everything. Slow motion wasn't in it, even though I knew we were at two hundred plus on the scale still.

Our brakes were on fire. There was no stopping them from damage this time. I didn't have the energy left to do so. Even if my Azris was filling fast, it just wasn't fast enough.

We powered through that crowd as it parted. Up ahead stood a giant tower. I tried to turn the wheel some more. It also wasn't responding.

Fuck, fuck, fuck. It drew in closer and closer.

We were going to hit it.

"Shields!" I cried to Ivori.

I felt the change, the system had taken our race win!

A woman and child stood admiring the tower.

"MOVE!" I tried to scream at her to get out of the way. She'd never hear me. Not in a million years.

Then she turned, her eyes lit with Azris, and I felt her energy flood forward.

We didn't hit that tower; we hit her shield instead. Ivori's front end crumpled, and I was thrown forward then backward with a snap.

Everything dulled, everything hurt.

I drifted for a little while.

Then I heard laughing.

I tried to open my eyes, bright light, everywhere hurt.

The driver's door was ripped open and strong hands yanked me out. My arms fell to my side, my body not responding.

"This is what everyone's worried about. This wimp?"

Oto, Ivori said into my mind. *Feel the energy from the planet again, move.*

I couldn't.

I couldn't feel it; it was as if I'd been cut off.

You haven't, she said. *He's trying to trick you. You're better than he is, you're better than any of them. You just have to believe you are.*

If that was only all it was, it would be easy, right?

I opened my eyes to look at him. He was just some ordinary guy, brown hair, black eyes etched with his Azris, nothing special to look at.

His stats flashed before me:

Name = Kidvec Rush
ID Number = 281771
Age = 27
Species = Tikinian
Sex = Male
Alignment = Chaotic
Bloodline = Fire
Health = 99%
Cultivation Level - Immortal 3
Active Meridians = 12/12
Nanites = 3.5 Million
Artefacts = 1
Chosen Specialist = Racer
First Chosen Affinity = Fire
Second Chosen affinity = Air

Statistic = Body + Tel + Cultivation
Strength = 68/400.44
Dexterity = 66/399.96
Constitution = 67/410.04
Int/Wis/Spirit = 101

He was stronger than Luca, Immortal Rank. I was screwed.
No. No I wasn't.
Nothing special.
He was just a Fire/Air affinity.
Nothing special. Those two words reverberated in my mind.
He wasn't special, but I was, we were.
Water, Fire, Earth, Air, Light, Darkness, Spirit.
I had them all.
My hand twitched.
That's it! Ivori encouraged me. *That's it!*
We were special, and I was no wimp.

Azris flooded me once more, and I felt Kidvec flinch. He dropped me. I landed hard, I just wasn't used to the gravity on the planet.

"I'm no wimp," I said and stood. "Here's what I am." I dropped my stance into the first thing that came to me.

Step one, Sixth Acceptance.

Pride flooded through me from Ivori as the energy around me drew in faster and faster.

"What?" Kidvec said.

Step Two, Sixth Determination.

Where I once struggled, it all made sense.

I saw it in the corner of my eye. The stats I had for my affinities, blinked out.

Affinities - Rank

Water - **Black**
Fire - **Black**
Earth - **Black**
Air - **Black**
Light - **Black**
Darkness - **Black**
Spirit - **Black**

The only difference was, I was on a planet that could fulfil my needs and fulfil she did.

"What the fuck are you?"

"Now that," I said. "Is the right question." Pulling my hands together, I felt the draw from Ivori herself. The nites responded, and though I hadn't brought the sword with me, now in my hand was the Kreeshon Quintin had forged.

Kidvec paled. "Like that, is it?" he asked.

"I didn't bring us here." Energy crackled around us. "You did. For a reason. You wanted to end my life here on Reeka for all the elders to see."

He laughed, and countered my stance with his own, pulling his sword to him. "Yes, I did. The fact that you know steps above your station is just more proof that you have to die, now." Fire spread up the blade, and I winced at the heat from here.

I held the blade up so he could see it better. With a flicker, I sent Water across its surface. Quickly followed by Fire.

"You have great control of both elements," he said and lunged toward me.

I followed his lunge, dropped to my knees, and spun, countering his strike with Air.

He fumbled with his recovery. "What?"

"Not just both elements," I said. "*All* elements."

I sucked all the light from the area, plummeting us into darkness, and he stumbled upon his next attack. I laughed as our swords clashed, but his sword glanced off mine with a wicked kickback.

"Impossible," he said.

"Nothing's impossible. They're worried for a reason. Whoever is above you sees me for me."

I struck this time. Just as he'd gotten used to the darkness around us, I flooded it with light. He let out a scream and covered his eyes with one hand.

I didn't hesitate and knocked his sword clean out of his grasp. "What did you really think about bringing someone like me here?"

"Ivori's demise," he said. "Your death. You're billions of miles away from those on your team, those who have your back."

I glanced around. The tower in front of us meant nothing to me. This planet meant nothing other than I knew there were many here who might want Ivori dead.

There were other people gathering, though, and it was clear their eyes were drawn to something.

"Ivori," I said, and turned. Her crumpled chassis. She was a wreck, again.

I felt the whir of wind, heard the snap of his blade again before it connected with flesh. It sliced deep into my already-sore shoulder and hit bone. Did it hurt? No. I glanced at him.

"I actually feel sorry for you," I said.

I watched as Earth drew to my now fresh-dripping wound. My suit was in tatters, my flesh stripped from my body.

I focused. My flesh stretched back over the muscle and sinew it just parted from, and a second later it was healed in full.

"Impossible!" Kidvec screamed.

"You seem to like that word."

He lunged at me once again. His sword so hot with Fire if he struck this time he'd sear any wound closed on exit himself.

I stepped sideways, spun left. Kidvec stumbled again, cursing under his breath.

He attacked again and I pivoted sharply, putting him off balance. He used Fire to shove himself backward away from me, and though my suit took most of the fire, I knew it singed my hair. I reached for the bottles at my belt, picking the last one out. My Azris was fueled by the planet herself, but my body was drained. I downed the potion, letting the energy and minerals it held hit my stomach with a gasp.

Kidvec gained his footing and composure, before he tried to swipe at me once more. The crowd around us gasped, as something else was happening. Kidvec looked away as his sword struck mine and I spun fast, slicing into his leg. Then as he began to fall, I sliced up into his back and spine.

He had no choice but to fall to his knees, and he saw what everyone else did.

Ivori.

Something else was happening around her. Energy spun faster and faster. Like that wall we'd just traveled through to get here. She was opening a portal? Back home?

She was something else. Something beautiful.

I stood over Kidvec, watching her as she formed before us all. Her eyes met mine.

"We have to go," she said. "He's coming. I can only do this once. But I need *his* energy." I saw his spirit around us all then, all the elements melding together. "Do it," she said. "For everyone around us now, for everyone we're protecting at home. Do it now."

Her words. I knew what I had to do. There were no choices here. If I didn't end this, his life now. We would not get away.

"You can't leave. He won't let you!"

"He who?" I asked, grabbing his hair, holding my sword to his throat. "Who do you think?"

"Batrak Viper," Ivori said. "Almost here, Oto!"

I didn't hesitate any longer. I drew my sword across his throat with ease. It sliced into muscle and stuck. I pulled, and with a plop, it came free. Kidvec's energy sparked no more.

Ivori drew his spirit toward her, and spinning around, forced it toward the portal. Then she looked at me, reached deep inside me, and yanked too. The Kreeshon vanished. "Get my core out, and move," she ordered.

I ran toward the tower, to her crumbled body. Dove in and reached for the center dash, her core. I yanked with all my might, severing her connection with the vehicle once more. The nites, we'd worked so hard to get them back, her metals . . . now I had to leave them.

The portal flickered, and I pushed my body forward toward it, slamming into the darkness with a vengeance. The air in my lungs was sucked out, and I couldn't breathe.

Hold on, Ivori's voice echoed to me. *Hold on, please.*

Then there was light, and the screech of tires.

My knees hit dirt as I looked up to see Don's Icarian hurtling toward me. His jaw dropped, his hands hit the wheel for hard left, and he started to slide.

I held up my arms, expecting nothing but more pain. I'd at least go out in style.

He skimmed past me by mere inches, the fresh air hitting my lungs like a welcome ocean wave.

Had we seriously only been gone seconds?

Rain poured down onto me. Soaking, steam rising, in but another second, Don stood before me. I looked up at him. He swallowed, his eyes meeting mine, then he dropped to his knees with me.

Red lights lit the track. Councilor Troha's voice echoed around us. "Race called. All drivers hold!"

Don's eyes fell. "I don't know what the fuck just happened, you?"

"You don't want to know," I said. "You just don't."

I wobbled. Don reached to offer me support. "That was a hell of a race. I don't care what they say, you won that."

"The whole world witnessed it," I said. "She can't take it back, no matter what happened after we crossed the line."

Ivori's core fell from my hands, and I fell with it.

That darkness swallowed me again, but I forced my eyes to stay open, to stay alert.

System notifications flashed before me, and I read them fast, seeing how much I'd grown, how close I'd gotten to losing everything. Including my life. My enhanced stats, flashed then returned to normal. King rank 4 though!

Name = Oto Benes - Giannetta/Fraser/Sawa
ID Number = 4188927
Age = 23
Species = Anodite
Sex = Male
Alignment = Chaotic
Bloodline = Royal Seven
Health = 99%
Cultivation Level - King 4
Active Meridians = 12/12
Nanites = **1 Million**
Artefacts = 2
Chosen Specialist = Racer
First Chosen Affinity = Water
Second Chosen affinity = Fire

Statistic = Body + Ivori + Cultivation
Strength = 64/**338.88**
Dexterity = 64/**327.68**
Constitution = 57/**291.84**
Int/Wis/Spirit = 77

Affinities - Rank

Water - Black
Fire - Black
Earth - Black
Air - Black
Light - Black
Darkness - Black
Spirit - Black

Droll's Leg Pouch – Empty

Ring of Light - A gift from Ezra
Adapted, so you may use it as you wish.
Boosts Azris circulation and usage, + 30 to all stats
Uses = 4

Death Thwarted - Used x 2

Then I swiped them all away. I was only interested in one thing, as I let the darkness take me.
Ivori? I asked.
I'm here, she said. *Weak, but here.*
You got us home, how?
Sheer determination and powered by the dead.
That tower? I asked. *The power it held, the—*
Yes, she almost whispered, and appeared beside me. *It held the energy of the dead. Many dead. Many dead at the hands of those monsters.*

Her rage and sadness washed over me, and I stood next to her, looking out into the darkness. It wasn't as dark as I thought. From here, no, it was brighter than anything I'd seen before. Stars, planets, life.

They know now, she said. *That we're coming for them.*

"Good," I replied aloud. I reached for her hand, took hold of it, feeling her strength mix with mine. "What they know and what they don't know are two very different things. We're coming for them, and we're not holding back."

"Are we ready for what comes next?" I asked her. "Copter?"

You bet we are, she said. Then squeezed my hand and coughed, *Well, when we find me a new body again.*

I laughed. "Will it ever get any easier?"

No, she said. *Not at all.*

More lights brought me around. Many different voices. "That's it. Come back to us."

"Who's that?" The voice sounded familiar.

"We're here," Alek said. "Take your time. You've been out a while."

"How long is a while?" I asked and sat up fast. My head pounded; my mind swam.

"A week," he said. "You were a mess. Doctor Styx struggled to stabilize you. He and Geo never left your side."

I opened my eyes to the dim room around me. "Ivori?" I asked right away. Panic stricken, I tried to move again, but couldn't.

"Whoa," the female voice said. "You've got some serious burns."

"Burns?" I looked into the older eyes of Councilor Troha. "Oh." Everything flooded back to me. "The race?"

"There was no denying you won, but what happened after you hit the finish line?"

"You didn't see it?" I asked.

She shook her head. "There's uproar over the networks from Drakol, though. What did you do?"

"I killed the man they sent to kill me," I said simply. "They all saw it."

Troha sighed. "You're going to Copter as soon as we can move you," she said. "But no one can protect you there."

I reached for her hand, felt her energies surface, but she couldn't counter me. Or see anything she used to. She smiled at me.

"I know," I said. "I don't need protection. Everyone I need will be with me. I will tell you something, though. They will need protection, because if they think they're going to come for me again, or anyone around me I love? I won't hold back, never again."

"No one will stand with them," she said and squeezed my hand. "They're on their own now. Thank you. For never stopping, for not holding back."

The doors behind Alek flung open, and Ezra rushed in. "I go to get one drink," she said. "And you come around."

She flung herself onto the bed and onto me. I wrapped her up in my arms. "Easy," I said, pain spreading over my body. Tightness everywhere.

Troha stepped back. "We'll let you rest," she said. "Then you'll attend our postponed race dinner. Show them all that you are okay, that you stand, and you stand a winner."

Ezra snuggled into my neck. "I saw you vanish," she said.

"I know," I replied and kissed her. "I'm here now."

I looked at Alek. "Your race?"

"Easy." He smiled. "It might not be as easy on Copter, but I'll give it my all."

"As will I," I said.

"All of us," Ezra said. "Though I didn't really expect my exams to get me anywhere, they've given me the one thing I know I'll need between the both of you."

"Oh," Alek said. "What's that?"

"Hopefully, the ability to keep you two out of the damned hospital!"

I started to laugh, though it hurt. Damn, it hurt. Alek started then too, and Ezra just curled into me, giggling.

If you enjoyed this book, please consider leaving me a review! Thank you so much!

If you're interested and want to follow what happens on Copter, just with a slightly different pov check out Infiltrate this is NSFW though :P

Sometimes just gotta follow the muse.

TEASER - SECT WARS - DIVIDE

Copter
Praitar City - Landing Zone

Saturday, August 14th *Morning*
Year - 27515

"Coming into land in five minutes, Lord Tullius," our pilot reported.

"Thank the gods," Lan said. She spread out her long legs before me, and my eyes drifted up her from her ankles. She winked at me, and I grinned. Then we both heard her knee crack. "Ouch," she cried, instantly rubbing at it.

"It's a long, long way via old transport," I said and let out a sigh. "And we're very late. We should have been there hours ago."

"Stupid old bus."

"You're right," Lan said. "I never expected it to take so long. This is the most uncomfortable form of travel I've ever had the privilege of taking."

"Agreed," the woman on my right said as she stirred. Sian looked almost exactly like Da, just older. No one off planet would know. "We're coming in now, though, right?"

Teaser - Sect Wars - Divide

"I never expected it to come to this," Taru added. "You're sure. We have to sort this all out, we should have asked for more help."

"No help, this is on us." I ran a hand through my now-cropped hair. "I'm under orders. Don't forget that. As much as I can set out on my own, Sawa is the most powerful sect around, and we follow your uncle first."

Taru rolled her eyes, but she still smiled at that. "Yes, they are, and I'm glad to be a part of them, and a part of a future with you." She tucked into my side, and I leaned down to kiss her softly.

"Then let's go make our mark," I said. "Get our Da back."

"Copter ain't going to know what's hit it," Sian, said.

They really wouldn't, but what had been happening here should not happen. There were threats going on Sawa wouldn't let slide, not only to them, but to the whole way of life everyone had become accustomed to, racing. "On your guard at all times, that goes for you too, Da," I said to her. Even knowing her real name I'd told all of us to use ours. There could be no slip ups. "Go nowhere alone, and trust no one."

"Finally meeting our wards?" Lan asked, standing when the ship stopped to grab her bag.

"Yes, should have been done before this, but we're here now. They go by the names Amalia Del Signore, and Camran Tarasov."

"They're Icarian drivers?" Taru asked. "Belong with Frasers' Track team, and . . ." She sighed. "My uncle has told me to treat them as family."

"Family," Lan raised an eyebrow. "Really?"

"Yes, really."

"It's complicated," I said. "You know all our families are."

Lan's brows creased. "I'd never expected to be a part of something so big, or so complicated."

I tugged her bag from her. "We're all complicated," I said. "But I'm glad we're complicated, because we're complicated together."

Lan laughed. "Corny, Kei. Corny."

I shrugged and watched her and Sian step out into the throng of other passengers getting off the ship. All three flanked me, and no one stopped us as we left. Heading for a fast car waiting for us.

It was a much shorter ride to Zhong's sect grounds. Lan pointed it out as we passed. We weren't stopping there just yet; we were heading to the city race track. There was already a race on, and we'd missed the start. I hated being late. Seriously.

I took the stairs two at a time. Late. Late for an escort, so we were making our own way to the tracks. Lan's steps were sure as if she'd been here before, but none of us had. Taru had my arm in hers, and Sian rightly lagged behind, watching my back.

"The noise," Taru said.

"Crowds," Lan replied, turning around and looking down on all of us. "This is larger than any amphitheater I've ever seen."

Taru tugged me to her as we reached the top and saw what spanned out before us. Sian came up behind me and leaned over Lan's shoulder. "It really is bigger than anything even I've ever seen, and I've seen some big places with my father."

There were several guards at the top of the stairs and out onto the spectators' platform. One long corridor spread to each side, and I could see several private boxes. One man moved toward us, and Lan intercepted him first. I heard him ask who we were, and on her "Master Kei Tullius," he dipped his head our way, and ushered her to follow him to a box.

It was better once we were inside. Here it was private, and I could easily stop anyone from spying, but Sian beat me to it, making sure a privacy shield erected up and around us.

Lan let out a sigh. "I never thought we'd get to relax." She sat down on the plush couch and brought up a 3D viewer of the race happening around us right now.

Drones caught images of the cars on the track over, and on the screen, we could see what was happening.

"Damn," Sian said. "They're really moving."

"Speed of the top car is 390 kilometers per hour," Taru said. "They really are moving. How can they even see or take things in at those speeds?"

"Skill," I said.

"Who are we watching again?" Sian asked.

Lan pointed to the car in front. "That's Amalia Del Signore, Car 77."

We all moved in to get a closer look at what was going on, on the screen was the light green paint job, the silver crest on one side. Then the number 77. She was neck and neck with another bright red car, number 21.

"She's going to try and take it?" Sian asked, looking at Lan.

Lan grinned. Her eyes widened. "She's got to take it if she wants this win."

"How do you know so much about racing?" Taru asked.

"The guys that used to . . ." She glanced at me and winced, a hand over her mouth.

"You don't need to be worried," I said to her. "I may feel a little jealous of those in your past, but it is your past." I moved to her, tugged her to me, and kissed her lightly. Only when she melted into my arms in full, trembling, did I let her go. "I'm your future. And I know, no one made you feel like that before."

"Never," she gasped.

A knock at the proverbial shield made Lan jump. We all turned to the doorway. There stood a young man. His face matched the pictures I'd seen. Camran Tarasov. However it was a little puffy? Had he been crying?

"Let him in, Da," I said.

Sian swiped her hand in the air, and the screen vanished. Camran stepped inside. Then she raised it once more.

I moved to stand before him, and the two of us eyed each other carefully for a while. He was oozing power, but something felt off.

When Lan screamed at the 3D viewer, we all turned to the race. "We'll talk after," I said. "For now, explain this."

"Amalia needs this win. We both do." Camran moved in closer and Lan inched away.

Car 77 lit with qi energy then and blasted forward. I looked at Taru. "They use qi to power the cars?"

Camran looked up at me, his face pale. "You know nothing about racing at all?"

I shook my head. "Nothing. I'm not here to help you race, though. We're here for protection only."

The way Camran looked at the three girls pissed me off right away. "Hey," I said. "You don't know us."

"Nothing meant by it at all." Camran held his hands up in a placating manner. "I can see you're leagues above me."

Lan giggled at his side, and he shot her a worried look. "Don't worry," she said. "We all play nice."

The sheer noise from outside, and the roar of the crowd had my attention back to the screen.

77 had taken the other car and was into the next bend. "What does that mean?"

Camran's shoulders sagged. "She's almost there."

I watched his emotions as they flickered over not only his face, but his whole body. His qi lines fluctuated with excitement, nerves, pain, love. I moved in beside him, put my hand on his arm. At first, he shot me a strange look, but then he relaxed.

"Eyes on the race," I said.

He looked back, but while they were all busy with making sure Amalia crossed that finish line as number one, I made sure I was doing my job.

I could only presume the gem was at work here, Camran's system was fucked, and he had no idea how badly. I could see his bond leading out there to the race, to Amalia, and she was drawing on that bond right now. He didn't have the qi to give her. I sighed. Tugged slightly on my levels, and to his surprise, allowed my qi down into his arm, core, and then through to her.

"That's—"

"Nothing." I pointed back to the screen. "Eyes on the race."

Protection? Holy shit, they needed a lot more than that. I could only put this down to gem, but this was neglect. They came from a good family for training. I'd done some homework and looked through their files. At least the online ones, and part of the vicenet I could scour.

I removed my hand, and he lowered his head, eyes downcast. The excitement of my team died down slightly too. All three of them looked at him with a little sadness.

"Shall I wait for Amalia to join us?" I asked.

Camran shook his head, sat down, linking his hands together tight. "I don't want her to hear some of what you're going to say," he said.

I sat opposite him, Taru by my side. I indicated the others to sit with him and his eyes shifted from one to the other. "They don't bite." I motioned to my left. "This is my first, Taru Akamine. Qiao Lan, my second," I said, gesturing to his left, then his right. "Da Zhong."

"It is a pleasure," he said. "I don't mean to seem so flaky, I'm usually not."

"Everything is on the line here," Taru said. "We can see that. We wouldn't be here if it wasn't."

"Luca said you're pure Sawa."

Taru caught my eye for just a moment, and I nodded to her. This was for her to speak. She was the blood relative. I was just connected with my parents and her through the Taharri.

"My mother is Shuko Sawa's sister," she admitted.

"I never thought I'd meet anyone of your standing." He swallowed. "I should be on my knees."

When he made to move, both ladies to his sides put hands out to stop him. "Seriously, not needed," I said. "You know Oto Benes too, right?"

Camran's face changed, but he nodded, his hands still twisting, his qi all over the place. "We all just watched him win. What do you think?"

"That when he eventually joins us here, we're in for a hell of a ride."

With a laugh, Camran's face cracked a genuine smile, his eyes twinkled. "You've met him?"

"Yes, briefly," I admitted with a nod. "He's going places."

"And you're here because . . ."

"Because you and he are connected; so are we." I glanced at Taru, who placed her hand on mine. "What's coming here is going to change everything."

"I need to win my race first." Camran said.

"Three hours," I said. "You need to be ready for anything."

His face paled. "What's going on?"

I leaned forward, sparked my qi. "Da is going to stay here in the booth, we're going to sneak out. The Sevran Vipers kidnapped a friend of mine, and have been holding her hostage. They believe we're just lackeys for Zhong where they bought a very dangerous artefact. One that's taking your qi, and will destroy this race, if not this whole city."

"Destroy the whole city?" he looked to my energy, "Qi? Oh, you use the ancient terms. Azris, here."

"Makes sense," Sian said.

"We're here to stop them, but first, you need to get out there to win that race."

MORE FROM ALEX

You can check out other books and my now complete series - The Bright - by clicking the link!

The Bright Lord

A home, a family. Lies, resentment. To save the future, he must reclaim his past.

Ryan Hart thought he had saved them all. He'd served as Lord Commander of the Sarashead guild, faithfully and with honor for thousands of years. His work expanded their empire and brought peace.

But peace never lasts. . . .

Emperor Duhan has been murdered, ripping Ryan out of his new life as a citizen on Earth. Once again, he must leave those he loves for the greater good.

Rebirth is the path, a reset into a new body that he must cultivate and train. The collision of two worlds draws ever closer, and if he can't claim what was once his, all will be lost.

The Bright Lord is a thrilling Litrpg, cultivation story that spans multiple worlds, love and friendship.

The Bright - Retaliate

Injured and on the run. Desperate but not hopeless. Recovery is a team effort.

Fleeing the destruction of their home in a battered ship, Tytan and his friends have a long way to go to feel safe. Pooling all their resources and his knowledge, the refugees seek help from the only avenue left open to them - the secret training grounds of the Bright Lords.

When a rescue mission demands action before they're ready, Tytan and his friends will discover just how much they're willing to risk to save their future.

Rejoin Tytan, Sin, and the crew as they fight for not only their own survival, but the survival of the galaxy-spanning Bright Lord society.

The Bright Fight

One rescue complete. Forced onto an unwanted path. Tytan and the Moeru-hi fight back.

Saving Rair had a steep price; Tytan and RJ are separated from their loved ones and only have a short time to recover before they must embark on an even more dangerous mission.

Racing back to Kraydon to save the sacred Lanthian, Tytan is brought to the razor's edge of sanity by the Mara's torture of Sin and Anders. Time is again running out for the Bright Lord and those he loves.

'To kill a god, you must become a god,' echoes in his mind. There's only one problem...

To save everyone, to achieve apotheosis, Tytan must first die. For good.

Rejoin Tytan, Sin, and the crew as they fight for not only their own survival, but the survival of the galaxy-spanning Bright Lord society.

The Bright Revelation

A system that humans shouldn't have access to. Abilities no one dreamed possible.

After an accident which should have killed her, Ella's life is torn asunder. She's on the wrong side of the galaxy when she's told her husband is a liar, a cheater. A murderer. Unwilling to believe what she's being fed, she uses her new, unfathomable abilities to break free of her "saviors" to make her way across the stars. Toward Earth. Home. Her family. And the truth.

You can also connect with me on Facebook and Twitter! Anytime for a chat! Thank you!

     facebook.com/alex.knowles.54738
     twitter.com/AlexKno74761755

CULTIVATION/LITRPG/GAMELIT LINKS

All things Cultivation, LitRPG, Gamelit, links, groups and chat.

Cultivation Novels - Facebook group -

https://www.facebook.com/groups/cultivationnovels/

Gamelit Society - Facebook group -

https://www.facebook.com/groups/LitRPGsociety/

LitRPG Books - Facebook Group -

https://www.facebook.com/groups/LitRPG.books/

LitRPG PodCast -

http://www.geekbytespodcast.com/

LITRPG

To learn more about LitRPG, talk to other authors including myself, and to just have an awesome time, please join the LitRPG Group

OTHER RECOMMENDED BOOKS

Here's some of my favourite authors amazon links! Check them out!

Olin Lester
The Missing: A genre-bending horror thriller!
Jez Cajiao
New Series - Age of Stone
Kevin Sinclair
New Series - Incoming!
Michael Chatfield
Love Ten Realms
Luke Chimilenko
Has to be Iron Prince!
Alex Raizman
Has a new Dinosaur core series out!
David Petrie
Zombies? I'm in!
K.T. Hannah
My SO loved Somnia Online

And a couple of the genre's publishers!

Other Recommended books

Portal Books
Highly recommend - Beast Realms and Shadeslinger - Fantastic both series!

Mountaindale Press
For the above - David Petrie's - Necrotic Apocalypse - totally loved it!

Made in the USA
Columbia, SC
01 May 2023